THE
OTHER
ME

ALSO BY SASKIA SARGINSON

The Twins
Without You

THE
OTHER
ME

SASKIA SARGINSON

NEW HANOVER COUNTY
PUBLIC LIBRARY
201 CHESTNUT STREET
WILMINGTON. NC 28401

FLATIRON
BOOKS

This is a work of fiction. All of the characters, organizations, and events portrayed in this novel are either products of the author's imagination or are used fictitiously.

THE OTHER ME. Copyright © 2015, 2016 by Saskia Sarginson. All rights reserved. Printed in the United States of America. For information, address Flatiron Books, 175 Fifth Avenue, New York, N.Y. 10010.

www.flatironbooks.com

Designed by Steven Seighman

The Library of Congress Cataloging-in-Publication Data is available upon request.

ISBN 978-1-250-08913-7 (hardcover)
ISBN 978-1-250-08349-4 (e-book)

Originally published in Great Britain in 2015 by Piatkus

Our books may be purchased in bulk for promotional, educational, or business use. Please contact your local bookseller or the Macmillan Corporate and Premium Sales Department at (800) 221-7945, extension 5442, or by e-mail at MacmillanSpecial Markets@macmillan.com.

First U.S. Edition: January 2016

10   9   8   7   6   5   4   3   2   1

For Alex M.

Our nightmare of total transparency conflicts with our dream of being entirely known.

—THOMAS NAGEL

PROLOGUE

I HAVE NO EXPERIENCE of killing anything. I take extra-long strides or sudden little hops to avoid stepping on insects that cross my path. When there's a wasp in the house, I cup it inside a mug so I can set it free out of the window. Feathered remains left in our garden after a cat has slunk away make me cry. I'm practically Buddhist. So how am I going to kill him?

Murder used to be a word that belonged to cloak-and-dagger plays or police dramas on TV. It had nothing to do with me. Not until he began to talk last night, telling me things I could never have guessed, asking me to do something terrible.

It started to snow this afternoon. The first flakes falling in nervous flurries from a gunmetal sky. Now, looking out into the evening, there is nothing but snow swirling towards me, white on white. Ice crystals billow out of darkness, twisting, spinning, casting a blinding spell. My breath makes a warm mist against the chill of the window. I close my eyes, leaning my forehead on the glass, and think about how I could stop his heart.

Perhaps suffocation would be kind? Slipping into his room at night, to hold a pillow over his face. Only I think that even when sleeping, the natural impulse is to fight for life, and I imagine his legs jerking and kicking out, the awful wrestle with the thrash and twist of his body.

There is a handgun in the top left-hand drawer of the portmanteau. I found the key once and opened it. Stared at the pistol, too scared to pick it up. My eyes followed the heavy lines of the barrel and worn grip. This time I'd feel the weight of it in my palm, slotting bullets into the snug nest of the cylinder. But I've seen the films, I know what happens when a bullet tears through a skull: blood, an explosion of it, and scraps of shattered bone, the gloopy insides coming out. Anyway, I've never fired a gun. I could end up maiming him instead.

I can't believe that I'm even considering this.

The garden is covered in a thick, dampening carpet of snow. Neat flowerbeds have become small white graves. The naked apple tree holds up silvery branches. The hushed world is transformed. Beyond our garden fence, streetlights gleam, catching snowflakes in illuminated fans. A car rolls past slowly, wheels crunching. The street is oddly deserted. But in the distance the city hums, vibrations pulling at the atmosphere—even the snow can't silence it—a constant reminder that a huge metropolis exists, the center of everything, and here I am creeping on the fringes, still tethered to the life I thought I'd left behind. I have always hated living in the suburbs, neither in nor out, neither one thing nor another.

It has to be pills. It's the safest way, surely? I'll have to acquire them in furtive visits to different chemists. No. That won't work, because I don't have weeks, not even days. It has to be now. I need another kind of drug, something immediate and powerful enough to let his dreams drag him under, so that he drowns silently, invisibly, within his own body. I think of his lungs, his heart, his muscles, the secret core of him, unclenching, letting go at last.

I've felt for a long time now that we inherit guilt—it passes forwards like crinkly hair, a squint, or blood that won't clot. We don't get a choice.

Will my guilt die too when I kill him?

PART ONE

THE LIE

KLAUDIA

1986, London

ALL THROUGH THE LONG DRAG of summer my stomach knotted and unraveled when I thought about what was going to happen in September. I'd circled the date on the calendar in red felt-tip with pink stars shooting out over the surrounding days. Inside the scrawl of rose and scarlet it said: *Tuesday 3rd. Klaudia starts at Kelwood High School.*

I've often walked past the big brick building on Mercers Road, pausing to glance at crowds of pupils in green and gray, watching them spill out of the gates, arm in arm, chatting and laughing. I used to wonder what they were saying, what it was that made them laugh. Now I'll find out, because it's going to be me in that uniform, skipping down the steps, my elbow linked with a friend's.

I've been taught at home. Mum and I at the kitchen table with a pile of exercise books, working our way through the syllabus, learning things by rote so that I could repeat them to my father when he came home from work.

I'm worried that not going to school has made me different. Perhaps it's even more strange that I'm an only child, or that my parents are as old as grandparents. I don't know, because I haven't learned any of the rules. Mum says I just have to be myself. I'm sure it's more complicated than that.

There's only the three of us at home: me, Mum and Dad. Well, four of us, if you count Jesus. Nothing ever actually happens at our house. Nothing ever changes. Reflections flicker inside surfaces and windows sparkle; the three cushions propped on the velveteen sofa don't move out of position, and the pictures on the walls are never wonky, especially the framed tapestry in the living room that reads, *All may be saved to the utter most.* My father checks its alignment every morning, squinting one eye and standing back to read the needlepoint lettering as if he doesn't know it, and a hundred other lines of scripture, off by heart.

Wooden ornaments jostle for space on the mantelpiece and dresser: the twelve apostles and Jesus in different poses, hand raised or holding a basket of fish, all staring out with blind eyes, frozen in place, as if the witch from Narnia has been on the rampage. Even these don't have a speck of dust on them. Each one is lifted and re-positioned after a thorough polish. Hunting dirt is something my mother does, feather duster in hand, the vacuum cleaner like a faithful pet, rolling from room to room with its long nose snuffling into corners.

I wish we could have a real pet. "We don't live on a farm, Klaudia," my father told me when I asked, "and it would add to your mother's burdens." My mother sighed, "It's a shame, cariad, but a cat would kill the birds." Mum feeds the robins, sparrows and thrushes that live in our garden with bits of bacon fat and the broken skulls of coconuts. My father made a bird table for her and fixed it on a branch of the apple tree. He likes to make things from wood. We're running out of places to put the ornaments, and there are a lot of characters in the Bible still to go. He has a shed in the garden where he keeps his tools and does his carving.

That's the other thing about starting school that worries me. My father. Otto Meyer. He works there. That's embarrassing. *He* is embarrassing. He's like Goliath, always too big for any room. And of course there's his heavy German accent. How can he still talk like that when he's lived in England for years and years? But maybe nobody will know or care that he's my dad. I'll make friends. Kids my own age. I want to take a look inside their homes and see how they live and what they eat and what they watch on TV. There is a whole world outside these pebble-dashed walls, beyond our straight suburban street, the Guptas' local store, the Methodist chapel and the Texaco garage blinking its orange lights on the main road.

———

The teacher, Mrs. Jones, is writing on the blackboard with chalk. I bend low over the desk and try to keep up with copying. I can feel the good-luck postcard that Mum gave me this morning crumpled in my pocket. Its edges press against my skin through the silky lining.

Most of the kids already seem to know each other. Lots of them must have gone to the same primary school. That hadn't occurred to me. I thought we'd all be new. After I'd found a spare desk, I perched on the edge of my chair wondering how to join in with one of the conversations. A girl stopped by my desk.

"Hello. I'm Lesley." She put her head on one side. "Have you just moved here?"

"Oh, no," I gabbled, "I've lived here for my whole life. Just around the corner."

She'd curled her lip. "Well, how come I've never seen you?"

"I didn't go to school. My mum taught me. At home," I said quickly.

The way she looked at me—it was as if I was a purple-spotted lemur in the zoo. I shouldn't have said anything. I knew it was wrong.

The collar of my white shirt is rubbing my neck. I wish I could rip off my top button. Thick gray socks make my knees itch. At the next desk a girl called Amber is frowning at the board. She has a bobble nose, curly black hair and blue eyes. Not like an Amber at all. She looks like Snow White. Her lips are blood-red as if she's bitten them. Perhaps she has. Perhaps she's as scared as me.

She glances across under sooty lashes and grins. I catch my breath. I want to be friends with her more than anything.

Mrs. Jones's chalk goes on scratching numbers. A dry, pale scent mixes with a faint tang of sweat and rubber, and the warm exhalations of a roomful of eleven-year-olds. I copy the numbers as carefully as I can, but they jumble up on the page, making no sense. Dad says that I'm lazy at math. He says I don't try hard enough.

Mrs. Jones has stopped writing to stare at us. Her cheeks have burning scarlet patches as if she's boiling hot or really embarrassed. But I don't think she can be either. She rakes her nails against her scalp, fingers disappearing inside short curls. Her navy cardigan is peppered with bits of dead skin. The eyes behind her spectacles search around the room. She taps one finger on her chin. She's looking for someone to ask. I drop my forehead so low it almost touches the wooden desk, hunching up, fixing on the blur of numbers on my paper, praying dear God, dear God, don't let her pick me.

Then lots of things happen at once. There's a soft thump, and the high-pitched sound of breaking glass. A missile has flown clean through the window on the other side of the room, making a jagged hole. Cracks run across the remaining panes in zig-zag lines. Someone screams. A cricket ball bounces and rolls slowly, coming to rest under my desk. There's broken glass all over the floor under the window. Bits gleam and sparkle.

My whole life I've been saying prayers, but they've never been answered before. I sit up in surprise, fighting to control my face, wanting to laugh at the miracle. Mrs. Jones has her hand clamped over her mouth. Amber and I exchange triumphant looks.

Kids have jumped out of their seats. There is an excited chatter. Mrs. Jones has recovered enough to shout, "Sit down—everyone keep calm and sit down." Another teacher comes in. He must have heard the noise. After a hurried chat, he leaves with a frown creasing his face.

"Whoever hit that ball is going to be in dead trouble," Amber whispers to me, eyes round as she makes a slicing motion across her throat.

"I know." I nod. "Look." I peer at the ball. "Under my desk."

She stretches out her leg to push it with her toe; then she glances at me and giggles. I'm so happy that I want to grab her hand and squeeze it tight. I want to ask her to be my best friend right now. Do people do that? I don't know how to behave. I don't know how to have a friend.

"Is everyone all right? No cuts or injuries?" Mrs. Jones is saying. "We'll have this mess cleared up in no time."

The door opens. We turn expectantly, and I catch my breath. I can feel the class watching my father stalking to the front, a broom grasped in one huge fist and a dustpan in the other. I look away from his towering shape, buttoned into a brown cotton coat. But I see his profile etched against the inside of my lids: the sharp line of his nose, the downward pull of his mouth.

I grip the edge of the desk. How weird is it that my father is the caretaker? What will Amber think?

I can hear the swish of bristles and the tinkle and scrape of glass fragments being swept into the plastic pan. I clench my teeth.

"See him?" Amber nudges me. "He's German."

I swallow, clearing my throat, trying to work out how to reply.

She hisses, "My sister says he's a Nazi. He gassed the Jews."

The desk tilts under me and I curl my toes inside my shoes to stop the sudden lurch in my belly. She puts her finger under her nose, straight across her top lip like a mustache, and winks at me. I examine my hands clamped against the desk: white speckles on my nails, pink, ragged skin around them with bits that shred and sting.

"Well, I think that will do. Thank you," Mrs. Jones is saying.

At the edge of sight, I see him moving away. He's stuck a piece of cardboard over the open wound of the window. He's going to leave. I squeeze my knees together, dropping my chin and rounding my shoulders to fold myself up. Don't look. Don't make eye contact. Underneath everything the word "Nazi" is repeating inside my head. But Nazis are heel clicking men in scary uniforms, with polished black boots, scars cutting across their smooth monster faces.

I hear the scrape of heavy footsteps passing, and then the door closes quietly. He's gone. I draw a deep breath and dare to raise my eyes. The class is back to normal: muttering, scratching heads, scribbling in exercise books. Nobody is looking at me. Mrs. Jones is writing on the board again. Amber makes a funny face for my benefit, miming a yawn.

My father was in the war. I'd never thought what that meant before. I know nothing about it, except that we won, and the Nazis killed the Jews. Of course my father had nothing to do with that. My insides start to crack like the glass in the window frame. He doesn't talk about the past. I put my thumb between my teeth and bite. He's just my dad: tall and serious with a funny accent. And ordinary. He can't be part of history.

The thing to do, I decide, is to keep quiet. Maybe nobody will think to connect us; it doesn't have to mean we're related, just because we have the same surname. I'll avoid him at school. I won't tell anyone.

I tilt my chin up and stretch my lips, grinning for Amber. She pats her opened mouth, pretending to yawn again, and I copy her, rolling my eyes at the numbers Mrs. Jones is inscribing onto the board.

The thing about September that I'd failed to mark on the calendar, but of course Mum had in her neat script, is that it's the beginning of the Methodist year. So we're sitting in our usual places in the second row of the church, listening to the long-winded Covenant Service. The lay preacher proclaims, "We are here to celebrate God's gracious offer to Israel that *I will be their God and they shall be my people.*"

In my head I'm offering God my own prayer of thanks, because He's given me what I've always wanted, even more than a pet: my own best friend. Amber is the most popular girl in my class, and she's chosen me. Every day since that first one, I've been impatient to get to school, my chest tightening with nervy excitement as I walk through the gates, waiting for Amber to run over and link her arm with mine. Sometimes I even forget that I have anything to hide.

My father breathes heavily through his mouth. He's placed his palms on his knees, leaning forward as if he's about to spring to his feet and take part in a race. My mother is dressed in her best clothes, hands linked in her lap. Both of them keep their eyes on Mr. Lewis in his gray suit as he talks about Christian perfection.

I wish we could have been Baptists. Like those African women wrapped in swathes of silver fabric, heads bound in brilliant turbans, clapping as if they're at a party. Or Catholics, with candles and blood-spurting statues, and incense-clouded air, altar boys in white lace singing like angels. But if I could choose any religion, I'd choose Hinduism—I like the sound of gods with elephant heads and sinuous ladies with multiple arms, the way they can change shapes and grant wishes. Lots of our neighbors are Hindu. The Choppras and the Guptas. My father says it's a shame that they are heathens. Mum says, "It's not for us to judge, Otto. With God's grace, we know that salvation is possible for everyone."

Aseema Choppra is in the year above me at school. On my first day she smiled at me as we passed each other on the stairs, and I turned to watch her walking away with her friends, her long black plait hugging the curve of her spine.

I fix my eyes on the plain wooden cross that hangs behind the preacher's head, trying to concentrate. He pauses to push a slick of hair back into place across his bald spot, then rubs his palm on his trousers, a fleeting expression of distaste on his face. Brylcreem, I bet. It's really sticky. Dad keeps a pot of it on the bathroom shelf. My father insists on cleanliness, seeing as it's so close to godliness. He gleams from top to toe. This morning I'd woken to find my shoes polished and placed outside my bedroom. My father cleans all our shoes, setting them out on sheets of newspaper and rolling up his sleeves, spitting and rubbing. He says you can tell a lot about a man from what he's wearing on his feet.

Dad also says that to follow Jesus Christ we need discipline. We should be fit and ready for the challenge He will set us. My father does his morning exercises in the garden. Whatever the weather, he's out there going through the same jerks and jumps: bending and straightening, touching his toes and dropping down to do push-ups. Watching him in his vest and rugby shorts, shoulders heaving at the timid air, his hair sweat-darkened, and the light catching his pale, bunched calves, he looks like a warrior in God's army.

My father can be frightening. But I've never thought of him as being someone to make fun of. Not until I saw the boys at school marching behind him, making silent salutes, their fingers under their noses, arms like pistons punching the air. *Sieg heil.*

"Klaudia, I notice that you don't speak to me at school," my father said today. "Is there a problem?"

I wrapped one leg around the other and gazed at a spot just behind him. "No."

"Well." He shrugged. "Perhaps you are embarrassed to have a father that is a caretaker. Perhaps you think it's too lowly a profession?"

I shook my head. He was testing me.

"Good, honest work is nothing to be ashamed of." He poked his chin forward, so that I saw the throb of his throat. "We are plain people. But we're giving you the advantages we never had. After everything your mother has done for you, you must work hard, help pay her back for all the sacrifices she's made." His disappointment in me pulled the edges of his mouth down. "Your mother is a saint, Klaudia. Neither of us deserves her."

His face transformed at the mention of her name, mouth and eyes turned upwards with delight, his eyes glowing with the same fervent look he gets when he is praying.

But then he frowned again. "A lot of those kids, they have no discipline.

No belief. No work ethic. They are foolish. And they get into drugs and so forth." His hairy eyebrows met in the middle, his eyes narrowing into a blue glitter. "I never want to see you behaving like them. Do you hear me?"

"Yes," I whispered.

"It would kill your mother."

He glared at me as if I was already a heroin addict, had already driven my mother into the depths of despair.

Mum is gesturing for me to stand, the hymn book flopping open in her other hand. The congregation is on its feet, singing "Christ, Whose Glory Fills the Skies." I catch my father's deep, throaty roar. For once his accent is disguised inside music and all I hear is the power of his voice.

My tongue is dry. No sounds come out. My mother holds the book towards me so that I can read. *"Pierce the gloom of sin and grief . . . scatter all my unbelief."* I mouth the words looking down at my shoes, seeing the hazy reflection of myself in their blue-black shine.

ELIZA

1995, Leeds

May

LIGHTS FLARE OUT OF DARKNESS. Guitars screech over a pounding bass. The place has all the pulsing energy of a funfair at night. I've never been a fan of fairs. Or gigs. I'm trying to keep my feet inside the crush, bracing myself against the push of elbows and shoulders, as a crowd, high on music, cheap lager and drugs, judders and jolts against me. I scan the moving heads; I've lost the friends I came with. Except Meg, just in front of me, waving her arms, hair sizzling with static. Then, as the lead singer leans over the edge of the stage, howling into his mike, spraying the front row with saliva, I feel a weight dropping onto my toe, crushing it.

The hulking culprit at my side is oblivious. His arc of hair glows purple in the strobe as he yells along with the lyrics. Pain shoots through my foot. I shout. But my scream hits a wall of sound.

"Meg. I'm leaving. Now!"

I prod her damp T-shirt. She turns, puzzled, watching my mouth moving. I point towards the exit, making a face meant to express frustration and agony. Pushing my way through the doors at the back, I limp into the bright lights of the pub. It seems quiet after the raging concert, but it's a usual busy Friday evening: locals and students converging on the bar, flock wallpaper, brass fittings, cigarette smoke and conversation.

Sinking into the nearest empty chair, I slip off my shoe and sock, worrying that my toe is actually broken. My nail is stained, color seeping like a smashed plum. It's hot. Throbbing.

Meg arrives at my side. "Let's have a gander . . ." She peers at my foot and purses her lips, sucks in air with a quick rush. "God! Looks like an elephant stepped on your toe!"

"One with a Mohican."

I flex my toe gingerly. It seems to be working. "I knew we should have gone to see *Braveheart*."

A slight frown of concern creases Meg's elfin face, and then she gives me her familiar cheerful grin.

"You'll be fine. And we couldn't miss The Flying Ducks. Only one night in Leeds. Would have been a crime."

She sits down, chin in her hands. "Want a bevvy?"

I nod. "The pain-killing kind." Although it's not the pain that worries me, it's if I'll be able to stand in pointe shoes tomorrow.

"Cider it is then. Hang on a mo." She grins and is off to the bar, pulling at the hem of her skirt, covering her bottom and swinging her hips.

I see the ice before I see him. A hand curled around a large plastic beaker. The faint crackle of cubes, piled to the brim.

"Excuse me," I call from my seat. The ice cubes stop, suspended in midair by a male hand. I take in the flimsy plastic container, mercury-like drops of condensation, the gleam of frozen water. My gaze follows the line of his wrist up his arm to the shoulder, and a face. Surprise raises his eyebrows and then recedes. He has friendly, crinkly eyes I notice, and a generous mouth that's mid-wince at the sight of my toe. Sitting with my bare foot up on the velvet seat, I have the instinct to cover it up.

I clear my throat. Try to pull dignity about me. "Could I have a couple?" I move my gaze to the cup.

"I was just taking them back to the rabble at my table. But it looks like your need is greater than ours." He frowns politely. "What happened?"

I incline my chin towards the back doors, where the growl and clamor of The Flying Ducks emerges, muted but self-explanatory.

"Are you a student?" He gazes at me. "I don't think I've seen you around."

"Yes. No." I curl my toes, flustered. There's something about the way he's looking at me that's making words shrivel in my mouth. "Well. I was. But I've dropped out. I'm taking a dance course instead."

"A dancer?" He sticks his fingers into the beaker and then changes his mind, puts it on the table. "Can't have you hobbling around with a bruised toe. Have the lot," he says. "On me."

He begins to walk away and then stops and turns. "Arnica," he says. "Keep it elevated. And painkillers. With Ibuprofen. Take the swelling down."

Meg nearly collides with him. "Who's that?" She widens her eyes at me. "He's dead gorgeous. Is he a doctor or something?"

I'm already wrapping frigid cubes in my scarf, pressing the blessed angles of cold to my aching toe. I shake my head. "Nobody. A kind stranger. Isn't it nice to think they exist?"

"Cynic." She pushes my glass of cider across the wet table. "Course they do. World's full of them."

But I'm not really listening to her; I'm watching the back of his dark head as he disappears towards a table of rowdy students in the corner. Shouts of hilarity greet him. A blonde girl reaches up and curls her arm around his waist.

Meg sees where I'm looking and shrugs. "Students. From the look of them, I'd say they're third years. They'll be celebrating their finals."

I won't see him again, then. The disappointment is a sliver of ice. A small injury, melting away into the liquid chill of what might have been.

October

Leeds is a gray city. But the first thing my gaze falls on is bright red and full of Spanish sizzle: the poster of *Strictly Ballroom* that I stuck to my wall with illegal tabs of Sellotape. Put there for the purpose of inspiration and motivation. Paul Mercurio clasps Tara Morice to his chest, her flamenco skirts frothing around her knees. What I wouldn't do to have the chance to dance in that film with that man.

There's a rap on my door and Lucy peers in. She has her pleading face on. "Is that your milk in the fridge, Eliza?"

"You can have it."

"Thanks! I'll pay you back." She grins. And she's gone.

I yawn. At least she asks. And now I'm properly awake, which is good, because I need to get up. The minute I'm out of my fusty nest of blankets and sheets I'm shivering, except my ankles, which are scorched as soon as I switch on the small fan heater. The heat bites at my skin like an angry Pekingese. There's a note stuck to the outside of my door. I rip it off and read: *Going to spend night with Pete. Don't ask. Meet you there tomorrow. Meg x*

In the empty kitchen, I tip out the last granules from a jar of Nescafé, pour on water and gulp the acrid, burning liquid next to the sink. Lucy's bowl is on the side, her half-eaten cereal going soggy in the last of my milk. I empty the coffee dregs over a pile of dirty crockery that's teetering at the brink of the washing-up bowl, balancing the unwashed cup on top.

It's raining again. The weather comes straight off the moors here, sweeping over desolate rocks and beaten heather. I check my watch. I have to be at the studio in half an hour. Out on the steep incline of our street, my legs tense to keep traction on the slick wet surface as I hurry to the phone box on the corner; I haul open the door, shaking water from my hair as I step inside. It's fuggy with steam, sour with stale breath and the smell of old paper. I dial the number that I know off by heart, holding the greasy black receiver close.

"Hello, love." She answers after the first ring. I call her every other day at nine o'clock and it's always her that picks up. Never Dad.

"How's everything? Are you working hard?" she asks as usual.

"Yes, Mum. I'm fine. Don't worry about me."

"Are you eating enough?"

"I promise I'm eating really healthily. I've got quite good at cooking actually. I'll make you something special when I come home."

I can hear her smile.

"Well. I've got to go. I have a class. Love you. Say hello to Dad."

Lying is an art. It takes time and practice to get right. Two important things to remember: either make your lies so big and bold that nobody dares to question them, or stick as close to the truth as possible and lie by omission.

Another thing I've learned is that once you've lied, there's no going back. With every lie comes guilt. You can't share the guilt, just as you can't expose the lie. It wouldn't be fair to other people. Confession would only hurt the ones you love. It's kinder, braver even, to maintain the untruth. In fact it's a duty.

———

Light gleams over the wooden floor of the studio, catches in the wall-to-wall mirrors. Girls cluster in groups, chatting, tying ribbons on shoes, flexing shoulders and adjusting leg warmers. Meg hurries over, hairpin in her mouth, hands busy twisting her hair into a bun at the back of her head.

"You missed the big announcement," she mutters, lips clamped around the hairpin. "Today's the day that Voronkov's going to choose two girls for solos for the show next week."

She tucks the ends of her long auburn hair under a hairnet and sticks the pin through. "He'll pick you, Eliza. He's bound to."

I love her for her confidence in me. Her loyalty. But the thought of dancing a solo makes my skin crawl. I've never performed in public before and the idea terrifies me.

The class begins and we work our way through *pliés*, *battements frappés*, *développés* and *grands battements*. I raise my leg high, powering it from the back of my thigh, pointing my toe. Sweat trickles down my spine. Voronkov corrects the angle of my head. His fingers pinch my chin. My arms maintain my position, the line flowing from my shoulder to my fingertips.

Voronkov's face is ageless. Thick gray hair grows from his temples like wings, yet his skin is unlined. Meg says either dance is the elixir of youth, or he's had a facelift.

I'm certain dance is better than anything a surgeon could do to erase wrinkles; it's like a magic potion. It sets me free. I am myself as soon as I begin to move. Tension leaves my face, drains from my limbs. The joy of it sings through my veins. I even smile through the warm-up at the barre and Voronkov's sarcasm. I still can't believe I'm really here, doing what I've always wanted. There are twelve of us in the class and we're reflected in four walls of mirrors. I catch multiple glimpses of myself grinning at different angles. Our working legs strike the floor in a series of *battements tendus*. Piano music plays from a cassette recorder.

"Again." Voronkov rolls his eyes like a wild horse.

I snap off my smile. My fingers clutch the barre. He notices at once. He notices everything.

He raps my knuckles. "Is sinking ship?" he asks me. "Is for guidance only. Not hanging from like woman drowning. Higher." He takes hold of my foot and raises it towards the ceiling. I try not to grab at the barre for support. My pivoting thighbone jams deep inside the socket. My toe quivers in his grasp.

He lets go. I squeeze and tense with the effort of holding the position, but my foot drops from grace, weighted by gravity and human failings. Even this feels good. Feels right. Nothing worth anything was ever easy. It's the kind of thing my father would say. But it's true.

The lesson over, we're alert with anticipation, flexing our aching feet, hands patting loose strands of hair back into place, trying to appear relaxed. Voronkov paces the room in silence, legs turned out like the Bolshoi dancer he used to be.

"I have no names," he declares at last, shoulders rolling in despair. "Not yet. Maybe nobody. Ever." His eyes stare at each of us in turn. "Not one of you is ready."

He curls his mouth as if he tastes something disgusting and stalks from the room. The two halves of his rounded buttocks quiver with disappointment.

There is silence. I hear the girl next to me sniff. As soon as they are certain he has gone, the complaining starts, everyone talking at once.

Meg raises her eyebrows. "Such a drama queen. He just wants to keep us all guessing."

We hurry home, dodging puddles. I imitate Voronkov's serious stare, the monotone of his accent. "I have no names. Maybe never." I pull my eyebrows into a bristling frown. "Maybe I send you all to Siberia for bad arabesques."

Meg laughs inside her hood. "It works though, doesn't it? Being chosen by him feels like some kind of royal honor."

I'm relieved that Voronkov is holding out on us. It gives me a bit longer to talk myself down from my fear of performance. Although I'm sure he won't pick me. I'm the least experienced student in our class. I dry off in the bathroom, toweling my rain-darkened hair until it's tamed into a brown bob tickling my chin while Meg makes us cups of tea, shouting through the surprising news that there's no milk, so we'll have to take it black.

Sitting cross-legged on her bedroom floor, I busy myself with sewing ribbons onto my new pointe shoes. I've already broken them in and scored the blunt ends with a knife.

"Well." Meg blows on her drink with contemplative satisfaction. "Only two more weeks before I'm off."

"Swapping Leeds for Paris." I look up at her. "You must be mad. And don't think we're going to miss you, because Lucy and I are subletting your room to a gorgeous man."

She sticks her tongue out. "You're going to miss me so much." She elongates the "o" in "so," like a note in a song.

"What, you mean your horrible habit of swigging orange juice from the bottle, and the state you leave the bathroom in?"

I'm struggling to keep a straight face. I look away, licking the end of the thread and squinting while I push it through the eye of the needle.

"All right," I relent, snapping off the cotton with my teeth, "I'm going to miss you every second of every day. Satisfied?"

"Then come and stay." She puts her cup down and shifts onto her knees on the bed. "Come for Christmas. Please!"

I look down at the shoe in my hand. The slippery pink is cool on my fingers. I press into the hard square of the toe.

"What's to consider?" She's waiting. I can feel the heat of her stare on my cheek. "Have you actually got any plans for the holiday, little Orphan Annie?" She's half teasing, half serious.

In my head the fake tree opens its plastic branches. My father turns his opera record up loud and my mother emerges from the kitchen with a batch of freshly cooked biscuits on a plate.

"Some dull and distant relatives I bet?" Meg's shaking her head. "Doing your duty. They'll understand. Christmas in Paris. Come on. How can you resist?"

I bite my lip. Mum won't forgive me if I'm not home for the day itself. I can't disappoint her. But I could buy her an amazing present in a Parisian boutique, and be back for Christmas Eve.

"Of course I'm coming . . ." I jab myself with the needle and wince, sucking my finger. "I'm not going to turn down a free holiday, even if the catch is having to put up with you. But I can't stay for Christmas. Sorry. I really do have plans." I notice a tiny speck of red on the fabric of my shoe. "Even orphans have obligations."

"Yes!" Meg rubs her hands together. "I'm well made up! Let's book your ticket together. I want to know the date you're coming. Dad's renting me a garret at the top of one of those tall houses in the Marais. It's going to be great. I just wish you were doing the course with me."

A year at a dance school in Paris goes beyond the bounds of my imagination. Things are different for Meg. Her dad is proud of her dancing. He's a golfing, gin-and-tonic kind of man, happy to pay for his little girl to learn ballet and French at the same time. I'm not envious. I'm living my own dream.

ERNST

1994, New York

EVERY TRIP TO THE HOSPITAL is exhausting. Maria takes my arm, her face set in a mask of determined good humor; she carries a padded bag packed with things I might need, as if I'm an overgrown, ancient baby. Out of the elevator, I limp through the lobby, she and Frank on either side, guiding me to the yellow cab that waits grinning at the curb. I am lowered like a bundle of washing, eased through the door so that I can slide my sharp behind across the seat, the two of them huffing and hanging onto my elbows, rolling their eyes at each other across my head. Frank steps back, tips his peaked hat, and brushes down his doorman's coat; waves us off as if we're going to a party.

Some party. Told them straight at the last visit. My old carcass isn't worth the effort or the money. It shocks me. How, against the odds, I'm still here. Something inside me persists, even though I should have died years ago. Most days I don't leave the apartment. But my walls are hung with beautiful things: paintings stippled with color; a canvas with the lush curves of a woman, still wet from her bath; a body on a cross, luminous above a leering crowd; dreamscapes littered with moons and goats. I gaze at them until I doze, and my mind wanders back through time like an unruly dog, smelling out unexpected memories. Snuffling amongst the past, I manage to lose sight of the day—the way it hangs around me, stagnant and dull. And when I emerge, the remaining hours are only to be endured, to be got through with card games and Maria's grim pulse-taking, her determination to pump me full of those wretched pills. *Ekelhaft.*

Funny how I catch myself using German after all this time. And I think of Otto. He waits for me inside my memories, impatiently kicking his heels. It's his voice that sounds in my head when I speak our language. With each slow passing day he grows more vivid and insistent in my mind.

It wasn't the way I'd planned to leave the farm, as an enlisted soldier, a *Landser* on my way to fight Ivan, with my new uniform rubbing at my sweaty neck, feet overheating inside polished boots.

But there I was, with the other new recruits, none of us knowing a damn thing, crammed into open flat railcars, hunkered down between armored vehicles and rattling weapons—*Paks* and *Panzerfausts*—men and machinery on their way to the Eastern Front. As the train made its way through summer heat, the red-brown dust of Poland stuck to our faces; found its way into ears and mouths; thickened our eyelashes with stubborn grit.

I saw pine forests, farms and villages in the distance. The sun and the rumbling of the train made me sleepy. At Krakow station the train stopped, and a small band of dirty children gathered, begging with open hands, until a couple of military police chased them away.

We believed that the war was nearly over. The rest of Europe would fall as easily as Poland and France. The Bolsheviks were on the run. As I tried to get comfortable against the angles of a canvas-covered machine gun, listening to the clank of wheels against tracks and the murmur of men's voices, I thought of what I would do in a couple of months' time when it was over, and I would be free to escape the farm and go abroad. America was my plan. I never wanted to see Germany again.

Otto was far away, wearing a different uniform. The Wehrmacht wasn't good enough for him. Scholz had pulled some strings for his golden boy— got him something important. We hadn't been separated before. My little brother, who was a head taller than me by the age of twelve, had never needed me to look out for him. Since I can remember he'd been pushing me away, anxious to prove he was better.

———

From my bed I can see across the tops of the trees in Central Park. The air is bright today, sharp enough to snap. I can hardly hear the traffic jammed along West 82nd Street. Gazing at my hands resting on the covers, I suddenly see them as other people must. As things that are deformed. I'm missing the tops of two fingers on one hand. One on the other. Taken by frostbite. These are old wounds. Like my blind eye. It's my arms that are punctured with fresh marks, colored with bruises.

I'm weary of this last battle. But I have the strength for one more journey. They won't believe me, of course. Maria will resist. I can see her now, barring the door with her body if necessary, black eyes snapping above the glare of her uniform: "Now Mister Meyer," she will say in her nasal way, the corners of her mouth pulling down, "You know that is not a sensible idea."

But she didn't see us in Russia, tramping through endless snow, starving and exhausted. Our feet rotten stumps wrapped in rags. She doesn't know what I'm capable of. I have stretched limits before, bracing myself against the hard wire of impossibility. And I can do it again.

We were swift as a greyhound, tough as leather and hard as Krupp steel. But what good did it do us?

I find myself humming the words to those old marching songs. The ones we learned in the Hitler Youth and sang again and again in the Wehrmacht, dug into foxholes, marching in line across never-ending plains, across broken, rutted wastelands in rain and hail, past rows of rough wooden crosses, with helmets hanging on them. A German boy doesn't cry.

Heute wollen wir marschier'n einen neuen Marsch, probier'n in dem schönen Westerwald. Ja da pfeift der Wind so kalt. I'm moving my lips, and the words crack as one language slides into another. *Dancing is a joy and the heart in love laughs.*

I would like to dance with her one more time.

But the wind is so cold.

Winter nights on the farm, when the frost made patterns on the inside of the window, Otto and I would creep out of our beds, wrapped in blankets, and climb down the ladder to the stable. Lotte and Berta sometimes slept lying down, and if one of them was stretched out on her side in the straw, we'd curl up against her warm flank, putting our cheeks against her muscled neck, fingers tangling in her thick greasy mane. Through the dark, I could almost taste the smell of piss and dung and the hot breath of the animal. Even in sleep, a part of us was conscious, ready to move if she stirred, to roll out of the way of her hooves.

There were other songs we learned and repeated in the club house and at camp, hurling words into the air, our young lungs heaving, mouths opened wide. "Kill them. Kill them all. Line the fat cats up against the wall." Perhaps we didn't understand what we sang. I don't know how much we really knew or when it was that the knowledge became something real, lodged inside like shrapnel.

KLAUDIA

1986, London

I'VE BEEN TO AMBER'S HOUSE three times, twice on my own, and once with Lesley. I liked it better on my own. Her mum made us cucumber sandwiches with the crusts cut off. We watched *The Sound of Music* on their huge color TV, while their hairy Lassie dog pressed up against me, resting his damp nose on my knee as if he loved me. She has a guinea pig called Honey. She let me pick it up. The creature felt strangely bony under her thick golden fur. Her claws scrabbled at my hand, and one got hooked through my cardigan. I bent close to unhook it and she nipped my chin with sharp teeth. I put her down quickly, before Amber noticed.

Amber wants to come to my house. "It's your turn," she explains. "It's only fair."

"Of course," I say quickly, in case she thinks I don't know how to do this. "I'll ask my mum."

I choose a Saturday afternoon when I know that Dad will be out at a chapel meeting. I'm nervous. I worry that she'll think our furniture is wrong and the wooden disciples weird. But Mum doesn't let me down. She's made cupcakes with icing and sugar flowers; she sits at the table with us, smiling and asking the right questions. I see Mum through Amber's eyes and realize how pretty she is. Even though she's old.

In my room, Amber finds my pink dance slippers.

"I didn't know you did ballet too?" She claps the slippers together. "I go to Miss Hockey. Grade Three on Tuesday evenings."

I shake my head. "I don't have lessons. Not yet."

Amber looks disappointed. She plays with the ribbons on the shoes, twisting them around her fingers.

"We could do some dancing now, if you like," I say, keeping my voice casual. "You could be the teacher. Show me some moves."

"Positions," she corrects, standing taller.

We get a chair and arrange it in the middle of the floor. I place my hand on it and hold my other arm out to the side; Amber kneels at my feet, pulling my heels together and pushing my toes apart. It hurts. She makes tut-tut noises when I complain, standing to demonstrate how I should be doing it.

"Come along," she says in a strict voice. "Stomach in. Chin up."

She teaches me five different positions. She prods my tummy and smacks my arm with my ruler if I drop my hand.

"Dance teachers are always mean," she explains. "Otherwise you never learn anything."

She yawns as I fail to master an arabesque, her mouth opening so wide I hear her jaw crack. I wobble lopsidedly. She fidgets, tapping her fingers on her folded arms while I struggle to stand on one leg with the other pointing out behind me. My ankle trembles as I flail my arms like a dying crow, flapping to stay upright.

Amber sighs, collapsing onto the bed. "Have you got any music?" She pushes her hair behind her ears. "I want to do some dancing too."

I'm not allowed to touch my father's opera records, or the record player. But he's not here and Mum is shut in the kitchen with the radio on, busy with supper. Smells of fish and frying butter waft through the house. I look at Amber's expectant face, and nod.

In the living room I squat on my haunches to flick through the records with nervous fingers. There's one at the back that has "Duke Ellington" written on it in big red letters. I think it's one of the records that Uncle Ernst used to put on. It won't have been used for years. I slide it out of its paper cover; Dad won't mind me playing it.

I lower the needle carefully. The melody pulses into the room with a wink and an explosion of trumpets. Amber frowns. "That's not proper ballet music." She puts her hands on her hips.

"It's fun, though," I suggest, "don't you think? We could dance together."

I grab her, feeling brave, and begin to step backwards and forwards like I've seen jive dancers do in films. She gasps, stumbles and squeezes my fingers. Then she's stepping in time with me, and we're moving to the rhythm. She laughs and suddenly we're dancing. She turns me under her arm and I spin round and round on the carpet. Amber's face flashes past. The living room blurs. My skirt flics up.

"Klaudia!"

My father is in the doorway. He strides past and grabs the needle, stopping the music with an abrupt screech. He turns to me.

"What do you think you're doing?" His face is mottled, his eyeballs press forwards, round and hard as marbles.

"Sorry." I hang my head.

Next to me, I sense Amber tighten, as if glue stiffens her spine.

"It's immoral music. Foolish rubbish." He stands over us. "Making a spectacle of yourself." He swings up his arm and I flinch. He's pointing to the door. "Go to your room."

Amber is staring at my father, the caretaker, the Nazi; her mouth slackens, and her eyebrows move across her forehead in horrified wonder. The space between us seals itself shut. When she does look at me, I see a kind of pity behind her righteous, shocked anger. She holds herself apart, dignified and wounded. *Liar*, her silent mouth whispers. I didn't lie, I want to protest. Not really. Neither of us speaks. She stands with her face averted.

My father leaves the room. He holds the jazz record by the very edge, pinching with sharp fingers. His anger hangs over us, a suffocating blanket.

"I have to go home now," she says in a distant voice. Her eyes are bright with my secret. She walks through the house as if the floor is seething with snakes, as if the furniture crouches to spring at her.

Everyone will know on Monday.

Mum puts my plate in front of me and sits down at the other side of the table. It's just the two of us, so she bows her head. "For what we are about to receive," she says, "may God help us to be truly thankful. Amen."

She opens her eyes and leans towards me, resting on her elbows so that her breasts, buttoned up inside a blue cardigan, balloon over the surface.

"Well?" Her eyebrows shoot upwards. "Did you have a lovely time with your friend? I thought she was staying for tea?" She picks up her cup and takes a careful sip, lips puckered, keeping her eyes fixed on me.

I glance down at a pile of chips shiny with grease, and a row of stubby fish sticks. I slice into one and notice bits of brown inside the white flakes. I let my shoulders rise and fall.

I feel Mum frown. "There's nothing the matter, is there?"

My chest is so tight that my words can't come out. I shake my head. My hair falls over my face. "Dad got angry."

"Cariad . . . what about?" She reaches out her hand, small as my own. Her fingers are warm.

I want to cry, to push my head into the curve of her shoulder, close my eyes against the comfort of her chest, blue wool rubbing my skin. But I feel angry. Together, she and Dad, they've ruined my life. I pull my hand away, stab a couple of chips and ram them into my mouth.

I chew, tasting salt. The difficulty of swallowing releases my chest. "I played a record. Amber wanted to dance."

Her forehead crumples. "I'm sorry, my love. You know how he is about that machine. I'll have a word with him."

I shake my head. "It's too late."

She begins to protest, "Oh, I'm sure it isn't . . ."

I look at her. For the first time in my life I'm aware that she doesn't understand me. The moment tenses, uncoils.

"What did Dad do . . . in the war?"

I've never asked before. The question hangs in the air like an ugly scrawl of graffiti. I hear the big clock ticking on the wall above the calendar. A fly has got in through the open window. It buzzes over the potted plants on the sill behind the sink, and settles on a spiky leaf to clean its legs.

My mother looks at her hands linked on the table in front of her. She's fiddling with her wedding ring, pushing it into the give of flesh. I shift in my chair. Maybe she didn't hear? She swallows and I hear the hard gulp as saliva goes down her throat.

"Where has this come from?" she asks quietly. "Did Amber say anything?"

"No." My voice is husky.

"I don't know what to tell you." She holds her clasped hands up, as if in prayer. "He was . . . Well. He did . . . he just did his duty, love." She doesn't sound very certain.

"But he was on the wrong side," I remind her.

There's another pause and I look down, noticing a mark on my skirt. I try to brush it off, but it's an oily stain. Mum is still silent. "He must have . . . done . . . bad things," I say in a small voice.

"No." She catches her breath. "It was the war that was bad, not the men in it. Not most of them." She's speaking quickly. "Millions of people died in the war. It was terrible. Hitler was an evil person, Klaudia. That doesn't make all Germans evil."

"Dad was a Nazi . . . wasn't he?" I put my fork down. I can't eat.

"Klaudia!" She looks shocked. "I don't know what's started you off on all these questions all of a sudden." Her face closes. "Of course your father wasn't a Nazi. It was a long time ago. Years before you were born. Another life. Da doesn't like to talk about it. It was very hard for him." She leans forward again. "Look at me, cariad. Don't worry about the war or what your father did in it. It's not for little girls to worry about. He's a good man." She blinks and I notice a tiny twitch on her left eyelid making the skin pucker and tremble.

I open my mouth. And close it again. I want to believe her.

She smiles, pushing herself up from the table. "Now, eat up, sweetie. I've got Angel Delight for pudding. Caramel. Your favorite. You can invite your friend another time, can't you?"

Amber moved to another desk. She and Lesley ignore me at break, turning their backs, murmuring behind their hands. People stop talking when I approach, beginning again when I'm out of earshot. I've tried explaining that my father didn't gas anybody, but nobody takes any notice. They seem to like the idea of a Nazi caretaker. Anyway, I am a liar. Amber said she'd never trust me again. There's something wrong with me. I must be funny in the head to have thought that I could get away with it.

As soon as I get to school, I untie my plaits and backcomb my hair in the girls' toilets. I've bought a pair of gold hoops that I clip on. They pinch. But everyone has pierced ears, and I'm not allowed. I can't have Dolcis shoes either. Instead, I wear childish Mary Janes, polished by my father. I've adopted the insincere way of talking the others have, as if I'm bored senseless. I've learned the latest slang. But it's hard to blend in when you're me. Even if I wasn't taller than average with long white-blonde hair and blue eyes, I can't deny that he's my dad. He scowls as he mops floors, shouts at the boys who kick the bucket as they walk by.

I'm walking quickly, scanning the corridor under my eyelashes on my way to chemistry, searching for the distant shape of my father. Someone grabs my arm from behind, and I let out a shriek.

Fingers squeeze tightly, shaking me. "Shut the fuck up."

Shane Stevens lets go of my elbow, staring at me as if he's trying to see through my skin. Shane is in the year above me: a wide-shouldered boy with a square head, the blunt contours accentuated by a vicious buzz cut. He smokes at break, standing apart, his cigarette cupped inside his hand. He walks with a careless swagger as if he owns the place, a group of boys tagging behind like shadows.

I notice that his irises are a startling shade of green. I stare back, forgetting that I'm supposed to look away.

"In a hurry, aren't you?" He's made his voice pleasant, almost normal. But there's a catch there. A threat. He leans towards me.

I blink. "Sorry." I apologize automatically. "I'm late for class."

He shrugs as if that doesn't interest him. "I've been wanting to have a word with you."

I swallow. My heart is pounding. I'm confused. I never knew he'd noticed my existence. I'd thought I was invisible.

He pulls out a piece of paper and shoves it into my hand. "You should come to this."

Shane is inviting me to something? Confusion scrambles my brain. I stare down at the paper, and in my panic, I can't make sense of the letters. I shake my head. "I don't understand."

"National Front meeting," he says, his face tightening with impatience. "Nick Griffin's speaking." He smirks. "With your old man being a Nazi and all, thought you'd be well up for it."

I don't know who Nick Griffin is, but I've heard of the National Front.

Something heavy drops inside. A cold weight pressing on my belly. "My father . . . he's not . . . I'm . . . you've made a mistake." Words gather and catch in my throat. I stretch out my arm, offering him back the paper. My fingers tremble.

He ignores it and moves closer. I smell his deodorant, the ripe aroma of cheese and onion crisps. The skin around his mouth is sore, his lips blistered at the corners. I see a fleck of blood leaking from a crack. The pink of his tongue emerges to probe it.

"I don't make mistakes," he continues in the pleasant, reasonable tone. He's grabbed a handful of my hair and he's staring at the fan of pale strands between his fingers. "Real blonde, aren't you?" He looks at me. "Your dad, he helped get rid of the front-wheelers. But it's a different time in'it? It's the Pakis we've got to get rid of. Send them all back to Paki-land, yeah? You and me, we're the ones who belong. Not them."

"Front-wheelers?" I frown.

He laughs. "Wheel. Skid. Yid. Nice bit of Cockney."

I begin to back away, but he's holding my hair. His manner doesn't match what he's saying. I want to run, but I'm trapped. And I have nowhere to go. I'm so late now that I can't go to chemistry. I'll wait in the library. Hide among the book stacks.

He narrows his eyes, lips curving upwards. Another red bead sits on the edge of his smile. His tongue slides out. I look away, scanning the corridor for an excuse. But he's let go of my hair and he's strolling off, hands jammed in his pockets. "I'll see you there," he calls over his shoulder. "Don't be shy, princess."

A couple of boys who've been waiting farther down the corridor, leaning against the wall, fall into step with him as he passes. I see him pat one of them on the back, hear a short bark of laughter. I crumple the paper into a ball, crushing it tight inside my fist.

I try praying. Please Jesus, make Shane Stevens fall off the bus. Let him have leprosy. Let him be struck by a bolt of lightning or a falling tree. But the weather is beautiful. October is soft and golden. Clusters of red and yellow leaves fatten branches. There is hardly a breeze to stir their scalloped edges.

The date for the National Front meeting comes and goes. Shane is waiting inside the school gates the next morning. He steps out in front of me, shoulders sharp, chest jutting. "Playing hard to get, princess?"

I stand with my head bowed. He leans over, sliding his arm around me. I brace myself to take his weight. "Or," he murmurs softly, "are you a little Jew-loving slut? A Paki-loving whore?" I feel the damp of his breath on my cheek.

At break time I hide in the girls' loos. I sit in a stall and watch the slow hands of my watch, spine stiff, listening for sounds outside the locked door.

When I get back to my desk, I lift the wooden lid to take out my English texts and find an unfamiliar book there. Puzzled, I read its title. *The Holocaust*. I glance around me quickly, but nobody is interested. They are chatting to each other, or setting papers straight, fiddling with pencils. I pull the book onto my lap and turn the pages. Black and white photographs leap out at me: skull faces staring through a barbed-wire fence. I stare back. Bones lie piled on top of each other, wrapped in rags. The bones make the shapes of bodies. I bang the book shut, feeling sick. There's a Post-it note on the back cover. It says, "Hitler waz a Jenius. Ask yor Dad."

ELIZA

1995, Leeds

Voronkov has invited a small audience to the performance—a select list he thinks might help our careers. Not for him the vulgar gushing of family and friends, a show simply to celebrate our achievements. That would be bourgeois pandering. Time-wasting.

He'd announced the chosen names at last. And mine was one of them. He's been drilling us for weeks. When he told me that I was to have a solo role, I took it as a sign. This was my chance to overcome my nerves.

Standing on the brink of the stage, I think I'm going to black out. I shuffle my toes in the rosin box again, pushing the powder onto my already whitened shoes. Deep breaths. In and out. My heart is pounding so loudly that I'm sure everyone must be able to hear.

The music begins, the lilting strings so familiar now that I know every rise and fall. I step into the light.

The blur of the audience swarms towards me. I can't hear the music anymore. There is a loud ringing in my ears. Faces pulse towards me and recede as if I'm on a lurching ship. Familiar features pull into focus: Shane is leering up out of the shadows. I try to blink him away. My chest heaves. Amber's face hovers like a balloon. They're not here. I know they're not. But I can see their laughing faces, their pointing fingers. I can't breathe.

My limbs are suddenly heavy and useless. They won't obey me. I manage to move my tongue inside my mouth, forcing it to dampen dry lips. Blood hammers at my temples. I try to take a step and stagger to the side, my arms splayed for balance.

There is a collective intake of breath. A voice hisses urgently, "Begin! Now!"

I spin away from the shine of eyeballs, the opening and closing mouths, the sharp chatter of voices veering into complaint. Fumbling from the stage, I shut my eyes against it. Inside I am dying.

I find myself in the wings. Horrified faces slide past. The other girls look at me as if I'm something broken, dangerous. I want to say that I'm sorry, but I can't find the words. I lean against the wall. Sweat trickles down my spine; my armpits are wet. Idiot. Fool. Voronkov is moving towards me and I wait, head down, hands open at my sides.

Meg follows me to the changing room, where I'm taking off my shoes with numb fingers.

"What happened?" She sits beside me.

I rub my eyes. "I don't know. I went blank."

"Has it happened before?"

I shake my head. "I've never performed in public before." I take a gulp of air. "The idea of it has been giving me nightmares."

I've let everyone down. Up on that stage, it felt as though the whole world was laughing at me. The blaze of spotlight triggered an overwhelming fear, paralyzing, beyond reason.

"But why didn't you say?"

"I thought I could get over it. I'm sorry."

"You don't have to apologize to me, you dozy thing. But," she winks, "maybe we should slip some Valium into Voronkov's tea."

"You need to get out," Lucy advises, after she hears what's happened. "Drown your sorrows and forget it. Stage fright happens to the best performers."

She has a plan. She's got a friend at the university and there's a student house party on. Lucy thinks parties are the great cure-all.

The place is heaving. Students are crammed into the narrow hall, lounging against walls and sitting on the stairs. Couples with their arms wrapped around each other. The bass has been turned up so loud that all I can hear is the dull, thundering beat of it, shaking the walls of the house, entering my bones.

Meg, Lucy and I find the kitchen. Cabinet surfaces are covered with half-empty bottles, plastic cups and spilled drinks. I grab a bottle opener and manage to twist off a cork, sloshing white wine into three plastic cups. We raise our cups, clashing them together, flimsy sides crumpling, wine slopping over our hands.

"To friendship," Lucy says.

"And crazy Russians," Meg adds.

"To both of you," I proclaim, "and me not bottling out next time." And I tip the rim to my lips. The first taste is sour and necessary, acidic in my gut.

Lucy grabs my hand, pulling me through packed bodies. I'm bumped past elbows, hips and shoulders. I feel the softness of bellies as I squeeze past, sucked into the hot heart of the party. I like this shield of human flesh, the loss of focus inside everyone's faces. I empty the cup into my mouth again, and it bangs against my teeth. I tip and swig. The edges of the room are fuzzy now, the moment is right here, pressed up against me, and at the same time it's floating away.

The music reveals itself inside the smaller space of the living room. The bass settles and I can pick out the slow, insistent beat of "Boombastic." I let myself go into the song—connecting movement with rhythm in the way that has always made sense to me. Nobody is looking. Nobody cares. I settle into invisibility.

I don't know how long I dance for. Sometimes I'm dancing opposite someone; Meg appears grinning at me, and then Lucy waving her hands. Then I'm alone. The room is dim. Shadows crawl across the wall. A red lamp gives everyone a devilish glow.

Meg reappears dragging a tall boy behind her.

"I'm off now. Pete and I are going back to his place," she yells. "Are you going to be all right?"

"Of course!" I shout back. "Have a great time."

There is no reason to stop dancing, except to sometimes pick another cup or bottle and see if there's anything left at the bottom, tipping unrecognizable liquid over my tongue. The music slides from one track to the next. The sweet smell of marijuana mixes with nicotine and sweat. I'm free inside movement. Except that the floor keeps swirling past my feet, making it hard to keep my balance, and the furniture jumps from one place to another. I bang my knee against a chair that rattles at me.

Then I'm in the lavatory, on my knees, white porcelain swallowing my head. My belly heaves and heaves. As I grip the cold rim and retch, looking into a gush of alcohol and bile, fractured moments from the afternoon come back to me like stills from a nightmare. I groan. Why won't it go away?

Out in the hall, with my clammy forehead pressed against the wall, I begin to shiver. There are fingers on my arm. A voice is saying, "Are you OK? Can I help you?"

I'm slumped against someone's shoulder, my head thrown back. Through half-closed lids, I see the dark ceiling spinning, faces revolving, and then there's only one face, close-up like a dentist. He peers down into my own. "You really know how to dance," he says.

A fierce light is clawing through my lids. I frown and clench my eyes tighter, turning into the crumpled pillow. My own pillow. My own bed. But now that I'm awake, I'm aware of my thirst. I usually keep a glass of water by the bed. Keeping my eyes shut, I begin to grope towards the place the glass should be.

My fingers meet flesh. A resisting substance. The knots and curves of a spine. Warm. Naked. There is another body in my single bed. I withdraw my hand as if a snake has bitten it and sit up straight, eyes snapping open.

There is a stranger next to me. He's dark haired. And he's asleep. As I stare into his face, my heart stutters. It's him. Ice-cube man. Black eyebrows arch in an expression of surprise, as if he's encountered something perplexing in his dream. He frowns and mutters. I can hear the dry click of tongue behind parched lips. His chest is bare and I wonder if he has anything on under the covers.

I can't bring myself to touch him. What is he doing in my bed? I lean away, dragging the covers with me, until I'm huddled against the wall. Checking my body with quick pats I'm relieved to find that I'm in my underwear.

I peer across at the floor. The rest of my clothes are abandoned in a crumpled pile. There is a pair of men's shoes and a tangle of jeans next to them. I'm trapped. I'll have to climb right over him to get out.

I bite my lip, trying to remember what happened. Above me, the red poster offers no clues. I attempt to rewind. Short memories jerk into focus. A man peering into my face, as if down a tunnel. I went to a party. The thump of bass. Music. Flicking lights. Before that . . . I groan.

Ice-cube man stirs and opens his eyes. He smiles as if we're old friends. "Hello," he says, stretching. "How's your head this morning?" He has the long, almond eyes that I remember, heavy-lidded and so dark they are almost black. A sketch of the room is reflected across them, silvery and slender.

"Terrible," I realize. I hold the sheet across my shoulders. "Who are you?"

"Cosmo. We did introduce ourselves last night." He rubs his cheek, making a rasping noise. "Don't you remember?"

I stare at him. I have no memory of last night. Instead I remember his smile as he set the crackling ice on the table before me. Should I remind him?

"OK." He frowns, stifling a yawn behind his hand, "Let's see . . . your name is Eliza. You came to Leeds to do a geography degree." He pauses, blows out through pursed lips as if he's thinking. "But you dropped out and now you spend your time dancing. You're an orphan. You have two brothers. Oh, and your best friend is about to abandon you for Paris." He looks pleased with himself. "Not bad with a hangover."

He has no idea that we've met before. I stare at him. I told him all that?

"We didn't sleep together," he says, "if that's what's bothering you. I mean, you were a little amorous, but neither of us was in any condition . . . you spent some time in the bathroom . . ."

"Enough!" I put my hands over my ears. "Please don't."

He sits up, blinking at his watch. "I would say let's get breakfast, but it's past lunch time."

Unbelieving, I grab his wrist to check the time for myself. He feels warm, solid. He's right. We've overslept. I've missed my tap class.

"How about a coffee?" He pushes the covers back and stands up. He's not quite naked. He's wearing a pair of crumpled boxers. I look away from his bare legs and stomach. But not before I glimpse taut muscles, dark hair tracing a line from his belly button down under the low-slung waistband of his boxers. "Think you might need one," he adds. Out of the corner of my eye, I see him bend to retrieve his shirt from the floor.

I do need something to sharpen me up. I heave myself out of bed, dragging the sheets with me, wrapping them around myself with some difficulty. He watches me, his mouth twitching. Trying to maintain my dignity I hobble towards the door.

"Drink some water," he yells as I shut myself in the bathroom. I lean over the sink, dizzy and nauseous. Turning on the cold tap, I pool water in my hands, splashing my eyes. It goes up my nose, drips down my throat. I bury my face in a towel. I can't believe that he's here, in my room.

God, I look haggard. The mirror shows gray smudges on my skin. My brown hair is a bird's nest. I drag a comb through it, and say his name aloud. "Cosmo." I've thought about him a lot since meeting him in the pub. But the truth is, he's a stranger. The first time we met doesn't count. We hardly exchanged more than a couple of words. And he's forgotten. Which is embarrassing. I scrub at my teeth and spit bubbles of minty paste into the sink. The failure of yesterday is sitting inside me, implacable and heavy. Memories have begun to flash up like neon signs behind my eyes. Voronkov's voice hissing, "Coward."

We squeeze into a sofa booth behind a small table at Café Flo. As we wait for our drinks to arrive, we both fall silent. I glance at my nails and then at the chipped green walls and the collection of oversized clocks, all of them telling different times. A local radio station plays in the background. Cosmo is humming along to some recent pop song, and he shifts in his seat, casually resting his arm along the back of the sofa. Students slump at tables, reading newspapers, chatting over plates of egg and chips and mugs of coffee, but every fiber of my body is acutely aware of the warm, human shape of his arm just behind me, and the space between us, his skin so nearly touching mine.

I open my mouth to ask him something useful and polite, like if he lives in Leeds, but instead I can't stop myself blurting out, "Actually, we've already met. Ages ago. You gave me some ice." My face burns and I look away.

"Ah, so you do remember." He gives me a wide smile. "Yeah. I recognized you too." He moves his arm and scratches his cheek. "I knew straight away. The girl with the toe. I stood in the doorway and watched you dancing." He looks down. "How's your foot now?"

"Fine. Thanks." I rest my chin on my hand, ducking to hide my pleasure. I play with the ends of my hair, twisting them between my fingers. "Haven't you done your finals?"

He nods. "I finished last year. History. I'm doing teacher training now. There's a college, the other side of town. I went to the party with a mate of mine who's doing an MA here. Abandoned him I'm afraid. One look at you and . . ."

"Oh." I can't think how to respond.

"Couldn't stop watching you . . . sorry, that sounds pervy. It was the way you danced. Lost in the music."

"Drunk, you mean."

"No . . . you were good."

Our cappuccinos arrive and I dip into the froth, swirling shapes inside it with my teaspoon. My mind is blank. "So," I struggle. "You're going to teach history?"

"It's not my dream. But it's keeping my parents happy."

"Where do they live?"

"South London. It's where I'm from. You?"

I fiddle with a packet of sugar, crunching it between my fingers. "Wiltshire."

"Ah, yes." He smiles. "I remember. The family home with wisteria over the porch."

"God!" I grip the sugar packet. "I really did talk a lot last night, didn't I?"

He smiles. "Didn't understand all of it. But yes. You are a chatty drunk." He takes a sip of his drink. "You probably don't get to London much. But if you do, you should check out my friend's burlesque club in Brixton. It occurred to me that you'd like it."

"Really?" I can't tell if he's joking. "I thought burlesque was another word for stripping?"

"That's what I thought, until Josh educated me. It's a skill, apparently. It's about anticipation—the performer weaving a spell on stage, making everyone hold their breaths . . . that's what you did . . ." He breaks off, and laughs. "Listen to me! I don't know what I'm talking about." He clears his throat. "You're the dancer."

My face stiffens, remembering the spotlight hitting me, and my body refusing to move. I reach across the table and push up the crumpled cuff of his shirt so that I can read the time. He puts his hand over my fingers. I notice that there are flecks of color on his skin. Red. Blue. White. Paint splatters.

Outside, I reach up to kiss his cheek and we bump noses. Our lips slide across and meet; I taste coffee. We hesitate and pull away.

"Well, that was awkward." He takes hold of my hand. "Do you want to try again?"

I begin to reply, but he's already put his mouth over mine. The sounds of the day slow and fade. There's a roaring in my ears: waves rushing inside a shell. His arms are tight around my waist. My hands have linked around the back of his neck. I feel the tickle of his hair, catch the faint scent of his skin. My tongue grazes the edge of his teeth. It is a kiss to fall into. And I let myself fall. My stomach rises and drops. My fingers move to his shoulders and grip.

When we pull apart, his face is open. Surprised. He touches his lips with his fingertips. "Eliza," he says. It sounds like a question.

ERNST

1931, Germany

BENEATH THE COW'S BELLY my thumb and fingers are busy squeezing and pulling. I lean against her warm flank. This is work I've done since I can remember. The rhythm is comforting. Streams of hissing liquid hit the side of the bucket, each spurt sounding slightly different. The cow, standing with lowered head, blows patient air from wet nostrils. I butt my head into her warmth, squeeze and pull. Nearly done. Otto crouches on his stool in the next stall. Meyer is at the end. The sweet smell makes my stomach rumble. I'm looking forward to breakfast.

Otto appears at the opening of the stall behind me, two pails of milk balanced from the yoke across his shoulders. His bare knees look too big, the bony surface of them rough with scars. He sniffs. His nose is always sticky with snot. "First again." He grins and walks carefully on, the pails swinging beside him.

I finish, slapping the cow on her backside, dried mud and matted hair beneath my fingers. I don't want Otto to take my slice of bread. I balance my pails and walk with small, steady steps out of the dim barn into the brightening morning. The sky is streaked with pink, the sun coming up over the thatched roof of the house.

Agnes and Bettina are in the yard, wrapped up against the cold, hats pulled down over their heads. They are going to collect the eggs, baskets hanging from their arms. I watch Bettina stop in front of Otto. She says something, covering her quick grin with mittened fingers. Otto's head jerks forward and he shoots out a hand to push her. She shrieks and jumps back. I see the milk spilling seconds after I already knew it was going to happen. Otto is so predictable. Bettina knows that too and she delights in teasing him.

I hear Meyer's heavy steps behind me. His hoarse shout makes me duck. Bettina and Agnes, meekly pulling their skirts about them, disappear around the corner. Otto is left, guilty, red-faced, puddles of milk around his boots, froth seeping into the mud. As he waits for Meyer, he sticks his milky hand in his mouth. He knows he won't have any breakfast.

Meyer is pulling the leather belt from his waist, grabbing Otto's ear with a twist to lead him back to the barn. I look away. I don't want to see my brother's humiliation. In the kitchen I eat my bread and cheese, munching on the dark rye tang, the sharp flavor of the cheese. I fill my mouth with milk, holding the softness on my tongue for a moment before I swallow. I slip a crust of bread into my pocket to give Otto later. Agnes sees me. But Agnes won't say anything.

Otto and I walk to school. The narrow lane borders a black field. Somewhere in the middle is a flock of geese. We can't see them—they've been swallowed up inside a low mist that hangs over the hollow—but their complaining voices come to us, loud as a gaggle of housewives. The red brick spire of the church rises above treetops in the distance. Otto walks ahead; he has marks on each leg, long livid stripes curving around his calves, over the backs of his knees. He stamps on icy puddles, snapping the brittle surface, splintering chunks that he kicks across the road, and wipes his nose on the back of his hand. It's his habit to sniff; he hasn't been weeping. We are used to the feel of the strap on our legs or backsides. We know how to hold the sharp sting inside us, breathing through the pain. We don't cry. Not anymore.

"He went on about the Bolsheviks again." Otto shoots a shard of ice against a tree, watching it shatter into a spray of crystals. "Always the same story."

Meyer likes to boast about his soldiering days in the Great War, how evil the Bolsheviks are, what horrors they committed in the name of communism. "You boys don't know you're born," he tells us when he whips us. Panting out words between strokes. "Got it easy. You need to show more gratitude."

Meyer beats us both, but Otto has it the worst. I've given up trying to comfort him. He likes it better if I ignore him; it was the same even when he was small. He hates to be pitied. People get a particular look when they find out that we're foundlings. They feel sorry for us when they notice our torn clothes and the strap marks on our skin, the fact that we always have to share our school books and never have a packed meal to eat at break. Otto turns away from sympathy, bending over a scab on his knee, prizing it loose, making it bleed. Or he'll find a hapless ant crawling by and casually crush it with his thumb.

KLAUDIA

1987, London

SHANE SAUNTERS UP TO ME in the crowded canteen with his pelvis forward, and that smirk on his face. He's got his hands around my waist, jerking me so close that I wince at his sharp hips. His breath is in my face. I see other people's faces, the way they shake their heads, their looks of disgust or fear. He grabs at me as if he has the right, as if we're girlfriend and boyfriend.

When I try to shove him away, he whispers, "Do that again and I'll break your fingers."

I stare up under my fringe, hating him. But he seems to find it amusing.

"I like a bit of graffiti," he says. "So be careful, or your old man will find his name on walls with the rest of his mates." He puts on a teacherly voice. "You do know who I'm talking about, don't you, Klaudia? My heroes."

My mind is numb. Blank. But I nod.

"Say their names for me." He licks his lips.

The smell of food is making me feel sick. Gravy. Mashed potatoes.

"Hitler?" I whisper.

"Uh-uh. Go on."

I can't think of another name and he squeezes my arm, pinching. "You can do better than that. Goering. Mengele, Hess . . ." he prompts.

The names are dry husks in my mouth. I don't know who they are. I don't want to know.

"Good girl." He pats my bottom. "I'll test you next time."

I avoid going outside at break. The library or the girls' toilets are my sanctuaries. A swastika has appeared on the lid of my desk, drawn carefully in blue pen. However hard I rub, and spit onto the cuff of my sleeve and rub at it again, the ink refuses to budge. I pile my books over it, or lean over my desk so that I can position my elbow or hand across it.

Only a week till Christmas. Paper chains hang from the ceiling of the canteen. There's a secret Santa mailbox in our classroom. Every morning when it's opened and envelopes distributed, I pretend I'm busy checking my pencil case. To my surprise I get a card from Amber. I take it home and put it on the chest of drawers in my bedroom, where Mum finds it and nods approvingly. "That's nice. You should invite your friend over again. Hope your father didn't scare her off." I give a vague smile. Amber might be charitable when it suits her, but she's not going to commit social suicide for me.

My mother has been baking for weeks. She started months ago with a Christmas cake wrapped in layers of waxy paper and tied with string. Trays of mince pies with stars cut into the pastry wait in a tin to be taken to the church service; vanilla biscuits are made for her prayer groups. At the weekend I'm going to help make gingerbread men.

"We're out of plain flour, cariad," Mum tells me on Saturday morning. "Pop into the Guptas' and pick some up will you?"

The Guptas' tiny shop at the end of our street is packed with towering shelves. Each row is crammed with everything you could wish for: packets of cornflakes, sugar, washing powder, cookies, tins of tomatoes and dog food stacked right up to the ceiling. And there are exotic things like dried chilies, packets of saffron and cardamom pods. The smell of spice makes my nose itch.

Mrs. Gupta is sitting behind the piles of newspapers at the counter; she gets up when I come in, the bell clanging behind me. When I go to the register to pay for the flour, she presses a lemon bon-bon into my palm. "Tell your mother I said hello," she says.

Saliva floods my mouth at the thought of the citrus tang. I nod and unwrap the sweet, placing it on my tongue, testing the hard surface against my teeth.

Mrs. Gupta tips her head from side to side, and the red dot between her eyebrows dances.

Aseema Choppra is coming into the shop as I'm leaving. I smile, my mouth too full to speak. But she clenches her jaw, lips tight. "You should pick your friends more carefully."

I gawp at her, not understanding. And then I realize she means Shane. I flush hot and cold, and I want to protest, tell her that he's not my friend, but the bon-bon stops my tongue. She turns away and I crunch down hard, shards of lemon in my teeth, sticking in my throat.

Gingerbread men lie in rows on the cooling tray: neat ranks of soldiers, arms and legs touching. Our kitchen is full of the smell of ginger and risen dough, the windows misty with steam. My father is reading the paper in the sitting room with opera on the turntable. He's turned the volume up. Foreign words vibrate through the house, bellowing voices filling every corner.

Mum is putting the baking things away, running water into the sink; she pushes the big bowl over to me with the wooden spoon.

I lean against the table and lick sweet, grainy dough from the spoon, and then stick my finger into the bowl and draw pale, greasy lines across the cool, ceramic inside. Mum smiles. "You've been doing that since you were a tiny thing."

She glances out of the window. "Look, sweetie." She beckons to me, her voice hushed. "The robins are back."

We stand together, her hand finding mine, watching two birds peck at the bag of nuts on the bird table. She squeezes my sticky fingers. "Oh, Klaudia. It makes me happy to see a pair in the garden again. Such clever little birds. And so loyal to each other."

She goes back to the washing-up and I begin to dry, but the music pulls at me, and I step away to dance around the kitchen table with the tea towel in my hand, exaggerating my movements to match the grand sweep of the singer's trills and soaring high notes. Each stretch of my arm, each bend and dip feels like a relief. I take my memories of school, of Shane, and throw them out into the warm kitchen, flatten them with the push of my hands. Those girls who smile at me and then turn their backs, they too are caught up in the swing of my arms, sent spinning towards the ceiling as I pirouette round and round. The music crashes and blazes, and the cloth flaps like a flag. All that matters is this moment, the smells of baking, robins in the garden, and being warm and safe with Mum.

She laughs, rubbing her soapy hands on her apron. "You're making me dizzy."

Breathless, I push the hair from my eyes. "Can't I have dance lessons?"

It isn't the first time I've asked. I've looked through the window of the Catholic church hall when the ballet class is on: pupils in pink shoes and black leotards doing exercises while an old lady beats out time with her walking stick. I want to be there with them, moving my feet on the chalky floor. I dance outside, on the pavement, copying what they do, holding my arms out to the side as if I'm lifting up enormous petticoats.

She shakes her head. "There isn't the money, love. And you know what your father thinks of the idea."

"Yes, but . . ."

"There isn't a but," she says. "Nothing to stop you dancing at home whenever you like, cariad."

She glances up, over my head, and her expression changes, mouth pulling down. I follow her gaze and see the tomcat from next door balancing in our apple tree, his tail thrashing. He's climbed higher than the bird table. Every fiber of his body twitches with desire. Mum rushes to the door and yanks it open. "Shoo!"

She's too late. The Perkinses' cat has something in its mouth. Other birds flutter and call in a fever of terror and rage. The cat has dropped to the grass, and slinks low at the edge of the garden, a growl in its throat, tail thrashing, feathers between its teeth. My mother runs unsteadily through the wet grass after it, flapping a tea towel. The cat, turned to liquid and shadow, slips through the bushes and disappears.

My father stalks into the kitchen, the creased newspaper under his arm, and hurries out to her. He accompanies her back into the house, guiding her by her elbow, his face set. "I'm sorry, Gwyn. The bugger got away this time."

"It's killing them for fun." She closes her eyes, her voice flat. "That's what I can't bear. It's not for food. Just for amusement."

He puts his hand on her shoulder. The music in the next room rolls to its conclusion, swirling voices and a crisis of strings.

———

It was later in the day that I saw it again. It was crouching in the shade of the rose bed, gazing at the bird table with a quivering mouth. My mother was upstairs putting a pile of ironing away, so I called to my father quietly, "The cat's back."

Minutes later there was an explosion. A single crack: shocking in the suburban air, making every bird in the garden swoop high on beating wings. I caught a glimpse of fur where the cat had been, the outlines of its body half-hidden in grass. My mother, breathless from her dash down the stairs, pulled me to her, hiding my head in her breasts as my father went past. Despite my mother's dress bunching against my mouth, her flesh folded into my face, I saw the pistol in his hand.

The glow of my bedside light falls across the open book on my lap, illuminating pages. But I can't concentrate. My eyes are sore from crying. I can't stop thinking about the cat.

I'd tried to run into the garden, but Mum grabbed my arm, shaking her head. She wouldn't let me go. From the window, I watched as my father took a spade and dug a shallow hole, rolled the lifeless body in and covered it with dirt.

The Perkinses came knocking at our door a little later. They'd heard a shot. They were sure of it. Had we seen their cat? I'd crouched at the top of the stairs, heart beating wildly. My father murmured at the threshold. Words of denial. His pistol had been returned to the locked portmanteau. Later I'd heard my parents talking in low, urgent voices. I couldn't pick out any phrases, just the backwards and forwards swell of an argument.

There's a quick knock and Mum puts her head around my door.

"Said your prayers?"

I nod, keeping my eyes fixed on the blurred lines of print.

She comes to sit beside me, her weight making the mattress ping. She presses her hand against the eiderdown, smoothing the pale pink fabric. "Are you all right?"

I put the book down and move my head. "I didn't know he was going to kill it . . . I'd never have told him . . . not if I knew . . ."

"Come on, now." She places a palm against my cheek. "You're not blaming yourself, surely?"

"But . . . how could he?" Tears crowd my voice. I stop and swallow.

"He wanted to protect the birds," she says quietly.

Anger burns a hole inside me. I shake my head. "It wasn't the cat's fault . . . that's just what cats do."

She sighs. "He did it for me."

"But you'd never want that!"

"Hush." She sighs. "I know, love. Of course I didn't want to shoot the poor creature."

"He's a murderer." I push my bottom lip out.

"Don't." She places her hand over my rigid fingers.

"Why does he have a gun? It's horrible."

"Oh," she lets out a sound of distress, as if the mention of it has wounded her. "I wish he'd get rid of it. Evil thing." She opens and closes her mouth. Her lips make a damp sound. "He got the gun years ago, as a precaution. He felt he needed to."

"A precaution against what?"

She sighs. "I suppose we don't talk about those days, when your da and I first got married. It's so long ago now. And we wanted to put it all behind us." Her eyebrows knit together. "But after our marriage there were some threats. Some . . . difficulties. There was resentment. Suspicion. But the gun was only for show. To make me feel safer, probably." Her lips wobble around a smile. "Only of course I was more scared of it than I was of any busy bodies."

I bite my lip. I'd never thought about what it would have been like to be married to a German back then. If I got teased at school now, it must have been so much worse for her, straight after the war. It's the first time I've thought about what being his wife meant. It's not just me that's been punished.

"If it was so difficult—why did you marry him?" I ask, breathless with my presumption. The need to know is more urgent. "Did you love him?"

She looks surprised. "Of course." She moves her hand to the base of her throat, touching the soft hollow there. "You know I grew up in Wales, in the mountains?" She glances at me and I nod. "It's tough country. Sheep farmers are the only people who can make a living."

I sit up straighter, dropping my book, and hug my knees under the covers.

"I found a hawk once, injured. There was a man in our village who could cure creatures and I took it there. He let me help him. I bound up the wing and weeks later we let it fly free. There's something about wild creatures, damaged things . . . I want to care for them."

I frown, not understanding the connection.

"Your da was like that. Fierce and proud. Oh, Klaudia, you should have seen him. He was tall and handsome. So blond his hair was nearly white." Her eyes are far away. "There was no one like him in the valleys. Didn't say much. But I could tell he was in pain, inside." She moves her hand to pat her chest briefly.

I lean forward. "How could you tell?"

She raises her eyebrows and smiles. "I just could." She laughs. "Come here, cariad." She folds me inside her talcum-powdered warmth to kiss me goodnight. Her cheek is downy soft as a small silk cushion. "When a man falls in love with you, it's a powerful thing. It sweeps you away," she says against my ear. Then she pulls back, her smile gone. "It was hard, because my parents were against him. In the end I had to run away."

"Is that why we never see them?"

She nods. "They couldn't understand. We eloped."

"Eloped!" I can't imagine my father doing something so romantic and impulsive.

She tips her head on one side as if she's thinking of what to say. "Yes," she says. "It does sound romantic doesn't it? And in a way it was. But after the war my parents weren't the only ones to keep hatred in their hearts." She looks at her hands. "It wasn't easy, settling down, trying to make a home. But we believed, Klaudia. We put our trust in Jesus."

The next morning I find a carving of a bird on my bedside table looking at me with unblinking eyes: a perfectly crafted creature with folded wings and a curl of claws tucked up. I realize that my father must have stood by my bed in the darkness while I was sleeping. Perhaps he'd touched my hair after he'd left his offering, or rearranged my covers. I take the bird into my hands. It feels cold and hard.

ELIZA

1995, Leeds

November

WE SPEND MOST OF our time at his place. He shares a house with two others from teacher training, and his friend, Mike. They'd tossed a coin for bedrooms. Cosmo won. His is the largest, at the top of the house, with views over rooftops and church spires to a glimpse of brown and green moorland, and most importantly, it has a double bed.

He'd swung his door open, standing back to let me enter, and I'd caught a tremor of uncertainty in him. I'd thought it was the anticipation of sex: nervy and necessary, a quickening in the air between us. But then I understood.

His walls were covered with paintings and sketches. Canvases, stacked together, leaned against a table. Color and shape leapt out at me, so that I didn't notice anything else. I went closer, staring at the pictures, recognizing faces of his friends, scenes from the city. And there were other paintings, like dreams; a shifting fantasy of mythological creatures, floating stars, moonlit woods.

When I turned to him, he was standing in an agony of waiting, twisting his hands, holding them out as if waiting for a jailer to clamp his wrists. His gaze was on my face, analyzing, dissecting. I didn't have to speak. He knew. Relief sank through him. He dropped his hands to his sides and grinned at me.

"Why are you teaching?" I went to him. Indignant. Excited by his talent. "You should be an artist. You *are* an artist."

My words were caught by his tongue moving between my lips, asking without speaking, and we were falling backwards onto the luxury of his double bed. His hand behind my head to cushion me made me want to cry. Rain tapped against the window. A sudden squall of winter. He was pulling my jumper over my shoulder, kissing my collarbone, licking at the curve of clavicle, feathering my ear with his breath.

The outside is full of the hiss of sparklers and snap of sausages. Gangs of children run giggling in the streets, full of the energy of the night, emboldened by the shrieking sky and smoky darkness. Everyone is going to Roundhay Park to see the fireworks display, but Cosmo pulls me back. "I have a better idea," he whispers.

There's a pull-down ladder that leads up to the Velux window in the sloping ceiling of his bedroom. He goes first, leaning down to help me up through the gap and out onto the slippery tiles of the roof. I catch my breath: the view of treetops, spires and buildings is eclipsed by the huge swing of the sky. Then I look down and my stomach lurches at the drop.

He holds out his hand. "Trust me?"

I nod, placing my fingers inside his.

"I know it's an old line. But I won't let you fall," he says.

A breeze tugs at my hair and I hang on to him, snatching glimpses into the void below, where a sea of rustling shapes moves. The bushes and trees of the garden transformed into an ocean.

It's a short shuffle across a stone ridge till we reach the big chimneystack and can crouch beside it. Hugging the cold, solid weight of bricks, we cling together and marvel at explosions of color which become bigger and brighter, shattering the darkness around us, as if we've flown closer to the moon. I want to tell him how much Mum loves fireworks. Instead I squeeze into his chest, laughing as a shower of hot cinders falls onto our heads.

"Never a dull moment when I'm with you," I say, patting the sparks out of his hair. "Have you got a thing for heights?"

He glances at me sideways. "Didn't I tell you, our next date is rappeling from the top of the cathedral?"

A rocket explodes, and streamers of red and gold scrawl across the sky, so close I could put up my hand and stir the colors like ribbons. Far away we hear the collective sighs of admiration rising above the trees in the park. But we are alone, high above the city, like birds. He turns and settles his lips on mine. "You taste of gunpowder."

As we're climbing down the ladder into his dark bedroom, a song comes up from the sitting room below: Mick Jagger's voice wailing through the ceiling, the bass thumping and moaning.

"I love this song! Dance with me." I take his hands, pulling him across the carpet, hips swaying.

He moves with me, smiling. "You love every song."

We're waltzing around like Fred Astaire and Ginger Rogers, turning inside moonlight, singing along to the words. Then he pulls me close, ribs pressed against ribs. And we're unpeeling our clothes, trying to find skin, pressing our mouths against each other, clashing teeth, swallowing breath. I smell the cinders in his hair, damp and smoky as he buries his face in my stomach, and we slide across the bed, entwined and laughing.

"I've never met anyone like you, Eliza Bennet," he says as he slips his hands around my waist, tugging at the waistband of my jeans. "Nerves of steel. Skin like silk. And legs that could crush a man to death."

Mike leans over and grabs a slice of pizza from the boxes spread on the coffee table. He sighs with pleasure as he takes a bite of stringy cheese, grease shining his fingers. Cosmo and I are slumped on the tatty sofa, hips welded together, his arm around my shoulder. Cosmo's other housemates, Lou and Peggy, are kneeling on the floor by the coffee table, passing a joint between them.

I lean my cheek on Cosmo's shoulder, letting their voices wash over me. Honey melts in my bones; there's a sensitized ticklishness on my skin. My lips are swollen from kissing. I'm suddenly ravenously hungry and I lean forward, pick up a piece of drooping pizza and take a huge bite. Cold, salty, chewy. It's the most delicious thing I've ever tasted.

"How's the dancing?" Lou asks me, eyes narrowed against the smoke. She pinches a fragment of tobacco from her tongue with fastidious care.

"Good."

And it is. Voronkov took me back. I'm working hard. I haven't tried to perform in public again. But I'm going to kick my fear away. One thing at a time, I tell myself. Sitting here, I feel as though I could do anything.

"I admire you," Lou is saying. "For taking a risk. I mean, personally, I couldn't do it. I need to know I can support myself. Teaching is one of those jobs. It'll always be there."

"God, that's a bit reductive isn't it?" Mike hoots, mouth full. "Whatever happened to passion? For educating the unformed mind—inspiring the next generation. *Dead Poets Society* and all that." He looks at me. "We could all do with being a bit more passionate, like Eliza with her dancing."

"Oh, I don't know if I'd call it passion." I swallow a piece of dough. "It's more like a compulsion. I have to dance—even when it's hard, or seems impossible. The need to do it is inside me, and I can't get rid of it. When I got to Leeds it was my chance to do what I believed in instead of what was expected. A geography degree just wasn't right for me. It was a big decision to drop out, but you have to admit your mistakes, don't you?" I look around at their listening faces. "Marriages. Jobs. Degrees. How many people won't admit it when they've got it wrong? They keep soldiering on until it's too late. It's so British, so stiff-upper-lip. You made your bed; you have to lie in it. What kind of idiot saying is that, anyway?"

I stop, flushed, aware that I'm talking loudly, scared that I'll give myself away if I say anything else. I've sailed too close to the truth already. I stiffen, staring at their faces: waiting for one of them to question me. But Mike raises his can of lager towards me in a silent salute. And Cosmo turns his head and presses his lips against my forehead.

A chink of moonlight through the curtains throws shadows over Cosmo's face. The planes and valleys of his features move across each other like a puzzle. Knowledge of him falters, and I press my fingers against his jaw, feeling the shape of his nose, twin arching brows like supplicant creatures.

"You're very quiet." I lean over him. His chest rises and falls beneath my ribs. A boat carrying me onwards.

"Just thinking about what you said." He takes my hand in his, kisses my fingers. "I wish I was as brave as you."

I crumple, my arm losing strength, too weak to hold me up. I sink onto

my side. "I'm not brave." I look at the dim ceiling. "I just dance. That's all."
I twist my head away, squeezing my eyes shut.

He rolls over and hugs me close. I'm turned away from him. My spine curved into the hollow of his chest. I can feel tension inside him. His self-doubt. "You're pleasing your parents," I murmur. "You're being sensible. Sensible is good."

"That's another thing. You're so courageous about being alone." His words rumble through me. I feel them in my stomach, my heart.

I fidget inside the cage of his arms. My fingers dig into the sinew of his biceps. "No," I whisper. "I'm not."

"Where are your brothers?" he asks.

I'm glad he can't see my face. "Abroad," I say. "Both of them. They live in Australia." I need to change the subject. I can hardly breathe. "Weren't you interested in becoming a doctor—like your mother and father?"

He gives a quick humorless laugh. "It's not just my parents that are doctors. My sister and brother too." He hauls me closer, his legs spooning mine. "I was never much good at science at school. Always had my head in history books or I'd be messing about with pencils and paint. I'm the odd one out." He blows gently into the nape of my neck. "You can imagine what family meals are like when we get together. I don't get a word in edgewise among all the medical anecdotes and in-jokes." He's kissing the edge of my shoulders as he speaks. "Why is it doctors never stop talking about blood?" He stops, moves away slightly. "Seriously though, I have great respect for them."

"Of course." I wriggle out of his grasp and turn on my hip to face him, relieved to be talking about something safe. "It must be amazing to be able to make a difference—actually cure people."

"They're committed to saving lives."

"All lives?" I can taste his breath.

"What do you mean?"

"I don't know," I flounder. "Say if someone was terribly injured, in pain, with no chance of recovery?"

I can just make out his frown. "It's a tricky subject. But modern medicine can relieve pain. I don't think it's up to us to end lives—think where that could lead."

I speak without thinking. "You sound like my—"

I bite back the word. I can't get air into my lungs. I struggle up, sitting over bent knees, coughing, palm over my mouth, eyes watering. He sits up too, pats my back, and passes me a glass of water from the bedside table.

I gulp dusty liquid. Wipe my eyes. We settle again, lying down, making room for each other, my head on his chest.

"Hey. Why are we talking about death?" He slips his hand under the covers and finds my breast, as if by accident. I shiver. Wanting starts up again, blossoming between my legs, warm and urgent.

"I'm going to introduce you to my grandmother," he murmurs, his fingers teasing my skin in soft loops. "I think you'd really like each other. She's the bravest person I know. She survived a concentration camp."

Desire leaves me, empties out. I move abruptly, crossing my arms. His fingers fall away.

"You never said." My voice is small. "You're Jewish?"

"No." He turns onto his back and folds his hands behind his head. "I'm a goy." He sounds cheerful. "My father's Dutch Jewish. Not Mum. But Dad's mother is the archetypal Jewish grandmother. All chutzpah and chicken soup. I used to be fascinated by everything at her house. The menorah. The language she used for things. It seemed so exotic and foreign." He finds my eyes through the wavering moonlight. "Then one day I saw the number tattooed on her arm. It was a shock. It brought it home to me. This whole history I have. Through her. She doesn't talk about what happened—not unless you ask. She lost her entire family. She's this tiny wisp of a woman. But she's stronger than anyone."

I inch away from him, acres of cold sheet stretching between us like a desert. Cosmo is still speaking, but his voice is distant. I can't hear anything clearly for the thunder of blood crashing in my ears. His history has changed my lie, swollen it to new proportions, making it huge and grotesque. Guilt twists up from the past, flooding through my veins, marking me out as my father's daughter.

ERNST

1933, Germany

THE RADIO IS ON IN the parlor. It's a freezing January and Mrs. Meyer sits by the fire knitting, thin ankles crossed under her skirt. Bettina and Agnes are on the floor, practically in the grate itself, shelling nuts into a bowl. Because it's bitter out, Otto and I are allowed inside with the rest of the family. We kneel hunched over a sheet of paper, cleaning tack.

Meyer is on a chair by the radio, head cocked towards it, listening. The only other noises are the soft clicking of knitting needles, snap of twigs breaking inside flames, and an occasional tumble of embers. A tinny voice shouts out of the radio into the hushed room.

A sudden whistling interrupts the program; sounds crackle and hiss through the transmitter. The voice disappears inside the noise. Meyer frowns and twiddles a knob. The voice rises up from the machine, even louder. "Reich President von Hindenburg has appointed Adolf Hitler, leader of the National Socialist Party, chancellor of the Reich."

Bettina throws a handful of peel into the fire. Flames flare green. I keep rubbing at the leather strap in my hand. Smelling horse sweat, beeswax and burning chestnut skins.

"Hitler is a friend of the farmer." Meyer nods. "And no friend to communists. Things will get better now."

Mrs. Meyer takes off her glasses and rubs at her eyes, her knitting abandoned on her lap. She gazes into the fire. "Put another log on, Ernst."

Meyer turns the radio off. I get up and place a piece of wood in the grate, the heat scorching my face as I lean close.

Two months later, Otto and I travel into town on a Saturday morning with Meyer, to take eggs and cheese to market as usual. As we draw up in the trap on the market square we see at once that something is happening: stalls are abandoned, and there's a crowd gathered around the steps of the town hall. Otto and I jump down and wriggle past elbows to get to the front. Men in brown SA uniform are taking down the German flag; we watch as they pour petrol on the twists of fabric. One of them drops a match and sets it blazing. Their polished boots reflect the glare. Farmers and townspeople shuffle and whisper.

"They've got rid of the mayor," someone says.

"Good riddance," another voice says.

A thin stream of smoke catches in the bright air, smudging it. A group of Hitler Youth push up behind the SA. The boys are the only ones to react openly. They cheer. I look at their uniforms, the knives in their belts, their flushed, excited faces, and feel envious. As the flag on the ground writhes and blackens, Otto and I watch the SA men begin to hoist a different one. The men shout to each other, voices full of satisfaction.

"Come along." Meyer tugs at us. "We're here to work."

We resist him, craning our heads, staring up above the gabled roof of the town hall, eager to see the new flag unfurling. There is no wind to lift it. It hangs, drooping and stubborn as a dead thing. But we know that when it snaps open it will show a black swastika, a red background.

We are German Catholics, living in a German Catholic family; but we have no official proof of our parentage, which is a problem. The organization insisted on taking photographs of us from different angles and sent them off for verification of our Aryan physiology. The results came back in our favor. But still we must undergo a worse humiliation.

Our section leader, Winkler, takes us into his office and makes us drop our pants. He has to check that we aren't circumcised, he explains. Otto stands to attention, staring straight ahead, flushing scarlet. Cold air breezes around my private parts, shriveling my balls. I nearly pull up my pants and walk out. I don't want to play at soldiers that badly. I want the knife—a dagger that says "Blood and Honor" on it. Only I've just discovered I won't get it until I'm fourteen. But there are other reasons for joining, I tell myself, as Winkler bends to stare at my penis: nobody will be able to doubt the purity of our blood if we are in the organization. And marching up and down with flags and drums will be more fun than toiling up and down the fields spreading muck. We'll have the perfect excuse not to do all kinds of farm duties. There will be trips into the mountains to go camping, weekends away. And we'll be the same as the other boys at school. Most have joined up now.

Winkler straightens and nods. "With no birth certificates, none of the correct paperwork, we have to be safe. You understand? Yours are . . . unusual cases."

"Sir." Otto salutes. "We are Aryans, sir." His voice is tight, wrung out with fierce longing. "We want to serve the Fatherland. To serve our Führer."

The night we are sworn in, I feel some of that emotion too. I wasn't expecting it. But it comes from the inside, a swelling pride, a sense that my blood is beating deep as the sea, beating to the same rhythm as the rest of the boys. Our hearts keep pace with our voices as we chant the words to a marching song. Torches blaze through the darkness, gathering us inside their jagged, fiery glow, and I glance across at Otto, watching him. His jaw thrust out, tightened to stop his mouth from trembling.

We will be part of German Youth until we turn fourteen. Then we can join Hitler Youth. Otto is already angry that I will get there before him. All our lives he's been trying to leapfrog me and become the older brother.

Every week we learn to march in lines, like real troops. Sometimes Winkler drills us through the town holding flags. It's a warning, he says. Important for people to understand that National Socialism destroys everything that stands in its way. The Führer tells everyone that the future of Germany is in the hands of its youth. There is strength in numbers. We have a new and giddy power. Our troop is ordered to disrupt the kids going to Bible study, jostle them and knock books out of their hands. It's weird at first, being a bully. I don't like seeing girls cry, so I only push the boys. It's better when they push back—it's not right when they cringe and put their arms over their faces. It makes me feel strangely angry with them. I get a kind of ache in my belly.

But fighting comes naturally to us. We're boys who are familiar with beatings. Not just the back of Meyer's hand and the strap; Otto and I have always fought, have given each other bruises since I can remember. When Winkler organizes brawls amongst us to harden us up, Otto and I are the first to get stuck in. I turn to see Otto smashing his fist into Carl Ohler's face. Carl is in our class at school. He's cleverer than Otto; most people are. But Carl likes to boast about his grades. Now his nose is bleeding, his mouth twisted. Otto bending over him screaming, "A German boy doesn't cry!"

Before this our lives hadn't counted for much. We'd been told often enough that we were unwanted, abandoned on a doorstep. Meyer and his wife took us in. We've been given their name, but we never belonged. We sleep over the stables and wait for the family to eat before us. Bettina and Agnes kick their legs against the table, chewing and staring at their plates while we stand behind them, our mouths watering, hoping for scraps.

KLAUDIA

1987, London

WE HAVE A SMALL TREE. Its unfolding plastic branches have been dusted and draped with colored lights and dotted with the same collection of decorations that get unpacked from the attic year after year. My mother keeps Christmas cards too. Cards from years back are strung on a piece of string that my father loops above the mantelpiece. The paper is yellowing, the writing inside faded. Any new ones will be propped up in pride of place between the clock and my mother's large Chinese urn. She keeps her sewing thread, an odd assortment of safety pins and spare stamps inside the bulbous porcelain container.

There are two new cards. One is from the Lewis family. The other, with a snowy scene of Central Park, is from my uncle Ernst. I wonder if he'd enclosed any money. He used to. But my father always gives it away to the church. I examine my uncle's untidy, scratchy handwriting. He doesn't write anything, just signs his name. I've only met him once. He came to visit when I was six. I'd had no idea that he was coming, and then there he was, in our house. The only relative I've ever met.

He was blond and tall like my father. You could tell they were brothers. His German accent wasn't so pronounced though. He had another shape to his words, a mixing of German and American. Ernst told me he'd picked up that way of speaking because of living in the USA for so long.

At first I'd been nervous of him. Grooves of silver scar tissue puckered the left side of his face. The eye on that side was pale and milky—blind, he said. And he was missing the ends of two fingers on one hand, one on the other. I'd wondered what kind of accident had done that to him, picturing him crawling from mangled, flaming wreckage or falling frozen from a mountain ridge. Ernst brought all kinds of goodies with him: American chocolate, presents for my mother and father and a huge, life-size baby doll for me with slow-closing spiky eyelashes. He was funny. He put jazz records on and asked me to dance. "Come on, kid. Don't let me down. Show me how it's done."

But when he left for America he forgot to say goodbye, and he never came back. I asked about it, and my mother said that unfortunately Uncle Ernst wasn't very reliable, and anyway, she added, raising her chin, no doubt he had a busy life over the ocean. I wasn't to expect him to visit again, she said. I think the truth is, he argued with my father. My father didn't like jazz and he thought the presents were overly extravagant. Ernst wasn't a believer, and I saw the way my father pursed his lips when we set off for chapel, leaving Ernst reading novels on the sofa, listening to Billie Holiday and eating chocolates.

I used to wish for the brothers to make up so that Ernst could come again. I've given up wishing now.

There are no presents under the tree. Mum keeps them hidden away until Christmas Eve. This year I've asked for a leotard. The need to make certain of it pricks at me so that I can't keep still. It'll only take a quick prod of the packaging to tell me whether or not she's bought it. This is my only opportunity to snoop. I'm guessing that the presents are stored away in my parents' bedroom.

I open their door cautiously. The room is hushed and cold. The walls are flocked in seamlessly repeating orange flowers on a green background; dried flowers poke from a basket. Over the dressing-table the words "Touch not the cup, it is death to the soul" are framed in gold. Crocheted scatter cushions, made by my mother, are arranged on the double bed and on the rocking chair in the corner. I can't remember their room ever looking any different.

I creep past the bed, covered with a blue candlewick spread, neatly tucked in at the corners. I have the feeling that something will shoot out a hand and grab my ankles as I go past, and I stumble quickly to the wardrobe. With a beating heart, I open the doors and hunt past the rows of dresses and suits all swathed in clear plastic, checking behind the shoes. A smell of mothballs rises and clings to me. There are no packages.

I open her top drawer, dipping my hands into lace and nylon. This is where she keeps her underwear: bras with stiff under-wiring and pants with high waists and slimming panels built in. The lace seems to burn my fingers. It is too intimate. I find an ornate perfume bottle. It is empty, lying on its side at the bottom of the drawer. I uncork the glass lid and sniff at the shadow of a scent, heady and faintly stale. I stumble over the name on the label, lips moving as I sound the letters aloud: M.i.t.s.o.u.k.o. I glance over my shoulder, thinking I hear something. A car passes outside with a clash of gears.

Hurrying, I pull open the next drawer down, staring at neatly folded jumpers and cardigans. I slide my hand among them, and then reach right to the back. Something moves under my fingers; I grasp a strange bundle. There's a clink of metal against metal. A silk scarf has been wrapped around knobbly objects.

I sit on the bed to unwrap the flowery scarf, finding several metal objects that look like old-fashioned pieces of jewelery. With a shock, I understand: they're military medals.

I hold a stumpy cross in my palm. It hangs from a red, white and black ribbon like a necklace. I run my fingers over a date engraved at the bottom: 1941. There's a dark shield too with an eagle over the top. The last one is a kind of brooch. It's silver with a crossed sword and rifle at the center. Each of them has a swastika engraved on it. They are cold and weighty in my hands.

Heart beating fast, I bundle them back into slippery silk and shove the package where I found it, behind the soft layers of wool.

In my own bedroom, I bury my face in my hands. You don't get medals for nothing. Three of them! I imagine Hitler pinning them on my father, Hitler's little mustache wrinkling up over his smile as he thanked him. For what? What did my father do to earn them? I don't understand. My parents keep the evidence hidden away, so they must be ashamed. But in that case, why didn't they get rid of them? The swastika on the medals reminds me of the one inked onto my desk and the one Shane Stevens draws on walls. I thought it was the Nazi sign, the one the SS wore on their uniforms.

It has begun to rain. The sky is dark and sullen. Water slaps against my windows in sudden squalls. It doesn't feel like Christmas. Everything is slimy and sodden and miserable. I shiver.

There is a loud rap on my door, making me jump.

"Klaudia," my father calls, "come and lay the table for lunch."

I keep my eyes down as I take cutlery out of a drawer and place mats and glasses on the kitchen table. He's wet from his dash from the shed into the house and mercuried drops shine on the wool of his shoulders. He holds a freshly carved crib with a baby Jesus in his large palms. "For the nativity scene at chapel," he says.

I want to shout and throw all the plates on the floor—see them smash into pieces. I want to knock the crib out of his hands. He is so righteous, but what about the pistol in the portmanteau, the cat buried in our garden, the Nazi medals hidden away?

"Did you meet Hitler when you were in the war?" I ask as I position the water jug in the middle of the table. I hear myself speak with a sense of disbelief, head swimming with a mix of rebelliousness and terror.

"What?" He pulls his gaze from his carving with a jerk.

My mouth is forming more forbidden words but I'm already losing the ability to speak them. "Hitler," I manage. "Did it make you sick to be in the same room as him?" My voice cracks.

He crosses the space between us with two strides. His skin mottles, his mouth pushed tight. And he raises his hand, the flat of it slicing the air.

I scrunch my eyes, tensed, waiting for the blow.

"Otto?"

My lids snap open and I see my mother coming in through the door behind him. My father's face is still fixed on mine, but his pupils have glazed. He's scratching his scalp with his long fingers. His other hand curled into a fist at his side.

"Is everything all right?" Mum is by my side, touching my arm, her face crumpled, looking from my father to me.

"Klaudia has been talking of things that do not concern her," he says stiffly.

I hear the click of moisture in Mum's throat as she swallows. She reaches out to pat his arm. "She's only a child," she says quietly.

"I'm not proud of who I was or the things I did." His voice is harsh. "But I met your mother and I found Jesus. Those two things saved me."

He leaves, shutting the door behind him. I have a pain inside as if my guts are tied in a knot. He'd wanted to hit me. I'd seen it in his eyes. And a watery sickness fills me, because worse than that, my mother lied to me.

"Klaudia? Cariad? I told you not to ask him questions about the past," she's saying. "I hope he didn't upset you. But you have to understand how difficult it is for him."

I can't look at her. I press my fingers around the cold glass jug, letting ice creep into my bones. I wish I'd never found the medals, wish I'd never asked about the war. Now I can't un-know it. Christmas is ruined. I don't want a leotard anymore.

ELIZA

1995, Leeds

December

HE'S NOT JEWISH. His grandmother is. Not just Jewish—she's a Holocaust survivor. Bloody hell! She was a prisoner in an actual camp. I stare at my face in the mirror. It's a conversation I've been having with myself for days, since he told me. It goes round and round. Sometimes I even picture the little row of inked numbers on her arm. Her skin must be wrinkled and worn thin, loose over the bone. The numbers hold their color. Dark. Indelible.

I'm leaving for Paris today. Cosmo said he'd come with me to the airport. But I don't want to drag him to London. Heathrow's a long way from Leeds. So we've compromised on the train station. We're going to do the *Brief Encounter* scene on the platform. It's a shame there's no steamy station café selling buns and tea in green china cups. We'll have to make do with coffee in a paper take-away beaker and a bar of chocolate.

His body is something that I'm compelled to touch, as if searching for pathways, secret avenues further into him. But there's more to us than a heady rush of chemicals. He listens to me. We discuss things. When tension tightens and a row blows up, he finds a way to make me laugh. His jokes are terrible. But he manages to get me every time; finds the crack, the fissure of weakness, and mines it, opens me out with a belly laugh.

I didn't know this could happen between two people. It's as if we meld into a new substance when we're together, something so much finer than me on my own. I have to be careful not to talk about it too much. I'll become one of those relationship bores, one of those people who repeat all the little inconsequential sayings of their "other half." One of those people who pepper conversation with the pronouns "we" and "us" in a smug, superior voice. Anyway, I'm superstitious. Fate will hear and take him away from me. The truth is, I feel so damn lucky.

I make it to the phone box on the corner by nine o'clock and dial the number. When the beeps go I push a coin into the slot.

But it's not Mum's voice. It's my father. I swallow, my throat constricting.

"Hello?" he's saying. "Hello? Is that you, Klaudia?"

It was my intention to tell Mum about going to Paris. I need to explain that I won't be able to phone her while I'm away, and reassure her that I'll be home on Christmas Eve.

"Yes," I say. "It's me. Is Mum there?"

"She's got a headache."

"Oh. Can I speak to her?"

The line crackles. "She's not feeling well, Klaudia. I don't want to disturb her."

"Tell her . . ." I pause. Disappointment dulls my voice. "Tell her I'm going to be very busy. It's the end of term and then I'm going to stay with a friend till I come home. So . . . so I may not be able to phone. Tell her not to worry and I'll see you both on Christmas Eve."

"Very well."

"Give her my love."

The line is dead. I stand with the purring receiver against my ear, frustrated that I couldn't say goodbye to her. I don't like to think of her feeling ill. But my father will bring her cups of tea and keep people away until she's better. He's always been protective of her.

And now I'm late, and I haven't packed. Cosmo will be here any minute. I grab a toothbrush, cleanser, jar of moisturizer and a handful of cosmetics. Shove them into my wash-bag and force the zipper over the jumbled squash. He's not Jewish, I tell myself again. His grandmother is. As if that makes it all right.

In my room, it doesn't take long to throw things into a suitcase. I stare around me at the forlorn space, taking in my single bed, the *Strictly Ballroom* poster on the wall, torn at one corner. My old, faded dance timetable pinned up over the desk. I'm hardly ever here. When I booked my plane ticket, I needed Meg and her Liverpudlian humor, her sensible perspective and her crazy ideas. I needed Paris. The taste of a goat's cheese salad. Sitting up late at night over a bottle of red wine. I don't want to go anymore. I don't want to leave Cosmo. But I've spent the money, and I can't let Meg down.

"Hurry up," his voice calls from the hall.

I'd thought we were catching the bus. But, as I bump my case over the steps onto the path, Cosmo is waiting at the curb: he's towering over a blue Mini with a proud hand resting on the roof, smiling like an advertisement. He opens the trunk. "Mike's lent me his car."

A window rattles above. Lucy leans out. "Give Meg my love," she shouts down.

I nod, waving back. The day is darkening already, the sun a faint, pale disc slipping between clouds.

She pulls her head in and the sash closes with a shudder. Blank glass reflects the thick weight of sky. Cosmo takes my suitcase from me. Our cold knuckles clash. He slams the trunk. I settle in the passenger seat. I've never seen him drive. I like the way he pulls out into the road, checking the mirror, touching my knee for a moment before he changes gear. He's a natural. His long legs somehow manage to fold under the steering wheel; he holds it lightly, lets it slip through his fingers as he makes a turn to the left.

In the busy station concourse, the trapped dome of air is filled with the bustle of travelers, the tension of waiting, the rush of wings. There's a sense of time opening and closing around us. People come and go. Lives switch left or right, like train tracks at points. Possibility seems to hover over our heads, unpredictable as the pigeons. Nerves knot in my stomach. I don't want to go. I curl my fingers through his. I feel like a child on the first day of school.

My train is standing at the platform. We look at it from a safe distance, behind the barrier. A cleaner gets off, bumping a bucket at his side. Passengers get on, settling themselves, putting coats on the rack, opening books and newspapers.

The flap display on the departure board clicks and turns with a fluttering noise, dropping new destinations and train times. The station clock moves its hands. Seconds pass.

"There's your train," he says. "You mustn't miss it." He's putting on an accent: 1940s cut-glass Trevor Howard.

I bite my lip. I can't remember my lines.

He holds my arms, staring into my face. "Shall I see you again? Please. Please. Next Thursday. I ask you most humbly."

I can't stop myself from laughing, and my voice wobbles and falls away from the accent I'm attempting. I don't stick to the script. "Not next Thursday," I correct him. "After Christmas. Next term. I'll be there. At your place. Just like we said."

"Have a wonderful time in Paris." He brushes his knuckles across my jaw, under my chin. It makes me shiver.

And then he's kissing me and I'm kissing him back. The sound of the station recedes. Our lips and tongues are all that exist; the warmth of his skin pressed against mine, his hands moving around my cheeks to hold me steady.

"I love you with all my heart and soul," he says softly.

"You forgot the accent." My throat constricts.

"No." He shakes his head. "I'm not Trevor anymore. That's me. I love you, Eliza."

I swallow. Heat scalds my cheeks. Things shouldn't start with a lie. This has gone too far already. The next time I see him will be a new year. A new start. I'll tell him then.

"I love you too," I say.

KLAUDIA

1987, London

SHANE COMES OUT OF a tunnel with three of his mates. It's not five o'clock yet, but it's winter dark. A train rattles across the bridge overhead. The steely screech of wheels on tracks is hard and unrelenting and urgent. I shiver, knowing not to run.

Shane steps forward, a beam of streetlight catching the gleam of his teeth. I recognize the three shuffling in the shadows behind him, all of them weak and mean, all of them bullies. They glance about furtively, and I sense their pent-up excitement. I back away, keeping my eyes on them. It's one thing to be trapped in a school playground, and another to be caught alone in an empty street.

"Remember those names I taught you?" Shane is by my side, pinching my arm tightly. "Hope you learned them like I told you."

He pulls a canister out of his pocket and presses it into my hand.

There's a smell in the tunnel that hits the back of my throat. Damp, soot, urine and old chicken bones rotting in paper takeaway cartons. Something scrabbles in the shadows.

"Just a rat, princess." He smiles as I flinch. "Now. Get writing."

My mind has gone blank. "Start with an easy one," he says pleasantly. "Try 'Hitler.'"

I direct the can at the dank wall, my finger on the aerosol nozzle. I'm shaking. "I don't want to," I whisper. My arm falls away, my finger still jammed down, so that a spray of red showers the bricks like a blood splatter, smattering Shane's shoes.

"Bitch." He's feeling inside my blazer, and he grabs my breast, squeezes hard, crushing me. "Your life won't be worth living if you don't do as you're told."

I gasp. My body recoils, and I struggle away, raising the can, moving my wrist, spelling out the letters. The paint hisses into the air, and the sour stink of chemicals fills my nostrils.

Three of them stand at the entrance; Shane is right behind me, his breath coming hard and fast. "Now write, *Hitler's coming to get you scum*," he directs. My body feels numb, emptied out, wooden as a puppet's. I do what he asks.

Another train rattles over our heads. A car passes in the street behind, its headlights moving across us, the wash of its glare flattening Shane's features. The light skims the green slime of the tunnel with silver, and then slides away. I am alone. Nothing can help me. Puppet Girl. My strings twitch and my hand moves, spewing big shaky words onto brickwork.

"Your dad would be proud." Shane takes the canister from my bloodless fingers and pulls me close, pressing his mouth over mine. I try to push him away, balling my fists against his chest. I smell the pus in his skin, taste beer on his tongue. His hand fumbles under my school skirt, fingers burning the thin skin of my thighs as he grabs between my legs and jabs hard.

"That's the end of the first lesson," he says. "Next one's coming soon."

I collapse onto cold concrete, shaking, alone, hearing footsteps and shouts of laughter echoing back to me. The arch of bricks presses down. My skin feels scalded where he touched me. I wipe at my face with both hands, pulling it, tearing at my skin with my nails, as if I could erase my features, take away the person I am.

I can't be seen with books about Nazis under my arm at school. So I take a bus to the nearest public library. I sidle past the desk, being careful not to make eye contact with the librarian busy stamping books with brisk authority. In the history section, I'm relieved to find that I'm alone. I browse up and down book stacks, running jittery fingers over titles. I don't even want to be seen to be taking an interest in the Holocaust, as if interest itself could tarnish me. I pull out three books and huddle over them in a quiet corner.

The first that I open is like the one I found in my desk. I force myself to read about ghettos and death marches. I flick past photographs of hollow-eyed inmates; benign-looking men sitting at desks in SS uniforms; brutal fences and stark buildings. The horror gives me a pain in my stomach. I feel exhausted by it: the unrelenting pile-up of statistics, cruelty upon cruelty. I close the book, my mouth dry, and glance around me. A mother is reading to her child at the next table. They sit with their heads close, and she runs a finger over the page as she talks, so quietly that I can't make out the words. The child is slumped against her shoulder sleepily, thumb in his mouth.

I pick up a book called *Stalingrad*, and flick through to the index, running my finger down the "M"s. Nothing. I feel relieved and a little silly. I try another, scanning the close-packed index without discovering a familiar name. I'm not going to find my father in history books. The librarian walks past balancing a pile of hardbacks in her arms. She stops and glances down.

"School work?"

I nod, not looking up.

"If you're researching World War Two, this one is very good." She stoops and picks a book off the shelf and puts it on the table.

"Thank you," I whisper.

She's gone on her soft-soled shoes.

I slide the *Diary of a German Soldier on the Eastern Front* towards me. It is heavy, thick with paper crammed with close text, broken up by black and white photographs. I look at the pictures first, turning pages slowly. There are old-fashioned-looking armored trucks; another shows a group of grinning soldiers holding rifles, cigarettes in their mouths. They don't look much older than me. The pages turn between my fingers. I find a photograph of a team of bedraggled horses straining through the mud up to their knees, pulling a big artillery gun. Even inside the blurry outlines, I can see the animals' eyes are widened with terror. Another photo is of a destroyed Russian tank with sacks of flour strewn around it. I read a bit of the caption: "Note the enemy dead in the immediate vicinity of the armored vehicle." Not sacks of flour. I lick my finger, spinning forwards quickly to the index. I find the "M"s and glance at the list. And there it is. "Meyer, Gefreiter, page 150."

I shut the book. It must be a coincidence. It can't be him. Meyer is a common name. But I have to look. My heart bumps against my ribs as I turn the pages. There's a picture of three German soldiers pointing guns at unarmed people in ordinary clothes. One of them, I see with a shock, is a woman. She's thin, young. Her blank expression is pinned before the barrel of a gun. I understand that I'm seeing her in the instant before she dies. Something else about the image jags, catches in my mind. The soldier nearest the camera is in profile. And despite the grainy black and white, I know that nose; that jut of chin. My hands begin to shake. My heart is crawling through my throat. I scan down, blinking, searching the caption. "Execution of Jewish partisans. Gefreiter Ohler, Gefreiter Krenz, Gefreiter Meyer. 1943, Russia."

My father stands before me, legs planted firmly in the barren white that must be snow. He stares over his gun into the face of the woman. His lips are set, jaw clenched in an expression he wears a lot: that cold anger of his I'm so familiar with. Gefreiter Meyer.

The mother's reading voice carries on behind me, a soft blur. I hear her child asking something and her answering hush, hush; the quiet click of shoes moving across the floor; rub and flicker of pages turning in the mild, bookish air. But in my head there is the crack of a gun; the crumple and thud of a woman falling into white, a single sigh as breath leaves her body.

I shove the book across the table and put my head between my knees. The floor lurches. My insides twist. Is this what he got his medals for? I can't get the photograph out of my head. I think the girl will always be there now. Fixed inside my skull.

1993

September

Mum keeps patting powder onto her cheeks, but more shiny tracks appear as she dabs at her eyes with a screwed-up hankie. I squeeze her hand. "It's only three years, Mum. It'll go so fast."

She shakes her head. "It's your time to get out into the world. You won't be coming home. It's all right, love. I understand. But remember your bedroom will always be here for you." She pats my arm. "I'll be here. In case you need me."

I swallow. Saliva catching in my throat. She won't let me speak. She puts a finger on my lips. "Run upstairs and say goodbye to your dad."

I go slowly through the sitting room, trailing up the stairs, looking around me as if this really is the last time I'll see it: the framed words from Scripture; surfaces cluttered with wooden statues; the umbrella stand and the clock in the hall.

Their bedroom door is ajar. I see him through the slender opening. He's standing in front of the mirror doing up his tie. He finishes, adjusting the knot. He looks at himself, blue eyes and expressionless mouth. I take a breath, preparing to enter, not knowing if he will hug me this time, or just shake my hand as he usually does. But before I can take a step, or push at the door, he raises his right arm. He lifts it in a line, saluting his reflection with slow gravity, his arm rigid, standing straight and tall. Like the soldiers in films; the boys at school.

I put my hand over my mouth, beginning to back away, soundless over the carpet, but his voice reaches me.

"Come in, Klaudia."

I edge into the room, my cheeks burning. We both know what I saw.

He doesn't blink. "Well, you're off. Remember where you come from; don't let university life go to your head." His face is a mask. "Work hard. Find the nearest chapel. Jesus will help you to stay on the right path."

I'm feeling sick. I can't look at him. I don't understand. He's in God's army now. The executioner in the snow, gun raised to his shoulder, that's in the past. My thoughts tremble around the image of him in the mirror, his action revealing something I can't let myself grasp. It slides away, nothing but a reflection, a shadow moving over glass.

My feet are on the stairs, stumbling away. Mum waits below to walk me to the train station, neat in her coat with her handbag slung over the crook of her elbow. She smiles. "All right, love? This is a big day. I'm so proud of you."

The front door swings open, letting in daylight, the sound of traffic.

PART TWO

THE TRAP

ELIZA—KLAUDIA

1995, London

IT TAKES ME AGES to negotiate the train and Tube, lugging my over-stuffed and battered suitcase. I slump onto a seat on the heated, crowded bus, the final leg of my journey, and gaze out of the window at familiar gray London streets. There are baubles hanging in shop windows, and decorations glow from lampposts: angels blowing trumpets and fat men on sledges picked out in lights. Pavements are thick with people wrapped up against the cold, their arms full of presents.

At home the fake tree will be blinking in the corner, the yellowed cards hanging over the mantelpiece, smells of mincemeat and goose fat coming from the kitchen.

Paris was colder than London. The first flakes of snow had been falling as Meg waved me goodbye at Charles de Gaulle. I'd been worried that the flight might have been canceled. But I'm arriving exactly when I said I would. I've got presents in my case: a bottle of perfume with a heart-shaped glass stopper: Mitsouko by Guerlain; I recognized the bottle in Galeries Lafayette, and thought it was about time Mum had a replacement. I can't wait to see her face when she opens it. But first I'll drop my bag on the floor and pull her to me for a hug. And I'll remember how she only comes up to my shoulder, and how she smells of talc, and the mints she carries in her handbag to suck when she thinks she should resist another biscuit.

As the bus turns off the main road, past the Methodist Chapel, a sense of dread trickles inside me. Each street triggers another memory: the teenage humiliation of being seen going to chapel with my parents, dragging my feet in sensible polished shoes, as I hunch past the group of kids on that same corner: Amber and Lesley sneering with shiny mouths, teetering in heels, their laughter following me. There were no parties for me; no make-up; no boyfriends. My father's hands tightened on my shoulders when I sat below him stuttering over the Bible text he'd set me to learn. I don't want to see him. It's only the thought of Mum, wiping her hands on her apron, coming forwards to pat my cheek that makes me impatient to get there. None of this is fair on her. I miss her. I can almost feel her fingers, dusty with flour, against my skin.

Our house is a dirty white, pebble-dashed semi. It sits in the middle of the row. There is a mean strip of front garden where rubbish collects—crisp packets, empty Coke cans—and a low concrete wall where, to my father's fury, teenagers sometimes perch. A stubby tongue of crazy paving leads to the half-glazed front door.

I ring the bell. I don't know why. I have my key. My father opens the door and I understand at once that something is wrong even though his expression barely changes when he looks at me.

"Klaudia."

"Where's Mum?"

The words are sawdust in my mouth. A boomerang of blood ricochets against my ribs. The open doorway sways and my father reaches out a hand. He's speaking but my brain is rejecting the words. *No.* I think I say it aloud. "No."

I'm sitting in the living room on the velveteen sofa. My head droops between my knees. The carpet spins under my feet. I look up and realize that he's in his best dark suit and the room is empty and bleak. There are no shiny baubles, no ribbons of tinsel wound around a plastic tree. It's freezing. I shiver and hug myself. The wooden saints gathered in a group on the sideboard regard me with blind eyes, hands raised in blessing. My father slumps opposite me, looking older and grayer. He seems to have shrunk. His shirt is loose around his neck and his jacket sleeves hang below his wrists.

He clears his throat. "She was knocked down by a car. Near the house, crossing our street. She died in the hospital later that day. Her injuries . . . were . . . they couldn't save her."

His voice is weary. It doesn't make any sense to me. I am unable to imagine my mother dashing in front of a car. I remember her telling me over and over to wait on the curb, look right and left, and right again.

"What happened . . . ?" I stare towards the kitchen, thinking she will appear in the doorway. She doesn't come. She will never come again. No. That's impossible. "The driver . . . have they been prosecuted?"

Dad shakes his head. "It wasn't his fault. He wasn't drunk or speeding. She . . . she just walked in front of him."

"When?" I whisper, hanging my head.

"A week ago," he says. "I tried to reach you at university. But I had no number for you. I waited by the phone, but you didn't call." He puts his hand over his eyes. "I sent a note to the address you left and that got no response either."

I can't look at him. Shame creeps through me, rolls like a suffocating fog through my limbs, filling my mouth, pressing behind my eyes. I can hardly breathe. I try to recall the last time I saw her. But I can't snatch any comfort from a memory. I see her face when I left, remember the way she'd touched my dyed hair. Patient. Resigned. "Your beautiful gold." She'd hugged me close. "Look after yourself, cariad. Come back to me soon."

But I didn't come back to her. I'd let her down. I'd lied and I'd abandoned her.

"The funeral at the chapel was . . ." His voice thickens and he stops. "People loved your mother. Everyone came."

"Are her ashes buried there?"

He stands up and looks out through the open door into the kitchen and the garden beyond. "No. There's a plaque. But she's buried here."

I glance up, startled. "Here?"

"In the garden. Under the apple tree," he says. "I put her ashes in the Chinese urn."

The urn is no longer on the mantelpiece. My heart beats faster. "Is that . . . OK? Is it allowed?"

"It's what she would have wanted. She loved that tree." He rubs his nose. "It's what I want. To have her close to me."

I think of my father decanting the granules and grains from whatever container the crematorium would have given him into the porcelain mouth. Did he use a spoon, or his hands? Had there been spillages?

I cross the frosty garden towards the apple tree. It leans slightly to one side; roots protrude through the grass like rheumatoid knuckles, ancient fingers tapping their way into the light. There is a darker patch of naked earth between the roots, recently turned. I lean against the cold trunk and stare down. I can't take it in. My mother: nothing but handfuls of ashes in an urn below my feet. A thrush sits on a higher branch and looks at me reproachfully. The bird table is empty.

I go back into the house and fetch some water in a small bowl. There is only the moldy heel of a loaf in the bread bin; crumbling it inside my fingers, I walk back to the bird table and leave my offerings. Wings flutter above me, a flash of yellow beak. A curtain twitches at an upstairs window next door. Mrs. Perkins watching from behind a fall of lace.

I curl my nostrils in the cold, dim house. The kitchen smells of rubbish. The bin needs emptying. My father is sitting in the living room. His hands rest on his knees and he stares into space as if he's in chapel and the preacher is in mid-flow.

I move around him, putting on lights. Reaching into the under-stairs cupboard, I locate the heating dial and turn, switching the setting to "high." I open the fridge, look through cupboards. There is no food. I will make a shopping list. I move slowly, as if I'm fighting my way through molasses. But it's helping to take action. Being practical is the only thing I can do. There's no time for crying. If I start, I won't be able to stop.

Mum, I tell her silently, you don't have to worry. I'm home. I'm Klaudia again. I'll take care of him. It doesn't matter what I feel about him. I'll do it for you.

I wish I could hear her now: her melodious words, soft as moss. I used to think she spoke the way clouds would if they had voices. I find a pen and begin to compose a list: bread, milk, apples, cereal. My closed throat aches.

1996

On New Year's Eve I lock myself in the bathroom and wash my hair. As I bend over the bath, blood rushes to my head, bubbles trickling into my ears and stinging my eyes. I soap and soap, scrubbing hard, then rinse until the wet ends squeak between my fingers, and the hot water runs cold. But as I dry it off, staring into the mirror, I see that no color has come out. The dye is stubborn.

I have a fleeting memory of my bleary face in the mirror as Cosmo waited in my bedroom. Missing him is a stone in my belly.

The third of January is the date we'd arranged to meet in Leeds. He'll be there now, wondering where I am. He thinks I spent the whole of Christmas in Paris. Maybe he'll presume I haven't come back yet, that I'm staying on for a while, and haven't let him know. I dig my nails into my palms. I've made so many mistakes. It's important that this time I do the right thing. No more lies. No more Eliza. There are pale roots growing through my dark dye—feathery and light as a child's hair—Klaudia coming back.

Every morning I haul myself out of bed and begin the slow trek through the day, counting minutes and hours until it's late enough to go to bed. Each measure of time weighs heavily. There is so little to do. I shop and clean. I feed the birds. I cook for my father and watch him pushing the food around his plate.

I'm using the supermarket on the high street. My father insisted that I should. "Don't go to the Guptas'," he told me. "I don't trust them. They overcharge." He frowned. "Their things are out of date."

Mum would call in at the Guptas' several times a week for things we'd run out of—a pat of butter, loaf of bread or pint of milk—and she and Mrs. Gupta always had a chat across the counter. They were friends. I'd never heard Mum complain of items being out of date or overpriced, although of course, my father was right about the supermarket being cheaper.

He's kept everything exactly as it was when Mum left the house for the last time. Her side of the wardrobe is full. Nothing has been packed away. I go into their room when he's not there and lean my face into her clothes, inhaling the talcum powder scent of her, Yardley English Lavender. I press my hands into her shoes, laying my fingers inside the worn leather, feeling the impressions her toes have made. The November issue of *Woman's Own* is in the magazine rack in the living room; a recipe has been neatly cut out of the well-thumbed pages. Mum's toothbrush and Pears soap are still on the sink in the bathroom; the bristles on the brush are dry, and her soap is riddled with cracks like parched mud.

There is a novel under the Bible on her bedside table. I sit on their bed, over the wires of the cold electric blanket, and open it at the marked page. It's a love story—light commercial stuff—my mother had never been interested in literary fiction. Every week she borrowed romances from the library. The covers all looked the same. Purple lettering. Breathless women swooning in men's arms. She was an intelligent woman. She just had a weakness for the idea of happily ever after.

I turn the leaves of the book to the front and see that it is long overdue. The library stamp is for the twentieth of November. My mother usually got through a novel a week. I expect that she'd begun her Christmas preparations. Once she'd begun on all her baking, she'd be too busy to read. And I think of Mum getting everything ready, excited about me coming home.

My father hardly leaves the house. I find him hunched in his chair in the living room listening to opera, and when his precious records reach the end, he doesn't seem to notice or care that they go on spinning soundlessly except for the click-clicking hiss of the needle running on empty grooves.

As I put crumbs and bacon fat on the bird table, I notice snowdrops showing pale against the earth. Green leaves poke up from untidy beds and through straggly grass. I'm guessing they are crocuses. Other bulbs are fattening under my feet, new shoots exploring delicate paths through darkness towards the light. Inside the porcelain belly of the urn, my mother's ashes are packed, cold and gray, like another kind of bulb.

I can't ever go back to Leeds. How can I? I was Eliza there and now Eliza is dead. She died the minute I arrived home. Guilt and grief have finished her off. I will never forgive myself for running away from Mum. I wish I could explain to her why I'd disappeared.

Cosmo and I were going to have our own Christmas, a belated one, just the two of us. I have his presents in my case: a book about Matisse and a wallet engraved with silver. I chew my thumbnail, imagining him hurrying to the door each time the malfunctioning bell lets out its strangled sound.

He'll be worried. Lucy doesn't know my real name, my address here, or my telephone number. He won't find me. The girl he's looking for doesn't exist. The pain of losing him digs in under the pain I feel about Mum. Two losses. Two wrongs. A snag of nail rips off between my teeth exposing the raw underneath.

It wasn't until I arrived at university and everyone was introducing themselves that I realized I didn't have to drag my background with me anymore. I could leave it behind in Croydon. Be the person I wanted to be. I've always liked the name Eliza. It's so English. It was easy to buy a packet of brunette hair coloring, and ask a hairdresser to chop it short. Then I dropped out of university, found a part-time job in a coffee shop and took my dancing seriously. Contemporary, ballet and tap lessons. It felt like I was suddenly set free from prison. In a different city, away from the bureaucracy of university, I could reinvent myself properly. I met Meg in a ballet class and moved into shared digs with her and Lucy. I had a post-office box for any mail with my real name. My surname was almost never used. If anyone asked, I said it was Bennet, because *Pride and Prejudice* is my favorite book, and Elizabeth Bennet the perfect heroine.

I made up a whole and detailed past for myself. It was like a game at first. Telling my new past to other people felt odd. I was sure that I would be exposed. Who would believe me? The story I was making up seemed incredible. But nobody doubted me. And I'd experienced a sense of power then—I'd altered my history. It made me feel in control of my destiny too. Despite the fact that I was living a lie, I'd never been happier, never felt more like myself. My lie seemed to be the truth.

But there is a cost for everything. And it was my mother who paid the price.

I can't stop touching her things. I'm looking for her—even though I know that she's gone.

I sit before Mum's beveled mirror in her bedroom and pick up her powder compact, an oval disc of plastic. I flip it open. The metal base is showing through the worn circle of make-up. I rub my finger onto the powder and press it onto my cheek. It looks ghostly against my skin. Her complexion was paler than mine. Her tube of lipstick is old too; the gold has been rubbed away where she grasped it. I twist up the tube of familiar apricot, smelling perfume and wax. Leaning into my reflection, I work color onto my mouth.

It looks orange on me. "Cariad," she'd cupped my chin in her hand when she'd discovered the ten-year-old me experimenting with her cosmetics, "you don't need any help in looking beautiful."

I never said goodbye. I close my eyes, tasting the thick and greasy layer, remembering that I sometimes found the print of her lips on my cheek after she'd kissed me goodnight.

"Klaudia."

I jump, opening my eyes. My father stands behind me. He stares at my face in the mirror. It occurs to me that he must have wished for a daughter that looked like his wife, feminine and small with glossy dark hair. Mum said that before she was pregnant with me my father could span her waist with his hands.

I feel caught out. My heart beats faster.

He ignores the lipstick on my skin and sighs. "Isn't it time that you went back to your studies?"

"I've taken . . . leave of absence."

"You need to return to university life." He frowns. "There's nothing more for you to do here."

"I've deferred for a year," I say quickly. The lie slides out of my mouth like a tongue.

He looks startled. "Why?"

"I just want to be at home," I tell him. "So that I can be here for you." The words feel awkward.

He moves his head as if a fly is bothering him. "I don't need a nurse maid."

I begin to protest, but he speaks across me. "You're making a foolish choice in my opinion. But if you're staying, then you'd better look for a job. It's not healthy to mope about all day."

My mother used to stand between us, softening edges, interpreting and explaining. I don't know how to talk to him. He moves aside to let me leave. As I go, heat glows in my cheeks, as if I'm guilty of something.

I am guilty. I always will be.

I stride out along the pavement, avoiding dog shit, overtaking dawdlers and young mothers gossiping across their prams. I know where I'm going. A few minutes later, I'm turning into Mercers Road.

Kelwood High looks exactly the same. The playground is deserted. The school day has already begun and pupils will be inside sitting at their desks. I stop and stare through the wire fence. Looking at the brick building makes me remember the itch of socks at my knees and the claustrophobic grip of my top button and knotted tie. Tall windows hold dark shadows. I think I hear the murmuring of trapped voices.

Shane Stevens was expelled after he and his crowd of followers attacked a group of Asian pupils; Shane broke someone's jaw, knocked him unconscious. A year after that, my father retired. But it's not easy to get rid of a reputation. A new girl came into our class in the Lower Fifth. She'd sat next to me, glancing across anxiously, eager to make friends. I'd wanted to smile. She didn't know me. But she'd find out soon enough. There was no point. It occurred to me then that my life would be so much better if I could simply begin again, be someone different.

Eliza was the person I'd always known I could be.

I haven't contacted Meg since I waved to her in the departure hall at the airport. I can't just disappear out of her life as well. I need to tell her who I really am—explain why I lied. I turn away from the bulk of school buildings and wire fencing and walk in the direction of home with my hands deep in my pockets. There is a cold wind, despite the blue sky.

I could write to her. Writing it down will mean I can choose my words carefully. It will give me space to explain. As soon as I have the thought, it becomes urgent that I act on it immediately. I go past the Guptas' shop. I haven't been in to buy anything since my father told me not to. But it doesn't make any sense. If I'm going to send a letter to Meg, I need stamps.

The familiar bell jangles above me and Mrs. Gupta glances up from behind the counter. She nods. "Klaudia. We haven't seen you for a long time."

She opens the register stiffly, with the expression of someone who has been misused. But then her face softens. "I'm sorry for your loss," she says quietly. "Your mother was a lovely person." As I hold out my palm for my change she takes my fingers and squeezes.

My throat is suddenly tight. Her kindness is too much to bear. I wanted to talk to her about Mum, but now I need to leave before I break down in tears.

At home, I shut myself in my room. I must write before I lose my nerve.

I find a pen and paper and sit at my desk, head in my hands, thinking. I make several false starts, wasting paper, crumpling sheet after sheet, ripping each one into shreds and dropping it in the bin. In the end, after lots of crossings-out and re-writes, I manage something that will have to do. I worry that it sounds too plain, too cold. But I don't want to beg or make excuses.

Dearest Meg,

I should have written before to thank you for having me to stay in Paris. I'm sorry. But after I left you something happened to change everything. I found out that my mum had been killed in a car accident. I know that this will seem very odd, as I've always told you that both my parents are already dead. But I lied to you. I am so sorry.

My real name is Klaudia Meyer. I was ashamed of who I was while I was growing up, because my father is German and he was in the army in the Second World War and he did some terrible things. My mother forgave him. But I was teased and bullied all my life for being his daughter. The daughter of a Nazi. Since the war he's become very religious. I was brought up a Methodist. For years he was the caretaker at my school, so there was no getting away from him. I suppose that coming to Leeds gave me an opportunity to run away from all that, to start again. It was my chance to dance and to be the person I wanted to be.

I'm not crazy. I was just desperate, and unhappy.

I know I shouldn't have lied to you. Nothing excuses it. But I am still your friend. I will always be your friend. Underneath the lies, I'm the same person. I hope more than anything else that you can forgive me. If you can, please write to me here, at my home in London. I will wait for a message. I can't bear to lose you. But I will understand if you don't want to see me again.

With all my love,
Klaudia

My hand shakes when I sign my name. What if she can't forgive me? I push away the fear. I have to take this risk; otherwise I've lost her anyway.

I don't know how much it costs to send a letter to France, so I put two first-class stamps on just to make sure, and seal the envelope.

Then I scribble a note to Cosmo. I can't leave him to wonder what happened to me any longer. It isn't fair. I keep it short. I don't put in any endearments. But they sound inside my head. Darling Cosmo. Dearest Love.

> *Cosmo, I'm so sorry I didn't meet you on the third like we'd planned. Things have changed for me and I'm not coming back to Leeds now. Please don't worry about me. I'll contact you when I can and explain. But meanwhile, don't wait for me. It would be better to forget me.*
> *Eliza*

I reread the note, hearing how awkward and abrupt it sounds. But I can't explain it properly. Not yet. Maybe Meg's response will give me the courage. If she forgives me, perhaps it will make it easier to tell Cosmo the truth. I walk to the end of the street to the mailbox. I push both letters quickly through the dark opening. They fall inside and it's too late to change my mind.

My father is standing in the kitchen staring out into the garden. The kettle begins to boil and he turns. He starts when he sees me.

"Do you want a cup of tea?" I try and sound cheerful, walking over to the cupboard and taking out two cups.

We sit across the table from one another. I fail to find anything to say. Silence stretches between us. He frowns into the bottom of his cup, clears his throat. "Have you started to look for a job?"

I shake my head.

He twists his mouth. "You can't stay at home and do nothing. I live on my pension. If you are here for this academic year then you must contribute." He taps his long fingers on the table.

I know he's right. I want to pay my way, but I can't because I'm broke. I've just sent the last of my money to Lucy to cover the rent and told her I wouldn't be coming back. Giving up my life in Leeds means no more

Voronkov. I need to find classes here. But I can't afford them. And a part of me thinks I don't deserve them—not after I let Mum down.

"You must keep up with your studies too. Don't get behind. Get a temporary job in a shop or restaurant," he adds.

I wonder what he would say if I told him that the only job I've ever wanted is to be a dancer. But he knows already. "Dancing is not a career," he told me years ago. "It is a frivolous hobby for silly girls."

ERNST

1933, Germany

IT'S A BEAUTIFUL APRIL EVENING. Clusters of daffodils gather under the trees, bright as fallen suns. Doves coo from the poplar branches. Soon, I realize, the swallows will be back, darting from under the eaves of the barn, flying in airy loops above the house.

I'm off to the lake. Mrs. Meyer is expecting perch for supper. Otto is furious because he's been made to stay behind and mend the orchard fence.

It's good to be on my own. It's always me and Otto, stuck together as if we're twins; whereas, actually, there is probably about a year between us. We don't know our real birth dates. He'd been a tiny baby when we were found. I'd been older, able to stagger about on plump legs. He's taller than me now though. One night those bony knees of his cranked out another half inch of cartilage.

I pick a switch of willow on my way past the pond and whip the tops of grasses, thrashing the air as I walk. Over the dyke, the windmill is turning slowly, white sails cutting a softer path through the sky. The rod and tackle box that's slung across my shoulder bumps against my hip. I like the measure of my own stride, the way I step as I please, stop and start, grow slower or faster. I don't enjoy marching in a troop. Being forced to go at the same speed as the rest. It's a relief to be just me, alone with the meadows and singing birds, the sunlight and the wind in the trees.

There isn't another person at the lake. The soil is churned up with animal prints by the water's edge. I walk farther along the bank, finding a patch of firm ground. I keep my back to the fields, so that I'm facing the dark expanse of forest across the water. I like to be able to keep my eye on its borders. You never know what might rush or creep from between its trunks. Branches and leaves rise in dense banks of green, different shades, darker and lighter. There used to be wolves in the forest. There's still wild boar though—even more dangerous, people say. I don't like the rustling depths of the trees, the impossibility of seeing anything properly once you've stepped inside.

I bait my line and cast off. The air is colder, the sun beginning to drop below the trees. I wait, hunched inside my jacket. Sometimes there's the splash of a perch rising. I stare at the surface, my hands on the rod, fingers alert for any tremble of movement. The lake is deep. There are eels under its calm: dark snakes writhing out of the muck at the bottom. We've caught some big ones in the past. I wouldn't like to be in the water with their muscular bodies pushing close, snouts full of sharp teeth.

A twig snaps. I raise my head, heart jumping at the sound of someone approaching. I spot them before they see me. Two people walking together, heads down, talking. As they come closer, I recognize them. It's Daniel Baumann and his sister. I can't remember her name. Daniel and I were friends at school. But even though they're not Orthodox, he and his sister moved to the Jewish school in the next town a couple of years ago. Daniel used to split his breakfast with me, tearing apart a *Brötchen* speckled with poppy seeds, halving boiled eggs, munching one side of an apple then handing me the rest. We were good at the same things, both liking science and nature studies. I haven't spoken to him since he left, even when I see him in the town. I am embarrassed, afraid of what people will think of me talking to a Jew. I avoid looking at him, not wanting to see disappointment or resentment in his eyes. Their father is a doctor. But we've never stepped inside his surgery. Never needed to. Mrs. Meyer sewed up Otto's leg, the time he'd cut it open on a scythe.

They haven't spotted me yet and I have the instinct to crawl into the long grasses and hide. But the rod and tackle spread on the ground would give me away. I stand up, straightening my jacket.

I see them notice me, the small shock of it registering in the flexing and twist of their shoulders. The girl slows, pulling at her brother's sleeve. And I know they want to avoid our meeting as much as me. Daniel falters, then puts his shoulders back and walks towards me, purposeful, resigned. Light bounces off his round glasses, hiding his eyes.

"Daniel." I nod.

I stare at his sister. She's pretty. Curling brown hair falling across her shoulders. She has skin like milk. But she is a Jew.

Daniel takes his sister's arm. "You remember Sarah?" The words are stiff and formal.

"Of course."

We stand for a moment and the silence is like a muffling up of the air; it seems to press closer, so that I can't catch my breath.

"I'm fishing."

I flush. Why am I stating the obvious like some stupid oaf? I can't think what else to say.

"We come here to get away from things," Sarah confides. She smiles and inclines her head along the path. "There's a deserted cottage . . ."

Daniel digs her in the ribs. She winces and closes her lips, frowning.

"It's OK," I say quickly. "I won't say anything. If it's a secret."

She gives me another quick smile, looking at me from under her lashes and my chest swells.

"We have to get on." Daniel pushes his glasses up his nose. I can't bear the coldness in his voice. But there is nothing I can do to change the way things are. I stand aside, watching them walk along the path and around the river. Gnats spin in the viscous air around them. Daniel keeps his back straight, his head up. Sarah leans close, her arm linked through his, pressing against his side, chattering on. I wish I could hear what she's saying. I watch the soft curves of her bottom, how it moves under her thin cotton skirt.

The newspaper on the table at the club screams *Germany, Defend Yourself!*

We gather in a group around Winkler. He holds up the paper with both hands and shakes it at us.

"You see," he shouts. "You see what the filthy Jews are doing to our great country?" His mouth twitches as he glares at us. "They dare to spread lies. Propaganda. Because of their dirty slander, we face a world-wide economic boycott."

He puts the paper on the table, smoothing its rumpled pages. "Now, what do you think our response should be?"

"Smash up their things!" Anton Vogel yells.

"Tear their ugly asses apart!" Karl Ludwig bangs his fist on the table.

I glance at the portrait of the Führer. He seems pleased. Winkler holds up a hand. "Good. Very good. The Fatherland won't stand for this. We will boycott all Jewish firms. All their shops. And you will play an important part in this."

Winkler hands us paper and pots of paint. Splashing black and red on our hands, we laugh and bite the ends of our paintbrushes as we discuss what to say. We write *DO NOT BUY FROM JEWS!!* And *WORLD JEWRY IS OUT TO DESTROY US.* Winkler writes one of his own: *PERISH JUDAH!* in big letters. As we leave the club house with our freshly painted signs, we hear the sound of smashing glass. There are lots of shops in town owned by Jews. The chemist and the ironmonger are the first that we come to. We'd intended to stick our posters up on their walls, perhaps throw a stone through their windows, but a truckload of Storm Troopers have beaten us to it.

They've shattered the windows of the ironmonger. Boxes of nails, bowls, spades and forks lie across the pavement; the door sags off its hinges. Glass glints across the pavement. People are picking things up and walking off with them under their arms. I see Herr Peters from the post office carrying a spade back to his shop. We are open-mouthed, watching the men in their brown uniforms, guns at their sides, as they smash every window in the chemist with truncheons. The glass cracks; panes fall, crashing and tinkling onto the road. I have a hard lump in my chest. The violent destruction makes me afraid and excited. And I feel sorry for Herr Engel and his wife. I'd carried a parcel for her once and she'd given me two Reichsmarks. The SA push inside the shop; we hear crashing and thumping, and armfuls of soap come flying into the street. Bottles and tins bounce and shatter over the pavement. It is over in minutes. They are back in the truck, engine roaring.

"That's how it's done!" Winkler is shouting. "Fast. Furious. That's the way we take revenge in Germany."

People stand outside and peer from doorways. Nobody says anything. Karl squats down and begins to pick out pieces of candy from the broken glass. Other boys copy him. Otto finds a tin of talc and shakes it with big extravagant sweeps, the white powder making a billowing cloud in the air. I smell the sweetness of lavender. It mixes with other scents: peppermint, ammonia. I shuffle my feet through shards of glass, powder, puddles of colored liquids. An unbroken bottle of camphor rolls across the pavement. I kick a round tin. It has "ointment" written on the lid. Then I stoop to rescue a bar of soap wrapped in purple paper. I put it to my nose and inhale. Violets. I rub my thumb across the flowery packaging and think of Sarah. Perhaps she'd like soap like this. But then I remember, and drop it.

KLAUDIA

1996, London

February

I TOOK A TRAIN from East Croydon to Victoria, then hopped on the Tube for one stop. It didn't take long, but Brixton feels like a different part of London. This is the real thing: the edgy, urban bustle and grime of a city.

There will be all sorts of possibilities here, I tell myself as I emerge from the steps of the Underground, jostled by a crowd of hurrying commuters. But as I trudge up and down the high street, going in and out of countless shops and restaurants asking for work, I begin to realize that getting a job isn't going to be easy. I leave copies of my CV with uninterested managers, even though I'm sure I'll never hear from them. My feet ache; I'm hungry and thirsty; I wish I could have a cup of tea or coffee, but I can't afford it.

The spicy smell from a Caribbean fast-food shop makes my stomach rumble. I go past a dusty-looking second-hand bookshop, thinking that I might come back later to browse. There are a couple of men leaning up against the wall of a hairdressing salon, cans of lager in their hands. I feel them slide their attention towards me. One of them winks. I hurry on, my fingers plucking at the red beret that Meg gave me for Christmas, covering the stripe of blonde that flares from my scalp.

I hear a low wolf-whistle behind me, and square my shoulders, feeling hounded. My eyes scan the shop fronts, and I turn my head left and right, searching for a burlesque club. I've been looking for it since I emerged out of the Tube station. It's the real reason I've come to Brixton. I want to find the club that Cosmo told me about. Because even if I just stand outside and stare through the window, I can have a moment of feeling connected to him.

A sign hangs outside the next building. Ornate letters read: *The Smokey Quartz*. Underneath it says: *Burlesque Club—open 8 p.m.–12.* I stop, biting my lip, suddenly nervous. Curiosity pushes me to edge closer. It'll be closed now, but the door is ajar and I want to peer inside, knowing that Cosmo has been here; that he's entered that doorway, looked at the same things I'll look at.

Fingers tap my arm.

The touch makes me jump and I spin round expecting to find myself confronting one of the lager drinkers. But it's him. I stare. I think my mouth actually drops open. The slide from daydream into reality makes me feel as though I've fallen through a gap in time.

"Eliza," Cosmo says. His face is tight. "Where the hell have you been?"

We stare at each other. I want to fling my arms around his neck. But I'm not Eliza anymore. I drop my eyes. Stare at his shoes. His old trainers, battered, familiar. My heart aches. An instinct to run starts up inside me, to run as fast as I can from his wounded expression, his need for explanations. I remain on the pavement, frozen.

"I'm sorry." My voice is small. "I'm so sorry." My mind is struggling to find a reason. I offer him a half-truth. "Something happened. There's been an accident . . ."

He steps closer, his expression softening.

"A relative," I stumble, searching for words. "An . . . aunt. She died suddenly, and I've had to drop everything to come to London and look after . . . my uncle."

"You couldn't have told me?"

I shake my head. "It was a shock. I wasn't thinking. It happened so quickly."

"Eliza. It's been weeks . . ." He looks puzzled. Then he sees my face and sighs, pulls me close. "And that note you sent was so cryptic. You told me not to worry—but it made me insane with worry. I've been searching for you everywhere. Nobody had a telephone number for you. Not the cafe where you worked, or the dance studio. You didn't leave Meg's details in Paris. Lucy said you'd paid off the rent without giving a forwarding address. She gave me Meg's number, but when I got through to her, you'd already left. Then I noticed that the postmark on the envelope you sent was from London."

The postmark. I hadn't thought. I nod into the weave of his jacket. I smell washing powder, city grit, lingering traces of old aromas caught in the wool. A tear slides down my cheek.

"What are you doing in Brixton?" he murmurs above my head. "Were you coming to the club?"

"I'm looking for work," I manage. "A waitress or something. I didn't know you'd be here," I add, hearing even as the words emerge that it's a silly thing to say.

"Come inside." He takes my arm. "I'll introduce you to Josh. Maybe he's hiring."

I blink as we enter a dim room. My heart is beating fast. Cosmo is still holding my arm as if he's arresting me. Chairs are piled on tables. A radio plays on the surface of a bar. The place is deserted. It's obviously closed. I start to feel relieved. Then a man straightens up from behind the bar.

"Hey, buddy!" he calls out in an American accent. He clasps Cosmo's hand and claps him on the back simultaneously. "This is so cool, man."

Cosmo has let go of me to greet the American. He turns back to me. "Josh. Meet Eliza. Remember, I told you about her . . . from Leeds."

Josh leans across the bar to shake my hand. His grip is firm. "So . . . you're Eliza, huh?" He grins.

There is a fluttering in my chest. I should say something. I should tell them that Eliza isn't my name. But that would sound crazy. And it would make Cosmo look ridiculous. I open my mouth and close it again.

"Eliza is looking for work," Cosmo says. "Anything going? She's very experienced at bar work. And a great dancer. She'd be an asset."

"Really?" Josh looks at me. "Ever danced on a burlesque stage?"

"Oh, no," I say quickly. "It was . . . bar work that I was looking for."

Josh rubs his chin. "As a matter of fact we could do with some more help. Business is picking up. If you're a friend of Cos', that's good enough for me." He smiles. "Can you start tomorrow?"

Cosmo turns to me with an expectant look.

Things are moving too fast. My head spins. I feel the need to hold on to something solid. There is nothing. Instead I wrap my arms around myself. Working here would be an impossible situation. I can't accept. I clear my throat, opening my mouth, the word "no" ready on my tongue.

"Thanks," I say instead, my voice cracking.

"Fantastic, Eliza." Josh grins. "What's your surname?"

I moisten my lips. "Bennet," I tell them. "Eliza Bennet."

I've stumbled further into the deception. I can't see a way back now.

"Welcome to the madhouse," Josh says.

I make myself look him in the eye; and I wonder if I will ever be able to stop lying.

"Just a minute," Cosmo tells me. "Do you mind waiting? I need a quick word with Josh; then can we grab a cup of tea or something?" He puts his hand on my arm. "Don't go anywhere."

They disappear into a back room behind a velvet curtain. My heart beats faster. I twist my head, staring around the empty room. I could escape. If I walked out of the door, I'd never have to see Cosmo again. I'd be free of my lie. I could go back to being Klaudia.

The radio continues to spew out a tinny dance tune. It crackles into a jingle for the station. I don't go. My feet are heavy, immovable. I can't leave him.

I stare at the dusty folds of velvet curtain and wonder what they have to discuss in private. The place is scruffy in this light. I can see scratches on the floor, and the rolled-up backdrops on the stage have frayed edges. But I guess at night, when the pink lampshades are lit and the mirror ball is turning, the room will be filled with a warm glow. The shabbiness will be transformed into something glamorous, mysterious.

A tall girl with flaming hair strides in through the door. She is wearing Lurex leg warmers and black tights under the swing of a long green coat. She pushes a tendril of curling hair back from her face and gives me a quizzical look.

"Can I help you? We're closed."

"Oh. I'm . . . I'm Eliza." I say. "The new bar staff."

"About time." She purses her lips and looks me up and down. "I'm Scarlett." She nods towards the stage. "The dancer in this joint. But Josh has had *me* working behind the bar." Her eyebrows shoot up, and she widens her eyes. "That didn't go down so well with yours truly. I'm glad he's seen sense and hired you." She also has an American accent. But hers is Southern slow. "I'll be seeing you around, Eliza."

She disappears through another door as Cosmo reappears through the velvet drapes like a magician in a show.

He says he knows of a good greasy spoon nearby. We take a shortcut through the market. Stalls of fruit and vegetables line the street under the railway arches. There are yams and plantains among shiny mounds of oranges and apples. "Two for a pound!" a man shouts.

"Come and 'av a look," calls a woman. Her weather-scorched face is folded in on itself, like a screwed-up wrapper. She must be ancient, but she is alive, stamping her feet, the scent of oranges on her fingers. The woman hunches into her anorak and winks at me.

"You're very quiet." Cosmo looks into my face. "Are you OK?"

"Yes." I straighten my spine, putting my chin up. "I'm fine."

"What an idiot." He smacks a hand to his head. "Of course you're not fine. I'm sorry. You must have been through hell. I wish I'd known. When you didn't show up at the house . . . I didn't know what to think. I was kicking myself for not asking you for Meg's number. I had no idea how to reach you. I'm not going to let you do that to me again."

His arm slides around my shoulders, holding me tight against his side. Our footsteps find their rhythm. Usually I'd slip my hand in the back pocket of his jeans, or curl it around his waist. Instead my arm hangs awkwardly, getting in the way.

"Has it been awful?" he asks softly.

I nod, not trusting myself to speak.

We pass a wig shop. The window is a rainbow of crimson, yellow, blue and silver; curly, afro, pixie, straight and long are displayed on top of a small army of faceless, bodyless heads. The pawnbroker's glitters with silver rings and gold watches. At the end of the street there's a halal butcher; carcasses hang on hooks above trays of pink mince. I hold my breath against the sweet, bloody smell.

The cafe is packed with men in overalls and fluorescent jackets, thick with the aroma of fried food. We find a corner table and sink into it across from each other. The window is cloudy with steam. A waitress with bleached hair and a nose ring takes our order: tea for two and a full English for Cosmo.

"Are you . . . staying with your family?" I ask quickly. Hoping to deflect his questions by getting my own in first.

"No. They're not too happy with me at the moment. There's another reason that I'm in London. Josh has commissioned me to paint a mural in the club."

"A mural?" I frown. "What about your course?" I pause while the waitress puts a teapot between us, and a plate in front of Cosmo.

"You inspired me," he says, his face glowing. "It was you that gave me the courage. I've given up the teacher training." He raises his eyebrows. "Josh said he'd pay me to do a mural, and it seemed like it could be the beginning of something. Then I got your note, and that made up my mind. You were here. So I had to be too."

He takes a bite of toast and mushroom. I use the opportunity to stare: I'd forgotten his bottom lip, how it curves, slightly bigger than his top one.

"Josh asked me about the mural over the holidays. I was desperate to talk to you about it." He picks up his cup with both hands. "I've moved into some cheap accommodation round the corner. I didn't want to do this part-time. It would have seemed like a hobby. Not the real thing." He puts his cup down and leans forward. "God, I've missed you, Eliza. I'm so happy to have found you again. As soon as I got to London I looked through the phone book, but of course you're not listed. I didn't know what else to do—except walk about the streets of South London and hope."

I drop my stare to look at his hands. His skin speckled yellow and blue.

"Hey," he says softly, "we're together now." He smiles. "How long are you going to be here?" He picks up a piece of toast and wipes up a puddle of egg yolk. Pops it in his mouth.

I jerk my head away. "I'm staying indefinitely. My uncle . . . he's not well . . . he needs me."

His face crumples with empathy. "After you've already lost your parents . . ."

I scratch the edge of my mouth. "I don't really want to talk about it." I clear my throat.

"Of course not." He looks flustered.

What the hell am I doing? My skin prickles.

"But it seems a bit like fate, doesn't it?" he continues tentatively. "Both of us in London."

I try and smile, but it slides away. I play with my teaspoon, chinking it against the cup.

"I'm glad you're doing this," I tell him. "The murals, I mean. I really am. I'm happy for you." The clean relief of the truth makes my voice tremble. Tears sting my eyes.

"What about your dancing?" His gaze is open, innocent.

My fingers pinch the teaspoon, placing it on the plastic tablecloth carefully. The clatter of the cafe fills the silence.

Cosmo pays for me, and I have no choice but to accept. I feel bad watching him put cash into the little saucer the gum-chewing waitress placed on our table with the bill. I don't want this small kindness. This symbol of how we were before. The magnitude of my betrayal weighs me down. He doesn't understand that everything is different. I feel as though I'm watching him from a distance, through a screen.

He reaches across the table and touches my hand. His touch burns. "Shall we start again?" he says. "Carry on from where we left off?"

My heart slows as I stare at his fingers over mine. I feel a lurch in my stomach. Then I pull away and get up, pushing the chair back with a noisy scrape and reaching for my jacket. When I look around he's moved to wait by the door, hands jammed in his pockets.

Two brown envelopes flutter onto the mat. Both bills. Nothing from France. It's too soon to expect a reply. It will take a while for my letter to get to her, and then she'll need space to think about it. I keep trying to put myself in her position—imagining how I'd react. I can't expect her to come to terms with it in a hurry. She'll be shocked, angry and hurt before she can even begin to think about forgiving me. But I've never known Meg to hold a grudge.

Mum's tweed coat and scarf hang on the peg by the front door, next to the umbrella stand. I touch a soft sleeve for comfort, and as my fingers rub the nubby texture, a small jolt of knowledge goes through me. It hadn't occurred to me before, but if it's hanging here, then she can't have been wearing it when she stepped outside for the last time. This is her only winter coat. It would have been cold on that December day.

"Wrap up, or you'll catch your death," she says behind me.

I turn with an intake of breath. The hall is empty. I frown, trying to imagine her unlatching the door, leaving the house without her coat. Instead I see her standing beside me and she is tying her scarf around her neck and tucking it inside the green and cream tweed collar. A final check through her handbag—lipstick, purse, clean hanky—and then she snaps the silver clasp closed and hangs the strap over the crook of her arm. All buttoned up, she smiles at me and is gone.

She must have been in a hurry that morning. But I don't remember my mother hurrying. She liked her routine. She was never late for anything.

Missing her is an ache in my bones. I know I'm doing the right thing by staying with my father. But neither of us can comfort the other. When I was younger, my father was the tallest man in any crowd, his head nearly brushing the tops of doorways, his shoulders wide enough to block light from a window. He is shrinking. Not just his body—bones and skin, thinning and shriveling—his spirit too. Without my mother, he lacks a world. She admired and obeyed him, reflecting him back at himself like a faithful, flattering mirror.

It occurs to me now that she was the strong one. She must have known what he did in the war. She hid his medals for him. She forgave him. In return, he put her on a pedestal. Love somehow held their odd relationship together. I wish I could find a clue inside all of that to help me mend my relationship with Cosmo, but I can't. My situation is twisted by the fact that I've lied to him since we met. And if I were brave enough to confess all my lies, if I were cruel enough to hurt him with the truth—what then? Do I also tell him that my German father murdered Jewish partisans, fought for Hitler, won medals for the Third Reich? I can't continue seeing him. Given a choice, why would he choose to have a relationship with someone like me, the real me?

There are pictures of Mum's family stuck into an album. Her parents are thin, tough-looking dark people staring suspiciously into the camera. There is one photo of a group with Mum aged about ten sitting on the floor. She wears white, arranged at the front of the family gathering. She'd scribbled the names on the back: aunts and uncles and cousins. All of these people were lost when she married my father.

"You have to remember that he was German. The war was fresh in people's minds. They couldn't understand why I was marrying him. They wouldn't accept it."

"So they just cut you off? Their own daughter. Just like that?" I'd got angry every time I was confronted with the fact. It seemed so cruel.

"It was the hardest decision of my life," she'd said. "But they made it clear. Him or them."

Mum sacrificed having a family for love. Perhaps my father made sacrifices too. It makes me feel humble, when I think of the time they lived through and the choices they made.

Cosmo is waiting for me outside the club. He doesn't smile as I approach. We look at each other, and I have to break away first, staring at the pavement mottled with cigarette butts, nubs of gum and a dusty bronze coin.

"What's going on?" he says quietly.

I press my tongue against the roof of my mouth. Clench my jaw to stop myself crying. I won't sob in front of him. He doesn't deserve that.

I indicate that we should walk and he falls into step beside me. This time he doesn't slide his arm around my shoulder. I think I will float away without the anchor of him holding me down, keeping me safe.

"Things have changed since I came to London," I try and explain. "I have a lot going on. Decisions to make. My uncle is fragile. He needs me. I just can't . . . can't . . ."

He stops and turns to face me. "Are you trying to tell me that it's over?"

I drag my gaze up to meet his. "Yes," I whisper.

He lets his shoulders rise and fall. "But I don't understand. Couldn't I help? I wouldn't get in the way of all these things you need to do. I might even be useful. Supportive?"

My heart sits in my belly, numb, inert. I find that I'm pressing my fingers around my stomach, as if I could heave my heart back into the right position, put things back together again.

I shake my head. "It's not that simple."

He frowns. "Don't treat me like a child, Eliza."

I've never heard him use that tone with me, words stretched tight with compressed anger. My insides contract. I fiddle with my hat. Pull it over my forehead. He's right. I can't give him more lies, more pathetic excuses.

"It's over," I tell him.

I see the shock in his eyes. There's a shift in the darkness, a deeper pooling of black. He blinks and licks his lips.

"Eliza?" His voice catches. "Are you sure?"

"I'm sorry. Things have changed." I force myself to go on. "I don't feel the same way."

"I see." His voice is shaking. Then he frowns. "Fuck it! I don't. I just don't see it at all. How can things change so much in such a short time?" He straightens up and looks at me with puzzled, angry eyes. "But if they have, if you've really changed your mind, fallen out of love . . ."

His voice trails away when I don't contradict him. He wipes a hand over his forehead.

I cringe, folding my arms over my chest, holding myself tightly. Otherwise I will reach out and grab his fingers, press them to my mouth. I want to encircle him with my embrace. I want to spread out like a limpet, clinging to him.

"Thank you," I manage. I glance behind us, towards the entrance of the club. "I'm late for work."

Can we really become strangers so quickly?

His face closes. "Sure. Better go then."

Pain winds a band around my chest, crushing my ribs, sucking all the air from my lungs. I turn and force my feet to move.

"By the way," he calls behind me, his voice grating, "I still love you."

The club is packed. It is a relief not to have time to think. I can just manage the simple actions the job requires of me, moving like a robot. I hardly feel the bottles and glasses in my hands. One falls through the circle of my thumb and finger, smashing on the floor. I get a brush and sweep away the broken pieces. Someone makes a joke and I shape my lips into a grin, more like a snarl than a smile.

When Josh gives me the nod that I can have five minutes off, I slip out of the back door into the empty yard behind. Sitting on the chilly step, leaning against the doorframe, I take gulps of damp air. My fingers are sticky with liqueurs and the tang of disinfectant.

The noise of the club clatters out into the night: a rumble of voices punctuated by clinking glass and the slur of drunken laughter. I can hear music too, not the usual club sounds with thundering bass to make your ears roar. Josh plays things like Josephine Baker and numbers from musicals.

An uncoiling of furred energy leaps at the edge of my vision: a sudden shadow, startling me. There's a scrabble of claws on wood and a cat appears in silhouette on the fence. The door opens, and Scarlett joins me on the doorstep, folding long legs and leaning close.

She gives me an unnecessary nudge. "Shit, it's freezing out here!" For a few minutes she struggles to light a small clay pipe. Giving up, she sighs and tucks it into her jacket. She wraps the jacket tighter. "Stay out here much longer and you'll get hypothermia."

I try to smile. "I'm just giving my feet a rest."

"Shhh . . . Can you hear it?"

"What?"

"The underground river." Scarlett stares intently at the cracked paving stones, the litter of cigarette butts. "The Effra. Josh told me about it."

I look at Scarlett carefully. The flat monotone of her voice disguises all traces of sarcasm or irony. Gives no warning of humor.

"Seems it runs right under here. Under Brixton. Imagine." Scarlett pushes her hands into her pockets. "Back in the Victorian days a coffin was found floating down the Thames." She raises brightly painted eyebrows. "When they prized the lid off, they found a woman inside. She'd been buried a couple of weeks before in Norwood Cemetery." She lowers her voice to a conspiratorial hiss. "Her grave was untouched."

I wrap my arms around my knees and wait. I don't know where she's going with this, and Scarlett likes to emphasize her stories with plenty of pauses for dramatic effect. But I'm glad of the distraction.

"The mystery was solved as soon as they opened the grave," Scarlett is continuing, unaware of the pain in my chest. "The woman had been buried right above the Effra. The ground had given way beneath the coffin, and it fell into the water. All rivers in London lead to the Thames, you see . . ."

"Very what's-his-name," I nod, struggling to think of the right name. "Edgar Allan Poe."

"I was thinking of getting a new act together based on gothic stuff. You know, vampires and mirrors," she says. "What do you think?"

She stands up, her man's jacket falling open to reveal a glimpse of gold-fringed bra and an expanse of pale, curved stomach. She shivers theatrically, flicking red curls over her shoulder.

"Hey, Cosmo tells me that you two know each other from before. He's renting a room in my flat. You should come over some time, have a drink."

She looks at her watch. "Whoops—on in two minutes!"

I am reeling from the unexpected sound of his name. She's gone, leaving a trail of Old Spice. I've seen the way men look at her. Anxiety bubbles inside. He told me he'd found somewhere cheap. But he didn't say it was with Scarlett. I push my knuckles against my mouth. Cosmo is renting a room from her. It doesn't have to be more complicated than that.

I squeeze through a tightly packed throng to get to the bar. The room is small. It doesn't take much to fill it. Elbowing a tall man to one side, I slip through the flip-top space and begin to take orders, juggling money, bumping the register closed with my hip, pouring a glass of white wine with one hand while I reach for a lager with the other.

I don't own Cosmo. He's free to see whomever he wants. He's better off without me. Lies. More lies. I can't stop them. Even to myself.

Scarlett is already into the first part of her performance on the tiny stage, languidly swinging a cane from side to side, a top hat perched on her head. I envy her confidence. I'd do anything to have such poise on stage, such command. I glance up as she twirls the cane in the air, letting it spin high above her before catching it, a wicked smile on her reddened lips.

Spring brought disorder to the garden. I'd found Mum's trowels and pruning shears stored in a basket, her old apron folded inside. Her gardening gloves were tucked in the pocket. Since then, I've begun the task of clearing the flowerbeds, even though I'm not really sure what I'm doing.

I concentrate on pulling out a mass of writhing weeds that cling just under the earth, coiling around the roots of other plants. The weak sun makes a patch of warmth on my back as I dig metal prongs into the earth. It's harder work than it looks. I put the trowel down for a moment to ease my aching arm, stretch my shoulders. I have begun my dance practice again, starting every morning with *pliés*, my hand resting on the back of a chair, imagining Voronkov's critical gaze on me. It's difficult to drag myself out of bed and put my body through the torture of stretching when my heart is heavy. But I keep seeing Cosmo in the cafe, hearing his voice as he asked, "What about your dancing?"

I've amassed a whole pile of pungent greenery. I hope they really are weeds. A flutter of wings cuts across the light, and I look up to see a magpie landing heavily in the branches of the apple tree. My father appears on the lawn, clapping his hands. The bird takes off on a lazy spread of black and white.

"Magpies," my father says. "Nothing but pests. Stealing other birds' nests."

"Oh." I wipe my forehead with the back of my wrist. "I thought that was cuckoos. Aren't magpies thought to be omens? One for sorrow. Two for joy."

"Superstitious nonsense." He comes over, stands next to me looking down with hands on his hips and he nods approvingly.

"It's looking much better," he says. "Your mother was a natural gardener too."

I push myself upright, unsettled by the unexpected praise. I brush damp soil from my knees. "Thanks." I take off the heavy gloves. "I was just finishing up. Need to get ready for work."

"How are you getting on?" he asks. "What kind of restaurant is it?"

I look down at the gloves, pretending to pat them into shape. I hadn't thought that he'd take an interest. I'd told him that I'd got a job as a waitress because I knew he'd disapprove of me being behind a bar. He and my mother never touched alcohol. "Oh, nothing fancy." I swallow. "But I like it there. It's good to be busy."

"Yes." He nods, eyebrows pulling together. "It was a mistake to take such a long break from your studies. But it can't be helped now."

I want to tell him that I'm not going back to Leeds. That I'd dropped out of my degree ages ago. I want to be honest with him, but I know he'll be angry and I'm not ready to argue with him. Neither of us is ready for that—not when we haven't recovered from the shock of Mum's death, not when we are just beginning to get on better.

When Scarlett invited me round to her place for a drink before work, my first thought was that I couldn't go. Cosmo would be there. But I'd reasoned that we'd meet again at some point. I couldn't put it off forever. So I accepted Scarlett's invitation, and allowed myself to imagine a fantasy scenario where he'd magically know about my false and complicated life. All the confusion cleared away without any pain. The luxury of it unfolded before me like a Hollywood movie, in soft-focus colors and weeping strings. And I saw him so clearly inside my head, his face full of forgiveness as he placed his finger on my lips and kissed me.

By the time I'm in the shower, soaping away earthy smells, I'm still lost in my daydreams, caught up in remembering the feel of Cosmo's mouth on mine. Wrapped in a towel, I pull out different tops to wear with my jeans, holding them up to my chest in the mirror: the pink sleeveless blouse, or my favorite washed-out green halter-neck? He always liked me in that. I stare at my reflection. What am I doing? This is not a fantasy, or a film. I've behaved appallingly. He's never going to forgive me. I rub my fist into my eyes, pushing at sore eyeballs, scattering eyelashes.

On my way to the train station, the sense of trepidation lodged in my belly weighs me down, makes my steps sluggish. Now I'm praying that I won't bump into him. I have no idea how he'll react. I don't even know if Scarlett's told him I'm coming.

Aseema Choppra is crossing our street, pushing a buggy. She stops to bend down, making shushing noises to a toddler. The child is wailing, snot seeping from flared nostrils.

I pause, looking at the crying child. "Is he yours? He's . . . lovely." The boy's wide, watery gaze doesn't move from my face. "You're married? I didn't know. Belated congratulations."

She runs a hand across the folds of her tunic, and the *tilaka* between her eyebrows glares at me like a fiery third eye. "It isn't really my business. But as you're here, I wanted to talk to you about Mrs. Gupta." She tightens her lips, and places her hands on the handles of the buggy.

"Sorry?" I wonder if I've misheard her.

"She's upset. Your father is avoiding her. She says you've only been in the shop once since you got home."

"Well . . . yes," I admit.

"I think your father is being unfair. Mrs. Gupta was a good friend to your mother. What happened was a tragic accident. It wasn't Mrs. Gupta's fault."

"Of course it wasn't," I reassure her. "Look, I appreciate you trying to help . . . but my father has suffered a terrible loss. I think it's up to him where he chooses to shop." I am firm. "It's nothing against the Guptas. It's not personal."

She tightens her hold on the buggy. "If that's your attitude."

"I can't force him to talk to Mrs. Gupta." I raise my chin. "I think he deserves some peace. He's grieving."

Aseema's mouth turns down. She has never liked me, not since school. She always presumed there was something between Shane and me.

I watch her walk away, her shoulders straight, head up. She glides rather than walks. Even with a buggy to push. Her plait hangs down her spine, longer and glossier than I'd remembered.

I know that Aseema is close to Mrs. Gupta, but even so, she has overstepped the bounds of neighborly concern. I'm glad that I defended my father. Whatever he did in the war, he loved Mum, and she loved him. It feels good to be on his side for once.

ERNST

1933, Germany

THREE SS DOCTORS HAVE COME to school. They sit in the gymnasium at trestle tables. We file into the fusty, boy-smelling hall class by class, going up in alphabetical order when our names are called. When it's my turn, I stand with head down, enduring it like one of the cows at milking time, toes curling inside my socks, while the unsmiling men in white coats instruct me to turn this way and that. I try not to breathe through my nose; the stink of rubber from mats piled in the corner makes me feel sick. The men weigh me and check my height. The thinnest one measures my skull with silver pincers, peering down his nose while he clamps the metal arms to either side of my forehead. The metal is sharp against my skin. They have a chart with glass eyes embedded in it. One of the doctors holds the chart next to my head, checking which one matches my iris; he reads out a number and the thin one writes it down. We all know blue is good. Brown is bad.

Winkler has already given leaflets to the German Youth boys telling us what the Aryan race looks like. Otto enjoys reading bits aloud. "An Aryan is tall, long-legged and slim." He scans the words, as if he needs to be prompted by the text. But he can recite it off by heart, like a poem. "The race is narrow-faced, with a narrow forehead; they have a narrow, high-built nose and a prominent chin. The hair color is blond."

There are posters on the clubhouse wall. One is of a fat man with a bulbous nose and drooling mouth groping a slender, fainting German girl. We spend extra time studying this particular poster, as the girl has such a tiny waist and pointy breasts. Another shows two men with bushy beards and hooked noses running away with Aryan babies stuffed under their coats. A caption screams: *Beware the baby-eating Jews!* Semites are well-known cannibals. The last one is an illustration of ugly women in headscarves, cackling like witches as they steal food from innocent blond children. I stare at the pictures, reminding myself that these cartoon creatures are Jews. But it doesn't seem real. I've never seen a real person that looks like any of them.

I've seen quite a few people that come close to the Aryan ideal, including my own face in the mirror. And then there is Otto, standing inches taller than me, whose shoulders are broader, whose nose is finer, and whose chin is firmer than mine. He looks exactly like the picture on the leaflet. He could have been the model for it. Right at the beginning, Winkler picked my brother out as a perfect representative of the Volk community, a warrior throwback from the lost continent of Atlantis. "You are the future of the Third Reich," he'd said, his hand resting on Otto's broad shoulder. Otto fought hard to keep a stern expression. But I could tell by the twitch at his mouth, the light in his eyes, that he could hardly contain his excitement.

Wherever we are, Hitler keeps an eye on us. There's a portrait of him in our classroom as well as in the club; the school portrait is even larger, and it's been positioned where the crucifix used to be. Every Monday, under his gaze, we have lessons in racial purity.

Sister Engel drums her fingers on the desk and looks across at us, most of us in our German Youth uniform, with the new flag on our collars.

She rises in her rustling robes and stands by the blackboard.

"The Master Race is not an accident," she says. "It must be preserved with careful breeding." She squints at the back row of desks. "Can anyone tell me what eugenics are?"

Karl's hand shoots up. "Racial science, Sister."

She nods. "Very good. From the Greek word meaning 'good origins' or 'good birth.'"

She stares out over the class, her hands folded before her. "Now, Gregor Mendel's Principles of Heredity were developed through the study of eugenics." She tilts her head to one side. "Can anyone tell me what these principles consist of?"

Karl is reaching for the ceiling, half out of his chair, face flushed. "They tell us that when two races mix, the lesser race will be . . . dominant in their children. The higher race is . . ." he frowns, "re . . . re . . ."

"Recessive," she finishes. "Yes. That is correct. Which means the lesser race will weaken and destroy the higher race. And we must never let that happen. We must keep our race pure."

She writes the words *Gregor Mendel* and *Principles of Heredity* on the board in her sloping letters.

"Of course we know that the highest race is Nordic." She smiles. "Who can tell me what its traits are?"

Everyone shouts at once: "Born leaders!" "Great warriors!" "Intelligent!" "Physically strong!" "Blond!" "Pure blooded!"

She's holding up her hand. "Indeed. The Nordic race is born to lead, which is why it's the master race." She smiles at us. "Can anyone tell me what the other races are?"

As we shout out names, she writes them on the board: Dinaric. Falic. Ostic. Ost-Baltic. Slav. Negro. Semitic.

She underlines Semitic with scrawling lines, pressing so hard that her chalk snaps in half. "This race comes at the bottom of the list," she says, "because it is the lowest. In fact, the Jews are subhuman. Think of them as parasites. Something we need to stamp on; otherwise," she shakes her head, "they will defile us, pollute our blood and turn Germany into a mongrel nation."

She wipes the chalk off her hands and pushes her glasses further up her nose. "To quote from our own Führer in his wonderful book, *Mein Kampf*," she clears her throat, "a nation which, in an era of racial poisoning, commits itself to nurturing its best and highest racial elements must, one day, become master of the world."

"Heil Hitler," we chorus, raising our arms.

Lessons used to start and finish with a prayer. Now there are no more prayers, except for short ones about protecting the Fatherland and the Führer. As we file out into the corridor, I hear the crackle of the radio. The principal keeps it on all day, for when the Führer makes a speech. Then a loudspeaker alerts nuns and teachers to listen with their pupils, and we drop what we're doing and sit in silence. I can't help wondering if he is angry all the time, or just when he gives speeches.

Otto and I are lying in the long grass by the lake. Mrs. Meyer has sent us off to find wild garlic and cuckooflower, and we're resentful of this unnecessary task. Since joining up, our lives are even busier. Between farm duties, school and the German Youth, there's hardly time to chew on some sausage and bread before falling into bed exhausted.

Mrs. Meyer can't see us here, flopped on our stomachs with a wilting, aromatic pile of garlic stalks beside us. We're splitting grass stems to make whistles; some of our attempts sound more like trumpet blasts and others farting raspberries. Our loud voices ring out in the still air, provoking and boasting. I'm glad. It will alert Sarah and Daniel, in case they're near. Our careless human sounds shatter the cool mystery of the forest. Without raising my head to look at it, I sense its louring presence beyond the wide, rippling surface of the lake. When I'm outside its borders, I always feel that something is watching me from between those dense lines of trunks and tangled branches. Being with Otto makes me feel safer. He doesn't believe in anything he can't see.

"You know, you and I, we don't have to do everything the Meyers tell us," Otto is saying, carefully splitting a grass stem with earthy fingers. "They're old and past it, no use to the Fatherland. It's us that are important. We're the ones who matter."

"So are you going to throw them out?" I tease. "Take over the farm?"

He spits in disgust. "I'm not going to be a farmer." He rolls onto his back and stares up at the blue sky. "I'm going to be a soldier in the SS." He turns his head to squint at me. "It would be fun to turn them out though, wouldn't it? I'd like to see their faces."

"What about Bettina and Agnes?"

"Bettina can stay." He smiles. "She's a pain. But she's pretty. She's growing tits. Did you notice? You can see them through her cotton blouse."

"I didn't notice." I look towards the forest. It's thick as a maze. Somewhere inside its interior is the cottage Sarah mentioned. The place they go to get away from things. I chew the end off a stalk of grass. It's spiky and fibrous, alien on my tongue; I pull it out between my lips like a green worm. Sarah is really pretty. Prettier than Bettina. Not that I can say that to my brother.

"Don't you fancy anyone?" He pokes me. "What's the matter with you?" He leans close and flicks a mucky finger at my ear. It stings. "You know we have to make lots of babies for the Fatherland. It's our duty."

"Stop it!" I cup my ear with my hand. He flicks me again on the other side. Bits of mud fly and splatter against my cheek. My lobe throbs.

I roll over onto him and grab his shoulders. He wrestles me, pushing and pulling until he slides out from under me. We both struggle to our feet. We've trampled the wild garlic and I inhale its bitter, pungent smell. He grabs the sweater tied around my waist by a sleeve, and yanks hard, stretching it.

"Look out, you'll break it!"

The knot of sleeves unravels and he's left holding the sweater in triumph. With a shout he hurls it high into the air. We both watch it float up over the lake and come down with a gentle splash onto the surface. The fabric fills with water, darkening, spreading out. Soon it will sink.

I scratch my head. "Idiot!" I say between clenched teeth. "You threw it. You get it."

Otto laughs. "No way! It's too cold."

The one thing in the world I can do better than Otto is swim. I know he doesn't like deep water. Is afraid of it.

"Oh, of course. I forgot," I say casually, turning away. "Don't worry. I won't make you get in."

I kick off my shoes. The mossy ground cushions the arch of my soles, is ticklish under my bare toes. I begin to hum, as if getting into the water is something delightful and easy.

He pushes me to one side. "I'll get the damn thing," he says roughly, pulling off his own shoes and stamping out of his shorts, wrenching his top over his head.

He wades in naked, wincing at the cold, a flush of goosebumps rising on his arms. But he strides on, up to his thighs in the freezing water. His hands paddle beside him, pushing through lumps and tangles of weed. I cover my mouth with my hand. It's important that he doesn't see me laughing or I'll be dead.

"Watch out for the eels!" I call, my voice concerned and innocent.

He stops for a second and then throws himself headlong into the lake. Its mirrored surface wrinkles under a gust of wind. The sweater has drifted farther out. He swims towards it with hesitant strokes keeping his head above the water level. The surface is black in the evening light and glistening with silver reflections. Suddenly he lets out a yell. "Something bit me!"

He turns, eyes wide, and swims for the shore, his arms flailing, splashing. For a moment I'm concerned. But I realize that he can stand where he is. And, as if he can read my thoughts, he stumbles and pushes himself upright. I know his feet will be sinking into thick, slimy mud. I see distaste and fear in his stretched mouth, his wide eyes.

He collapses on the bank next to me, clutching his calf. There's a cut there, blood leaking out in a smudged red line over his wet skin. He gasps and winces, rocking his knee into his chest, his shoulders rigid as he curses through clenched teeth.

"Don't be a baby." I stand over him. "You must have scratched yourself on something."

"It's not a scratch!" he shouts, hauling himself back onto his feet and fumbling with his clothes. He hops on one leg, attempting to pull on a sock. "The bloody thing had teeth."

"What about my sweater?"

I can just make it out: a dark splodge of bloated wool sitting under the surface, like the humped back of a water goblin.

"Get it yourself."

He pushes a hand through hair turned greenish brown with river water and scowls at me; but I notice a blurry film over his eyes and immediately my victory evaporates. I want to sling my arm around his shoulders, and give him a reassuring squeeze. But I know better. I leave him to stomp back to the farm without me. And I watch him pull his elbow across his face; brushing away the tears he thinks I didn't see.

KLAUDIA

1996, London

"THE BUZZER'S BROKEN. Come in," Scarlett says.

The hall light goes off with a click.

"Keep the door open a minute," she yells.

I stand, my hand on the handle to stop it slamming shut behind us. Naked electric light floods the bare hall.

"Quick!" She beckons. "Up the stairs before the damn thing goes off again."

At the top of the stairs she turns a key in a lock, and I peer through a dusky jumble of shadows, inhaling incense, overripe fruit and the sour tang of milk that has gone off. It reminds me of my shared house in Leeds, of Meg and Lucy, and I feel a pang of homesickness for my lost life. She sets off down a narrow passage, dropping her coat on a crowded table as she passes. "Kitchen. Living room. The can," she intones, motioning into darkened rooms. I nearly trip over a pile of shoes and boots as I follow her, squeezing past boxes on the way to another flight of stairs.

"It's what you guys call a maisonette. Two floors. Neat, isn't it?" Scarlett leads me upwards. "We can get onto the roof extension as well. Barbecues in the summer. Well, except for the bees maybe . . ."

She carries on talking. "Luke and Cosmo are in the two rooms across the landing." I glance at the closed doors. I want to ask her which one is Cosmo's. I try to sense if he's there, behind a door, just an arm's length away from me. I'm suddenly breathless with the fear that he's about to come out. We'll be crushed together in the narrow corridor, and I'll feel the weight of his disappointment, his embarrassment at seeing me.

She turns a handle. "This is my room. Welcome to my boudoir."

I dive past her, clumsy in my haste, and she shuts us into a space that's crammed with a bewildering jumble of clothes, accessories, different colors and textures; winking rhinestones and sequins.

A battered wooden wardrobe gapes, its doors flapping apart, hinges straining under layers of costumes. A dressmaker's dummy leans drunkenly to one side like a headless, subdued ghost. Rows of shoes and boots line one wall, arranged in heel height from fluffy flat slippers to thigh-high boots with towering platforms. I smell face powder and the floral, waxy scent of lipsticks. A large mirror is propped on a table that's spread with bottles, tubes and pots of make-up. The bed is draped with tasseled shawls, and silk cushions covered in Chinese dragons.

She indicates that I sit among the shawls. Immediately I leap up. Something sharp has attacked my bottom.

"Oh jeez! Sorry. Forgot about these." She scoops the heap of gleaming pins into a pot as I rub my right buttock.

"In the middle of hemming something." She tilts her head towards a sewing machine that I'd failed to notice on a table on the other side of the bed. "I make pretty much all my own costumes."

I finger the silky folds of a diaphanous cape. "You made this?" It takes a moment for me to adjust my image of the Scarlett I know swaying across a stage in a suspender belt and nipple tassels, to someone crouched over a sewing machine, industrious and neat, with pins in her mouth.

"Wanna try something on?"

"No," I laugh. "Not now. Thanks."

"You can borrow a hat if you like. I haven't seen you out of that red beret once."

I reach up and touch the felt. "I'm growing my hair out. It's a mess at the moment."

"I know that one. Well." She shrugs. "Lucky you look cute in red."

She leans over and reaches behind one of the pillows, takes out a bottle of vodka and waves it at me. "Let's see if either of the boys is around. I might even share this with them."

There's a large man in the kitchen. He has a thick, brown beard. A green T-shirt strains across his round belly. It says "Blue Note, New York City" in white letters. The beard can't hide his cheeks, broad and pink as a giant toddler's.

"This is Luke," Scarlett says. "My other flatmate. Luke. Meet Eliza."

"Want some tea, Eliza?" He motions to a packet of PG Tips.

"I'll have mine with some of this." Scarlett plonks the bottle on the table and sits down, crossing her long legs. Luke adds generous splashes of vodka to three cups of tea. He tells me he plays saxophone in a jazz band. He's just got back from a three-month tour of Europe.

"Berlin was the best," he says. "Best beer, best women and best musicians." He grins into his drink at some undisclosed memory. "Spent my last night talking to this chick who'd grown up in East Berlin. Said the worst of it wasn't empty shops and lack of news." He shakes his head. "It wasn't even having spies for neighbors—it was the fact of this immovable thing blocking your life, holding you back, like a weight in your mind." He presses a fleshy hand to his head. "The night the wall came down, she said you couldn't move for crowds. People chucked fireworks, went crazy. Next day they were chipping at the wall, smashing it with hammers. Anything they could get hold of. Man. It would have been cool to be there."

We'd watched it on the news at home, on the little black and white TV in the living room. I remember my father's rigid gaze, his hands clasping the arms of his chair. There had been flickering images of people hammering away, confusion and euphoria on faces grinning into the camera, and old newsreels of soldiers and barbed wire. My mother had been knitting me a cardigan. I was more interested in choosing buttons for it, sifting through circles of plastic in her sewing box, than listening to the news. It was Germany. Anything to do with Germany embarrassed me.

Luke digs around in his pocket and pulls out a large wallet. Unzipping it, he extracts a small lump and holds it out to me. "She gave me some. Looks like an ordinary chunk of concrete, doesn't it?"

I touch the fragment. It's cool, the surface rough. It isn't gray, but pale pink with a patchwork of tiny bits of glinting white stone, charcoal and dark brown.

"Ever been to Berlin?" He slips the piece of wall back into his wallet.

"No."

I open my mouth again, looking from Scarlett to Luke. I want to tell them that I am half German. They think they're talking to Eliza Bennet—a girl who doesn't exist—it makes me feel as if I'm not really sitting here at all. I curl my fingers tightly around my cup.

A shape moves at the threshold, blocking the light. Cosmo stands in the doorway. I duck my head, afraid that I'm blushing again.

"Here he is at last." Scarlett taps the table. "Join us. Have a drink. Does this mean you're finished?"

Cosmo pulls up the chair next to mine. I sit up straighter, aware of the force between us, a hum of energy, pushing and pulling like a magnet gone wild. Can he sense it as much as me?

His face is stern. He nods, avoiding my eyes. "The designs are ready. I'm moving my gear down to the club later. I'll make a start tonight."

"The mural?" I dare to lean closer, catching his scent, ink on his fingers, a clean tang of soap and lemony aftershave, the underneath musk of his skin. His sleeve is pushed back and I can see his watch, the shine on his skin, black hair. I remember how I'd tweaked his cuff to tell the time before I knew him properly, and I can't believe how familiar I'd been then, how presumptuous.

"Yeah. I'll be working on it late at night—after you lot go home." He looks at the other two, not me. The lack of his gaze feels cold.

"Like a vampire," Scarlett says.

"It's the best time to work." Luke grins. "I'm a late-night, early-morning person myself. The world is a different place then. Looser. More exciting."

I clear my throat, and glance down at my cup to hide my disappointment. If he's going to be painting the wall after the club is closed then I won't see him. I know it's for the best. But I feel cheated just the same.

Days have passed and I haven't seen Cosmo. He comes to the club after I've gone home. I appear the next day to see the evidence of his night's painting. We are like ghosts whispering around the edges of each other's lives. Or perhaps it's more like a cruel farce with one of us entering the stage, just as the other leaves.

The mural grows in the same way a flower opens: slowly, in an unfurling of texture and color. It's a delicate, tantalizing reveal—like burlesque itself. His first dancer is finished; she smiles at me as if she has a secret to tell—her face is luminous, one eye winking. He's begun to paint the background. Color seeps out around her head like a halo, gold and red bleeding into an inky blue. He's started on another dancer. This one leans against a pillar. She's still just a sketch. But soon he'll breathe life into her too. Looking at the first dancer, I get the feeling that she's about to sashay off the wall into the room. The painting fills me with pride. I want to share my feelings, exclaim loudly over his talent. I say nothing. Sometimes, when no one is looking, I rub my finger against the paint to see if it comes off on my skin. It never does.

When I'm not working, I spend my time training in my room. I've pushed the furniture back to give me some floor space, rolled up my rug, and I use a chair as a barre. I'm going over the routine that Voronkov choreographed for me. I dance to different tapes, trying out modern and classical music. I'm back in shape after weeks of inactivity. I remember a saying that Meg recited to me once: miss three days' training and the audience will know; two days and your teacher will; one day, and you'll know. As I pull my forehead to my knee, flattening my back, I feel the fibers of my muscles opening, softening, molecules expanding into the stretch. I can't work at the club forever. I need to get back into proper training. I should apply for dance school. But the fear of performing is there inside me. And I can't see a way round it.

Mrs. Perkins from next door is standing on her doorstep. She and her husband haven't spoken to our family for years. My mother tried hard to make amends after the cat incident, offering gifts of cupcakes, cuttings from the garden, and going out of her way to be friendly whenever she saw them, but all she got in return were short, grudging nods. A faint meow comes from a cat basket in her arms. I see a glimpse of gray fur.

"A kitten?" I give an encouraging smile.

She looks startled and tightens her grip on the basket. "What's it to you?" She has her snub nose in the air, as if scenting prey.

"Nothing." I make an awkward noise in the back of my throat—a questioning half-laugh. "I like kittens."

She leans over the low wall between our front gardens, and the full bouquet of her sugary perfume catches in my mouth. A mask of orange pancake makes her look like a cross between an ancient Geisha girl and a frog.

"You tell your father he'd better not try any funny business this time." She jabs a finger in my direction. "He kills my cat, and he'll answer for it."

My heart flips inside my ribs.

"We know he shot poor old Bill. We just never had any proof. He's a cold one, isn't he?" She arches a penciled-in brow. "All Germans are the same, my Harry says." Her padded shoulders roll and tremble. "We're keeping our eye on him, so you can tell him that from us. God knows what he gets up to in that shed."

"The shed?" My voice comes out as a whisper.

She nods, jowls wobbling. "Always in there, isn't he? Always got the door shut. Stays in there for hours."

"He makes things. Out of wood." I release a sigh, realizing that I've been holding my breath.

Her mouth pinches. "Well, you can say what you like. We know what we know. And there was all that carrying on before Christmas. Terrible to hear, it was."

"What . . . what do you mean?" My spine sags.

"Screaming. Shouting. And I could hear crying at night." She lowers her voice to a hiss. "It was your mum, God rest her soul."

My mother never raised her voice. She cried easily over small things, sentimental things, sobbing quietly, dabbing at her eyes with the edge of a tissue. But she didn't make a sound in front of my father. He hated any kind of scene or drama.

Mrs. Perkins is lying. Her eyes bulge and she pants slightly, her wet mouth open. Tiny flecks of spittle have collected at the corners of her lips. I turn my back on her and slip in through the front door, closing it behind me. All I remember are Mum's anxious attempts to befriend Mrs. Perkins, her desire to make things all right again. My father was wrong to shoot the cat, but he'd been right when he'd said the Perkinses were spiteful people. I lean my forehead against the cool of the frosted glass.

I hear a drag of breath, and turn to find my father standing there: a long, looming shape in the hall. I put my hand to my cheek. "You startled me."

His mouth twitches. "That woman." He takes a step closer. "What was she saying?"

I shake my head. "Nothing."

He waits. I hear the click of the minute hand coming from the clock. I feel like a little girl again, made to stand before him with my hands spread wide for him to inspect.

"She said you mustn't shoot her cat," I say quickly. "They've got a new kitten."

"Hope they get the bugger neutered then," my father says.

It is dim in the hallway, the light muted through the glass. But I think he winks at me.

As soon as the mailman's cart rattles down the street, I'm on the alert for footsteps approaching our front door. I rush to the mat every time I hear the slide of envelopes, the metal snap of the letterbox opening and closing.

Nothing from Meg. It's been weeks. She'll have received my letter by now. I'm trying not to panic. On my last night in Paris, we drank a bottle of red wine and ate bowls of onion soup before walking through the freezing night, arms linked. Looking down into the black depths of the Seine, she'd squeezed close. "It's been amazing having you here. I really miss you, you know."

I look at my reflection in the bathroom mirror and grimace. Meg would despair if she could see me now. She wouldn't let me leave the house looking like this. Blonde roots clash with dark brown ends. I run my fingers through the half-tone strands and realize that it will take months to grow out completely. I can't go on wearing hats. I've bought a cloche hat and alternate between that and the beret. People must wonder why they never see me without them.

There is a small hair salon on the high street. I pass it on my way to the train station. I have the morning before I go in for work.

An elderly woman sits under a large dryer, a magazine splayed on her lap. A girl looks up from filing her nails when I push the door open. She sits me down opposite a mirror and whisks the cloche hat off my head. She stares at my hair, nostrils flaring in disapproval; then she sucks her bottom lip in. "Well, what did you have in mind?"

I explain that I'm growing the blonde back in. Could she match up the colors?

"Nah." She sighs and shakes her head. "You could bleach the lot. Then cut the bleached ends off once you've got enough re-growth," she offers. "You could do with a cut, too. Chop off the split ends and some of the dye."

I allow myself to be tied into a pale blue gown and led to a deep sink. The girl scalds me with boiling water. Her nails graze my scalp. My neck, tipped back at an awkward angle, aches; I'm finding it hard to swallow. Eventually, she releases me from the torture and applies a product. She says she has to put eraser on the brown first. My eyes sting. But when she pastes on the bleach, I can smell something rotting, like dead animal.

"Yeah. Stinks, doesn't it?" She wrinkles her nose. "It's the ammonia. But it'll be worth it."

Hours later, after she has set to work with her scissors and a hairdryer, I look at myself. My hair is white. It's as fair as it used to be when I was a child. Except that now it has no tone to it, no mix of other shades. It is cropped short, my jawline exposed. My mouth and eyes look bigger. I seem vulnerable. Naked.

I put a hand up towards the unfamiliar style, touching my neck. The floor around my feet is speckled with curls and tufts of brown.

"That's more like it," the girl says. "You look all right now. Modern. Trendy."

I leave the salon on stiff legs. My shorn hair feels weightless, as if I have feathers on my head. The breeze moves through it.

Josh is at the bar unpacking boxes of crisps; he glances over his shoulder as I push open the door. The look of relief on his face changes to surprise when he notices my hair.

"Whoa! I had to do a double-take!" His eyebrows rise in startled arcs. He pauses, as if working out what to say. "Like the new look." He clears his throat and gestures towards the opened boxes. "Give me a hand, would you? For some reason they've only sent us prawn cocktail flavor."

Scarlett, coming in through the velvet curtain, stops and grins, throwing her arms into the air. "Hallelujah! She's got rid of the hat at last!" She touches my hair briefly. "Platinum as Marilyn. Very sexy."

I smile and shrug off my jacket, glancing across at Cosmo's painting on the wall. I go closer, taking in the latest changes.

Another world stands there, inviting me inside its crimson glow: in dusky shadows strange creatures lurk, winged lions and unicorns. The burlesque dancers are half dryads, half human. Boughs heavy with grapes wind fleshy leaves around the line of the ceiling. The dancers pull down fat globes of fruit, putting them to their lips as they shimmer and smile, enticing as sirens.

Josh appears beside me. "Got to hand it to him. The guy's got talent."

"Is it finished?" A sudden panic grips me.

Josh scratches his neck. "Only a few final touches left, he says."

It's a quiet night. I polish glasses and watch Scarlett's performance. My eyes keep returning to the painting. In the pinkish glow and the dim shadows and glittering lights of the club, the dryad-dancers seem to move before my eyes. The green boughs above their heads, weaving across the line where wall meets ceiling, appear to shimmer with moisture. If I were to touch them, I'd feel their fleshy fiber, the softness of leaves, the wet dew beneath my fingers.

Scarlett finishes her set with a flutter of ostrich feathers as she brushes a large fan across her naked stomach. She winks at the audience, bowing to accept the smatter of applause. As the stage lights darken, Peggy Lee is singing "Fever."

I sense a customer approaching and turn with my attentive smile fixed.

But it's Cosmo. His eyes widen. "Your hair!"

I swallow my smile, ducking my head, disconcerted by the reality of him. He's taller than I remember. My mouth is dry. I pat the short feathers around my ears with uncertain fingers. "Radical, I know."

"Yes, but . . ." He smiles. "It suits you. You look good as a blonde."

I think about telling him that I *am* a natural blonde, but that seems vain. My happiness at seeing him is hindered by wariness. I don't know what he's thinking. The lack of connection makes me feel untethered.

I point to the mural. Something safe. "It's amazing."

He looks pleased. Then he leans on the bar, conspiratorial across a couple of empty beer glasses. I catch the taste of his breath. My insides lurch.

"I miss you." He holds up a hand as if I'm going to interrupt him. "Don't worry," he says quickly. "I'm not here to try and persuade you to come back to me. I heard what you said. It's over. But there's nothing to stop us being friends, is there?"

I shake my head, unsayable words shriveling inside my mouth.

"As I'm going to be free in the evenings again . . . I wondered if you'd like to have a drink or something. I know you're busy here," he makes an apologetic gesture, "and you have . . . things going on with your family. But if you want to . . ." He breaks off, leaving the question hanging, tantalizing and dangerous.

I pick up the beer glasses as if they have become an urgent task, and bend to put them in the machine. I pull air in quickly, lungs fluttering. His generosity makes me ashamed. But can we really be friends? Doubt pulls at me. I dash it away, because I need to see him again, just to be in his company, to hear his voice again.

When I've composed myself, I turn back. "Sure." I cross my arms. "A drink. Why not?"

He straightens up and shrugs, suddenly casual. "Sunday?"

I nod, watching him walk away.

The congregation have stopped talking about my father and me. At chapel, the whispering clusters have moved on to other topics. Invitations for my father to join discussion groups or go on rambling jaunts along the Thames have dwindled away. He declined every offer. He no longer has nutritional offerings thrust into his unwilling hands from women in the congregation: home-cooked pies wrapped in foil or cakes in Tupperware boxes presented to him after services with damp smiles. He made it quite clear that he thought the food parcels were ill-advised charity.

The last hymn is announced and we stand. My book is open. But my father knows the words by heart. He opens his mouth and sings with the vigour and enthusiasm that I remember from my childhood. I am conscious of my shorn and silvery hair. It feels bright and frivolous in the confines of the chapel.

When Mum was alive, we usually stayed for tea and biscuits in the hall afterwards, but my father isn't interested in making small talk over chocolate bourbons. Straight after the service, we make our way down the aisle, my father's chin jutting, a look of endurance etched into his stern expression, as if he is barely prepared to tolerate the polite greetings people give us as we pass. And I see the effect he has on others, the restraint, even nervousness, he inspires in them.

It's a short walk home. The trees are pink and white with blossom. Behind the traffic fumes and taint of petrol, there is the green and certain scent of spring. My father hums one of the hymns from the service. Turning into our road, I notice two familiar figures, one in a red sari: Mrs. Gupta and her husband approaching along the pavement. I can feel my father tensing. He increases his stride. As we get closer, I prepare to give them a casual greeting: something to break the ice. I clear my throat.

But when we are a few feet away, my father veers right, stepping off the curb. I stare after him, open-mouthed. He's marching to the other side without a backwards glance. A motorbike screeches past his heels, horn blaring angrily. I see Mrs. Gupta's startled face. A semi lets off a hissing squeal of brakes as I mumble a greeting. I have to run to catch up.

"That was rude," I tell him. "We should have said hello at least."

He looks at me blankly, the house key in his hand.

"The Guptas," I say. "You ignored them."

I follow him up the path to our doorstep.

He shakes his head. "I didn't see them." He turns the key in the lock. "I don't know what you're making such a fuss about."

Cosmo suggested we meet in the Chinese restaurant on Atlantic Road. I keep telling myself that this is not a date. But it feels like one. I'm sick with nerves. My underarms are damp. I have two showers, spray myself with deodorant and empty my wardrobe, throwing things onto my bed. I have an eclectic mix of clothes. I try on a brown mini-skirt and T-shirt; but that just makes me look wrong: like an adult wearing a Brownie uniform. A pair of black leather trousers hugs my bottom so tightly I don't think I'd dare sit down in them. I find a plum-colored jumpsuit that I bought when I was shopping with Meg, and dangle earrings at my lobes, loop beads around my neck. But

I take it all off and pull on my jeans and a white shirt. Better that I look natural and relaxed. If we're going to be friends I need to work at being casual. I'll have to learn not to care so much.

The bottle of perfume that I brought back from Paris is at the bottom of my otherwise empty case, still gift-wrapped for Christmas. I open the packaging, crumpling shiny cellophane and undoing the box. The ornate bottle is a solid weight in my hand. Gold liquid glows in the light. It seems a shame to waste it. Wearing it will make me feel closer to her.

I unstop the heavy glass top, putting my nose to the rim. I don't recognize the dense notes of cinnamon and peach. It's exotic, floral and spicy. I can only remember lavender talc on her skin; but I expect that she wore this when she was younger. I dab generous splashes onto my pulse at my neck, behind my ears, on my wrists.

I put my head around the sitting-room door to say goodbye to my father. He looks up from his chair. He has a book in his hand. A Bible. I go closer and stoop to turn the sidelight on. "You'll strain your eyes."

He jerks his head from the cramped lines of text. "What's that smell?"

I pause, swallowing guiltily. "What smell?"

He stares at me, his eyes accusing. "Your perfume."

I clasp one wrist tightly with my fingers. "Mitsouko," I admit.

I've upset him. How stupid of me. It's reminded him of my mother. It must be a shock. Smells are tripwires into memory.

He moves his lips over his teeth; the grooves between his nose and mouth stretch. "I don't like it."

"No," I whisper. "I'm sorry."

"You smell like a harlot."

I blink, wiping my palm over my neck as if I could rub away the scent. He opens the Bible and lowers his gaze.

The restaurant is half empty. Cosmo is waiting at a table for two in the corner. He stands up and I hesitate, not knowing how to greet him, feeling shy. He makes a move towards me and we brush our cheeks against each other's in a self-conscious, clumsy air-kiss. He inhales. "You smell wonderful."

"Really?" I look at him doubtfully. "Not too . . . strong?"

He looks at me as if I'm mad and shakes his head.

I can't think about food. I'm nauseous with anxiety. I nod and agree with his suggestions and wait while he orders sweet and sour pork, chicken with cashew nuts and bowls of egg-fried rice. The waiter pours out steaming cups of jasmine tea.

Cosmo lifts his cup. "Firstly, I'd like to celebrate the fact that we can be friends."

I lean across the table, clinking china against china. His dark eyes are impenetrable, despite his smiling mouth.

"Secondly, I got another commission today."

"That's great." I dip my head and sip. The tea is fragrant and hot.

"A local French restaurant," he adds. "They want an underwater scene."

"How are your parents taking it?" I maneuver a piece of bamboo shoot into my mouth with chopsticks. It's weirdly chewy. "You said they didn't get the art thing."

He tilts his head. "They don't. But they've accepted that I want to give this a go." He waves his hand as if it's unimportant and shifts his chair closer to the table. "You never said how it went in Paris."

"It was lovely." The truth feels like a luxury. "We had a decadent time. Ate too much. Took in the usual sights." I curl my hand around the warmth of my cup. "It was great just to be with Meg again."

"She's a good friend."

There's a sharp pain inside. I stare into my unfinished food. It is cold, congealing. Bits of spilled rice stick to the table.

I watch him transferring sweet and sour pork to his lips. I used to steal food from his plate in restaurants. It was a joke that I'd always prefer what he ordered. Chinese meals solved the problem.

"How are you getting on at the club?" He pours more tea.

I clear my throat. "I'm enjoying it."

We're making conversation like strangers. Reading from a script. I should have listened to my doubts. I should never have come.

"Glad you like working behind the bar. But I thought you'd end up dancing burlesque." He's looking at his hands, turning them over. "Seemed like the natural thing for you to do. Has anyone talked about it?"

"No." I duck my head. "I don't want to."

"Because you don't approve? Or because it would interfere with your dance training . . ."

"Nothing like that. It's great. What Scarlett does." I spin my cup slowly on the table, leaving damp rings. "I'm full of admiration. But I think you have the wrong idea about me. Remember the party? I was happy to dance, not just because I was drunk, but because it was a private party. No audience. If you'd seen me just a few hours before on stage, you'd understand. I was completely frozen with stage fright."

"You never told me," he says slowly. "That's why you were drinking as if your life depended on it." He taps his chin with his thumb.

"Yes. So you see, I don't have nerves of steel. And I won't be doing any burlesque at the club . . ."

I have a memory of us in his bed; my spine curled into him as he held me in his arms. *You're so brave*, he'd said. The thought of losing his respect is unbearable.

He leans back in his chair and we sip our tea in silence. The atmosphere tightens.

"Have your brothers come back?"

I snap my head up. Confusion scattering my thoughts. "My brothers?"

"Yes." His eyebrows pull together, creasing the top of his nose. "For the funeral? To help?"

"Oh." I collect myself. "No. It's a long way away. Australia."

"Seems you have to do everything on your own."

I drop my gaze to my lap, and squeeze my fingers tight, nails digging into flesh.

"Eliza Bennet," he muses. "Does anyone ever call you Elizabeth?"

I can't look up. I gaze into the tea leaves in the bottom of my cup. "No."

"*Pride and Prejudice*." I hear the clink of his chopsticks as he puts them down. "Miss Elizabeth Bennet. Took me ages to make the connection. But then you know I'm not exactly the literary type. Did your parents choose Eliza to go with your surname on purpose? Were they Austen fans?"

My face flames. "It's just a coincidence. Just one of those things."

I am crushed by my own deceit. I fiddle with my cuff and look at my watch, wanting to go home, because this was a mistake. We're not friends. We can never be friends. And after he finds out what I've done and who I really am, he'll never want to see me again. He'll hate me. Like Meg does.

He calls for the bill. Outside, the street is busy. Church bells are ringing, competing with the sound of booming car basses and distant sirens. Cosmo buttons up his jacket.

"It's early still. Would you like to come back to the flat?"

He rocks onto his heels. I see him notice my hesitation, and he adds carefully, "Scarlett and Luke are probably there. They'd love to see you."

I look out into the traffic, fighting with myself. I want to place my hand in his and walk through the streets. I want him to take me into his bedroom, close the door and pull me close.

He's waiting. He tips his head back, exposing paler skin under his chin. I remember the vulnerable patch behind his ears, the pinkness under his hair and the tender place at the bottom of his spine, where tan slips into white over the curves of his buttocks.

"No. Thanks. I should get back."

He frowns, ducks his head and looks at me sideways, his expression puzzled. "Is this really what you want?"

"Of course," I say brightly. "We're friends. Aren't we?"

He walks me to the Tube station and we hold ourselves apart. At the musty, dark entrance, we brush each other's cheeks with empty air-kisses.

"Eliza?" He's staring at me. "It's odd . . . but since you've left Leeds, it's as if you've disappeared."

"What?" I press the back of my hand to my cheek.

"The girl I remember. My brave dancer. The girl on the roof. That Eliza. She's not here anymore."

We look at each other and something rips, like a bandage tearing away from a wound. The moment is raw and bright. Sounds drain into silence. Nothing else exists except us. The hairs on my arms rise. My eyes blur. I blink and a tear slides onto my cheek.

"I'm sorry." I turn away, searching for a tissue in my pocket. "I wish I could bring her back."

"Eliza . . ." He's calling my name, but I'm blundering through a crowd, scrabbling to find my ticket, pushing through the barrier, the doors sliding closed behind me.

ERNST

1933, Germany

THE NUNS ARE IN a fluster. The Führer has ordered that all unpatriotic books be burned. There's a long list of banned authors, books full of *undeutsche Gedanken*—un-German thoughts. The authors are mostly Jewish. These books, the nuns tell us, betrayed German youth and must be burned immediately.

Lessons are canceled. Flushed nuns climb stepladders in the library, tripping over their robes, pulling out volumes. They stagger back and forth, arms overflowing with books. We've been enlisted to help, pushing heaped handcarts from the library past classrooms, and finally, outside into the yard. There's a pile of books already there: broken spines splayed, pages flapping, torn-out lines of text, ripped and dirty covers. Excited by the lack of routine and lessons, we lend our strong arms and willing legs to the cause.

As I trundle a handcart up and down the corridors, the reality of what we're doing hasn't really sunk in. Albert Einstein's *Relativity* lies on top of the haphazard heap of books in the cart I'm pushing. I tried to read the book in the library just days before. It was too hard for me; but the glimpse I had of the ideas in it, ideas about space and time, about what truth is, and the difference between what we can see and what we think we see, had intrigued me. I wanted to know more. If the book was burned, I'd never have a chance to unpick the locks to all those ideas, never discover the secrets it contained.

I glance around to check that no one's looking, and stuff it into the back of my trousers, tucked safely in my belt, hidden under my jacket.

The pile in the yard grows. There are names I've never heard of. Others I recognize, although I've never read them: Walter Benjamin; Ernst Bloch; Sigmund Freud; Thomas Mann. I begin to feel uncomfortable. To a boy who's always had to share his textbooks, this waste seems frighteningly extravagant.

Sister Sommer, the youngest and prettiest nun, sets the match. The dry paper catches instantly and within moments the whole pile is burning fiercely. Scraps of paper fly upwards in the scorching air. Swirling fragments of text, quickly shriveling into blackness, begin to shower our heads and shoulders in ashy rain. I look across at Otto, who stands at attention with his class; he stares directly into the flames, his face bright with fiery reflections. Led by our teachers, we sing "Deutschland, Deutschland Über Alles," our voices rising over the crackling flames.

As I breathe and sing, my ribs move up and down and Einstein's *Relativity* digs its hard contours into my spine. I have to stop myself from wriggling, or twisting my arm around to reposition it inside my waistband.

I snatched the book up on impulse and I'm already regretting it. It was a stupid thing to do. Now I'll have to find a place to hide it. Otto won't let me keep it. He might even report me if he finds it. But I can't think where's safe from his searching fingers. My eyes sting. I'm sweating, not just from the heat, but from the fear of what I've done. Then a thought comes to me like a cool breeze wafting through a window: Daniel and Sarah's cottage.

Mrs. Meyer sits at the kitchen table while she works on the *Ahnenpass*, the obligatory Ancestor Report. She's dragged old birth certificates, marriage documents and sepia photographs from envelopes and drawers. Neither of the Meyers is a practiced reader or writer. She agonizes over the report, her hands blotted with ink, her forehead furrowed. Bettina and Agnes annoy their mother by shuffling her carefully ordered piles, examining bits and pieces, rubbing their fingers across the documentation that ensures their places in the Fatherland. Otto cannot contain his jealousy. He paces the yard outside and kicks stones against the wall.

"It's not fair." He wipes his nose on the back of his hand. "We look more German than anyone. But we're nothing without papers."

I shrug. "Nobody is accusing us of not being Aryan."

"But I need proof." He frowns and digs his hands into his pockets. "I want to be without a speck of reproach."

I turn away to hide my smile. Otto has begun to copy Winkler's formal speech and mannerisms. My brother, who's considered a bit of a dunce at school, and who's never wanted to read a book or learn vocabulary, now gathers long words like a squirrel hoarding nuts. The Third Reich counts physical prowess, discipline and obedience far above academic abilities, but the people who hold the highest positions in the Nazi order all have the ability to spout pompous prose. My brother listens to those speeches of Hitler and Goebbels with glazed eyes, his lips moving soundlessly, parroting phrases.

I slip away from Otto and the farm on the pretense of going fishing, and follow the path that leads from the lake into the tangled woods. The track narrows, tall trunks on either side pressing so close they cut out the light. I shiver in the gloom, glancing over my shoulder, jumping when a bird flies up or a stick snaps. After an hour and a half of searching, just as I'm about to give up, I find Daniel and Sarah's cottage.

It is just a tumbledown ruin. Bindweed and ivy claw at crumbling walls; the roof is a slump of old thatch, slimy and ragged. It's fallen through completely in one place. Windows are cracked and broken. Tall nettles guard the doorway: an impenetrable fortress of stinging leaves, thick and green. Pushing my way through brambles to the back of the building, I see that the nettles have been cut down to make a narrow entrance to a downstairs window. Making my way through them carefully, I find a path beaten by human feet.

The catch has been left unfastened, and it's easy to swing my leg over the sill. I blink and listen, holding my breath, nostrils curling as smells press in on me: mold spores, damp, rotten fabric, dust. I hear nothing but the sounds of my own body, the gurgle of my stomach. The air is green-tinged from the ivy leaves and nettles leaning against the windows. As my eyes get used to the lack of light, I begin to explore, spotting signs of recent habitation: a bundle of clean blankets on the floor, a small jam jar with a handful of wild flowers in it. I find a blackened kettle sitting in the grate, and squat to touch the cold, battered metal. There are two cups on a shelf. Ten books have been stacked next to them. I run my finger across the spines, seeing that they are all by forbidden authors.

I take the Einstein from my pocket and slot it into the middle of the row. It strikes me that Daniel will be impressed by my choice of book. I hang around for as long as I dare, imagining that I hear approaching footsteps, twigs snapping, muffled voices. Crows fly overhead, their hoarse cries echoing. Nobody comes. I go home clutching my rod and say that I've been unable to catch anything. Meyer cuffs my ear and Otto glares at me, angry that I left him behind.

The following day I spot Daniel in the village. He keeps his head averted and shoulders hunched, but as I stride across the road towards him, I notice a pulsing at his neck, a quick, nervous swallowing. He's afraid. I overtake him, brushing close, muttering with stiff lips, "Meet me in the cottage this evening, at seven p.m." I cough, glancing around to check that we're not being watched. "Sarah too," I add, as I leave him, swinging off to the left. All my farm duties should be over by then. It'll just be a matter of getting away without Otto noticing.

I knew they would come. They have no choice. I've made sure I'm at the cottage first, so that I've claimed the space and I'm ready and waiting when Daniel climbs through the window. He straightens, giving me his direct stare.

"What do you want, Ernst?" He puts his hands on his hips.

But my eyes are on Sarah clambering over the sill behind. I glimpse her knee, a tantalizing flash of skin between hem and sock. Her skirt has got caught on the latch, and I rush forward to unhook it, pulling the thin fabric free. She takes my hand, giving me a fluttering smile. She feels gentle, pliable. I hold her fingers for a moment too long. She tugs slightly and I let go, blushing.

"I don't want anything," I tell Daniel. "Just a place to keep a book."

"So the Einstein belongs to you?" Sarah asks, her eyes wide.

I nod.

"We were scared," she says. "We thought someone might have put it here as a warning."

"I'm sorry . . . I hadn't thought . . ."

Daniel's lips are pursed, his eyes narrowed. "What does a Nazi want with a forbidden book?"

I can't stop myself from sighing. His mistrust of me is frustrating. "I just want to read it. That's all. I'm not your enemy, Daniel. I'm not going to tell anybody about this place. About the books."

"But you—" he begins to say.

Sarah slips her hand inside her brother's. "I believe him, Dan."

I look at her gratefully, and then back at Daniel. I want to win him over, show him that I'm not like the others. "What does your father think about everything that's going on?" I lean against the wall. "Did you know that people . . . your people, are leaving town? Emigrating. Herr Huber, the iron-monger, has gone already. The rumor is he went to America."

"Of course I know." Daniel rubs his cheek. "But my father says we just need to wait it out. He says this can't last forever. Hitler will lose power." His skin has angry marks where he's touched it. "My father fought in the Great War. He was a German hero. Jews have been in Germany since Roman times." Behind his glasses, I see his expression change from suspicion to hope. "We're not going to run away. Things will get back to normal. They have to."

Sarah turns to me. "What do you think, Ernst?"

It's the first time she's used my name. I imagine those syllables melded by her tongue, how her lips formed the word. The intimacy makes me blush again. I cough and run my finger around my collar.

"I don't know."

All I can think of are the posters in the clubhouse, the ranting speeches, the Storm Troopers smashing the chemist's windows. That has become the norm. I don't see how time can run backwards through all that hatred and return to how it used to be.

"Will you come again?" Sarah's face is open, her cheeks flushed. "To read your book? Perhaps we can play a game of cards next time?"

I would like to stay in the cottage forever. But it's getting late, the light ebbing away, leaving us inside a mire of mossy gray like the liquid texture of the lake. I can't make out their features anymore, as if we really are under-water, swimming apart through fronds of shadows.

———

Otto is waiting for me by the gate into the rye field. Behind him the last rays of the sun are burning.

"Where have you been?" He scowls.

"Getting away from you," I say lightly. And looking over his head, I spot a blur of movement, a shape disturbing the usual lines of tree and hedge. There is someone standing beneath the spread of a chestnut tree on the other side of the field. "Look," I say to distract him. "Who's that?"

Otto snaps his head around and stares. "It's a woman. She's on our land."

I look more carefully. He is right. The shape is a woman's; she's standing under the tree as if she's waiting for something. I squint, unable to make out her features. I don't recognize her silhouette. She is probably a stranger. There are plenty of people on the road, travelers, people looking for work or shelter for the night.

Otto is already striding over there. "You! You're on private land!"

The woman under the tree flinches. I see her begin to turn away and then back as if uncertain about what to do. I'm following behind Otto, and as we get closer, I realize that she's older than I first thought. She's thin, and her fingers clutch at long, tatty skirts.

"She's probably looking for charity," I guess, "food or somewhere to stay."

"More likely looking to steal."

The woman takes us in with startled eyes. Her mouth opens and closes in a thin face; auburn hair sweeps behind her in a long plait. She might have been beautiful once, only there isn't room to consider it properly, as my head is full of Sarah, her shining loveliness. The woman's lips flicker around the hint of a smile, hands lifting.

"Don't come any closer," Otto yells. "There's nothing for you here. What are you? A Jew? A gypsy?"

Her face folds inwards, fear knitting up her features. She ducks her head and backs away, hunching; and I know that she's used to making herself small, making herself invisible.

Otto picks up a stone, pulls back his arm. I grab him in time, my fingers tight around his bicep.

"What are you doing? She hasn't done anything wrong."

He spins round, chest out, curled fists ready.

I shake my head. "You're just angry about the Ancestor Report. Go and punch a scarecrow. Don't take it out on an old woman."

I walk back around the edges of the field, avoiding trampling the new shoots, and his voice shouts, "You're an idiot! We're never going to belong. Not really. And you don't care!"

His words echo inside the branches above my head, scaring a bird into flight. A rabbit runs out from under my feet, dashing in a panicked rush for the hedge, white tail glowing through the dusk. But I hardly notice; I am already letting my mind settle around those moments with Sarah, re-exploring the feel of her hand in mine. I wonder now if she hadn't squeezed my fingers before she let go. The more I think about it, the more I seem to remember the slight extra pressure of her flesh against my own.

KLAUDIA

1996, London

I'VE ARRIVED AT THE CLUB early, before my official hours start. I'm planning to tidy the office, wash the tea-stained cups that clutter Josh's desk, and sort out the rail crammed with Scarlett's costumes. The place should be empty, but the door isn't locked. Pushing it cautiously, I see two people, a man and a woman with their backs to me. The man is Cosmo.

For a moment I can't understand. He's finished the mural. His job is done. Stupidly, I think he must have come to see me, and my heart lifts. Then I realize that he's showing his work to a diminutive, elderly woman; he stoops to her level, their heads touching conspiratorially, both lost in contemplation of the painting before them. I slip off my jacket, bundling it and my bag through the velvet drapes into the office, and hover awkwardly. It's been minutes and neither of them acknowledges me.

Cosmo places a cushioning palm on her elbow, murmuring. All her focus is on the painting, absorbed and reverent. I'm certain he knows I'm here. Even though he doesn't turn around, I feel his attention shift towards me. And I understand that he doesn't want me here. Sorrow turns me inside out. I shift from one foot to the other.

He turns at last, his face closed, helping the woman at his side as she moves with careful, fragile steps. I know it's his grandmother before he introduces us. My heart begins to hammer in my chest.

She's exactly as I'd imagined: a tiny old lady with wrinkled skin, her hair just ivory fluff over a domed skull. But her eyes are bright, all-seeing. I shrink from them. As Cosmo makes the formal introductions, she gives me her hand. It's such a slender collection of bones that I'm scared of crushing it. Her mouth curves into a generous smile, showing off a row of perfect dentures.

"Eliza," she says. "What a pretty name."

I find that I'm blushing. I look at Cosmo. He raises one eyebrow, shrugging away my confusion.

"What do you think of my grandson's work?"

"He's very talented," I say quietly.

"You have a fan, Cosmo." She pinches his elbow with playful fingers.

I look at the tidy folds of her blouse, how it buttons around her narrow wrists. I think about the hidden number tattooed onto one of her arms. Does she hate it? Or perhaps it's a reminder of what she's endured, a symbol of her strength.

He's put his arm around her shoulder protectively. "Come on, Bubbe," he says. "I promised to buy you dinner."

"He spoils me," she hisses, delighted.

They leave together, whispering like lovers. I open the dishwasher and begin to unload sparkling glasses, placing them in racks.

Darkness blindfolds me. Something jolted me out of my dreams. And there it is again, the noise that woke me: a desperate howl. A primeval wail. I sit up, hugging the bedsheets and blink through the night, beginning to make out the familiar shapes of my room.

The hairs on my arms stand up as it comes again: a shattering cry. It has to be the sound of a child being murdered, a mother torn from her baby.

I get up and feel my unsteady way to the window, pulling back the curtain. My legs are shaking. I know that I should go out there, try and help. I expect to see people running from their houses, a police car wailing to a screeching halt. But the street is deserted. A shadow moves from under a parked car. A bushy tail dragging low, and a sharp-nosed face is caught in the flare of streetlight.

I press a hand over my juddering heart. A fox. I'd heard their cry before. But I'd forgotten the pain and anguish, the hideous urgency of it. I watch as another emerges. It walks on tiptoes, back arched like a hyena. They are making a chattering sound now, like angry men smacking their lips.

Back in bed, the fear that the foxes' screams have stirred up is banging in my chest. And I curl myself into a ball, wrapping my arms around my bent legs, holding myself tightly. I can't wipe away an image of Cosmo's grandmother in the concentration camp, starving, beaten. Her head shaved. He'd wanted me to meet her. It wasn't supposed to be like this.

Scarlett is trying on outfits for me to judge. She's thinking of a new routine. She wanders around her bedroom in her silk kimono, a stocking trailing from one hand, a red-feathered hat perched on her head.

"I met Cosmo's grandma the other day," she says. "What an amazing woman! Did you know that she's a concentration-camp survivor? She was forced to go on one of those death marches and ended up in Bergen-Belsen. Incredible that she's alive."

My pulse begins to thud at my wrists. I raise my shoulders, making a noise in my throat.

"I asked her if she didn't want Cosmo to convert, you know, become Jewish?" Scarlett carries on, unperturbed by my lack of response. "Anyway, she just gave me this really steady look and held my hand in hers and she said, 'Religion has caused enough pain in this world; why would I let it come between me and my grandson? He's his own man, my dear; what more could I want from him?'" Scarlett turns to me, eyes wide. "How amazing is that? It's like, she's not bitter or anything, just a lovely lady. And you know, a lot of those Nazi bastards are still out there, getting away with what they did." She shakes her head. "It's so wrong."

"Yes," I say quietly. "I know."

"Cosmo told me that he wishes he shared her ability to forgive what they did to her. Thinks she's a saint. He says he has a hard time biting his tongue when he's with her."

I knot my fingers together, wishing she'd stop talking about it.

She rummages in her wardrobe. "By the way, Josh told me you're a dancer." She picks up a fuchsia boa and then discards it. "You kept that one quiet."

"I took classes," I say slowly, relieved that the subject has changed, "and

I was thinking of studying dance full time." I roll onto my stomach on Scarlett's bed.

"According to Cosmo, you're good." She raises one eyebrow. "You know what they say about lights and bushels."

Cosmo was talking about me. Pleasure and pain collide. I sit up, wrapping my arms around my legs. "I have a problem though . . ."

She stops prowling around and sits next to me. "What?"

I shrug and look away, playing with the tassels on one of the shawls. "The one time I stepped onto a stage, I froze. Just blanked out completely."

"Any idea why?" Scarlett asks.

I shake my head. I can't tell her about my father, my childhood. The school years spent hiding from Shane. The bullying and ostracizing. Each day full of difficulty. My one safety measure was to stay unnoticed, unseen.

"I think we should work on it," Scarlett says. "I mean, burlesque is about revealing yourself while staying in control. I could give you some tips."

I hunch my shoulders. "I'd just be wasting your time."

"It's up to me to decide that." She crosses her legs and pulls her dressing gown around her. "I'm looking for new dancers, and here you are."

I slide off the bed. "I'm a ballet dancer—a contemporary dancer. Not burlesque . . ."

"But you do tap, right? Bet you've learned a bit of swing or jive? Salsa?"

"Well . . . yes."

"So add burlesque to your repertoire. It doesn't mean that you'll be doing it as a career forever."

I run my fingers through my hair. "Sorry. I appreciate you trying to help, but I don't think it's a good idea."

"OK." She lets the kimono drop and sashays across to the wardrobe. Picks out a short, ruffled dress and slips it on. She regards herself in the mirror. "But do one thing for me."

"What?"

"Dance for me."

"Now?" I give a short, embarrassed laugh.

Scarlett turns and she isn't smiling. "I've never seen you dance. I'll only know you when I see you express yourself through movement—because it's who you are, isn't it?"

I sink back onto the bed playing with my thumbs, winding them round and round each other. I pinch one until it hurts. My body is alive with the fizz of adrenaline.

But she's right. I get up slowly and begin. I'm feeling awkward, clumsy; too aware of Scarlett's intent gaze. But within seconds, I've lost myself: stretching and dipping, contracting and swaying. Music plays inside my head. I break away from remembered choreography. I'm not looking at Scarlett. I'm alone. My body can't lie. I dance out the ache inside, my longing for Cosmo, my sorrow for the lost people in my life, for Mum, and all those people I don't know, the invisible ones that move beyond the edges of sight. I'm expressing my feelings with every extension through fingers and toes, every curving line.

When I stop my skin is hot. I'm panting, ribs rising and falling. I hear the passing traffic in the street. Notice the dust motes caught inside the sunlight coming through the grubby windows.

Scarlett and I hold each other's gaze, and I stop breathing. I wonder if she can really see me. My hands hang by my side. I wait.

Scarlett says in a quiet voice, "My offer stands. Let me know when you're ready."

She's sitting before her mirror, applying foundation and powder with practiced fingers, humming to herself as if I'm not there.

Mrs. Perkins's new cat is in the apple tree. It must have gone up after the birds. It clings to a branch meowing pitifully, pink mouth open, its yellow eyes fixed on me. Hooked claws dig into mottled bark. I stand below and make enticing noises, clicking my tongue. The cat thrashes its tail and stares down at me.

It rained heavily last night and leaves drip onto my upturned face. The damp trunk offers no footholds. I fetch the stepladder out of the shed and place it at the foot of the tree. Carefully, I edge upwards, testing the rungs one at a time. I stretch out my fingers. "Here kitty," I whisper. He gives me a haughty stare. It's clear that he isn't going to meet me halfway.

I stand on the top rung, praying that the ladder won't slide from beneath me, and make a wild grab, managing to catch the animal around its middle. I haul it off the branch, but it seems to stretch like elastic in my hands, tenacious claws clinging to the tree. I have to yank to release them, and wince, imagining I hear the snapping of tiny hooks. Rammed tightly under my arm, it writhes and struggles in a frenzy of desperation, as if it's become ten cats. A panicked paw flashes past my face. Pain sears. I nearly fall. Nearly drop the cat. He's scratched me just below my eye. But his protest must have exhausted him. He gives up and flops in my grip like a furry rag-doll. I back down the ladder using one hand, soft gray fur crushed against me.

I slip through the hall and out of the front door before my father appears, and ring Mrs. Perkins's bell. She emerges with a look of indignation on her face.

"My baby!" She holds out red-tipped hands for him.

I hand him over. His ears and tail droop. "He was stuck in our tree."

She hugs the cat, drowning his head between her mountainous breasts. The cat shoots me a disbelieving look and lets out a low wail. She turns to leave.

"Mrs. Perkins . . ."

She stands, head cocked, one foot on her doorstep.

"Are you sure you heard my mother . . . screaming?" I put my hand to my stinging cheek. "Couldn't it have been . . . something else. A fox maybe?"

"You think I don't know what a fox sounds like?" She shakes her head with such vigor that her gold necklaces shimmy across her chest. "I've not a shadow of doubt. It was your poor mother. Heard it night after night, and my Harry heard it too. We were going to call the authorities. It didn't seem right."

The door shuts with a bang. I pat the raised line on my cheek and look at my finger, at the small dots of gleaming red.

I remember the terrible sound of the foxes—how exactly they mimicked the sound of a woman or a child being murdered. Mrs. Perkins is lying. She would have gone ahead and called the police if she'd been sure that it was my mother making that noise.

ERNST

1937, Germany

MEETING SARAH AND DANIEL at the cottage has become a habit. Sometimes, with farm duties and German Youth activities, it's impossible to get away. Or I can't give Otto the slip. But I usually manage it twice a week. We have prearranged times, and we leave notes if we miss each other. We read, chat, eat the food they smuggle in their pockets; we play cards. Daniel and I talk about science; we spread a map of the world on the floor to plan the trips we'll take one day, adventures we'll have in Africa and Australia. We've stopped talking about what's happening at home. It's become a kind of unwritten rule.

Once, in the kitchen, when Daniel wasn't there, I kissed Sarah on the cheek, brushing my lips across that plump rise of flesh below her eye. Both of us pretended it hadn't happened. We avoided looking directly at each other for days afterwards. But her embarrassment was thrilling because I knew then that she felt the same: *her* chest tightened, *her* heart raced, when I was near. I've stopped bothering to remind myself that they are Jews. There's no point— it doesn't make sense.

On my fourteenth birthday, I graduated into the Hitler Youth, and Otto followed eleven months later. We both have our daggers at our belts with the inscription "Blood and Honor" engraved on them. Otto has risen in the ranks, becoming Section Leader. He loves the role. "Eyes right. Stand down."

He pokes his face into other boys' and tells them they are a disgrace to the Fatherland.

Winkler favored Otto. And in the older squad our new Section Leader, Scholz, feels the same about my brother. Otto looks like the perfect Nazi. And he's strong, fast, brave, and disciplined—always the first to volunteer and the first to answer questions. He's a star pupil, the ideal boy soldier.

We're all outside the clubhouse after the Tuesday meeting, getting on bicycles, or heading back home on foot, chatting and calling out friendly insults to each other through the pale evening, when Conrad Lange steps in front of my brother.

Conrad puffs his chest out, his mouth pressed into a line. "What I want to know, Meyer, is where are your papers? Where's your family report?" He pokes a finger at Otto. "How come we all have to prove we're true Aryans— and you don't? You and Ernst, you could be anyone. Gypsies. *Mischlinge*. Hell. You could be Jews!"

A small crowd gathers around both of them. I hold my breath, waiting for the punch. Instead, Otto reaches for a rope hanging from his belt. He doesn't say anything. Casually, with thoughtful concentration, he winds it around his own bare arm. We've been practicing knots, and they are still twisted into the rough fiber.

With deliberate movements, Otto begins to saw at his skin with the rope, pulling it up and down the same patch of flesh. Conrad glances at Otto's arm and then at his face. He shuffles his feet in the dry grass.

"What are you doing?" his voice croaks. I see the edge of Conrad's tongue as he licks his lips.

Otto says nothing. The force of his looking could bore a hole in Conrad's skull. Otto beckons to another boy from the group that's gathered around. He indicates that the boy work the rope for him. "Harder," Otto tells him between gritted teeth. He holds his arm out. And the boy works the gnarled rope knot up and down Otto's arm until it shreds his skin, and the flesh underneath flushes purple, raw, with shiny pink patches and flecks of blood.

Conrad glances away.

"Watch." Otto's lips are tight. "This is for my country. This is how much pain I can stand for my Führer."

Conrad steps backwards.

Otto holds out the rope. "Let me see you do it."

Conrad's face is drained of color, and he continues backing away, murmuring, "You're crazy."

"No. You're a coward!" Otto shouts after him.

The other boys pat Otto on the back, examining his ruined arm with expressions of nervous admiration. I see Scholz looking out of the clubhouse window, his slight smile before he moves away.

Otto's arm takes weeks to heal. It becomes a slimy, weeping sore. Bettina bathes it with salt water. He sits meekly while she dabs at it, exclaiming over his stupidity. Eventually, it grows a thin layer of pale scar tissue and he no longer needs Bettina's nursing. I notice that he begins to hang around her more, offering her advice on how to do her chores more efficiently and even carrying things for her if they're heavy. He is developing bigger muscles in his chest and arms. He does push-ups every day before bed, grunting and panting while I'm trying to sleep.

The horses are out in the field, and the stable door is open. Bettina is standing guard at the threshold, watching as Otto stalks a loose hen. The hen is darting backwards and forwards along the back wall, her speckled feathers fluffed up, apple-pip eyes bright with fear. Otto lunges, rolling shoulder first into the straw. The hen squawks as she makes a desperate leap into the dusty air, and Otto bounces up empty-handed, feathers between his fingers. Bettina laughs and claps. "Nearly!"

Panting, Otto glares at the hen. He plucks straw from his sweater as he waits for her to settle. When she begins to peck amongst the hay again, he throws himself at her fast as an uncoiling spring. This time he grabs her around the middle. Triumphantly, he hoists the bundle of feathers up with both hands, pinning the wings neatly, and presents her to Bettina. Bettina tucks the hen under her arm. "Bad girl. Next time the fox will get you."

Grinning, Otto leans forward to plant a kiss on her lips. Bettina gasps, stepping away, so that Otto's mouth slides across her chin. She lifts a hand and slaps his cheek. I hear the sting of fingers against flesh. Without waiting for his response she marches past, the hen jolting in her grip.

"Bitch." Otto stares after her, rubbing his cheek. "She thinks she's too good for me. Well, too bad for her." He folds his arms. "She's a slut anyway.

She's been with Bruno Stein. He boasts about it all the time. I want a girl who's pure and innocent. An angel. That's what I'm looking for."

Since I can remember, my brother has had nightmares. I used to think he'd outgrow them. But they've got worse as he's got older. He's much too big for his bed, and however he positions himself, tucking himself up, burrowing into the thin mattress, he loses the blanket, and his feet or his shoulders stick out. I've got used to waking suddenly in the dark, hearing him crying out. Sometimes I creep over to him and sit on his bed and stroke his damp hair back from his forehead, try to rearrange his covers over him. He trembles and moans, the nightmare clinging to him. In the morning, he doesn't seem to remember. If I ask him about it, he smiles and shrugs and says that I'm imagining things. He's never slept better.

Meyer doesn't want us to go to the Nazi party rally at Nuremberg. There's too much to do on the farm. But he has no choice. It is an order. Otto and I have never been farther away than the local town. There is a whole week of festivities. We stay in tents pitched in neat lines. There are games and marches. And on the last day, Hitler comes to talk to the whole rally. Sixty thousand Hitler Youth stand motionless in their ranks. Flags with eagles' heads and the sword and hammer snap and flutter above a mass of fair heads. Drums and trumpets sing out, cymbals clash. Every uniform is clean and pressed. Not one person steps out of place. A woman with a camera hurries among the lines of boys, filming us.

When Hitler appears on the podium a great roar goes up and every arm is raised in a *Sieg heil*. The ground shakes. And then a hush falls as he speaks, chopping the air with his hands, his voice trembling with emotion as he tells us that the Germany of the future will have no ranks and no classes. "You, my youth," he shouts, "never forget that one day you will rule the world."

He stares out at the crowd, his sweeping arm including us all. "You are flesh from our flesh. Blood from our blood," his voice echoes.

My throat constricts with pride. Despite the distance between us, I swear he's looking right at me, picking me out.

Otto is at the end of the line. I can't see him without turning my head.

But he is thinking the same thing as me. Nobody ever claimed us as flesh and blood before. The seduction of it washes through my body. I begin to understand that it makes Otto feel more than important: it makes him feel safe. Inside that vast mass standing shoulder to shoulder, with the Führer spreading his arms to embrace us, I feel safe too.

On the way home in the train, Otto wets his mouth and stares out of the carriage window, his eyes moving greedily over the landscape as if he wants to devour everything he sees. And although our voices are hoarse with shouting and singing, we all begin to sing again, a marching song. Otto's voice rises until it is the loudest in the carriage, the veins in his neck swollen with effort, blood pumping blue and thick at the base of his neck.

We arrive home to a dark, sleeping farm. We slink into our beds, hungry and exhausted. But neither of us can sleep. I hear Otto tossing and turning, his feet hanging over the edge of the cot. I am filled with adrenaline. Heady words repeat in my mind. Drums and cymbals clash and stamp. Flags strain high up, soaring towards the clouds, towards the promise of a new Germany, and a new future for us. A boy can grow to be powerful and important in Hitler's Germany.

When we go to feed the horses the next morning, Meyer turns up, mouth set in a line, his face heavy with resentment.

My fingers fumble around the bridle. Berta twitches her head, knocking my hand and I drop the whole thing, the heavy, silver bit clunking against Meyer's toe.

He glares at me, his fingers scrabbling at his belt buckle.

"Leave him." Otto steps between Meyer and me and looks him in the eye. "Put that away. You'll never beat us again," he says.

I am startled by his tone of cold authority. My little brother has grown up. It isn't just the fuzz of hair on his cheeks, the muscles in his shoulders and his towering height—he's taller than Meyer now—it is his certainty. Meyer's mouth droops. His hand goes to his belt again and then falls away. He spits in the straw. "Think you're a big man now."

But that is the end of the beatings.

KLAUDIA

1996, London

I'M ON MY WAY to work when I catch sight of the back of Cosmo's head. My step falters. I loiter on a street corner for a second, uncertain about whether to run to catch up, or let him go on without me. Since our Chinese meal we've fallen into a kind of uneasy truce, making polite but brief conversation, not quite meeting each other's eyes if we happen to bump into each other.

Backing into the safety of a shop doorway, I stare after him, catching glimpses through the crowd. Another head is keeping pace with his, and the realization grips me: he isn't alone. It isn't his grandmother this time, but a dark-haired girl. As if drawn by a hypnotist, I leave the shelter of the doorway and trail behind. They're having an animated discussion, and I see by a flash of profile that she's beautiful. She's tall, long-limbed, with the kind of smooth amber skin that tans in moments. She waves her hands around in a passionate, Mediterranean manner. He throws his head back, laughing at something she says, stepping closer to wrap his arm around her, pulling her to him. Her shoulder slots exactly into the hollow under his. I turn away, pushing my knuckles hard against my lips.

At night I twist my head on my crumpled pillow, trying to erase the image of them together. Except I keep replaying it, recalling details: her faded jeans tight on her thighs, her long swinging ebony hair and the line of her cheek-bone. They'd seemed so comfortable together, as if they'd known each other for years. She'd looked like the kind of girl I'd like to be friends with. What hurts most is that it didn't seem to be a "fling," something casual. There was something deeper between them. I could see it. Even at a distance.

I've changed my mind about the burlesque lessons. I can't go on being a coward about everything. But the timing couldn't be worse. Scarlett likes to teach in her room, which means I'm at the flat more often, and I'm terrified of bumping into him. Worse, seeing him with her.

When I ring the bell Scarlett throws the keys down. I hurry up, one hand clutching the keys, the other sliding along the rickety bannister, feeling my way in the dark. I have to be agile to move quickly in the dim, narrow corridors of the flat: piles of old magazines, hairdryers, wine bottles, boxes and odd shoes lie in wait for me. I hop around the obstacles, my ears straining for the sound of his voice, or a door opening. So far I've managed to avoid him. I wonder if he's avoiding me too.

"Here." Scarlett hands me an envelope. "This is for you."

"What is it?"

As I pull two pieces of paper out of the envelope, she explains. "It's an application to the Laban Center. All you need to do is fill it in."

My mouth falls open.

"Just do it," she says. "You should be training as a dancer, not working behind a bar. Not even doing burlesque. But for now, burlesque will have to do."

"Thanks." I look down at my feet. My throat tightens.

She rubs her hands together, dismissing my embarrassment, my gratitude. "OK," she tells me. "Let's start. Make an entrance. Walk into the middle of the floor and turn. Look at me. Make eye contact."

We have cleared a path through the chaos of her room. I walk, swinging my hips. I stop and turn and force myself to look at her.

She shakes her head. "There's no conviction in it. If you don't feel it then pretend. Make-believe is part of life. It's how we find out who we are."

I try again. She shows me how it's done. She steps with a careless swagger, and yet each movement, each curl of her fingers, is a deliberate art.

"You know what they say—that you can't expect anyone to love you until you love yourself?"

I nod.

"Well. It's the same principle with enjoyment too. You need to learn to enjoy yourself." She separates the words. "Enjoy. Your. Self." She twists her bangle around her wrist. "People feel uncomfortable watching a performer that's uncertain. I used to be nervous until I told myself that it didn't matter. If I fucked up, so what? You can't take life that seriously or you'll never do anything. Try again."

I take a deep breath and do the walk. This time I step as though I mean it. I feel the intention in my bones. It gives me a sudden flare of empowerment.

"Better," Scarlett says. "Much better. Trust your body. It knows what to do."

I walk and stand. Turn slowly, arching my back. Run my fingers lightly down my arm.

"I know you don't want to be looked at." Scarlett tucks her legs up under her on the bed. "But we don't want them to look at you. We want them to *see* you. To see what you want them to see. Don't forget, it's an act. You're in charge."

I slink around the chair, trailing my hand across the back of it. With one move, I kick up a leg and swoop it over to the other side. I feel a lurch of uncertainty. It's embarrassing to be advertising my sexuality like this.

"Keep the focus," Scarlett tells me. "You can't stop believing in what you're doing. Not for a moment." She gets off the bed and strolls over to the wardrobe.

"I think it would help if we dressed you up. Get you into the mood."

"Oh, no." I grip the back of the chair. "I don't think so . . ."

She ignores me and starts pulling out items of clothing, satin, lace and gauze, holding them up against me, her head on one side, squinting. "That's your color. That would look awesome on you." She puts her hand to her head, slapping her forehead. "No. Wait. I know!" She rummages in the back of her wardrobe, half inside it, wrestling with fabric, so that it looks as though the clothes are trying to drag her inside and swallow her whole. She emerges with a hanger, pushing her hair back into place as she holds it up triumphantly. "This will fit you. I was thinner when I was working this baby."

She slips a man's smoking jacket and a corset in shiny black off the hanger. Dipping into the bag attached to it, she hands me a pair of black stockings, white collar and tie and a top hat.

"You're kidding."

She shrugs. "I never joke about dressing up. Come on. Outta those jeans. Let's see if you've got the legs for this get-up."

When Scarlett has finished lacing me up, I can hardly breathe. The bones dig into my ribs. The bow tie itches my neck. She sits me down on the pin-free bed and dabs at my face with make-up brushes, her eyes half-closed in concentration. A little of this. A little of that. It feels pleasant to have brushes fluttering and pressing against my skin. She stands back, admiring her handiwork and steers me over to the mirror.

We stare at my reflection together. My heart is hammering inside the constraints of the corset. I look like someone else. Not the English girl of my imagination, but someone that I might be in awe of if I spotted myself at a party. I look like the kind of girl that would never have to fetch her own drink.

"You look like Marlene Dietrich," Scarlett announces. "Enigmatic. Cool and . . ." She pauses, nodding. "Germanic."

The image in the mirror wavers. I blink, clearing my throat, and turning away from my reflection. "I don't think this is really me." My hands claw at the bow tie. It hugs me tighter than a constricting snake. I want to strip it off, throw it from me in a slick black unraveling.

"Don't be crazy!" Scarlett grabs me and forces me to confront my reflection again. "You're sexy as hell." She slaps my thigh playfully, but hard enough to sting. "Look at those legs! It's a crime to waste them."

I stare at the girl in the mirror. Eliza and Klaudia collide, their images sliding across each other. They blur, mixing like two colors, making a swirl of muddy nothing. I hover outside, watching the thin texture of two strangers tremble and fade. I lower my eyes, my body stiffening under her fingers.

Voices come tumbling into the room from outside. West-Indian accents. A loud discussion shouted across the street and a peal of raucous laughter.

I begin to take it all off, unrolling the stockings, shrugging out of the jacket. My fingers scrabble at the hook and eyes behind me, trying to loosen the stays. I can't breathe.

"Let me . . ." Scarlett is there, quickly stripping out the laces. I feel the corset undo, my breasts spilling free. "You only live once, but if you do it right, once is enough," Scarlett says quietly. "That's Mae West. And she knew what she was talking about."

We both hear the moan of the saxophone. The sound drifts down as if it's coming from the sky, as if it's falling from the few hazy clouds that sift across the rooftops.

"Luke must be playing to his bees," Scarlett says. "I think we're done for the day. Let's go see."

I'm glad of the distraction. I struggle back into my jeans, yanking my T-shirt over my head. "Luke has bees?" I ask as I follow her up the narrow stairs that lead onto the flat roof of the extension at the back of the house.

"Sure. He's just got the one hive. His honey is too too divine, darling," Scarlett drawls over her shoulder, imitating someone. I think it's a character out of *Breakfast at Tiffany's.*

Out on the roof extension, the daylight is dazzling. We're above the cityscape and the sky is huge. Luke winks at us, but doesn't stop playing. I recognize the swooping notes of "Night and Day." Luke's cheeks inflate and his fingers move, nimble and sure across the keys. I lean against a wall, listening to the mellow, throaty cry of the instrument.

"Saxophones. They get me every time," Scarlett says. "And look, the bees are dancing."

Standing at a safe distance, I see a few bees tracing circles and squiggles in the warm air above their hive. It does look like a dance. The sound of their buzzing is muffled inside the music, louder during the breathy pauses. Luke takes his mouth away from the instrument. "They really like jazz best." He wipes his lips with the back of his hand. "I mean, seriously. I'm not even biased. I've tried out different types—classical, rock."

"How can they hear the music?" I ask.

"Must be the vibrations." Luke taps his foot, places the saxophone against his mouth and begins to play again.

"Sound is vibration."

I start at the sound of Cosmo's voice; he's blinking in the light, as he crosses the roof. He's barefoot. His hair rumpled. It occurs to me that he's just got out of bed. I glance behind him, expecting to see the dark-haired girl.

"Luke's saxophone is sending a series of compressions and rarefactions through the air. I think that's what the bees are picking up on." He continues, waving a hand towards the bees. "But it's different for humans. Depending on their speed, the vibrations will ripple the fluid in your ear, like ripples in water after a stone enters it."

He touches my earlobe, squeezing gently between finger and thumb. A tiny shiver shoots through me.

"That jiggles the little tiny bones in here," he adds, "which sends an impulse to your brain, and," he smiles, releasing my ear, "you hear music."

"Well, I certainly do." Scarlett sways her hips. "Love this song. Reminds me of home."

I clear my throat and step away from him. "How do you know all that?" My voice is husky.

"Lived with doctors all my life." He shrugs. "Couldn't avoid absorbing something."

There is green in his hair. His bare arms and hands are covered with paint splatters. Yellow smudges over pink streaks. I want to touch his skin, smoothing my thumb against the ridges and flakes of color. I hunch my shoulders and turn to look at the hive, concentrating on the dancing bees.

"What made you leave New York for Brixton?" Cosmo is asking Scarlett.

"It was a done deal as soon as Josh told me whereabouts in London he was planning on setting up shop," she says. "There's a line in *The Prince and the Showgirl* where Olivier asks Marilyn Monroe where she lives. And she turns to him and says in that breathy voice, 'Brixton Water Lane.'"

"You're joking!" Cosmo laughs. I hear the sound as a betrayal. He's happy without me.

"Really," Scarlett says. "So you see, it was my destiny."

I can't turn my head, can't risk it. I feel transparent. All my jealousy, misery and desire will be exposed. I keep my back to both of them and walk to the edge of the roof. My ribs hold the impression of the corset. I allow myself a deep breath, filling my lungs. I wonder where his girlfriend is. I half expect to hear her voice behind me. I don't think I could manage it if she came up here now.

Below me, over the low parapet, people walk, chat, cycle by. I draw my gaze up, across the slate roofs where the evening is gathering, dusky purple as a bruise clotting.

———

The club is quiet. It's too hot to do anything that involves any effort. We've run out of ice. There is a distinct smell of sweat in the room. I hear Josh telling a customer that he's had cheap air-conditioning installed in his flat. "It's the old-fashioned kind," he says, keeping a straight face. "I lie on my bed and wave my legs around." He looks over and winks at me.

I practice my burlesque sashay, stooping to collect an empty glass from a table with a dip and a bump of my hip. My spine is supple as milk, one hand on my hips. There's a dribble of beer on my arm, and I lick my skin, tasting salt and the lingering smell of the dandelions I'd pulled from the garden that afternoon, their crushed leaves releasing a sour juice.

Even Scarlett is subdued. Slinking about the stage, her movements are heavy and deliberate, except for the wrist of one hand. She flutters a fan throughout the routine; it bobs and flits around her like a painted butterfly.

"May as well go on home if you like," Josh tells me, looking at his watch. "The place is empty. I can cash up."

As I leave the club, someone moves out of the pool of light under the lamppost on the corner. I see his smile as he walks under the next illumination, and my heart bumps against my chest.

I glance into the shadows behind Cosmo, looking for her.

"Are you going to see Josh?" I try and sound normal. "He's just about to cash up. We're closing early."

"I was." He squints towards the door of the club as if he can see right through it, and nods. "But it's not important." He pushes his hand through his hair, leaving it sticking up. "How are you? What are you doing?"

"You mean now?" I'm confused by his attention. I brush my palms over my jeans. I feel grubby and crumpled. I remember his girlfriend's casual elegance.

He shrugs. "It's so hot," he says. "I was thinking that it would be cooler in the park. We could go together . . . if you like."

He said "we." Something opens inside. Relief. Happiness. I pinch the skin on the back of my hand, needing the nip of pain to steady me.

"You're on your own?" I manage to keep my voice casual.

He looks puzzled. "Yes."

"I thought . . . I thought you might be with your girlfriend."

His face is blank. And then he steps closer. "Who told you I had a girlfriend?"

I pray he can't see the blush spreading across my cheeks. "I saw you with her. A dark-haired girl. In Brixton. A while ago."

"Beth?" He frowns.

I'm thrown for a moment. I thought she'd have an Italian name, or Spanish. Carmen. Florenza. Something exotic.

"My sister?" he's saying slowly as if I'm hard of hearing. "God. I hope people don't make that mistake often."

Relief turns my bones to liquid; I wish there was somewhere to sit down. Happiness is back in my chest, bright and bubbling and dangerous. I can't afford to feel like this. I look away from the creaturely energy coiled under his skin. If he didn't have that lop-sided smile, that tapering of muscle above the line of his jeans, perhaps it would make him easier to forget.

I keep my voice level. "I don't have to go home yet. Just as long as I get the last train."

We walk gritty streets. Cars thunder past, the boom of bass echoing from walls like thunder. Everyone has the same idea. People spill onto the pavement. Whole families awake at midnight. Mothers sit with babies on their laps on their front steps. Grandmothers doze in armchairs dragged out from sitting rooms. A Rastafarian passes us, tall and aloof in the darkness; he carries a staff like a wizard. His locks fall down his back in a thick dark mass.

"Won't it be shut at this time of night?" I say as we come out of Milton Road, the bulk of the lido in front of us. Behind that is the open expanse of park, just visible as smudged shapes rearing up towards the skyline.

"Gates are made for climbing," Cosmo replies.

He goes first, and helps me clamber over, holding my bag out of the way of the spikes. I jump down and he steadies me, clasping my shoulders. We bump up against each other and break apart quickly. The park is seeped in ink, trees throwing long shadows across patches of creamy moonlight. We set off up the hill. Bushes, bins and benches crouch, making shapes that seem to grow eyes and move towards us. I edge closer to Cosmo, resisting the instinct to grab his hand.

Even in the wide-open spaces of the park, the air gathers in thick swathes. Cosmo heads off the path and onto the grass, dry and uneven underfoot, the slope rising steeply. It's difficult to move one leg in front of the other, as if the sinews of night are drawn tight. I hear a rumble somewhere, vibrations grumbling through my bones.

We reach the top of the slope, panting, and Cosmo throws out his arms. "Look!"

The whole of the city falls open, glimmering in the distance. Tower blocks and church spires pushing towards the moon. We stand together in the hot night, lost inside the basin of winking lights, the rise and fall of the skyline marked out in glitter. London seems far away. It's as if we're alone on a planet circling the city.

"Spectacular, isn't it?" He sounds pleased, as if he's personally responsible for conjuring up the view.

Our arms brush. I can feel the heat of his skin. He's always hot, as if the energy inside him makes him glow. I close my eyes. A drop of rain splashes onto my closed lid. I open my eyes in surprise and the tiny pool floods my vision. There is a crack of thunder. This time rolling across the sky above us. Water is coursing through the atmosphere, soaking us.

Cosmo grabs my hand. "Come on!"

Another crack of thunder like a tree crashing on top of us, and the whole park lights up in a technicolor glow. Jagged lines flicker on and off across the horizon like silver flares. We are running now, feet flying across wet grass. It's downhill and the momentum of the slope gives us a giddy speed. Cosmo races ahead, pulling me behind. Water blinds me. I can't see the ground. I slip, but Cosmo jerks me onto my feet. We reach the bottom panting and laughing, hearts racing.

He looks down and pushes a strand of hair away from my wet cheek. "This is how I remember you." His voice is husky.

Above us rain shimmers like a fall of needles. The crack of thunder is fainter now, rolling away. My clothes cling to my skin. I'm trembling.

"I'd give you my coat if I had one," he says.

"I know." I smile. "You always were a Walter Raleigh kind of man."

We clamber back over the fence and begin to walk, splashing through water. The road is a river. Rubbish bobs in the streams gushing into man-holes and gutters. Tarmac shines across the empty road. The storm has swept people back into their houses, and we have the place to ourselves. Salsa music plays, curling out of a club somewhere.

"I should go home." My voice sounds odd. Prickly. I don't know how to leave him.

"Actually," he says quickly, "there's something I'd like to show you. If you've got time?" He stops. "It's not far."

I look at him under my fringe of dripping hair.

"It's the mural I'm working on. In a restaurant round the corner. I've got the keys."

Hope pumps through my veins, quick and hot as adrenaline. He wants my approval. This is his way of telling me that he's forgiven me. We walk for ten minutes and he stops in front of a restaurant door. The sign says "Closed." He stoops and turns a key in the lock.

I squint in the dim light, making out chairs piled on tables. An aban-doned broom leans against a counter. Tiny colored fish flicker and turn in an aquarium built into the wall. Blue light fills the room with a watery glow. A square of brilliance shines through an open serving hatch at the back. I guess it's the kitchen from the sound of pans crashing. "They're finishing up in there," Cosmo explains.

He moves to the side and I hear a click. Overhead lights glare and I blink. But now I can see a half-finished painting across one of the walls. I recog-nize his style. The fluid sweeps of paint, the lush colors. I move closer. He's working on an underwater scene. There are trailing coils of seaweed, flicker-ing fish like the ones in the tank, and strange underwater creatures. He's almost finished painting a mermaid. She floats towards me, a tremulous smile on her lips.

I stare. Shock makes my skin burn. I recognize her face from the one I see every day in the mirror. It's my reflection swimming out of the glass. My face. I turn to him, puzzled.

He's gazing at the painting. "I can't stop painting you, Eliza." He's talking so quietly that I have to strain to hear. "I see you when I close my eyes."

I swallow with difficulty. It feels as if I've got Scarlett's corset on. I can hardly breathe.

He drags his gaze away from the mural. "I lied. I didn't want to see Josh tonight. It was you I came to see." He scratches the back of his head. "I have no idea what's happening here." His voice is growing stronger. "I thought after I found you again that . . . that we'd continue what we'd begun in Leeds. I mean, I'm not imagining things, am I? You still feel it too, don't you?" He opens his hands. "I know you said you just want to be friends; and I've tried to stay out of your way, tried not to think of you. But it doesn't work."

Blood thunders in my ears. I hang my head. Tears seep from under my lashes.

"Eliza," he murmurs, stepping closer.

"I'm sorry." I stumble towards him, blind with longing, and his arms are there, sliding around me. "I'm just so scared. I've made all these mistakes . . ." I gulp, rubbing my face against his damp chest.

He hugs me tightly, his ribs against mine. "It doesn't matter. None of it matters."

"No." I push away, out of the circle of his arms. My mouth isn't working properly. "You don't know that. There are things you don't understand. Things I've done."

"What do you mean?" He's got hold of my arms, and his fingers tighten. I'm forced to look into his face. "I knew there was something else," he says. His black eyes are steady. "Tell me."

My knees sag. I feel as though I'm going to fall. The hard, true facts line up in my head, ready to spill into sound.

"I'm not . . ." I stumble over the words. "I'm not . . . really . . ."

"Hey, Cosmo. I thought we'd been broken into!"

A tall man stands in the doorway, a meat cleaver in his hand. He has a French accent. "*Merde!* Let me know next time you come back. I could have sliced you open with this." He waves the heavy blade in his hands. It glints.

Cosmo runs a hand through his hair. "Sorry, Vincent. Didn't think."

Vincent looks at me and back at Cosmo. "OK. OK. I see what's going on." He rolls his eyes and retreats back to the kitchen.

Cosmo turns to face me again. "What were you saying?"

I take a deep breath. "Nothing. It doesn't matter."

"Yes." He takes hold of my hand. His fingers dig into mine. "Yes. It does."

"I can't do this." My voice comes from far away.

There's too much to tell—my father, my lies, my real identity; it's too much of a betrayal to expect his forgiveness. I don't want him to hate me. I couldn't bear the look on his face—the disappointment and disgust.

"Eliza," he says, his voice trembling, "remember my grandmother? Remember what I told you about her?" His fingers grip me harder. "I know you're brave too."

Panic kicks at my guts. I wrench away from him. My heart is shrinking. "It's better if we're friends. That's all."

He swings away from me with an exclamation of frustration. His hand closes into a fist. "Damn it, Eliza! I never know where I am with you."

I stand, dumb and heavy, flinching at his fury.

"Do you think this is a game?" He narrows his eyes.

"No!" I sound harsh.

"And you think we can be friends?" His face twists.

"No," I admit, hanging my head.

He turns his back to me. He dips his chin and I hear the sharp intake of breath. "Right." His voice is hurt. "I won't bother you again. You don't have to worry."

He's walking towards the door, keys dangling from his fingers.

"I can't explain," I whisper, balling up my hands by my side. But he doesn't hear.

ERNST

1938, Germany

IN MARCH WE'RE CALLED into a special assembly at school. The hall is crammed with muttering boys; there have been rumors. The principal climbs the stage and stares out, a look of jubilation on her usually sour face. She adjusts her robes and waits for us to fall silent.

"This is a glorious day. Since early morning, our troops have been marching into Austria." There's an audible intake of breath. "They have met with no resistance," she continues, her voice trembling. "In fact, the Austrian people have hailed us as liberators. Our brave soldiers are even now being celebrated and welcomed in Austrian towns and villages. From this day on, Austria returns to Germany to be part of the Fatherland, and will be known as the Ostmark." The principal raises her right arm.

Our arms shoot into the air. The cry goes up, "*Sieg heil!*" The nuns can't restrain us after that. Every boy is chattering and boasting; the talk is of brothers and fathers who are soldiers, and of how soon we can join up.

I slip away to the cottage straight after school to see what Daniel thinks. Our rule that we don't talk about politics is finished with. We can't ignore what's happening. Now there is bound to be a war.

"My father has had to close his practice." Daniel paces the fusty kitchen, kicking a loose tile, pushing the broken chair out of the way. "And did you know that Jews can't even sit university exams now?" Despite his rage he looks tired, dark circles smudging his skin. "The country is gripped in this madness." His mouth quivers. He takes off his glasses and rubs his eyes. "There seems to be no end to it."

I guess he's copying what his father's said, and I glance around instinctively. Speaking out against Hitler has consequences. One of the boys in my class repeated some things his father had said about the Führer, and the next day men in leather coats took his father away.

Sarah leans against the doorframe twisting her fingers together. "Dad says there's no future here. We have to leave." She stops fidgeting with her hands and crosses her arms, wrapping them around her ribs. "We have relatives in Europe. But he's thinking about America, or even Israel."

They may as well be going to the moon or Mars. I'll never see them again. A pain grips my belly as if I need to empty my bowels.

Weeks pass, but when I ask about their plans to leave, Daniel tells me that his father is still trying to get the right paperwork. "We'll be leaving any day now," he says. And each time he answers my question with his stiffened smile and those same empty words, my heart does a little flip of relief. I haven't lost them yet. On a hot evening in July, I arrive at the cottage to find Daniel in a strange mood. His gaze is flat and withdrawn. He shows me an identification card. It has a big yellow "J" on the front and inside his fingerprint and all his details.

"I have to carry it all the time. As if I'm a criminal." His voice is dull. He shoves the card back into his pocket, crumpling its edges.

Daniel isn't in the mood for games or talking. He sits on a blanket in the corner with his long legs folded under him, and loses himself in a novel. I don't know how he can immerse himself in a story. It's too hot to concentrate on anything. The air is oppressive and muggy. A fly buzzes at the cobwebby window. After abandoning a game of cards, Sarah and I go into the forest for a walk, ducking under swags of greenery. There's no escape from the languid heat. The canopy of branches makes it worse, shutting it in.

Sweat trickles down my shoulder blades. I hope I don't smell. I dip my chin to sniff my armpits. We drag our feet through drifts of lush grass, pushing aside brambles. "My father's found someone who can help us—he thinks he'll get our visas next week," Sarah says, as she unpicks a thorn from her skirt.

"I don't want you to go." I speak before I think.

She winces. The thorn has pierced her finger. She examines it. A bead of red appears, trembling on the surface. I pick up her hand and put her finger in my mouth. I feel her sag, hear the small gasp she makes as my tongue circles the tip of her finger. Her blood tastes sweet. And I don't know how, but our mouths are together, her lips moving against mine. I close my eyes and put my hand on her waist to pull her close. I've never kissed a girl before and I couldn't have imagined the bliss of it. The ground tips under me. When I let go of her, I think I might faint. The forest spins around us: colors and sounds blurring and intensifying.

November

He is dead. We heard it on the radio. Vom Rath, the Nazi diplomat shot in Paris, took two days to die of his wounds. It's all anyone is talking about, that and the revenge that must be taken on his Jewish killer.

Evening falls, dark and cold. Even at the farm, I can feel strands of tension coming from the town. And I think of them stretching out from all the villages and cities beyond like a net being drawn tight over the whole of Germany.

Otto takes the stairs to our room three at a time. "Quick, get your things," he shouts, grabbing his hat, checking his dagger at his belt. "We're going into town. The Jews are going to pay this time."

I shake my head. "I'm staying here."

"I don't understand you." Otto curls his mouth in disgust. "What's the matter—don't you care about this . . . this insult to the Fatherland?"

"It's nothing to do with me."

"It has everything to do with you . . ." He heads for the trapdoor, and turns to go down the stairs. "A Jew just walking into the German Embassy and shooting a Nazi? A diplomat? You think that's all right do you?" He glares at me. "Why is it that I always have to prove myself for both of us?"

A car arrives, revving its engine at the entrance to the yard. I hear voices and a door slamming. The engine thrums and tires squeal away into the night. I stand in the yard watching the blinking red lights until they disappear.

I'm alone. The Meyers are in their parlor gathered around the radio. It is bitterly cold. The sky clear. I can see the speckled path of the Milky Way. I look across at the horizon, to where the town beyond lies with its church spires and gabled roofs. Over there the sky is smudged with the dirty glow of a fire. I curl my fingers tight. The Baumanns will barricade themselves inside their house. But fire eats through doors, melts locks. I pace up and down the yard. The horses stamp in their stables. I stand by Berta's massive head and scratch her forehead, nails working across her white star; she pushes the weight of her skull into my arms and I stroke her bristly lip until it hangs loose and quivering. She regards me with the liquid curve of one eye, and I see myself reflected inside her wise gaze.

I should go into town. But what good would it do? What help could I possibly be? I push my knuckles against my eyelids until flashes of color burst. No solution comes to me. No course of action. My mind is numb. I am afraid, and it makes me despise myself. I lean against the stable wall and knock my forehead against the brick, banging it over and over until it's throbbing. The pain makes me feel better. I know I can't protect the Baumanns single-handedly; I wouldn't stand a chance. I can imagine what kind of crowd is gathering in the streets, the mood they are in.

There is one other place I could go. A force pulls at me, propelling me towards the forest. I'm sure that the cottage will be empty. But I have to go. Just in case.

I close the gate behind me, creeping along the side of a ploughed field, feeling my way. Noises rustle. I'm an intruder in the darkness; from fathomless banks of undergrowth, I feel eyes watching. My feet slip on the heavy earth, catch on roots, so that twice I fall, cursing, onto my knees.

I pass the lake, glittering in the moonlight, slate gray and still. Frost whitens the reeds. I've never been inside the forest at night before. I pull my dagger out of the sheath and grip hard. My mouth is dry. I step with slow care, trying to move quietly. The cottage rears up, a black shape hunched inside a tangle of trees. I don't know if I am brave enough to go inside. The building has lost any semblance of friendship; all my hours there with Sarah and Daniel seem like a dream. The gaping windows are expectant: watchful and malevolent. Then I catch a tiny pulse of light through the glass and my shoulders relax.

As I climb over the sill I call Daniel and Sarah's names in a hushed voice.

They're in the parlor, huddled around a single candle. I get a shock, because they aren't alone. Mrs. Baumann is there too. Daniel stands up and puts his hand on my shoulder. "This is bad," he says. "A bad night for Germany." He sounds like an adult; it makes me feel young and foolish.

"Where's your father?" I ask.

"He wouldn't come. He had to protect our property. All his medical equipment. He told me to bring Sarah and my mother."

I sit next to Sarah. But we don't touch. She presses up close to her mother, who has her arms around her. Sarah's mother watches me over her daughter's head. I meet her steady, assessing gaze and lower my eyes. I am ashamed. It's very cold and we wrap ourselves in blankets. We don't speak much and none of us sleeps properly. I doze and wake with a stiff neck and dribble on my chin. As dawn begins to break up the darkness, I leave them there with promises to come again as soon as I can, and trail home through crisp, silvery grass, stumbling over frozen ground.

Otto's bed is empty. It hasn't been slept in. I'm relieved that he hasn't got there before me. I sit on my cot, shivering and uncertain. The day is beginning. A cock crows. The horses move in the stables below. I hear a car stopping outside the gate, the murmur of voices and a door slamming. I stiffen, waiting. One of the horses makes a welcoming whicker. The stairs creak. Otto comes up slowly, his head appearing first through the trapdoor. He brings the stink of stale sweat and smoke with him. He sits on his bed heavily. We're facing each other, our knees almost touching. He looks exhausted but replete, as if he's had a long day's hunting. There are smuts over his clothes, streaking his face. Blood has dried on his cheek in a crust.

"You've hurt yourself." I gesture towards the slash of dark red.

He wipes it and looks at his hand. "Not mine," he says.

Then I notice a spray of blood over his sleeve. It glistens. He sees where I'm looking and narrows his eyes, leans forward and picks something from my hair. A leaf. He twirls it between his fingers and regards me steadily. "Busy night?"

I ignore him. My heart is thumping in my chest. I keep my expression blank.

"What have you been doing, Ernst," he persists, "while we've been hard at work stamping on vermin?"

He drops the leaf, crushing it under his boot. As he moves his foot, a fragment of glass glints on the floorboards next to the smear of broken green.

"Nothing." I clear my throat. "And you?"

He yawns. "Synagogues burned. Skulls broken. And there is no longer a single pane of glass standing in any Jew establishment. They got the message all right."

I think about the Baumanns crouched in the cottage. Are they still there, or have they gone back to their house to meet Dr. Baumann? I want to make sure that they're safe. But it's impossible to leave the farm. All day the talk is of how many windows were smashed, how the streets and pavements glittered with glass, and how the Jews ran like rats into their basements, hiding behind locked doors. I hope that the Baumanns' home is still standing, that their windows are intact. Otto boasts to Bettina and Agnes. Mrs. Meyer won't let the girls go into town. Instead they hear Otto's stories, eyes wide, gathered around him. I can't listen.

Evening. The dark is heavy with damp; a low mist swirls through the tops of grasses, gathers around bushes and brambles. As I approach the cottage, I strain my ears, picking up a strange noise. I realize, with a bump of joy, that it's a human sound and hurry forward. They're still here. Climbing through the window, my ears are trying to decipher the odd noise. It's louder now and I understand. Sarah is sobbing inside the circle of Daniel's arms, her head against his chest. I blink in the grainy, underwater light, making out another figure in the other room. Mrs. Baumann sits on the floor, rocking back and forth; and a deep howl rises from her, an endless, eerie hungering. It makes the hairs prickle on the back of my neck. I stare from one to the other, terror bubbling. They don't acknowledge me. It's as if I'm not here.

"What?" My voice breaks. "What is it?"

All I hear is Sarah's painful sobbing and her mother's terrible, mad cry. The sounds tear at me. I want to put my hands over my ears.

None of them looks up. I am shut out. "Tell me," my voice squeaks.

"Our father is dead." Daniel raises his head. Behind his glasses, his eyes are red and swollen.

My mouth falls open. Shock winds me. I take a step forwards. I want to put my arms around both of them. But they are untouchable.

"How?" I whisper.

"We think . . . we think he'd been trying to stop them . . . they . . . they hanged him. Lynched him in the street." Daniel looks at me as if he doesn't know me. "Go. Go now, Ernst. We can't meet again."

I press my hand over my mouth, feeling sick. "No. I'm not leaving you."

He shakes his head. He looks exhausted. "Things have changed. My father is dead. Do you understand?" His face suddenly blazes. "We're different, Ernst. You and me. We can't be friends. Do you know what they did? Have you seen? Everything is destroyed. People died. People were taken away." He stops, a dry sob in his chest. "We're not German anymore. We're not even human to them. My father was trying to get us out before . . . now I have to do it."

"No." I'm shaking. "It's all wrong. I won't pretend I don't know you."

"You don't get it, do you?" Daniel frowns. "It's not about you. We'll be punished. Not you."

A chasm has opened in the ground. The void between us deepens, becomes a bottomless, echoless pit. Sarah turns her blotched face towards me, her mouth trembling. My fingers itch to dry the wet on her cheeks, push the tangles of hair away.

"What are you going to do?" I ask.

"We're going to stay here," Daniel says. "We can't go home. I have to keep my mother and sister safe. It's up to me."

"Then you'll need help. I can bring you food. Clothes. I can help."

His lips press tight.

"Let him." Sarah wipes her face with the back of her hand. "He's not like them."

I take a deep breath. Tears sting the back of my eyes. "I won't let you down," I say.

I hate going into town. Lots of shops have been boarded up. Houses sit empty with gaping holes where windows used to be. The synagogue is a blackened ruin. People call it *Kristallnacht* after all the broken glass. Everyone is different since it happened. Nobody smiles or gossips. Sometimes I feel the heat of a stare on my back. When I turn, the watcher has dropped their gaze, and begun to whistle or examine their nails.

I steal bread from the larder. I take eggs from the hens. I pull clothes from neighbors' clotheslines. I dig up vegetables in the garden at night. I wrap my own supper in napkins and push it into my pocket when nobody is looking. I know that I'm taking too many risks, but I haven't got a choice. Their survival depends on me. Each time I manage to get to the cottage they are thinner, paler. The forest seems to have claimed them. Their clothes are moss tinged, sour with damp; twigs stick in their hair, dirt rims their nails. There's a particular look in their eyes now: wary and strained and watchful. Mrs. Baumann's chapped lips are sealed shut; I haven't heard her speak since that night. But they are safe. The cottage has become their only hope; Daniel hasn't been able to get visas. It is too late. Germany has shut her gates. At his last attempt, some SS questioned him on his way back. He only managed to escape because a scuffle broke out farther down the street.

The army is moving fast. The Wehrmacht has invaded Poland. All anyone talks of is the war, the power of our troops, their swift victories, the success of *Lebensraum*—our new Living Space.

I don't care about the war. Otto is desperate to join up. But I can't go anywhere. I have to stay and look after the Baumanns. I have to take care of Sarah. I dream of her at night, and every day my only thought is of how I am going to get back to her. After I make my drop of food or supplies, she comes with me through the woods. We hold hands, fingers knotted tightly.

"There's something you don't know," she says in a hesitant voice. "We moved from our house."

I frown. "What do you mean?"

She bows her head and I glimpse the thickened grime under her collar, dirt etched onto her pale skin. "Ages ago, after . . . after my father couldn't work anymore. There was no money. We've been living in a flat across the railway line. It's a Jewish area. My father took enough medical equipment to start a new surgery. He'd been treating our neighbors for free. He said it was the one thing he wouldn't let them take from him. His skill."

"Why didn't you tell me?" I thought we'd shared everything.

"Daniel's proud." She shrugs. "Sometimes it's better not to speak, when nothing can be done."

I press her up against the trunks of trees and bury my face in her neck. I inhale the musky aroma of her: bark and earth and wood smoke. She lets me lift her skirt. She is velvety on my fingers. I tremble, feeling the length of her body resting against mine; the softness of her, the sweet, lush curve of her mouth. I will never allow anyone to hurt her.

I steal soap for her. It's just a worn green sliver, smelling of detergent. I wish I'd kept the bar I found on the pavement that day, the one wrapped in flowery paper, dense with the scent of violets.

"We'll always be together," I tell her. "And when it's over, people will forget about the race problem. We'll be married. We'll go to America."

She smiles as she listens to my stories.

"I love you," she says.

It is the one thing I believe.

Otto has applied to the Waffen SS. It is common knowledge that getting into the SS requires one hundred and fifty years of documentation as proof of ancestry. But Otto thinks he's a special case. That he's the only person in the Fatherland who can prove his Aryan blood just by being himself. I had actually begun to believe that they might make an exception for him.

On the day he gets his response, I find him alone behind the stables. I know better than to question him. He has his dagger in his hand and he throws it straight at the wooden planks. He goes to the knife and pulls it out, returns to his position and throws again. Even as I walk away, I hear the whistle of the blade, all his anger sounding inside the judder of steel on wood as it finds its target, over and over again.

KLAUDIA

1996, London

Dear Meg,

 I haven't heard a word from you. I can't bear to think how hurt you must be. Your silence hurts me too. I find myself talking to you, telling you things. I can't believe that we won't see each other again. You're my best friend. I thought we'd know each other all our lives, be old ladies together, laughing about our days in Leeds with Voronkov, reminiscing about how we danced on different stages round the world. I thought we'd boast about our children, our grandchildren. Have I really destroyed all that?

 I miss Mum. People think you should get over it in a month or two. But I miss her every day. I always will. And it's worse because I feel guilty. I let her down. I'll never forgive myself for it.

 I wish I could talk to you about so many things. Remember Cosmo? The crazy thing is that he's here in London. I'm working for his friend in a burlesque bar of all places. The people there are lovely. Except, they think I'm Eliza.

 Cosmo has no idea who I really am. So he doesn't understand why I'm holding myself back. I'm afraid I've lost him because of it. But I can't let myself get involved again, not while he thinks I'm Eliza, can I? I know you'd tell me to be honest, tell the truth and get it over with. But I can't. I'm afraid. You haven't been able to forgive me. I don't want him to hate me—to despise me, cut me out of his life. And the other thing *is, his grandmother is Jewish. She was in a concentration camp. How can I tell him that my father is German—what he did in the war? I haven't told anyone. Not even you.*

Dearest Meg. I love you and I'm so sorry about lying to you . . .

I stop because I'm crying. My tears fall onto the paper, blurring the ink. I wipe my eyes with the edge of my T-shirt. I can't send this. It wouldn't be fair to Meg. She's made it clear that our friendship is over.

I begin to rip it up. Then I stop. My fingers are trembling. I have to try one more time. I can't let her go yet. I smooth out the paper and scrawl my name.

The heat in the street is worse. There's a clogged smell in the air, tar melting on the roads. The pavement is streaked with dog shit. I drop the letter into the mailbox on the corner. I don't hear it fall. It simply disappears, swallowed up, and I'm suddenly afraid Meg will never open it.

In the Guptas' store, the bell clangs above me. It's stuffy and dim. An electric fan whirrs in the corner. I rummage through the clutter on the shelves, picking out a packet of teabags, just to give me an excuse to talk to Mrs. Gupta.

At the register, she takes my purchase from me with methodical care, ringing it up, and placing it in a brown paper bag.

"I'd just like to say," I begin awkwardly, my voice sounding thin, "that I'm sorry if you think my father is avoiding you or anything like that . . ." I force myself to speak up. "He doesn't mean to be rude. He's taken my mother's death very badly."

She shakes her head gently. "I can understand his problem." She counts out my money as she slips it inside the register. "Our shop is an unpleasant reminder."

"Oh, I don't think it's that. He's just . . . he's just keeping himself to himself at the moment."

"But there is no denying that I myself will remind him of that unfortunate day." She crumples the top of the bag with nimble fingers, folding it closed.

I open my mouth to ask her what she means, but the bell clangs as a couple of people come into the shop, and a telephone begins to ring, loud and insistent behind the plastic strands hanging at the door, the noise coming out of the mysterious, unseen spaces of the Guptas' house. Mrs. Gupta turns away from me, distracted by the phone, which stops suddenly, as an elderly woman leans against the counter, repeating a question. "I said, do you have prunes, love?" The woman speaks loudly, as if her hearing isn't good. Her thin hands fidget over a stack of newspapers. "Tinned prunes?"

I wait, clutching my bag, while Mrs. Gupta points the woman in the right direction, and rings up a can of lager for a man in a tracksuit, his bullet head shaved like Shane's.

"You saw Mum the day she died?"

Mrs. Gupta nods. "I thought you knew."

I want to ask her if my mother had said anything on the day she died, if she'd seemed happy or sad, but a wavering voice comes from behind cans of baked beans. "Can't find them." And Mrs. Gupta hurries away, her fleeting look of exasperation quickly erased.

It's just half an hour before opening time. Josh has switched on the sound system and Frank Sinatra is crooning into the empty room. The bar stands polished and ready, and all the lamps are lit, shedding small pink moons onto each table. I'm in the office standing behind Scarlett, helping her into her corset. She is damp with sweat. My fingers slip as I tug at ribbons, heaving her waist into its hourglass shape.

"Did you hear about Cosmo?" she pants, her hands on her hips.

I stop pulling; the ribbons slacken and coil around my hands.

"Cosmo?" There's no moisture in my throat.

"Yeah. He's got a job in Rome. Lucky thing."

"Rome?"

Scarlett's mass of red hair, her white shoulders, and the office with its clutter of costumes and paperwork, hurtle away from me. Air rushes through my lungs. My fingers scrabble at my chest, expecting to grasp a sword. I feel skewered through.

She's nodding, red curls bouncing and tumbling. "He's gone already. Won't be back for weeks, months even. It's a new mural job—something big."

She's still talking. Her words blur into nonsense. I can't concentrate on anything. I'm in the room with her, but it all seems magnified and unreal; I stare at her spine, at the individual shafts of hair that stick to her skin; a freckle floats towards me like an island on a pale map. I bite the inside of my lip and try to focus on doing her up. I yank and squeeze, fumbling around the shapes of knots with shaking fingers. Her skin spills from the top of the corset. I smell men's cologne and nicotine.

Rome. He didn't say anything about it. He didn't even say goodbye.

"Eighty-five degrees!" my father tells me, tapping the barometer.

I used to sit under the apple tree for hours when I was a child, with a book in my hands. The pleasure of outdoor reading was one of the best things about the summer. I loved romantic classics like *Jane Eyre* and *Wuthering Heights*. Then I discovered Austen and fell in love with Elizabeth Bennet and Mr. Darcy, along with the rest of the world. Except Mum. She sometimes sat on the lawn with me, slumped in a green deckchair. She always wore a hat to protect her skin. And in her lap would be some simmering modern love story.

The radio is full of the latest facts about the heatwave. It's all anyone talks about. The newscaster reported delays on trains due to speed restrictions for fear of buckling lines. Fires are breaking out in forests around the country. There are constant reminders about the garden-house ban.

My father takes no notice of the ban. Every evening he is out there aiming a jet of water into the flowerbeds. "It rained all spring. And now they have no water!"

I watch drops of moisture shivering on leaves and hot soil. The earth has split and torn apart into fissures. Ants surge out of one crevice in a seamless ebony trickle. The wet earth releases a stench of fox. I know the Perkinses will be peering from behind their curtains and I'm certain that they will report us. I keep expecting a formal knock on our door. A man in a suit handing over an envelope. A fine to pay.

"Maybe you should use a watering can instead," I suggest. But my voice is dull. It lacks conviction.

Cosmo left without saying goodbye. He's far away in Italy, and I feel as crushed as the brittle seedpods on the ground.

My father shrugs off the suggestion. "I won't have Gwyn's flowers dying because other people didn't do their job."

I think he wants an argument. Hopes for one, even. He sits and broods for most of the day. He looks through the photo albums. He's put more pictures of Mum inside frames he's made in the shed. He props them up on the mantelpiece among the figures of Jesus and the wooden crosses. He keeps a vase there full of fresh flowers. Mum's half-finished knitting is arranged on the coffee table with her reading glasses. Our sitting room looks like a shrine. Anyone would think we were Catholics. Mum never really approved of my father's carvings. It didn't sit with her beliefs. But she knew it made him happy. Her mute face shines out at me from behind squares of polished glass, and I know she wouldn't like any of this.

It's impossible to sleep. The nights are hot and sticky. I leave my window wide open, letting in soupy air and the smell of melting tarmac. I lie in tangled, sweaty sheets listening to the distant roar of traffic coming from the main road, and think of Cosmo. I wasn't brave enough. I keep reliving the moment he stepped away from me in the restaurant, the way his voice sounded. Closed off. Resigned. I feel a quickening inside, and my lungs can't get enough air into them. He's gone.

I hate Eliza. Hate myself for what I've done. I can't erase it, can't change all the mistakes, can't take back the untruths and the hurt I've caused. The heat is suffocating; it closes around me. I wish I were on a beach far away with cool sand between my toes, nothing but the undulating ocean before me. When I was a child I used to think that ice creams at the beach would taste different from those bought from the van at the end of the street: impossible not to lick up the thick fumes that belched out of the van's exhaust, swallowing them along with a melting Popsicle.

In my head I saw translucent water, white spume, the ticklish tumble of tiny fish, and longed for the sensation of waves, the playful roll and splash of them as they slapped against my knees. I couldn't swim. But in my dreams I found myself walking in fearlessly, floating out towards the horizon, swimming with ease through sinuous ribbons of seawater.

We didn't have the money to go on holiday. We never went to a beach. Not even for a day.

I'm awake when the electric milk truck rattles down the street. I listen to the stop-start whine of its engine and the jingle of glass as the milkman sets pints down on doorsteps. There are a few hours of almost complete quiet just before dawn. But now I can hear the sounds of the city waking up: cars and motorbikes. A distant siren. A dog barking. Birds' voices. The mutter and hum of unseen machines, the rumble of trains. An airplane passing.

I stumble into the bathroom and splash my face, leaning under the cold tap, letting it gush into my mouth, tasting the metallic tang. The house is silent. My father must still be asleep. It's early, even for him. I pull on my clothes and go quietly down the stairs into the kitchen. I fill the kettle and switch it on. Set out a cup, dropping a tea bag inside. I get a teaspoon out of the drawer and place it next to the cup. The comfort of ordinary actions. Padding across the floor, I unlock the back door and push it open, letting in summery smells and the early-morning air.

There is a pile of earth under the apple tree. It looks a bit like a molehill. We've never had moles before. I wander out over the dewy grass and my heart judders. An animal has been digging between the roots of the apple tree. Scrape marks gouge out the ground. Fresh earth thrown up and scattered over the damaged lawn. I peer into the raw wound at my feet. At the bottom, something glints: a small square of white, about the size of a stamp.

I don't know what to do. A fox must have unearthed what should have stayed hidden; but now that it's visible, I feel a need to see inside.

Kneeling on the wet ground, I begin to scrape at the earth with a trowel, working carefully around the curve of china. I thrust the sharp point deeper. The soil is wetter, darker. It smells rich and musty. Fine shreds of roots interlace the earth, making my job harder. A writhing worm, vulnerable and naked, burrows away from the light.

Now I can push my hands underneath the urn and lift it clear. I slump sideways, cradling it on my lap, staring at the long-tailed birds and the boughs heavy with pink blossom. I run my filthy fingers across the delicate lines of them, trace the gold encircling the lid.

It feels heavy. But it's so small. How can she be stored inside a container this size? I brush away clinging mud. My fingers move to the lid, twisting, and it gives, scraping as it turns. My heart is beating hard. I close my eyes for a second. Not knowing if I can look. I've never seen human ashes before. I don't know what to expect. Taking a deep breath, I open my eyes.

Gray matter fills it to the brim. It seems natural to dip my fingers into the ashes. They are silky fine as the ashes from a fire. It could almost be water lapping against me. I scoop up a handful, holding that tiny weight in my palm. "Mum," I whisper, curling my fingers and shutting my eyes. Something inside me shuts too: an end to any hope that she will return, whole and alive to me.

I replace the urn back in the hole, because I don't know what else to do, and push the earth back on top. I kneel, my filthy hands pressing the ground, my head bowed, and all the tears that I'd been holding back rush to my eyes. My face is wet. A bird stirs in the branches over my head. I hear the fluted trilling of a thrush.

She was proud of me as a child, proud that I'd gone to university. I don't want to think that she might somehow be looking down, witnessing my lies and broken promises. I don't know what went wrong—I had every intention of being Klaudia again. My hair has almost grown back, the blonde threading into white, bleached ends. But it's not about my hair. I should be defined by who I am to the people I love: daughter, partner, lover and friend. My lies have corrupted every role.

I wish for the feel of Mum's cool hand on my forehead, and close my eyes, finding that I can breathe calmly under her imagined touch, as if all the tangled threads have been cleared away.

I'm waiting in the kitchen when my father comes down for breakfast. There's something I need to ask. It came to me as I'd reburied the urn. I was thinking of Mum and her tough upbringing on a mountain. How she'd transferred her love for a Welsh wilderness to a small London garden. And I realized, suddenly, that I had no idea how she met my father. She'd never told me how he'd arrived at her village.

My father sits heavily at the table and I push scrambled eggs and grilled tomatoes onto a plate and set it before him. I pour a cup of tea, strong and sweet, as he likes it. Then I take my place opposite him.

"I was wondering," I say, leaning forward, "how you met Mum?"

It sounds blunter than I'd intended. I'd rehearsed the question while I cracked eggs into a bowl, and sliced tomatoes.

He blinks at me.

Other questions are bursting through me.

"I mean, what made you want to go to Wales?" I push on, aware of his blank face. "Did you go straight after the war?"

He chews his mouthful steadily, staring down at his plate. I stop myself from fidgeting. The subject of war is unmentionable. Only this is different, I tell myself. This is about the time that came after. I brace myself, expecting him to snap. Or he might ignore me. He's done that before. I shift in my chair, cross my legs and uncross them.

"It wasn't afterwards." He wraps a hand around his glass, takes a long drink of water. "We met during the war."

I frown. "But how?" He's not meeting my eyes. "You mean you were in Wales during the war?"

He nods. "I was a prisoner, in a camp there." His voice is curt and matter-of-fact.

I put down my fork and stare at him. "I had no idea that you were . . . captured. When . . ."

His mouth tightens and I see the muscle jump in his jaw. "It's not something I talk about. As a soldier," he pauses and straightens his shoulders, "there is a sense of shame. It happened early in the war. I was in a U-boat. It was tough work. But it was considered important." He looks at a spot past my head when he talks, no emotion in his voice. "We were sunk. I was rescued by the English. We prisoners worked on the local farm. Your mother was the daughter of a farmhand." His gaze moves to my face. "Gwyn was so good. So pure. She changed everything. By the end of the war we knew we wanted to get married. She was old enough by then to know her own mind."

His extraordinary revelations spin inside me, making me dizzy. I want to ask him more questions—what was it like in the camp; how did he first come to talk to Mum; were they allowed time alone together? But I can see by the hard line of his mouth that he won't answer. He averts his eyes, continuing to eat. I watch him finishing his food. He puts his knife and fork together neatly, dabs his mouth on the napkin, stands up and leaves the room. I gather his plate and cup, put them in the sink, run the hot water, squeeze out some washing-up liquid.

The idea of being cooped up inside the narrow metal tube of a U-boat gives me claustrophobia. I don't know how he could have borne it. And then to be torpedoed: water pouring through the damaged hull, the alarm screaming, trapped men scrambling through water in darkness. I imagine my father falling through a cold sea, being hauled aboard a British boat, half drowned. Then he's in a field dotted with sheep, loading hay onto a truck with a pitchfork as a pretty young girl walks by. He stops, wiping the sweat from his eyes to stare; she glances over her shoulder, blushing.

What he's told me makes sense of so many things. I've never thought about it properly, but how would my father have gotten from Germany to Wales? Math has never been my subject, and I squint, jumbling numbers in my head with an effort, struggling to get at the answers. My mother must have been only about fourteen when she met her German prisoner. And seventeen or eighteen when they ran away together. She was young and impressionable, and it must have felt to her like being Romeo and Juliet. She was too young to understand what she was doing. But people grew up quicker in those days, I remind myself. Boys were sent to war at the age she married.

I see my young, handsome father standing behind barbed wire, resentful, ashamed, deprived of his part in the fighting, as he stares out towards the coast and the war happening without him over the sea. I slump forwards, my hands hanging loose in the warm bubbles. Tension leaves my body as I understand. He isn't guilty. He wasn't in the SS. He wasn't part of any atrocities—he wasn't there at all. And the photograph. It wasn't him. It wasn't him, after all.

ERNST

1940, Germany

Bettina throws her bicycle down in the yard. "Come quick! They're deporting the Jews!"

Meyer fastens the horse to the trap and we all clamber up. He flicks the reins over the chestnut back and she trots past fields of rye, her nostrils flaring at the pigs, snuffling as usual, noses deep in the mud. As soon as we round the corner to the station, we see the crowd. People have gathered to watch the Jews as they file past onto the platform. My eyes go to the shuffling line, and I recognize nearly all of them. Have known them since I was a child. None of them meet my gaze. I see the chemist and his wife. They carry suitcases; mothers hold the hands of children and hug smaller ones against their shoulders. They are bundled into coats and hats. It is cold. Winter is coming. The train isn't a passenger train. It's a goods train, and they climb up onto the boxcars, helping each other.

"Where are they going?" Bettina asks.

"To a camp," her father tells her. "The Lublin Reservation."

"What will they do there?" Agnes wants to know.

"They'll work and be given somewhere to stay and food to eat."

We stand inside the silent crowd, watching as people climb quietly onto the train in their best clothes. A baby cries.

A face moves towards us, bloodless lips closed under vacant eyes. Mrs. Baumann. I have a sudden moment of vertigo, as if my foot has stepped off a cliff. I catch my breath, hardly knowing what I'm doing as I push to the front, shoving elbows and arms out of the way. Sarah and Daniel are there too, walking on either side of their mother.

I open my mouth to call Sarah's name, but Otto's callused skin stops the sound, his palm clamped over my face. I struggle, my heart thundering.

"Shut up, you fool," Otto hisses in my ear. "Don't say a word. Do you want to go with them?"

When he releases me, I lunge forwards. But he's already caught hold of my arm, dragging me back, his nails scissoring into my muscle. I try and wrench away, but he is stronger. I'm caught by the wrist, and my skin burns as I twist and pull. Fear makes me weak, and all my flailing is ineffectual. A childish sob escapes. Mr. Meyer growls at us to stop. Other people are turning to stare too, including the nearest SS soldier. I go limp just as the Baumanns pass. Daniel is carrying Sarah's case, his face expressionless. I can't tell if Sarah knows I'm here. She looks in front of her, a slight smile on her lips, as if she's walking in a different world.

"Sarah!"

The word comes from deep inside; the sound I'd make if I were drowning. A last cry. But Otto has his fingers across my mouth again. And the noise that came from my lips wasn't the one I heard bursting out of my heart, thundering through my throat. It was more a pitiful wail, a cat being strangled.

"It's for the survival of Germany."

One of his hands binds my lips; the other is curled around my bicep. I'm filled with the meaty stink of him. I roll back my lips and bite, tearing into him. He lets go with a yelp, and I'm running, running after her. Everything feels weightless and insubstantial like a dream. And Sarah floats out of reach, a blue shadow. A soldier steps in front of me, his gun lowered.

"Go back." He nods towards the throng behind me.

My feet are suddenly heavy. My whole body sets hard, immovable as a house. The noises of the watching crowd, the shuffling feet of the Jews, little mews of children and whispered conversations roar through my head. And behind it I hear the drip, drip of condensation from the train onto the track. I can't understand why Sarah isn't turning. Why doesn't she turn? A sob breaks in my throat. The line of passengers keeps shuffling by, giving me frightened sideways glances. A mother quiets her child. "No, darling. You can't take your toys. We'll send for them . . ."

I gaze past the soldier, towards the back of Sarah's dark head. Watching her and Daniel as they move farther away. The soldier stiffens his shoulders and his fingers tighten around the barrel.

Otto is by my side. He says something to the soldier and they laugh. All strength has left my body. I want to be sick. My stomach has turned to water. I feel my bowels loosen. Otto doesn't put his hand over my mouth again. He knows I'm done, that my dry tongue sticks to the roof of my mouth, gluing my words fast. I would fall to my knees if it weren't for him holding me up. His pinching fingers are the only reality, his hot breath on my neck.

Mutely I watch Daniel help Sarah onto the train, handing up her case. I see her fear now, the trembling of her hands. She puts her arm around her mother's hunched back. I stare at the flash of blue that is the hem of her coat. It's all I can see of her. I remember holding the worn rub of wool between my fingers as she pulled the thin folds of it around me, so that we were pressed together inside its small blue tent. We'd fallen onto the forest floor and I'd felt my way beneath her clothes. The soft give of her lips as she'd opened them to me. The last time we were together. Others clamber up. Stumbling people, clutching at each other, bodies crammed in together. Dear God. How many can fit into one car? My eyes hurt with staring, but the patch of blue has disappeared.

SS walk up and down the platform, shoving people inside, sliding doors shut. There are no windows, just little slits in the doors, high up. I see fingers at the openings, eyes staring out. The train pulls away with a shriek of metal. Otto releases his grip and I stagger, hands flailing as I catch my stride. I'm running behind the train, chest out; my fist hits the side of the last car, my feet sliding at the edge of the platform, and I teeter on the brink, wanting to plunge onto the tracks, to fall into darkness.

The rumbling wheels fade into the distance, swallowed by ordinary sounds: the soughing wind in the trees, music of birds and a dog barking. The crowd disperses, talking in low voices. A soldier spits as I pass. The wet sticks and slides across my neck.

In the cart on the way back, our feet dangling over the edge, Otto sucks the side of his hand, and says quietly, "If you give yourself away again, I won't be able to protect you. You're lucky. I never said anything. Nobody knew."

I hardly hear him. I'm thinking of Sarah and Daniel and their mother. I can't imagine what it's like in that train, shut inside darkness, standing like animals. I set my jaw, and turn my head away, staring at a row of poplar trees, pigs in a field. A castle rises above a distant copse, tall and elegant.

"Your little Jewish bitch," he says. "She would have destroyed you in the end."

The cottage looks as it always has from the outside: a dank ruin surrounded by brambles. But at the back, the door that we never used has been smashed open; it gapes on broken hinges; splintered wood flares like knives. Inside there's the remains of a fire in the grate, torn, blackened pages curling in the ashes. The books and cards have all been burned. The cups shattered. Shards of china and scraps of paper have been kicked about the rooms; singed blankets and clothes twisted among them. A candle rolls under my feet. *Death To Jews* crawls in large red letters over the parlor wall. Dribbles of red paint on the floor like blood. I kneel in the ashes, my face in my hands, and sob. And the thought is there in my head and it won't go away. They think it was me. They think I betrayed them.

1941, Ukraine

We've been marching for days. My ankles and toes are rubbed raw. And the weather is turning bitter. I smell snow in the air, see it in the flat gray sky. The Ukraine is dreary. The long horizons don't change however hard we march. And there are the same ragged pine forests we saw in Poland. The same poor farms. As we file through villages, they seem empty. And then I notice movement behind half-open doors and windows. People staring at us from the shadows, faces gaunt with hunger.

"Bloody Stalin," Damaske says. "We're lucky to be born German."

I disagree with him. But I say nothing. I like Damaske. He is uncomplaining. A natural optimist. He has an open, ruddy face and green eyes.

He's built like a pack animal—short and sturdy with broad shoulders. He is always quick to share his cigarettes.

The road is almost impassable: rain turned it to mud and then the army trekked along it, convoys of tanks, horses and marching men churning it up. Now the wind has dried it into steep, hardened ruts. There are potholes big enough to half swallow a man. We see lines of Russian prisoners shuffling along in their tattered brown uniforms. The enemy. At first I'd stared at them, at these exhausted boys. They didn't look so fierce. Some of them have straw stuffed inside their jackets and hats. Some wear huge wooden clogs instead of boots. We pass a burnt-out tank on its side, charred metal twisted into lumps. One of ours. There's the stink of burning.

In a town we halt near a Red Cross tent and are given the order to stand down. Nurses draw cold coffee from a horse-drawn field kitchen and ladle it into our canteen cups. Three Messerschmitts go over with a roar, the black swastikas on the under-wings visible. We let out a cheer. The Russians have nothing to compete with the Luftwaffe. Damaske and I wander over to the ruin of a house and lean against a crumbling wall to sip our coffee and have a smoke. There is even a trickle of sunlight breaking through the gray.

A crowd of German soldiers and civilians have gathered farther down the road. We amble over to see what's going on. Some SS stand in a half circle watching while the Ukrainian Auxiliary Police herd a group of women onto a truck. One of the women is heavily pregnant and carrying a toddler on her hip. As she struggles to get into the truck her foot slips, overbalancing her; the child grabs at its mother's hair in fright. A policeman curses and gives her a hard shove and she stumbles again, staggering on loose stones. Undone by her belly and the weight of her child, she falls: straight down like a tree, one hand out to break her fall, the other clasped around her screaming child.

They sprawl in the road together, the child's face contorted in a wail. I see the bare skin of the woman's legs exposed, a torn stocking around her ankle. An SS soldier steps forward and takes hold of the child by its arm; with one casual movement he flings it into the truck, limbs splayed, body arching. There is a muffled thump, like the slap of meat on a counter. The mother cries out and grabs the soldier by the ankle. He looks down, a fleeting expression of surprise on his face. He raises the butt of his rifle and brings it down on her head.

I lurch forward before I can think, my hands out to help the woman. Her face turns to me and I see the blood running into her eye and the gaping circle of her silent mouth. I think of Mrs. Baumann. Sarah. My legs are shaking.

The soldier places himself between her and me. He smiles. "Get back to your duties. Nothing to be concerned about here."

"But, what . . . what had she done?"

"Just a Pole going to a work detail." His voice is polite. Final.

Damaske is waiting for me. He shakes his head. "Come on. Nothing to do with us." He takes a deep drag on the stub of his cigarette and throws it on the road. "I don't know how those SS sleep at night."

I don't look back at the truck. The milky coffee in my belly is curdling, bile rising into my mouth, and I swallow hard.

KLAUDIA

1996, London

I'VE BEEN TRYING TO IMAGINE what it must have been like for my father in that submarine as it rolled towards the bottom of the ocean, with his short life flashing before him. No wonder he found Jesus after that. I think of how young my mother was when she met him: a child still. And him the older boy, tall and handsome, surly and brooding as a blond Heathcliff, transported to her Welsh mountains.

It's too hot to sleep again. I twist from one side of my narrow mattress to the other, trying to get comfortable, kicking away my covers. I feel uneasy; something is out of kilter. Not right. Not just the things that worry me every day: Meg and Cosmo; my lies. Something else. Something hidden. I concentrate, willing it to come up out of the darkness. I sense it shouldering its way through the shadows into my memory. And then I have it, suddenly. The medals. I press my fist against my teeth. How could I have forgotten?

I wake to the distant whining of a small engine below. A thump and bang. The vacuum cleaner is on downstairs. I sit up, yawning, and swing my legs over the side.

I stagger along the hall, pulling on my dressing gown. Pushing open my father's door, I enter quietly. I can hear the roar of the machine through the floor. I open my mother's drawer. Her cardigans are folded in neat piles. I push my fingers to the back. There is no silky scarf bundled around metal objects. I frown. It was years ago that I found them.

I close the drawer and search the others, rooting through fabrics, sifting through scarves and belts, checking Mum's jewelry box. I get down on my knees to look under the bed. I pull open the wardrobe and my father's drawers. He has few clothes and it doesn't take long to see that there are no medals behind or underneath them. I look through his bedside cabinet, finding a pair of spare reading glasses; earplugs; a pen; a jar of Vicks; and a small heap of loose coins. I sit on the bed and put my hands over my eyes, pressing hard until sparks flare. Did I misremember? Did I imagine them? I was only a child, and I was confused and scared about who my father might be. I had no information and so I made things up. Perhaps I made the medals up too. But I weighed them in my hands, saw the details of raised emblems, frayed ribbon and those etched swastikas.

My father is vacuuming in the living room, wearing one of my mother's aprons. Up close, the noise makes me wince. My head is sore, as if I've spent a night drinking. He doesn't hear me as he stalks around the room, pushing furniture out of the way and thrusting the nozzle into corners, chasing up dust and cobwebs. The plastic end clashes with a wooden skirting board. He switches off the machine and picks up a can of polish.

"Klaudia." He nods, waving the can towards the kitchen. "I've left some breakfast on the stove for you. Then come and help. The house is a mess. Your mother wouldn't like it."

I blink stupidly. My father has made me breakfast? Such an ordinary, domestic gesture, but it feels monumental. He has a pair of reading glasses propped, forgotten, on his head. He sprays a burst of polish onto the portmanteau and begins to rub fiercely.

The stench of fried meat overpowers the smell of polish and I follow the trail into the kitchen. I uncover the dish and prod burnt sausages with a fork. Liquid grease bursts out, trickling in thin streams. I put one of the least charred onto a plate with a piece of toast, pouring on a generous dollop of ketchup to disguise the taste.

As I am chewing slowly, between large gulps of hot tea, my father comes into the kitchen, hands on his hips. I feel my throat closing. I have a sudden urge to retch. But he is watching me. With a concentrated effort, I force the food down.

Satisfied, he picks up a duster and leaves the room. I push the plate away and put my head in my hands. Everything he told me makes sense. How else could he have ended up in a remote Welsh farm straight after the war? He was locked away from all the fighting, hauling hay bales, not pointing a gun. The medals I found might have belonged to a friend. It doesn't matter. Anyone can buy war memorabilia.

And the photograph? It had to be someone else. The name was a coincidence. But I remember the familiar profile in grainy print and bite my lip. I get up and follow my father into the living room. He's clutching one of the wooden disciples, a yellow cloth in his other hand.

"So you mean you were never at the Eastern Front?" I ask from the doorway. "You never went to Russia?"

He looks surprised. "No. I told you. I was in a U-boat. And then I was captured."

He flicks the bottom of the ornament with the duster and replaces it carefully. "It's my brother, Ernst, who was at the Front. He was the one that went into the Wehrmacht."

The club is busy. "Three Cool Cats" is playing. I move from one customer to another, handing over drinks, scooping change out of the register. Between the shapes of people I catch glimpses of the mural, remembering the mermaid, and her face that was my own. The way she'd swum towards me, her eyes steady and hopeful. Cosmo's absence is a bruise. I've been trying not to prod the spot, not to think of him. But everything is different now. I feel taller, lighter. Knowing that my father wasn't the one who pulled the trigger, knowing that he wasn't involved in the horrors in the Ukraine and Russia and Poland, it's as if a rope has been taken from my wrists, a gag from my mouth.

I need to find out from Josh or Scarlett exactly where Cosmo is in Rome. I'm going to take a weekend off work, get on a plane and find him. The thought of it makes my palms sweaty. But I have to do it.

Josh is leaning across the bar. He looks worried and he's beckoning to me. I hurry over, concerned, because Josh never loses his cool. He's shouting over the music. I can't hear. I put my hand up to my ear and he tries again. I feel his breath, words vibrating against my cheek, the buzz of his voice a ticklish sensation.

"Scarlett's just phoned," he repeats, even louder. "She's ill. Food poisoning. She said you could do it."

Stunned, I shake my head.

He beckons again and I follow him into his office. The noise of the club retreats behind the swing of velvet.

"I can't let the crowd down, Eliza." He paces around his desk. "Not at such short notice." He opens his palms, appealing to me. "Look, I trust Scarlett. If she says you can do it, then you can."

My pulse is jumping at my throat. "No. You don't understand . . ."

"Please." He ruffles his fingers through his shock of curly hair. "Pick a costume. Just walk about on the stage and smile. You don't have to take anything off."

I put my hand to my mouth. I hear Scarlett's voice. *Your body knows what to do.* We've practiced different routines. We've discussed costumes. Talked as if I will be stepping onto that stage and performing. But it was always a date in the future—something just out of reach.

Josh is staring at me with a desperate look. He fiddles with the neck of his shirt, smoothing the collar, and I notice his bitten nails. I can't let him down.

"OK."

He lets out a huge sigh and grabs me, kisses my nose. His lips are damp. "Thank you. Thank you."

"But tell them I'm just the cover," I tell him quickly. "Don't let them have any expectations . . ."

The curtain has already fallen behind him.

Josh's cramped office is empty. The telephone silent. Beyond the red fabric comes a muffled mutter and hum and the crooning of Peggy Lee. I taste the bile of fear in my mouth. The thought of walking out there and standing on stage is making me want to retch.

I need to find a costume. Scarlett's crammed clothes rail is squeezed between the filing cabinet and the doorway. I touch the lace on a corset. The fabric is rigid with bone, speckled with sparkling sequins. As I slip it from the hanger, the brittle edges rub against my hands like the scales of an exotic reptile. It's a struggle to do up on my own. Then I roll on white fishnet stockings, and drape a sheer white scarf around my neck. Scarlett's feet are bigger than mine. I will go barefoot. I don't intend to take anything off except the scarf; I'm never going to be the kind of girl who's happy to appear in public in nipple tassels.

Outside in the smoky, crowded room, I stumble when someone steps in front of me.

"Eliza."

Cosmo blocks my path. His gaze travels downwards, taking in what I'm wearing, or not wearing. I can't speak. He slides his hand to hold mine. Our fingers entwine. He tugs, and I follow, as he pulls me back into the office, folds of velvet sliding across us.

He lets go of my hand. We stare at each other.

"I thought you were away . . ." I struggle to push words out. "In Rome."

The fact of him here, when in my head he'd been in Italy, has unraveled me.

"I was." He pushes his hands into his pockets and takes them out again. "I'm back for a couple of days. I wanted to see you."

My heart is thundering.

"You're about to go on?" His eyebrows shoot up. "I always hoped you'd do it."

My lips waver around the shape of a smile.

"I'm ashamed of myself." He rubs his nose with his knuckle. "I owe you an apology."

"Apology?"

He rolls his head from side to side as if his neck is stiff. "Just hear me out, Eliza. Please." He wrinkles his brow. "I need to do this. Last time . . . I was childish. Going off like that. It was rude. I worried later, about you getting home when it was so late. Then I got on a plane without telling you. There was no excuse, even if I was disappointed. But the truth is I'm not good with rejection." He's speaking quickly, not looking at me.

I try to interrupt. I can't bear the irony. It's me that should be apologizing. But he continues, rushing his words.

"When I was a kid, I was never good enough. I didn't want to be a doctor like my parents. I wasn't into science like my brother and sister. But I still wanted to be like them." He shrugs. "It made me feel useless when I failed science exams, when I was afraid of blood. They thought it was funny. But I took it all as a rejection. Over-sensitive, you see."

"No." I jerk my head up.

A laugh ignites inside me. All the misunderstandings piling up behind us. The confusion and muddle. And it's so simple really. I love him.

The laugh stays inside. "Please don't. You have nothing to explain, nothing to be sorry for. It's me . . ."

But he's still speaking, and I recognize the determined look on his face, his need to tell me something. "Eliza, I know there are reasons for you pushing me away. You were trying to tell me something before, and I lost my temper. Whatever it is, I'm here now and I promise I'll listen."

We're standing next to Josh's messy desk in the cramped space. I'd only have to take one more step and I'd be able to reach up and slide my arms around his neck.

The noise of the club presses into the office: music and the muttering of an impatient crowd. I blink. Remembering.

"I'm supposed to be on stage . . . I have to go." I look behind him towards the curtain.

"I'll wait." Cosmo stoops and kisses my cheek. "Good luck . . ." He pulls back. "Am I allowed to say I'm proud of you?"

I raise my hand and caress my cheek, put my fingers where his lips have been. My heart stutters. He's holding up swags of red velvet. I look through into the dark club. Sound swells around us: a choppy sea pulling us apart.

My mouth is dry and I moisten my lips. "Cosmo." I turn back. "You're right. We need to talk. There's so much to tell you."

Out in the crowd, I push through customers to the bar and ask Josh to put "Harlem Nocturne" on. I'm not looking at people as I make my way to the stage. My legs are shaking. The music has started and I can feel the attention of the place turning towards me. I climb the steps.

The chatter in the room has quieted. I blink in the spotlight. Someone makes a shushing sound. I can hear the clink of glasses. Then Josh must have turned the track up because everything else is swallowed inside its lush rhythm.

I stand, frozen. The hammering of my heart drowns the song. I close my eyes against the glare. An uncomfortable murmuring starts, a shifting of feet and someone's nervous laughter. I remind myself that Cosmo is there, somewhere in the faces, watching me. I can still feel his lips on my cheek. I lift an arm, moving my hip to the left, moving into the music.

I'm dancing. I'm using Voronkov's ballet routine like a map; but I'm already adapting it, adding a burlesque flavor. I can't brave the gaze of the audience yet; I'm staring at the floor. But then I feel it—a prickle of electricity running between the crowd and me, a tug of connection that makes me look out into the space beyond the stage, at the watchers behind the lights. I begin to play to them. I anticipate their reactions. It's like a game, or a conversation. I'm enjoying myself. I slow down, sensing the pull of their collective looking, and a thrill shivers through me. All those afternoons in Scarlett's room have left their mark: I know how to tilt my head; I've mastered the slow slide of fingers over skin; I remember the power of stillness. Can almost hear them holding their breath as they wait for me to move again. The music is reaching its conclusion. I've slipped the scarf from my shoulders. It flutters into dusty darkness.

The song ends and I bow deeply, my head hanging over my knees. My scalp is wet with sweat. Salty drops flicker as they fall. I stand upright and the applause begins. It buzzes around me. My mouth is parched and I'm breathing hard. My legs feel hollow. I negotiate the steps carefully, straining to see where I'm putting my feet. A hand takes mine, warm fingers closing around my own.

Cosmo is looking up at me.

And suddenly I know that it's going to be all right. I can't wait to unburden myself of my lie. I can't wait to be alone with him.

There's a noise at the back of the club. People are jostling and pushing. Someone shouts. Cosmo glances up, and I see Josh gesturing to the bouncer. We get troublemakers in occasionally, beery men who misunderstand their environment. Cosmo spreads his arms protectively as a figure emerges out of the crowd: a heavyset man with a square face under a crew cut. He smirks as he draws nearer.

"Klaudia," the man says, the slash of his mouth spreading into a leer. "Well. Well. Who'd have thought it? All these years. I would have known you anywhere. Even in that get-up." He winks and puts his head on one side. "You always did have a good pair of legs, princess."

Cosmo positions himself in front of me. "Look, I don't know who you think you're talking to, but you've got the wrong person." His voice is low and reasonable.

"Piss off, mate," Shane says. "I wasn't talking to you."

"I'm sorry, but you've made a mistake," Cosmo persists. "She doesn't know you. This is Eliza, not whatever-you-said." He doesn't even glance at me for affirmation. His certainty is terrible. "I think you'd better leave now."

Shane laughs. "Eliza might be her stage name—but this juicy little number knows me all right. Don't you, Klaudia?" He reaches a hand to pinch my cheek. I flinch at his touch. "We had a good thing going back in the day. We were at school together. We come from the same manor. Did she tell you that her old man's a Nazi?" His eyes glitter. He taps the side of his nose. "I know all about her. She used to wear her hair down her back. Two plaits. But I like the cropped look. Kind of sexy."

Cosmo squares his shoulders and I see Shane sizing him up, closing his fingers into fists. They flex and glower at each other.

"Don't." I put my hand on Cosmo's arm.

He glances at me, his face sliding into doubt.

A long sigh runs through me. "He's telling the truth." I'm not sure if anyone hears. The words melt into the shove of movement gathering around us.

The bouncer is at Shane's side, all bulky biceps and hard brows, and he's motioning for him to leave. Shane looks amused, holding up his hands to show he's making no resistance. With the bouncer steering him, Shane strolls away. The back of his thick neck glistens, an inked swastika dark against the mottled pink of his skin. The crowd parts for him. I can hear his laughter.

Cosmo is staring at me; his mouth is working, trying to find words.

My mind is a blank nothing. I feel ludicrous, standing here in the corset like a clown.

"I have to get out of these things."

I turn and blunder into the office, ripping at the bodice with trembling fingers, pushing the corset off me, laddering the stockings with my nails; kicking them away under the table. I ram my feet into my jeans, struggle into my top and grab my bag.

As I pull the curtain aside to leave, Cosmo hasn't moved. He is completely still, every atom of him arrowed towards me. His dark eyes won't let me go.

"That man." His lips twitch. "What was he talking about?" He opens his hands and lets them fall. "How do you know him? Who's Klaudia?"

"I am." I rub my face. "I'm Klaudia."

It's a strange relief to say it. I've been holding back the moment for so long. Even as it falls, crushing me, I have a sense of destiny reached, of the inevitable happening. Cosmo's expression changes; doubt and confusion pull at his forehead; the muscles of his jaw harden.

"I don't understand."

He takes a step back. The clamor of the club continues: a muttering of voices and a track from a musical blaring out. Curious faces turn towards us, pale smudges swirling out of the gloom.

"Everything he said is true. I've lied to you." My voice is flat. "I'm not Eliza. I'm not who you think I am."

Cosmo's mouth goes slack. He looks at me as if he can't believe what he sees, as if I'm a monster.

ERNST

1941–1948, Russia

IN THE BEGINNING I kept a diary, scribbling things in a small notebook, the pages protected by oilcloth. I recorded skirmishes with the enemy; I wrote about the brilliance of sunflower fields; I tried to do justice to vast stretches of land broken only by the distant shapes of collective farms and wooden windmills. I'd never been in a landscape so huge, so seemingly endless. I faithfully recorded our rations: *Slibowitz, Komissbrot*, tinned liver, cold tea, vodka. I described a dead horse rotting at the side of the road, flies feasting on its dusty eyes, and how it had made me stupidly sad, as if the death of a horse meant anything there. But I'd remembered the smell of the stables at home, Lotte's muzzle twitching against my palm.

I stopped eventually, stopped writing things down. I didn't have words to describe men blown to pieces in front of me. I was too exhausted from hauling dead and dying men out of the mud, searching for identity tags on unrecognizable carcasses to compose lines of text. Exhaustion and terror and the need to survive shaped my days. I tried to sleep, curled into muddy fox-holes, or stretched out on a hayrick, my helmet banging against my fore-head, but the lice were an unbearable torture. And the rain. Dribbles of water crept inside my collar; damp cloth clung to my freezing skin; inside wet socks and boots, my feet grew clammy, swollen and rotten.

If I did sleep, I usually fell into a coma-like state. But I had nightmares about Sarah. I'd heard stories. There were rumors about what the Nazis were doing to Jews. I had a recurring image of her kneeling by a pit, a man holding a pistol to her head. In the dream, I stood by, unable to move, watching him pull the trigger. I would wake gasping, filled with a sense of loss, catapulted back into the misery of the new day.

We marched and fought. Marched and fought. The drills we'd done in Hitler Youth were no preparation for this: we were ambushed, shot at by snipers from deserted buildings, knifed in the guts as we stalked the enemy through tangled forests. The ground exploded under our feet. Battles were unremitting, lasting days. Nights turned white with flares. Our ears and senses were pummeled and blasted by continual shrieks and bangs. Men were separated from their original units. Through the confusion, Damaske and I managed not to lose each other. I began to think that having him beside me kept me human. Sharing a cup of vodka, making jokes at each other's expense, a quick pat on the back. These things allowed me to remain me. I would have gone mad, or become animal without his friendship. No one else would ever understand what we had seen and endured. Our uniform was oily, filthy with grime and mud. There was no opportunity to wash. We weren't fed for days. While searching for partisans in a village, I found a couple of grubby potatoes and ate them raw, almost choking on the splintering flesh.

After a bitterly cold night spent in a shelter, canvas stretched over the entrance, we woke to find a fresh fall of snow had rendered the world brilliant—strangely glittering and blue. Snow concealed the mire of sucking sludge, softened bomb craters and burnt-out tanks, smudged the starkness; it healed the broken landscape around us. We hated it. This was the beginning of winter. Each day the temperature fell further. It made marching impossible; we sank up to our thighs in the dense white. We pulled our caps down and wrapped scarves around our noses. Still our nostrils froze. My numb fingers couldn't feel the trigger on my gun, and touching metal was an agony. When we pissed, other men put their hands inside the stream for a moment's warmth.

It was five degrees below zero. We'd been forced back, away from territory we'd won weeks before, and we were dug in, attempting to hold an area of flat, desolate land. The line was thin and long. We crouched in the trench listening to the Russians advancing: the grumble of their tanks sent shock waves through the frozen ground. We heard them singing, the roar of their voices, an outnumbering mass of Red Army bearing down on us. I clutched an anti-tank grenade in my hand. I was certain that I was going to die. The others felt it too. That mutual certainty of death was a tangible force in the freezing air. It made us feel skinless, raw, almost euphoric.

A blast threw me against hard dirt. When I staggered up, Damaske was curled amongst rubble. I turned him over and saw that the right side of his face was torn away. A shock of pale bone and muscle showed through blackened flesh. One eye stared up at me. He tried to speak. I held him on my lap, hunched over, sheltering his body with mine, while shouting men stepped over us, and explosions tore through the earth above. I don't know how long I cradled his head in my arms, looking into his wild, pleading eye, wishing for it to shut, wishing for it to end. He died gurgling blood from the dark hole where his nose had been.

The retreat was chaotic, a shambles of men attempting to escape, hitching lifts on anything that moved, shuffling along in boots stuffed with straw or paper. Ambulance trucks crawled past overflowing with dying men, too stunned by pain and despair to even groan. It was then that I saw the boys from Hitler Youth: kids who can't have been older than fifteen, marching in the opposite direction into the line of fire, with a fervor of conviction blazing on their unfinished faces. And I recognized that expression, that light in their eyes, the same one Otto had had. None of them would come back alive. But Otto would. The Red Cross had gotten a letter to me. My brother was a POW somewhere in England, captured in the first months of the fighting.

I'd imagined that he was enduring similar things to me; that he was living through his own hell, as I was. But, turning the letter in my hands, I understood that we'd shared nothing.

The order for unconditional surrender came in the spring. We stood with our rifles tied with rags, hands up, while Russians went through our pockets, stealing watches and wedding rings. The Nazi insignia of eagle and swastika was ripped from our uniforms. We were marched for weeks, going farther east with almost no food. We chewed bark on trees, ate grass. Soviet Intelligence Officers examined us under our left arms, looking for the blood group tattoos found on Waffen SS. These men disappeared. We never saw them again. I thought of Otto and his failed ambitions.

We were herded into cattle cars, packed closely inside. The doors slammed shut, just as they had on Sarah and her family. The journey was long in the stinking cars as they swayed and jolted, and we fell against each other in the dark. Our daily rations were a slice of salt herring and a slice of bread. When we reached the gulag, we were shoved into a rambling line to march inside. A crack rang out and an officer at the front of the line crumpled to the ground. The Russian who'd shot him ambled up and pulled off the dead man's leather riding boots.

On November 7, 1945, we were told that the German Wehrmacht no longer existed. All insignia were to be removed. We were to work to repay the war damage inflicted on Russia by the fascists. Day after day we went out into the snowy forests under armed guard to chop down trees using axes and cross-saws, dragging the wood back to the camp. Every morning there were gray-faced cadavers in bunks—men killed by exhaustion and malnutrition. I planned an escape, managing to first hide some rotten cabbage leaves in my sock. It would be better to freeze to death as a free man than die in the camp. I wriggled under the gate inside deep ruts made by trucks, and waded knee-deep in snow for two days before they found me, delirious and frostbitten.

They called the whole camp out, made them stand in line and watch while I was beaten. Five men with guns and ropes. I tried to shield my face, curling up on the ground, hands over my head. But there was no escape from the blows. They struck until I was unconscious, a pulpy mass of bleeding flesh. My face was so swollen I was blind for days. My left eye never recovered.

I was in solitary confinement after that, months of living in a room hardly bigger than a crate, with no heating. I had nothing to keep me alive, except thoughts and memories. And plans. I had no idea what had happened to Sarah and Daniel. In the madness of my lonely days, I tried making bargains with whatever forces existed in the world, good or bad, for their survival. I dreamed of finding them. I dreamed of rescuing Sarah, of holding her in my arms.

I thought of Otto too in his POW camp. I was certain that his camp was nothing like mine. The English would abide by the Geneva Convention. Otto might even have been set free. I wondered where he'd gone and what he was doing, and what angel stood by his side to protect him.

KLAUDIA

1996, London

THE BLEAK LIGHT OF early morning peels my eyelids apart. The memory of Cosmo and yesterday overwhelms me: an agony of shame and loss hitting my solar plexus in one hard stab. I groan. I want to pull the covers over my face, curl into a ball and stay in bed, curtains drawn, window and door shut. Instead I haul myself out of the covers. As I reach under the bed for my slippers, my fingers drag something else out by mistake: a pair of dusty trainers, long forgotten.

My new trainers have been abandoned with the rest of my things in my old room in Leeds. I used to run there, sprinting up the hills. I loved the sense of freedom. The forgetting it offered. I can't think about last night: Shane's words, the look of disbelief and disappointment on Cosmo's face before I turned and left him there. I pull the trainers on. The soles are thick with ancient mud. I scrape my hair into a ponytail, hunt around in my drawers for tracksuit bottoms and a T-shirt, testing the familiar rubbery bounce, leaving a trail of crumbling dirt.

"I'm going for a run," I call through my father's door. "Won't be long."

The morning is gray with a slight chill. Leaves dangle from branches, lusterless, sad, beginning to turn brown. The world looks tired. Weeds poke through cracks in the pavements. Gutters are caked in gritty dust, clogged with rubbish. People are up and about, walking to work with purposeful strides. A car passes. The garbage truck turns into our street, the garbage men clattering bins and shouting to each other. I catch a whiff of rotten eggs, the stench of stale food.

I find my stride, stretching out, the muscles in my buttocks and calves resisting at first. Then my breath begins to come in a pattern, my arms and legs moving to a rhythm. Dry leaves rustle under my soles, papery as dead skin. The power in my body makes me feel better, gives me back hope. I stop when I can't go on anymore, standing with legs straddled, bent over with my hands on my knees, pulling in gulps of air. My forehead is slick with sweat, and I lick my lips, tasting salt.

I'm on a side street by the untidy little playground that my mother used to bring me to when I was a child. It's deserted. Behind a drooping wire fence, shapes of swings, a slide and a broken seesaw loom like strange creatures in a zoo.

I jog home slowly, reluctant to enter the house, putting off the moment when I'll have to face up to last night. In the kitchen, I notice that my father has had his breakfast. He's washed up his plate and cup. They sit on the draining board. There's something pathetic about this reminder of his solitary meal that makes my throat constrict. I can't afford to cry. I'll never be able to stop. I stand at the sink and gulp down several large glasses of water, staring out into the garden without seeing anything.

There's a rustle from the hall: the slide of letters hitting the mat. The snap of the letterbox closing. Two letters are lying by the front door. I bend to pick them up automatically and place them on the hall table. One is formal and addressed to my father. Then I see a familiar scrawl of handwriting. My name. A French stamp.

I'm still in my running things, the sweat drying on my face, as I shut the door to my bedroom. Leaning against it, I tear along the envelope with shaking fingers.

Dear Klaudia,

It feels freaky to write your new name. (Your old name really, I guess.)

I know this reply is late. I got your second letter first, ripped it open, and couldn't understand what the hell you were going on about. That's when I discovered that my downstairs neighbor thought he was being helpful, slipping your first letter under my door. It went under the mat. Anyway, I found it after I knew to look. And all this time I've been wor-

ried sick about you. You'd just disappeared into thin air. I began to think you'd been murdered. I thought about phoning the police.

When I finally understood, it felt like a slap across the face to hear that you'd been lying to me all this time. I marched around my flat, talking to myself like a mad woman. I wanted to wring your neck. What the hell were you thinking? It just made a mockery of all our secret-sharing—all those moments I trusted you with MY truths. And you never fessed up. Never felt like it was your turn to tell the truth. That's what friends do. They trust each other. But your second letter frightened me. You're not alone. I'm here.

I don't think I'll ever really understand why you did it. And why you kept up the pretense for two years. (Two years!!!!) But I don't intend to lose you. Best friends are hard to come by. And underneath the fake name and the fake stories, I think it's just you.

I'll be back this Christmas. I'm coming to London and we can see each other. I'll meet your father. I have your address. Have you got a phone number there? Send it to me. I don't want to be out of contact with you for so long again. I missed you, you crazy mixed-up kid. I'm rushing this letter off as quickly as I can—I don't want you to think I've deserted you for a moment longer.

I'm so sorry about your mum.
Sending you hugs from Paris,
Meg

I sit on the bed, slumped over the letter. I'm trembling. Relief, frustration, happiness, hope, shame. Emotions stream through my insides, each one slippery as an eel. They writhe and twist so that I can't pin down exactly what I feel. I close my eyes. I haven't lost Meg. I haven't lost her friendship. Her love. I have to hang on to that. In the end, what I feel is relief.

I kick off my trainers and get out of my exercise clothes. In the shower, I turn the handle as far as it will go, wanting to be deluged with heat. Instead, tepid water drips and dribbles from the showerhead. My parents were never ones for modernizing. The pipes clank. I lather soap in my hands, rinse the salt from my face. The shower curtain flaps against my skin, cold and clammy.

Meg's words are giving me courage. I must go back to Brixton. I don't know if Cosmo told them about Shane. But I imagine that everyone overheard the conversation. By now it will be common knowledge. Despite the cold water spurting over my shoulders, the thought of walking back into the club and facing them makes me hot with embarrassment and shame.

My father's in the kitchen, pairs of shoes on newspaper spread over the table, glasses perched on the end of his nose. He attacks the toe of a black lace-up with fierce swipes of a brush. "Any shoes need cleaning?"

"No thanks."

He pauses, peering at me over his glasses. "When are you going back? Your new term must be starting soon."

I press my thumb to my front teeth. My heart begins to thump.

"I'm not going back." I control my hands, stopping myself from fidgeting. "I dropped out of my degree. It was a mistake. I want to dance. I've always wanted to dance."

He puts the brush down slowly, sits back in his chair and frowns. "You want to dance."

He repeats the words as if I've said that I wanted to rob a bank, expose myself in a public place, murder the nearest pensioner.

I clear my throat. "Yes." My voice wobbles. "I'm going to apply to do a BA in dance and choreography." Each syllable is a struggle. "At the Laban Center. It's in London."

"Ridiculous." He rises and walks to the window. Looks out into the garden, shoulders rigid with tension. "Your mother would be disappointed."

Anger coils around my guts. I am breathless with it.

"No. Mum would understand."

He swings round. His face is puce. His eyes swivel to find me. Irises almost colorless in this light, pale blue as skimmed milk. He blinks.

"I knew her like no one else. And I'm telling you that she would be disappointed, Klaudia. As I am. You lied to us. You have let yourself down, as usual. Let us both down. Your mother was always in agreement with me."

"Well maybe she shouldn't have been." I clench my hands into fists. "Maybe she felt she didn't have a choice."

I turn and leave the room, keeping my back straight, but my legs are trembling, weak and boneless under me. I grab the banister and haul myself up from one step to the next.

"I'm giving you time to reconsider," he shouts after me. "If you do start that . . . that dance course . . . you won't be living at home anymore."

He follows me into the hall. "Don't walk away from me when I'm talking to you." His voice is quivering with rage.

I don't answer; don't look back. His feet are on the stairs behind me. I hear the creak of spindles, joists complaining under his tread, the rough tearing of air in and out of his lungs. I slam my bedroom door in his face. But he's yelling through the wood.

"Where were you after term finished, Klaudia? You knew how much your mother looked forward to you coming home. Although she never complained when you were late. She was so proud of you for taking a degree. And now you tell me you weren't even at the university!"

I've got my eyes screwed shut, hands tight over my ears, but I can't block out his words. He won't stop.

"While you were gallivanting around, your mother was sitting at home waiting for you," his voice goes on, and through the muffler of my fingers, I hear his bitterness. "Imagine how she would have felt if she'd known about your lies. So don't tell me about what did or didn't disappoint her, or what she would have thought. You have no right. You are worthless and selfish. Always have been."

The door suddenly judders, as if he's slammed his fist against it, and I catch my breath.

I put my palm to my forehead to rub away the clattering feelings. But it's guilt that takes over. I sink onto my bed, dropping my head into my hands, and a noise rises out of me, thin and broken. The sound shocks me. I press my fingers over my mouth.

We have never understood each other. As a child, he frightened and over-awed me. I wanted his approval while slinking away, embarrassed by his lumbering height and German accent. The shame I felt when I believed he might have been a Nazi never really left me. The residue is inside me still, like a kind of poison.

The room closes in: walls encroaching, furniture looming, ornaments and shoes and discarded clothes rising up to smother me. I can't breathe. It's the way I've always felt at home. I swing my legs up onto the bed and lie down, pulling my knees to my chest, wrapping my arms around myself.

I post my application to the Laban Center on my way to the station. As my fingers relinquish their grip, I wonder if I'll get the chance to tell Scarlett, to thank her. I stayed up all night agonizing over the wording. If they like the sound of me and approve my qualifications, the next step will be an audition and interview. Whatever happens, I'll have to move, find a place of my own. Mum would understand. She always knew that she was the go-between, the glue that stuck us all together.

Rush hour has finished, so the train to Victoria is quiet. I have a double seat to myself; I slump, head pressed against the glass, watching back gardens go by. There are lines of washing. Children's toys left in the grass. We go under a bridge with graffiti on the dirty brickwork. More back gardens. A cat on a doorstep. A woman staring over a fence, smoking. We catch each other's eyes but neither of us smiles. And then she is gone.

I travel down vertiginous escalators. The dusty Tube platform is half empty. I stare at the advertisement opposite without seeing it. I have a novel in my bag, but I won't be able to concentrate on that either. There's a scurrying below me. A gray mouse hurries alongside the metal rails. It makes a sudden dash for the wall, disappearing through a hole, as the train arrives in a rush of color and sound. Doors slide open into a bright carriage. I find a seat and clutch my bag on my lap, trying to make myself take deep breaths.

It's raining when I emerge into dull daylight on Brixton High Street. I turn up my collar and put my hands in my pocket, walking quickly along darkened pavements. Shoppers holding umbrellas over their faces barge into me and I duck out of the way of spokes, dodge around people blinded by rain and their anxiety to get out of it as quickly as possible.

I cut through the market, hurrying past bright mounds of fruit and vegetables; stallholders, bundled up in anoraks, are hardly bothering to shout for customers. A dog barks at me. A boy holds it on a straining chain. The animal's wide mouth is a ribbed cavern. I pull my coat closer and slip past, my heart crashing in my chest.

At the Smokey Quartz I push the door, only to find that it's locked. I shove against it. Rain splatters down my collar. I wipe the glass and peer through into the dark interior. It seems deserted. I try knocking. No one comes.

"Who you lookin' for, love?" A man with dreadlocks stops, staring at me with his head on one side. Raindrops catch in his eyelashes.

"Nobody. It's OK."

"You look for nobody, you find nobody." He grins and wanders off, his head tipped towards the sky.

I've been imagining Cosmo at the Smokey Quartz. Seeing him inside the club, frozen in an expression of disgust and betrayal, stuck inside the moment that Shane swaggered up to me and ripped the fiction of Eliza apart. But now I remember that only Josh should be here, sorting out the deliveries, making calls in the office. Scarlett will be at the flat, rehearsing or painting her toes or sleeping. With sudden blank horror, I understand that I have no idea where Cosmo is. I'll have to go to the flat. Even if Cosmo's not there, Scarlett might know where he is. I must apologize to her as well. I wish I knew what to say. I feel so tired. I'm empty of words.

I walk slowly, water dribbling down my neck and into my eyes. As I turn into their road on the opposite pavement, I see number fourteen coming up on my left. There's a figure standing at the front door, hunched in the rain. It's Josh. I stop, sucking my lips, uncertain. His finger jabs at the doorbell, as he cranes his head to stare up at the first-floor windows. One of the windows is thrown open, the sash rolling up with a bang and Cosmo leans out.

I catch my breath and duck behind a parked car, squatting on my haunches, my bag trailing along the gritty pavement. I can hear Cosmo's voice.

"Hang on. Scarlett's coming to let you in."

"This had better be good. I'm wet through!" Josh shouts back.

Cautiously, I lever myself up enough to peer over the car hood. The door opens and I catch a glimpse of red hair. I glance up at the house. The window is shut. They're in there together. Heat flares in my face, travels across my body, sweat pricking under my arms. I visualize them in the kitchen, pouring vodka into tea. Maybe Luke is there too. They will say they always knew there was something odd about me. They'll be outraged, angry, hurt.

They'll be sitting around the table in a circle, protective of their friendship, united in their exclusion of the outsider. I am catapulted back into school. The odd one out, being whispered about behind hands.

I remain crouched on the wet pavement, shielded by the car. The tire has tiny stones stuck into the thick rubber tread. I see myself reflected in the chrome center: curled like a fetus. I nip my bottom lip between my teeth and try to picture myself standing up and walking over to the door, pressing my finger against the doorbell.

I straighten, leaning on the hood to steady myself. A woman hurrying past falters in her stride, startled eyes flickering towards me before she carries on. I peer up at the first-floor window again, almost hoping that one of them will be looking out. But there's only the empty glare of reflections.

My hair's plastered to my skull as I trudge back towards the Tube station, blinking rain-spangled lashes. A wave of dirty water swills across my feet as a car rolls past, wheels hissing.

My insides ache. None of them will want to know me as Klaudia. I've lied to them for months.

Cosmo. I mouth his name, repeating it like an incantation. He trusted me. He loved me.

I should have been brave enough to tell him before it got out of hand. There were so many moments in Leeds, or that day when we bumped into each other at the Smokey Quartz; I should have corrected him then, explained everything, revealed myself as my father's daughter. The lie distorted me. It's ruined everything. I've ruined everything. There's a pain in my heart. I put my hand over the soaking fabric of my coat, and stumble down the steps to the Tube station, into the gloom of the tunnels.

ERNST

1973, Cardiff

It's an ugly street. The narrow terraced houses have mean proportions, the windows too small to let in any decent light. I sniff, smelling drains, damp brickwork, cooking. On the way over, staring out of the cab window through the drizzle, I'd noticed gaping holes in fences, glimpsed areas of naked ground: old bomb sites, overgrown with weeds. Back at home I'd be putting in an offer for land like this, calculating how many properties I could get onto it. But I wouldn't cram boxes together. I build good, solid houses. I've made my reputation on the quality of my work. Little details like verandas, and front doors with porches make all the difference.

Standing on Otto's doorstep, I'm suddenly afraid that I've made a mistake by coming, and I have the urge to run back to my hotel room. I sent a telegram warning them of my arrival, deliberately not allowing time for a reply before I set off. Maybe I'm getting soft, but I've begun to yearn for family. Despite everything, Otto is my only flesh and blood, the only one who understands my past. I want to try and mend our relationship. Over thirty years have passed. Maybe now we can be brothers. Otto is too stubborn to make the first move. That's always been my role. I glance up at their house—poky and grimy as the rest of the terrace—and lean closer. I can't hear anything. No muffled noises. I don't even know if they have kids. I presume that they must have. They've been married since the end of the war. I put my shoulders back and press the bell.

A small woman opens the door. She has soapy hands, her sleeves rolled up to the elbows. She wipes her wet fingers on her apron and simultaneously slips her hands behind her waist to pull the apron off.

"Oh my goodness. You must be Ernst."

She smiles. I'd mistaken her for a young woman at first; there's something childlike about her. Her pale skin appears unlined. But when she smiles there are fine creases around her eyes, a slight softening of her jaw, and I start, prickles running up my spine, because she looks so much like Sarah, as Sarah would look if she was alive.

I gather myself and bow my head. "And you must be Gwyn."

She's busy rolling her sleeves down, and she pats her hair. Dark, thick hair twisted up into a bun. Strands hang around her cheeks and she hooks them back behind her ears.

I follow her into the narrow hall and through into a front parlor. I'm inclined to duck, even though my head clears the ceiling. It feels low and closed-in. The room is clean and tidy. Nothing out of place. As I look around at the spotless carpet, neatly arranged furniture and polished table with a fruit bowl set in the exact center, I guess that they haven't had children after all. I wonder why. Gwyn seems the motherly type: she's all curves, with a tiny waist, billowing hips and generous breasts. I try not to stare, forcing my gaze to meet her eyes. I see a familiar flicker of discomfort in her face, a flush creeping over her cheeks. It isn't to do with my admiration of her figure. She's noticed my scar.

"Would you like a cup of tea?" she says. "Otto will be here shortly. I can offer you a slice of fruitcake. Just made this morning."

I know she's looking at the bumps and folds of flesh, the milky cast to my eye. But her interest doesn't feel intrusive or unkind.

"Is it a war injury?"

"In a way."

"I'm sorry for the pain it must have caused you." She shakes her head. "And now I'm forgetting my manners. You'll surely be tired after such a long journey. Sit." She gestures towards a hard-looking sofa. "I'll fetch that tea."

I stare around me. A plain wooden cross takes prime position on one wall. A carriage clock ticks solidly from the brown-tiled mantelpiece. There's a cold gas fire beneath it in the grate. A reproduction print of misty mountains hangs next to a framed tapestry. I squint at the embroidered lines of text with my good eye, but don't get up to peer at it, in case Gwyn finds me snooping; I presume they are lines from a prayer. A collection of wooden biblical figures jostle each other on a shelf, and the carriage clock sits next to an ugly jar with a lid, encircled with flowers and birds.

At a noise outside the door, I pull myself to my feet, thinking it will be Gwyn back with the tea. But it's Otto. My brother still has his braced way of moving, as if holding himself to attention in a strong wind. He is as tall as I remember, and broader for being older; his body thicker, his chest almost barrel shaped. His blond hair has grayed, but rises from his scalp in a thick, vigorous thatch like an animal's pelt.

I wonder if I can look him in the face, if I can even stay inside the same room as him. I force myself to take deep breaths, remembering that coming here was my idea. This is our chance to heal. After a moment's hesitation we shake hands. He grips hard. I'm at a disadvantage with my raddled, aching fingers. He doesn't seem to notice my disfigured grip. Close-up, I see doubt pulling at the corners of his eyes.

Gwyn bustles about setting out tiny tables and pouring tea, spooning sugar into cups. We sit balancing plates on our knees. Otto is working two jobs, he says. He is a bus conductor and a security guard at a local warehouse. Seeing their simplicity, their restricted means, I feel hesitant about explaining my wealth. I tell them I work in the building trade and leave it at that. I tug at my cuff, pulling it over the heavy silver Rolex that nudges my wrist bone. I notice the leather patches on Otto's elbows, sewn on with neat stiches, and the worn shine on his trouser knees. Otto hasn't lost his strong German accent.

"Do you have many Welsh friends?" I ask, stirring my tea.

"Gwyn has her chapel friends. We keep ourselves to ourselves most of the time," Otto says. "We don't go in for a social whirl, do we Gwyn?"

She wipes a crumb from her lip.

"Where are you staying?" Otto helps himself to a slice of cake.

When I tell them, Gwyn says that I must stay with them. They have a spare room. And I'm family. I protest. She insists, looking to Otto for support. His mouth twitches in annoyance. I put my cup down on the doll's table next to me, and although I know that I should comply with Otto's wishes, seeing his need to control the situation rekindles the old competitive relationship between us, and I find myself offering Gwyn a smile.

"Then, if you're sure. I'll go back to the hotel and fetch my bags."

I turn at the doorway, considering my brother. There is something else that's different.

"Your nose." I tap my own. "No sniffing."

"I was allergic to horses. Not many around here."

We both smile and I feel a tug of yearning coming from the mire of our past. When I'd booked my ticket, I'd done so with the hopeful conviction that we were old enough, and had traveled far enough from our childhood and the war, to be able to wipe the slate clean. Standing in that little parlor, I set my hopes against the physical reality of this brother of mine. I put my hand on his shoulder; under my touch, his muscles tighten in a reflex of distrust.

Back at the hotel, as I pay for the unused room, tearing off a check and handing it to the receptionist, I realize what else is different about Otto, the way he'd looked at Gwyn, his gaze following every movement. He's in love.

My room is hardly larger than a cupboard. It has a tiny single bed. I lie down on it, remembering Otto's long limbs overflowing the confines of his cot above the stables. A pair of orange curtains droops at the window. Tugging them to one side, I am met by a blank stare from the grimy crush of terraced houses opposite. I have a moment of longing for the generous proportions of my penthouse, with its sweep of pale carpet across the living room, and the grand piano that I can't play; my collection of paintings and the huge bank of windows that offers a dazzle of sky, of stars, and always the tops of the trees in Central Park: the clattering of winter branches, summer's green, or a riot of red in the fall.

I'd arrived in Cardiff on a Saturday. The next day Otto isn't working and Gwyn cooks a roast meal with beef and small cakes made of batter that Gwyn tells me are called Yorkshire puddings. Otto bends his head over his plate and says a prayer. I am caught out, my fork in my hand. It's strange to hear him speaking words of thanks to a God I don't believe in. Gwyn smiles at me, nods that I should start.

The meat is pink and tender, the Yorkshire puddings light and crispy. Gwyn hums as she eats. I fork potatoes and gravy into my mouth, eating until my belt strains around my waist, wondering how I can offer them money in return for their hospitality. We go for a walk in the afternoon, through a scrubby, hilly park. A gust of wind whips Gwyn's dark hair across her face, she laughs and pushes it back, and for one dizzying moment I see Sarah. The light gets inside Gwyn's eyes. Only they aren't brown like Sarah's; they are violet, a color more brilliant and intense than any butterfly's wing. In Gwyn's presence my brother is transformed. He rarely touches her. But he watches her with an expression of hunger and wonderment. I envy him for the first time in my life.

Gwyn keeps asking me about New York. I tell her about my bus journey from the docks through Lower Manhattan when I'd first arrived, and how I'd peered up at the skyscrapers, thrilled by their beauty and power. I tell her about the horses that pull open carriages through the park, and how I carry carrots in my pockets for them. I describe the palatial shops on Park Avenue, the streets busy with yellow cabs and buses. Steam rising from gratings. Jazz. Hot dogs.

She is like a little girl being told fairy stories. Otto frowns disapprovingly. "You never married?" he asks.

"No. I've had girlfriends, of course. Maybe I've been focused on my career too much. No time for anything else."

"You just haven't met the right woman yet," Gwyn says in a conspiratorial tone.

It's unnerving how like Sarah Gwyn is. Being with her sets memories free, and I can see Sarah as a girl again. She stands knee deep in brambles, raising her finger, a frown plucking at the space between her eyebrows as she examines the pulse of red. But she was a girl, not a woman. I see her by the gaping entrance of the cattle car, passing her case to her brother, climbing in with the hem of her blue coat swinging. Bodies press after her, pushing her out of sight.

I put my hand over my eyes, wiping away the images. When I turn to the other two, Gwyn has stopped next to a woman with a pram; she bends to look inside, cooing at the unseen baby; and I wonder again why Gwyn and Otto have no children.

"You could come to New York, you know," I say casually. "I'd help you. I could arrange to get Otto a job . . ."

"We don't need your charity." Otto takes his wife's arm, linking her hand through his hooked elbow. "We are happy here. We have a home." He pauses. "We have Jesus."

It sounds odd. As if Jesus is a useful possession. Like central heating, or an insurance policy.

I've been with them a week. The night before I leave for home, Otto goes off to his job as a security guard. He's been out of the house before, but not at night. I feel awkward with Gwyn, anxious to show her that I'm not going to be a nuisance. I offer to help with supper, but she laughs and makes me sit.

While she cooks, I show her a few snaps of Manhattan and one of a building site with the sign that says "Meyer Construction. A Name You Can Trust." She admires the photos and congratulates me on the company. She wants to know how I worked my way up from construction worker to manager and then owner. I'm not used to anyone showing such a genuine interest, and her expressions of admiration and praise embarrass and please me.

I get a bottle of Scotch and a couple of jazz records out of my suitcase. We have cold ham and mashed potatoes at the kitchen table and I pour a tumbler of whiskey.

I toast her. "For your kindness, Gwyn. My brother is a lucky man."

She blushes. The sudden pink makes her eyes look more vivid. The drink slips down my throat. I smack my lips together. "That's good." I pour another one. "Just say the word. If you'd like some."

She shakes her head.

"Did you know that you hum when you eat?" I ask.

She laughs. "I hum whenever I'm happy."

I put Sarah Vaughan on the turntable singing "Misty," and turn it up loud. We sit opposite each other under the glare of the electric light and she puts her head on one side, listening. "I love it. You feel it here," she pats her chest, "don't you?"

I nod. "That's what I like about jazz. It's visceral. And this song . . . well, I guess this is a little sentimental . . ."

"It's beautiful. Otto feels the same way about his opera records."

"Did Otto tell you much about his life before the war?"

She fixes me with that steady gaze. "I know about the Hitler Youth. He regrets it all. He understands how evil it was. He was looking for somewhere to belong." It sounds like a speech she's used before. She smiles. "Finding faith in Jesus saved him."

"I think it's you he's found faith in." I stop. I have to be careful. The whiskey is loosening my tongue.

She glances away, swallowing. Her cheek flickers with a twitch of muscle.

"How did you get your scar?"

"I was taken prisoner by the Russians. At the end of the war. I took a beating from some of the guards for trying to escape."

"Oh!" She puts her hand over her mouth. "Does Otto know that you were a prisoner of war?"

"I wrote to him. I don't think he got the letter. Communication was sporadic, unreliable. It felt as though we'd been forgotten. After the war was over, they kept us locked up for three more years." I turn my face so that I look at her with my good eye. "What did Otto tell you about me?"

She shifts in her seat, crosses her legs. "He told me that you were never close. Even as children. That you had your life in America, and it was too far and too expensive for us to visit, and anyway, he said there was no communication between you . . . he said it was better that way."

This is the first time we've talked about anything personal or mentioned the past since I've arrived. Otto has guided the conversation up until now, keeping it in careful, polite territory. The intimacy of this exchange has taken me by surprise, and I'm hungry for more. She reaches across the table and takes hold of my hand. I flinch. She examines my fingers, runs her own small fingers over the blunt, reddened ends of mine. I feel the squirm of shame in my belly.

"And how did you lose these?"

"Frostbite."

She winces, screws up her face. "How did you manage to survive all of that . . . all that horror . . . without God?"

"I believe in man, not God. I believe in the good in people. Even inside all of that evil, good existed."

She places her other hand over the top of mine, so that I'm cushioned inside her fingers. "What you see as goodness—that's what I see as God." She lets go of me. "I think I will try some of that drink now."

We stand at the sink, shoulder to shoulder, as if we've known each other for years. She scrapes at streaks of mashed potato, washes and rinses our plates, handing them to me to dry; I stack the dishes on the draining board; she flicks soapy suds at me, giggling like a schoolgirl, and I see that she's languid with whiskey. Her movements have that loose, unfettered feel, and when she slips on a pool of water, losing her balance, she clutches at my sleeve with a chirruping laugh.

Our domestic duties done, we go into the neat parlor and I set the needle down gently on a Billie Holiday record. Gwyn turns off the overhead light, bends to switch on a side lamp. We collapse on the sofa, heavy with drink and food, our heads lolling back, and I ask her how she met Otto.

"There was a lot of freedom for the prisoners, especially the ones who worked on the farm, like Otto." Gwyn tugs at the neck of her jumper. "He looked like a film star. He was different with me. He talked to me. Opened up. It was like being with a wild creature that would let only you touch it." She sits forward, perching on the edge of her seat. "When he told me he loved me," she gives a small shrug, "I was overwhelmed. I loved him too. I left my home and family for him."

"And do you love him now?"

I shouldn't have asked her. I begin to apologize, but she puts her hand on my knee. "I'm a grown woman. Not a little girl anymore. Love means something different. He needs me. He's the loneliest person I've ever known. He breaks my heart."

I can't concentrate on her words; her touch is making my nerves hum. "Come on." I get to my feet. "Let's dance."

I wait, holding out my arms. She uncurls herself slowly and stands for a moment, like a swimmer at the edge of an ocean. And then she steps forward over the brink.

"I haven't danced in years," she murmurs.

I inhale. A scent of lavender comes from inside her clothes. Her hair reminds me of apples and butter; stale cooking smells coil inside it, rise from the wool of her sweater. The women I take to my bed trail exquisite perfumes. They smell of silk and skin cream and lipstick. But it's Gwyn I find intoxicating. My hands slip down to circle her waist. The button on her skirt is under my fingers.

One song stops and another begins. Billie Holiday is singing "All of Me." Gwyn shivers. Saxophone notes fill the small room. I keep my eyes closed, losing myself in the scent and the texture of her. Billie Holiday's voice is imploring, *take my lips, I want to lose them.*

The song ends. The record is spinning on, hissing as the needle catches in the grooves. Abruptly Gwyn pulls free. We stand apart, staring at each other.

Gwyn snaps on the glare of over-head light, and begins to set the sofa cushions back in place with brisk pats and shakes as I gather up my records and bottle of Scotch. The floor seems to tip under me, but not because I'm drunk. Being apart from her makes me unsteady. We wish each other an awkward goodnight.

I stumble up the stairs and shut myself into my room. Lying awake, watching the street light seeping through the curtains, I hear Gwyn's feet on the landing, the gurgle of water through pipes, the click of her door closing, and tell myself that I will never come back. I will never see her again.

I keep my promise for a whole year. I work hard. The business expands. I have girlfriends, elegantly dressed women who know how to call a waiter with an arch of an eyebrow, who hail cabs with confident arms, stepping off the curb in high heels. We kiss in the back of those cabs, and afterwards the woman will pull out a little mirror and stare into it, dabbing at her lips, reapplying crimson or fuchsia, giving herself a smile of approval. And I think of Gwyn wiping floury fingers on her apron, the way her cheeks flushed after that first drink. Sometimes I see Sarah's face instead, her pale skin, black hair and laughing eyes. But it isn't physical similarities that confuse the two of them in my mind. Somehow Gwyn transforms me into a better person, just as Sarah did. Both of them make the darkness brighter. Every night before I go to bed, I stand and stare over the skyline of Manhattan towards the Atlantic, feeling the pull of her.

———

Then a business trip to London comes up, or rather I engineer a trip by offering to meet a business associate in England instead of New York. It's only a few hours on the train from the capital to Cardiff. How could I go all that way, and not make a quick detour to see my brother and his wife?

Otto is less than pleased to see me. But I hardly notice. There she is, exactly as I'd remembered, with that shy look on her face, her eyes cast down; only this time I have my own secret knowledge of her. Under that restrained exterior is a strong woman of faith; and an innocent girl who loves to dance, who wants to have fun, who takes delight in all the small details of life.

And I think that I can manage, that I can be with her in the same room without touching her, and that Otto won't notice. I am a fool. The air between us is like molasses, suffocating, impossible to pull away from. We don't meet each other's eyes. I stay for three days. Otto is there all the time, but I think we both know that his presence keeps us safe.

On the day before I'm leaving, I offer to take them both out to celebrate, as a thank you for their hospitality.

"We don't live your kind of life, Ernst," Otto says. "Why would we go out for a meal when we can eat a better one at home?"

I can't keep the disappointment from my expression. I'd wanted to treat her. I'd wanted her to experience some luxury, something extravagant. She whispers later in the kitchen, "Don't feel bad. I wouldn't know what to do with myself in a restaurant. It wouldn't feel right to have someone else wait on me."

Otto is working on my last afternoon. I want to shout as soon as the door closes behind him. But Gwyn is washing clothes in a big tub in the outhouse. As I slip in through the door, waiting like a schoolboy behind her, she doesn't acknowledge my presence, just keeps scrubbing and soaping.

"Do you have to do that now? I thought maybe . . . I could take you out for a cup of tea."

She raises her hands, raw and red from the water. "You didn't really have a business trip to London, did you?"

I shake my head. "I've thought about you." I stop, swallowing the other words I'm longing to say. *I've missed you. Come away with me. Marry me.*

Her cheeks flame as if she's heard them anyway. "I'm married, Ernst." Her lips hardly move. "To your brother."

It's like a slap. I move backwards, fumbling for the doorway. "I made a mistake. It was stupid . . ."

She nods. But the edges of her mouth waver.

"Please tell me though . . ." I falter, hating my weakness, "just tell me this one time that you feel the same . . ."

"What I *feel* doesn't matter." She puts a wet hand to her throat. "It's what I do that counts, it's how I behave. Feelings are there to tempt us."

I hang my head. I can't speak.

Her face softens and she steps towards me. She is close now. She's so much smaller than me. Her head barely reaches my chest. There are soap suds in the dark coils of her hair.

"I know these feelings are wrong," I murmur. "But I can't be sorry about them." I want to touch her cheek, brush my fingers across the nape of her neck. "I can't be sorry about loving you, even though I know . . . I know we'll never be together."

"Ernst." Her voice is a whisper.

"When I was in the prison camp in Russia, the only thing that kept me from death was remembering that I used to have feelings, that my numb heart had once danced, and broken, and wept, and that perhaps it could again one day."

She's put her finger to my lips. My stomach contracts with the shock of her touch. She's tipping her mouth towards me, leaning closer, and I take her face between my palms and we are kissing, leaning up against the big tub, the smell of detergent in my nose, the smell of her.

We stop and I manage to step away. Our breath is harsh. It's the only sound.

"I'll go," I tell her, choking on the words. "I'll leave now."

Her face is terrible, desperate. Her eyes are blazing. She takes my hand in hers, and I let her lead me across the garden into the house, up the narrow stairs into my bedroom.

She pulls the orange curtains across the window. She doesn't speak, taking off her sweater in one impatient unpeeling; she does a strange little wriggle as she pushes her skirt and slip over her hips with rough tugs, letting them drop around her ankles and kicking them away. Her breathing quickens, and she gasps in frustration when her stocking twists and catches over her foot. I kneel below her and try to help, my stumpy fingers fumbling about her heel, yanking at slippery, taut fabric. And then we are naked, with no space between us.

PART THREE

THE TELLING

KLAUDIA

1996, London

WHEN THE LETTER COMES FROM the Laban Center, I grab the envelope from the mat almost before it has had time to waft down from the letterbox. I'm unable to stop my fingers shaking as I rip it open.

Words repeat in my head. They are inviting me to come for an audition. Relief makes me tremble. In the kitchen, I stand by the window and look out at the garden. It's been battered by rain. Patches of bruised dirt show through the lawn. My audition is after Christmas, in January next year, so I'll have plenty of time to prepare. I've already sent Josh a note apologizing, explaining that I won't embarrass everyone by coming back to work. I'll have to look for a new job. Find a place to live. Rehearse. One day at a time, I tell myself. I feel like an invalid. But this is something to keep going for.

My father moves behind me, his heavy tread making the floorboards creak. I clutch the letter and turn to face him.

"I have an audition. For the dance school."

He doesn't appear to hear. He's boiling the kettle, bending to take out a cup and saucer.

"If I get in, I won't turn the opportunity down. I can't," I say loudly, watching for his reaction.

He drops a tea bag into his cup. I hover by the window, waiting.

"I'm sorry if you don't think I'm doing the right thing," I blurt out. "I'm sorry if you're disappointed."

He pours the boiling water and turns his head, raising his pale eyes slowly. "I don't agree with this dancing nonsense, Klaudia. But I've changed my mind. You can stay." He stirs his cup. "I was too hasty. You're . . . you're my last link with your mother."

I unstick my lips, holding my breath.

"Sometimes, I look at you and suddenly there she is." He stares at me, his expression brightening. "My Gwyn. Her smile shining out of your face."

"I . . . I didn't think I looked anything like . . . her. Like Mum."

A strange warmth seeps through my limbs: the child in me squirming inside his unexpected approval.

"Not your coloring, no." He waves a hand as if conducting a jerky piece of music. "And you don't have her spirit. Her goodness. But I see her features in you, even the way you laugh, sometimes you sound like her."

I take a step closer, wanting to touch him. "I know how much you miss her . . ." My voice breaks. "I do too."

He clears his throat, and his cup and saucer clatter together, spilling tea. He puts the saucer back on the counter and rips off a piece of kitchen roll. His hand is trembling.

I sit in the hall, cross-legged on the carpet, hugging the phone to me, twirling the cable round and round my hand, as if I can pull Meg closer, reel her in. Within moments, the easy banter that we shared at university comes back; and I hunch over the mouthpiece with her voice in my ear.

We have so much to catch up on. It's a relief to tell the truth. Not to watch my words, make sure I don't slip up. I tell her everything that has happened since we left each other at the airport up until the moment I danced at the burlesque club. "And Cosmo was there to see you dance?" She laughs. "Wish I'd seen you too, strutting your stuff. And I bet his face would have been a picture . . . what happened? Did you sort it out?"

"No," I admit. "I put off telling him the truth, and then he found out in the worst way possible. Someone from my past showed up straight after I came off stage. He told Cosmo that I wasn't Eliza." I lean over my legs. "And so now he despises me."

"How do you know he despises you?" Her voice comes down the line. And I hear the cynicism in it, Meg preparing to argue.

"You didn't see the way he looked at me," I say quickly. "Anyway, he's in Rome now. He only came back for a couple of days." I change the subject, because there is nothing to be gained in going over it. It hurts too much. Instead, I tell her about my plans to switch degrees. The audition at the Laban Center. Meg is supportive, interested.

"And what was all that about your father?" she asks.

I am silent, squeezing the receiver. I'd forgotten that I'd mentioned him in the letter.

"You said you thought he was a Nazi or something?"

I am aware of my father moving around upstairs. His slow steps cross the landing and the bathroom door shuts.

"Not a Nazi," I whisper. "He's German. It's complicated. I'll explain when we meet."

We keep talking, slipping easily into other subjects, reminiscing, laughing. The objects around me melt away: the rise of stairs, banisters, side-table legs, coats hanging on pegs and the front door with its oblong of frosted glass. I am lying on my bed in my room with Meg flopped next to me, a half-drunk bottle of wine on the floor; we're sitting across a table in Café Flo bleary-eyed with our cups of coffee, sharing a Kit-Kat, or looking into the Seine with the frosty air making clouds between us.

When I put the phone down, my hand is cramped and aching. My ear sweaty where I'd pinned the receiver to it. I get up off the floor stiffly, aware that my one-sided conversation would have sounded loud in the silent house.

My father comes out of the bathroom, switching the light off behind him with a sharp tug on the dangling cord.

"My friend from Leeds," I explain. "She's a dancer too."

I hope he'll ask me about her. I would like to share it with him. But he just grunts, and disappears into his room. I realize that he hasn't done his morning exercises recently. He looks shrunken. He moves carefully, as if his joints hurt. And he is always alone. He manages chapel once a week, but he hasn't gone to prayer meetings since Mum died. If only he had some friends. I remember the old Caribbean men that sat around tables in the Atlantic pub in Brixton with their games of dominoes. How they laughed and slapped each other on the back, their glasses of rum by their elbows. The easy curl of their talk, the banter slipping and sliding between them as they slumped over the table.

The house is a shrine to my mother. Both of us seem to be stuck, and I have no idea what to do about it. I go to bed wishing for something to happen, some unexpected event that will shake us free of each other and the past. I've been investing my hopes in my audition, imagining the kind of life I could have if I got a place at Laban and moved out of here. But that was before my father said that I reminded him of Mum, before I saw that he was vulnerable too.

I kneel on the floor in front of the under-sink cupboards and root around for cloths, disinfectants and polish.

After I left home, my ingrained habits of cleanliness were hard to break. When I moved in with Meg and Lucy, I couldn't stop myself from tidying up their dirty dishes and mess. They never made their beds or cleaned the bath.

One of Lucy's sisters, visiting from Manchester, a Greenham Common badge on her sweater, began to lecture me when I rolled up my sleeves to wash the kitchen floor. "It's only dirt." Her mouth turned down. "Do you think women starved themselves to death and threw themselves under horses to get the vote so that you can play into the male perception of the little woman?"

It shocked me to realize that I hadn't really escaped my upbringing. It was ingrained. It hadn't occurred to me to be interested in politics. I'd been too busy trying to fit in, trying not to draw attention to myself. Politics reminded me of Shane, his leaflets and his hard fists. I was ashamed that I was so narrow-minded and conventional. The endless round of domestic tasks that I'd been brought up with at home seemed trivial and useless.

But here I am with a scrubbing brush in my hand, because I can't think what else to give my father as a peace offering. I balance precariously on a stool in the bathroom and rub at the limescale on the showerhead, breaking a nail. I use vinegar and newspaper on the windows, the way Mum always used to. In my parents' room, I drag the bed and chest of drawers to one side so that I can vacuum properly, going underneath things, sucking the clumps of grime that have gathered in the gloom. I push thoughts of Cosmo back into the shadows, concentrating on bringing a shine to furniture, purging the place of dust and cobwebs, scrubbing at surfaces as if I could wipe everything clean.

It's as I move the small table on my mother's side of the bed that I notice the writing on the wall. The furniture had been covering it. Letters scratched into the paper. I lean close. *Help me.*

I catch my breath and re-read the words, my finger touching torn paper, the jagged meaning rough under my skin. *Help me.* The uneven letters look as though they've been made with the point of a pair of nail scissors. I reel back, my heart thumping, and clamp my hand over my mouth. Reading those words brings Mrs. Perkins's sour face close, her lips opening and closing. "Your mother," she's saying. "Screaming at night." And Mum's coat hangs in the hall, when of course it shouldn't be there at all, because she would have worn it when she left the house. Her stepping out in front of a car, as if she was ever careless of traffic. None of it made sense. It has never made sense.

I don't know where my father is. I clench and unclench my fists. What did he do? My hands feel clammy. I wipe them on my jeans, staring around the bedroom. Think. Think. I abandon the vacuum cleaner, still plugged in, leave the bundle of cloths and bottles on the floor; I don't bother to push the bedside table back against the wall. The scratched words stare out at me, the last thing I see before I turn and leave the room and go quickly down the stairs and out into the wet afternoon. Hurrying away from the house, I run along the pavement, head bowed into the rain.

Mr. Gupta looks up when he hears the bell.

"Is your wife here?"

He looks behind him warily, then angles his head so that he can call out through the plastic curtain while still keeping his eyes on me as if I'm mad. Perhaps I am.

When Mrs. Gupta pushes her way through the colored ribbons, I want to seize her hand. She looks calm and wise, her eyes fixing me with a deep stare.

"You said you saw Mum, the day she died," I begin, tripping over my words, unable to go slowly. "When she came into the shop, did she say anything? Did she look worried or upset?"

Mrs. Gupta adjusts the swathe of fabric over her shoulder and moves her head. "You don't know?"

"What?" My pulse hammers in my ears.

"You don't know what state she was in?"

"State?" I repeat. "What do you mean? State?"

"Child." She folds her chin into her neck. "Your mother wasn't well at all. She was . . . quite unlike herself."

"I don't understand." My mouth is dry. My tongue fumbles around my teeth.

"It was terrible . . . she was crying and wailing. She had bare feet. No coat on. She rushed away before we could help her."

The shop lists to one side. The floor at an angle. I think all the packets and tins will come crashing down. I put my hand over my mouth, clutching at the counter to stop myself from falling.

Mrs. Gupta is guiding me into a chair and talking quickly in Hindi to her husband. They place a glass of water in my hand.

"Your mother was not herself, Klaudia. And this is why she was run over. She was behaving in a strange way. As if she was very sick. Mentally unbalanced."

I sip the water automatically. It is tepid. I taste London pipes. I shake my head, and struggle to my feet. "I have to go."

Wet grass moves under my feet, soft and muddy; rotten apples roll beneath me; above my head, dead leaves shift and sigh. The shed door is shut. I push it open without knocking. My father looks up, startled. He's sitting at his workbench, a piece of wood in his hands, sawdust speckling his knees and scattered over the floor. The raw, sweet smell of it. Behind him I see the glint of silver, the edges and handles of his saw and hammers. All his tools lined up in the dark.

"What happened to Mum? What did you do?"

He puts the wood down. Places a lathe next to it, his eyebrows shooting up.

"The day she died." I can hardly speak. "She ran into the Guptas' crying. Without her shoes. And Mrs. Perkins. She said she'd heard Mum screaming." I take a step closer. "What did you do to her?"

He's staring at me and I feel a slippage of something, certainty crumbling away over an edge. I don't know who he is. I don't recognize him. He's that man in the mirror, his reflection saluting out of cold glass, the *Sieg heil* etched in flickering light and dark. I snatch at oxygen as if I'm being strangled, struggling to stay upright. He will grab my neck with his big hands and squeeze. Fear runs through me, cold and clean, wiping everything away, emptying me of myself. It's as if I can feel his fingers pressing the air from my windpipe.

He looks down into his lap. "I failed her," he says.

The hair on my neck prickles. I'm closed in, choking among shelves lined with bottles of white spirit and castor oil. Clorox. Pesticide. Brooms and rakes hanging from hooks. I put my hand to my throat.

Another person had materialized through his skin, pressing a stranger's face towards me. I didn't know who that man was, or what he would be capable of. But as quickly as he'd flashed into my father's features, he'd disappeared, and another stranger sits before me. Someone with crumpled shoulders and drooping mouth.

He balls his hands into fists. "She changed. She didn't recognize me. I was scared." His voice wavers. "I didn't want them to take her away. I didn't want them to lock her up. I thought she'd get better if I could just keep her at home, keep her safe. But she got worse."

"I don't understand. What do you mean?"

"She was confused. She screamed. Terrible things." He rubs his forehead. "It started after she was poorly," he says in a dull voice. "Nothing too serious. A bit of a temperature. She thought it was just a cold. But a few days later she began to act strangely. She had funny turns. She thought I was trying to hurt her."

I want to put my hands over my ears. I can't imagine Mum behaving like that. I can't imagine what she must have been feeling.

"I found her going out barefoot. Or with her dress half unbuttoned." He takes a deep breath. "I kept the doors locked. But she was crafty. She got all the way to the Guptas before I realized. She was on the pavement, confused and scared. She had no boots on, and it was so cold." His eyes glaze over, as if he's seeing her poor naked feet again. He twitches his mouth and looks up at me. "She seemed to relax. I thought she was coming out of it. I held out my hand. But . . . she ran across the road."

"But . . . why? What was wrong with her?"

"When I explained her symptoms at the hospital . . . afterwards . . . they told me she probably had delirium."

"Delirium? I've never heard of it." I shake my head. "Why didn't you tell me?"

He begins to make strange, choking sounds. Harsh, dry sobs. I shift in the dim light, not wanting to watch him. I've never seen him cry before.

"I thought I could cure her with my love."

I catch something in his voice: behind the grief, he is like a petulant child. I can hear myself breathing. He lets his shoulders slump heavily.

His head lolls forward. "I didn't want people to see her like that. She would have hated it too. I didn't want you to know. What was the point? I didn't want you to remember her that way." He wipes his eyes with the back of his hand. "She was different, you see. She wasn't my Gwyn anymore. I thought if I waited it out, she'd come back. The way she was before. Perfect and pure. My angel."

"I think I knew . . . I knew something wasn't right." My voice is thin.

The shed is dense with dust, chemicals and the sharp scent of wood. I back away, through the door. "You kept her prisoner," I say quietly. "You kept her here, when she needed help."

I want to hurt him. He is responsible for her death.

There's no point. It's too late. He's lost her. There is no greater punishment. On the way past the apple tree I pause and place my hand on it. I slump against its rough bark. I can't forgive him. My conscience whispers inside my head—what about me? If I'd come home when term had finished, if I hadn't gone to Paris, she might still be alive.

It's early morning. As I leave the house, I feel a splatter of rain on my forehead. Another hits the pavement, making a dark splotch. I begin to jog in the direction of the playground. I need to run. I can't face my father. I hardly slept last night. My chest has been buttoned tight since he told me. I looked up delirium. He was telling the truth. It's a sudden dementia that older people can get, with symptoms of disorientation, delusions and paranoia. Sometimes it's a sign of another, life-threatening illness. Then I read that it can be reversible, if sufferers get help quickly enough. The thought of her desperation and fear, the image of her scratching those words into the wallpaper—that useless, pathetic gesture—makes me sick with shame. Yesterday, I caught a glimpse of something evil in him. But I've always known it was there. The running; the dancing; my new identity: they were all just ways of trying to blot out the knowledge, sever the connection. Only how can I escape something that lives inside me? I am his daughter.

The roads are wet, sharp with grit, puddled with oily water. The rain feels liberating, cleansing, the way it hits my skin, coating it with a cold membrane. I have to make a sudden jump to avoid a trail of rubbish dragged across the road. A large bin lies on its side on the pavement, innards sprawling, ragged scraps of plastic, an old tin can, sodden cardboard boxes and half chewed bones. I jog on, growing warmer. When cars pass, there's a swish of tires and spray splatters my legs.

I run and run, wanting to tear off all the lies, rip away the fibs and half-truths. I feel grubby with them, polluted, unclean. My legs are shaking. Rain slicks my hair, dribbles into my eyes, soaking through my clothes. I'm glad of it. But I can't push myself anymore. I'm exhausted.

As I approach our house, a black taxi pulls up. It stops, engine running, diesel fumes pumping from the exhaust. The cabbie climbs out, wincing in the rain as he holds the passenger door open; he reaches in and slides a suitcase onto the pavement and a man unfolds himself, looking up at our house. I blink through the downpour, not understanding why my father is arriving in a taxi, when I left him not more than an hour ago at home.

But it's not Dad. Of course not. It's a similar-looking man, eerily similar: tall and thin, with the same distinctive straight nose and big, sloping brow. The cab moves away from the curb, the yellow light flickering on. I am closer now, staring, a nagging memory pulling at me. I lick my lips, my breath coming faster; I think I recognize him. Except, doubt trips me up, as I realize that this man is older than I'd first thought. And under his loose clothes, he is bone-thin. He leans heavily on a stick, knuckles pressing through thin skin. Perhaps I'm mistaken. But as he turns towards me and I see his pale, blind eye, the weave of scar tissue distorting his cheek, I know I'm right.

"Ernst?" I touch his sleeve. "Uncle Ernst."

I thought he wouldn't recognize me. I'd been a child after all, a little girl with long blonde plaits. But the anxious speculation in his face disappears and he says, "Klaudia," as if my name is something rare and elegant, like a piece of antique glass.

He doesn't seem to notice that we're standing in the rain. I take his arm, leaning to pick up his suitcase with my other hand.

"I didn't know you were coming . . . Dad didn't say," I say over my shoulder as I unlock the door, guiding him over the step and into the hall.

"Your father doesn't know," he admits. "I didn't tell your parents, I'm afraid. It was an impulse."

An impulse? I push wet hair out of my eyes. "Don't you live in New York?"

He murmurs an agreement, but he's looking around him, distracted and expectant. "Are your parents here?"

I feel a jolt of pain. In his mind, Mum is alive, could come down the stairs or through a door at any moment. I don't want to tell him about her. Not now. He looks exhausted. One thing at a time, I think.

"Come and sit down. I'll fetch Dad."

I settle him on the sofa. He notices Mum's knitting, and his eyes go to the photographs—nobody could fail to see the banks of images, arranged in rows—and he leans towards them eagerly. While he's staring, I persuade him to part with his damp jacket. He slips it off absentmindedly.

"I'll get you some hot tea," I tell him, the jacket folded over my arm. It's good-quality fabric, I notice, soft and supple.

He pulls his attention back to me, and he's smiling. "You sound like your mother. This reminds me of a time, many years ago, before you were born, when I came to visit and she fetched me tea. There was cake, I seem to remember . . ."

"No cake this time." I would like to stand and listen to him reminisce, but water trickles under my collar. "Back in a minute."

Upstairs, I shrug off my wet top and towel-dry my hair. Pulling on a shirt, I run down to the kitchen to make tea. I stand over the kettle, waiting for it to boil, glancing towards the living-room door. I find it hard to believe that Ernst is in there, sitting on the sofa as if he's just popped in from across the street, instead of across the Atlantic Ocean. My father comes out of the shed, hurrying through the rain across the garden with a new wooden sculpture in his hand.

"We have a visitor," I tell him in a hushed voice. "Your brother. Uncle Ernst."

My father's face is utterly blank, stripped of expression, as if he's spun back through the years into a state of pre-baby nothingness. His mouth sags. Then he recovers and gives me a severe, accusing stare. "Why are you saying this?"

"I know. It's unexpected," I say soothingly, trying to make him understand that this is not a trick that I'm playing on him, something that I've conjured up. "But he is here," I insist, keeping my voice gentle, even though I don't feel like being kind. "He's in the living room."

"He can't stay. I won't have him in my house."

The words are blunt and sudden as stones thrown through a window. The kettle is screaming beside me, steam billowing between us. I automatically switch it off and pour water into the teapot.

"He's very frail . . ." I flounder. I know they didn't get on. But my father's lips are twisting in disgust or hate, or both. "We can't ask him to leave. He's come all the way from America."

"What does he want?" My father sways back onto the heels of his feet, wraps his arms across his chest, as if he's hiding something. "Does he know about Gwyn?"

I shake my head. He slams the sculpture down onto the kitchen counter, where it wavers like a drunk and topples onto its side, rolling onto the floor with a muted clatter. As I bend to pick it up—another bearded disciple—he strides past me into the living room.

I hurry behind, bearing a tray heavy with the pot and cups. An atmosphere gathers around the brothers, tight and menacing as a fist. Ernst had been standing, but I watch him crumple, stepping backwards, a hand flailing beside him as if he's searching for a support that isn't there. I put down the tray in a hurry, tea slopping out of the spout, and step forward to curl my fingers around his. He sinks onto the sofa. I sit next to him, his hand caught in mine.

His is all bone and sinew. I notice his shortened fingers in mine, the nubs of swollen flesh and missing joints. A blue-black vein pulses under the blotchy back of his hand. He's ill, I realize. I can smell it on him—an oily, rotting, sickly scent, and a tang of chemicals.

"Gwyn," he murmurs, his voice cracking. "I never thought . . . never imagined she wouldn't be here." He raises his head and looks at me. His blind eye is weeping. "I'm sorry, Klaudia. So sorry."

Tears sting my eyes. I swallow. "We should have contacted you. Let you know." We should have. I feel guilty.

"Where are you staying?" my father asks from his position by the mantelpiece. He's standing stiffly as a soldier. A force field radiates from him: an impenetrable shield.

"With us, of course," I say quickly.

"No. I wasn't presuming . . ." Ernst leans back against the sofa wearily. "I'll book into a hotel."

"Nonsense." I look at my father. "Mum wouldn't hear of it if she was here. Would she, Dad?" I add pointedly.

My father tears his gaze away from Ernst and stares at me, the corners of his mouth tightening. "Ernst must do what he thinks is right."

The force field is hard and bright. I look away from it.

"You are staying with us. I can make up the spare bed in a few moments. I'll show you where it is." I hear Mum's voice in my head. I let her use my tongue. "Perhaps you want to use the bathroom or rest for a little while? You've had a shock."

He pats my knee. The effort seems too much for him. "You are kind." His voice is a whisper.

Ernst is settled in the spare room with his suitcase, and I'm on my way up, my feet on the stairs with an armful of clean sheets, when my father beckons me into the living room with a curt nod. He shuts the door.

"I don't want him staying." He glances down.

"Why?" I hug the bundle of sheets closer. "I know you two don't get on, but he's your brother."

He sucks his bottom lip under his teeth. "Ernst isn't like us. He's an American now. He has different values. He's not . . . a believer." He paces the floor. "He's an atheist," he hisses.

I don't react. I lift my shoulders and let them fall. "So?"

"I didn't want to tell you this, but he's an alcoholic. He's unreliable. I don't trust him. He's not a good person, Klaudia."

I seem to remember my mother mentioning something about Ernst being unreliable years ago. But what my father is saying doesn't add up. I didn't smell drink on Ernst. He doesn't have the bloated look of a heavy drinker. He just seemed tired and ill.

"I don't care about that." I fumble for the door handle with my free hand and turn it. "Apart from you, he's the only relation I've got. Whatever's happened in the past . . . it was a long time ago. I'm going up there to make his bed. He needs a proper rest. We can't turn him out on the streets in his state. Let him stay for a couple of nights."

My father has forfeited his power in this house. There has been a shifting of guilt and blame, a resettling of authority. I leave without waiting for a reply, gripping the pile of sheets, breathing in clean washing-powder scents and my own determination.

I am excited by Ernst's arrival. Something warm and bright flickers inside me, a kind of hope, unexpected and startling: I'd given up on seeing him again. It's extraordinary to think that there's someone else in this house with the same blood as mine. Someone who met me as a child, and who knew Mum too. There will be time to talk, to discover stories perhaps, stories that might color in some of the missing pages. I've lost so many people. I won't be that scared girl anymore. I won't be a liar. I feel a hunger for the truth. Whatever happened between my father and his brother, they will be able to sort it out now, under this roof. I want Ernst to stay.

ERNST

1996, London

PAIN AXES DEEP UNDER my breastbone, cutting me down. Gwyn. My love. My lost love. I've been imagining you safe in your home, alive and well, content in your routine. The effort it has taken to get here, Gwyn, I wasn't sure if I'd make it. When the plane hit turbulence, quivering and dropping over the ocean, I moaned in my seat like a child. I wanted to land safely, because I needed to get to you. I believed that it would be enough to see you—not to touch you or hold you; not to tell you that I love you— just to watch you move around your living room, to set tea on the table, put a hand to your hair, patting a stray wisp into place. Being in the same house, I'd smell your cakes baking and hear the murmur of your voice next door. I didn't come to make trouble. Just to see you. To see Klaudia. To say goodbye.

Gwyn. Darling Gwyn. I don't have a photograph of you in my wallet. I've had nothing to remind me of you all this time. Just your signature on a Christmas card once a year, some little note with news about your lives in England. A few scribbled lines.

That afternoon in Wales, after we'd disentangled ourselves, you sat up and leaned over to switch on a sidelight, picking up your watch to peer at its face. Do you remember? I resented the intrusion of that bright beam into the place we'd lost ourselves, the way it found us out.

"We have to get up. Your taxi will be here." Your voice was trembling, and you hurried out of bed, wrapping the sheet around you with anxious fingers. "Otto might even come back."

"Gwyn." I grabbed your wrist, felt the slight tug as you resisted.

"This can't happen." You looked exhausted. "I wanted . . . I wanted . . ."

But you never said what you wanted. I watched you stumble about the room gathering clothes, holding them in a bundle to your stomach.

I struggled onto my elbows and sat up. "Don't worry," my voice croaked, the effort of being noble almost killing me, "I won't interfere with your life, your marriage."

God. I wanted to pull you back into bed with me. "I'm here if you need me," I managed. "I'll always be here for you."

But you shook your head as if I was the inexperienced one. "Find yourself a wife, Ernst. You're still young. You deserve to be happy. Settled."

As we dressed in our separate corners, it seemed that with every new item of clothing, we moved further apart. The loss hollowed me out. I followed you onto the landing, but you disappeared into the bathroom, shutting the door. I carried my bag downstairs into the hall and waited for you impatiently. It was a new experience for me, that sense of yearning. Never before had a woman made me feel incomplete when we were apart—no one except Sarah.

The house seemed to close in on me. Everywhere I looked I was reminded that it all belonged to Otto, that this was a home you'd made with your husband. I could hardly catch my breath. I loosened my collar, and prayed that Otto wouldn't come back to say goodbye. He'd told me in his gruff way that he probably wouldn't be able to get away in time. If he came, he would sense the atmosphere, he would know. My nerves startled at every noise.

My taxi was due. You came back and we stood in the hall, my suitcase between us, your skin smelling of Pears soap, your blouse buttoned to the neck. I tried to give you some money, but you folded your arms, shaking your head. "For the extra food," I insisted. "Please."

I longed to look after you, to spoil you. If I couldn't do that, at least I could give you something useful. Your pride got in the way. Or perhaps you were like him. Perhaps you saw money as sordid too.

"Otto wouldn't hear of it."

It was as if we'd done nothing more than take tea. You were being so careful, my brother may as well have been standing over us. But we still had a few moments alone together, and I wanted to hold you close, push my nose into your hair. In bed, the pale cushion of your skin had turned pink where I'd touched you, and I'd wondered if those faint marks lingered under your clothes.

A sharp ring on the bell made us both jump.

You opened the door before I could stop you. It was just the taxi driver by his cab. But the world had come rushing in. Life pulling us apart. Seconds ticking away.

"You should go." Your face was stretched with the effort of not crying.

"Darling." I mouthed the word silently.

Your eyes glittered with tears. One spilled onto your cheek. "Goodbye, Ernst," you said, keeping your voice steady.

I dragged my feet over the threshold, aware of every passer-by in the street, the driver's watchful gaze. I had to keep up the performance. So I leaned forward in my seat and raised my hand cheerfully, as if this was a casual goodbye, as if we would see each other again. Then the taxi pulled away, and I turned in sudden panic to stare through the back window. But a bus had blocked my view, and I'd lost you.

I kept my promise, Gwyn. I went back to New York. My only communication was to send Christmas cards. I had no return mail, no messages at all for the first couple of years. And then a Christmas card arrived, with your new address in London. Inside you had scribbled a couple of lines to explain that you'd had a daughter. A daughter! Imagine what I thought. Of course, I wondered if she was mine. But you didn't say anything. So I began to doubt it. And it was your prerogative to keep it a secret. Otto would believe that the child was his. He had no reason to think otherwise. Perhaps she was. I had to respect what you wanted. I sent a telegram with my congratulations, addressing it to both of you. I meant what I said. I wasn't going to interfere with your marriage. Not if you didn't want me to.

Going to stay with you in London six years later, all I could think about was you. The joy of you. I didn't know how to feel about Klaudia. In my mind I'd settled it that she belonged to Otto. And I'd hoped that having a child might have softened him, made him feel more secure about his marriage, less possessive over you.

I slept in this room the third time I came to stay. I recognize the wallpaper. The same dark wardrobe stands in the corner. Klaudia was a little girl then. Long-limbed, anxious, watchful, she'd covered her mouth when I made her laugh, chewed the ends of her plaits. When I put jazz records on, she began to sway, moving her shoulders and hands. I persuaded her to dance, and as soon as she did, I saw that dance was a substance to her, like the sea is to a swimmer—it was her natural environment. It buoyed her up.

For Christmas I gave her a doll that was almost as big as her. I bought a bottle of perfume for you; I can't remember the name of it now, but it was something expensive and musky I'd found in Saks. I'd tried dozens of scents, stopping by different counters, sniffing out the one that would suit your dark hair and violet eyes. I knew it needed to be exotic, but warm and natural. I bought a silk scarf too, by Chanel. I'd wanted to spend so much more on you. The store was full of glittering treasures: diamond necklaces and sapphire earrings, evening dresses in crêpe de Chine and delicate combs made of mother of pearl. But I knew I mustn't be too extravagant. You wouldn't like it. It would make Otto suspicious.

I was to stay for a week over the Christmas holidays. I'd wanted my visit to be a success; I'd planned to arrive with presents for everyone; I needed to show you and Otto, and myself, that I could play the part of the generous uncle without disrupting anything or threatening anyone. That was my hope. From a distance you can convince yourself of anything.

Inside this narrow bed, clean sheets tucked tightly around me, I am too tired to move. I lie, trussed up, rigid as a corpse, and think about the confines of my brother's life, and my own. I am not foolish or arrogant enough to delude myself into presuming that my money and business have made my life big. Far from it. It's people that count, and I haven't had anyone to grow bigger for. Otto, in this tiny house with his simple work and lack of ambition, has married the woman he loved. Has a daughter. He even has a faith to cling to. In the end, it's he that's escaped the past.

I wish I could believe that his love was the best that you could have had. I saw his need of you, Gwyn, his jealousy; the way he wanted you to himself. It scared me. That's not love. But it was the best he could do. I knew that. And you forgave him for it.

Will he want to hear what I have come to tell him? I hired a private detective to help me. Even back then, inside that chaos, German efficiency endured: there are files of names available if you know where to check. I have been busy. In the years before I became ill, I went to the farm. My first time in Germany since I emigrated.

When Otto was a child, his prickly pride, his yearning to belong, his constant need for reassurance and authority, seemed to make him less, make him weak. But I envy him now. He had you, Gwyn. He had the good fortune to find you; the power to keep you.

There is a scent on these sheets that I remember from last time. The washing powder that you used: rinsed clean, blue, a whiff of the sea. I bury my nose inside folds of cotton. Wanting to block out the other smell. I hate catching the sour stink of it on myself. It reminds me of the filthy sucking mud, that stench of damp and fear and death, lice biting under my belt, dirty, scabby flesh. It pitches me into endless battles: all the same horrors, enacted differently over and over. The screams of the Reds as they came at us, tanks rolling over foxholes, crushing men, explosions that ripped out sound, leaving me deaf, until reality came back with the tumbling rain of earth, and the heavier thump and slap of torn limbs landing. How to describe the sound a leg makes as it hits the ground?

Throughout the parched heat of summer and the blank cold of winter, I was like the men around me, full of thoughts of home, the longing to return to civilian life. Even those days at the farm with Meyer raising his belt, Bettina giggling in the yard, seemed blissful and beautiful and utterly perfect. Of course Sarah and Daniel wouldn't be at the lake or the cottage. I knew that. Even though I dreamt of them: Daniel glancing up over his book, Sarah holding out her hand to me, half turning inside sunlight, the thick cream of spring blossom enfolding her. But that is how a soldier endures— by fixing to a belief that he will return to peacetime. And that everything he left will be the same.

I don't know why I wasn't killed in the trenches or the gulags. I stopped asking that. I don't think there is an answer, a reason. There is no higher purpose. No God. Just good luck, or bad luck. And then one day, it was over: the war, the prison camp. But the cruel trick is that the thing you longed for all those years, the memory you created to sustain you, doesn't exist. There is no return. There is no going back.

I went to America as soon as I could. But even there, the everyday turned to dust. I was blunted and impoverished, unable to exist in a civilian world. I threw myself into work, into giving shape to my ambition: the force and effort of it kept me safe from madness. Nothing else touched me. Sex was just a brief forgetting.

It was different with you, Gwyn. I don't know why. You were never mine. I cried in your arms, and you let me. Stroking my hair, you hummed softly, kissing each severed finger joint, one by one. Being with you, it was like being washed clean by the rain.

KLAUDIA

1996, London

IT FEELS SURREAL, having breakfast together—the three of us—me between the two brothers: Ernst, tall and big-boned, all straight nose and
jutting chin, like my father, except for his scarred face. He should be frightening to look at. His blind eye droops slightly at the rim, showing the in-
ner pink; and the distorting ribbing of scarring pulls at the rest of his
features, stretches his mouth into a lopsided smile. But instead of feeling
revulsion, there is something compelling about him. His eyes are kind. I
keep looking at him—it's as if I have to keep checking that he's really here,
my uncle, here in the flesh. If only Mum was still alive. I'm sure this would
make her happy too. I stop myself from saying so aloud; I don't want to do
anything that might make my father worse. He is sulking; it's pathetic.
He's like an overgrown child. I give him disapproving glances, trying to catch
his attention.

It's Ernst who is making all the effort. He is trying to draw my father
out, reminding him of things in their past, and in the process revealing things
to me about my father's childhood. Ernst talks about the cows they milked
each morning before breakfast and the kitchen garden they had to hoe and
weed after school.

I'm intrigued, interrupting him to ask questions. He leans across the table
to remind my father of the names of the horses that lived in the stables below their bedroom. Lotte and Berta.

"We knew how to plough with a team of horses," Ernst tells me. "That's a skill you don't find anymore."

"Because there's no need for it," my father says.

"The German army relied on their horses," Ernst carries on. "Not many people knew that. They thought it was all Panzer tanks and Messerschmitts; but in reality the Wehrmacht was horse-powered. And that made it slower and more expensive to run than the Russian army. It was one of our failings."

"Nobody is interested, Ernst," my father tells him. "It's just history now."

"Klaudia is." Ernst winks at me with his good eye. "Aren't you?"

I smile, standing to clear away the butter, wiping a splodge of marmalade from the table. "I am."

Ernst's fingers have a constant tremor; he keeps them clamped tightly around the handle of his cup. But still the tea slops over the rim. He puts his drink down with careful concentration and looks at his brother. "I'd like to see where Gwyn is buried, Otto," he asks in a low voice. "If I may?"

My father pushes himself back from the table and stands for a moment, his mouth working, chewing his lips. "Gwyn was cremated," he says in a tight, reluctant voice. "Her ashes are buried in the garden."

Ernst waits. My father turns his head away, shoulders raised.

I am furious with him. Ernst has every right to ask to see where Mum is buried. My father, who has always had the ability to be unnecessarily rude, is outdoing himself.

"I'll show you." I touch Ernst's sleeve.

We stand under the apple tree. It's stopped raining. The ground is mushy and dank. A layer of dead leaves has collected around the roots. There is nothing to mark the spot. Perhaps we should put a plaque on the tree. Ernst bows his head for a moment.

"I only met your mother a few times," he said. "But she was a beautiful person. I was . . . I was very fond of her."

I clear my throat. "Thank you."

A thrush skims our heads and lands on a branch, looking at me with its head on one side. I have already put breadcrumbs on the table. It's waiting for us to leave.

I begin to move away towards the house. I glance behind. Ernst isn't following. He's still gazing down at the roots of the apple tree. Then he raises his head and looks around as if he'd forgotten where he is. He makes his way towards me, using his stick. He looks frail. His wincing mouth tells me that he's in pain. But I don't know if I should help him or not. He seems to want his independence.

"Have you always lived in New York?" I rub my hands together while I wait. There's a chill in the air.

"Yes," he says, pausing. "Since I moved there in the late 1950s. I loved it from the moment I arrived." He limps on. I turn away, not wanting to watch his halting progress, fearing he'll think me impatient. "I couldn't get over the skyscrapers." His voice takes on a note of wonder. "Such symbols of hope. Of determination. It's a city of immigrants of course, and it allowed me to find my place. Anything is possible there. You aren't judged on your past, on where you come from."

It occurs to me that I have no idea what we can do to fill the time. He seems so weak. But he has a plan; he'd like to go to the nearest park, he says, wheezing as he reaches me in the open kitchen door. He can manage a walk if I don't mind going slowly.

"Shut the door," my father's voice calls from the sitting room. "There's a draft in here."

I shut the door with a bang. I can imagine his expression.

On the bus I tell Ernst about my audition. "It's after Christmas, in January." I brace myself as the bus lurches around a corner. "I'm preparing two pieces. I have plenty of time. But I'm nervous."

"Of course you're nervous." He clasps his stick. "That's good. It would be strange if you weren't. I can remember you dancing when you were little. Six or seven, you would have been. And it was obvious to me then that you were born to it."

I'm touched that he remembers. I ask him what I'd been dancing to and he says he thinks it was something with swing—Armstrong or Calloway—and we talk about jazz music and the club in Manhattan where he's heard Ella Fitzgerald and Sarah Vaughan sing.

"Your mother liked jazz too," he says.

"Really?" I can't hide my surprise. "All my father ever plays is opera."

"She liked the records I brought with me when I came to stay." He's clutching his stick. And I know it's to control the tremble in his hands. It makes me want to take his fingers between my own. "Maybe she was just being polite," he adds.

"Oh no," I reassure him. "Mum wasn't like that. She was kind. But she was honest. She always said what she meant . . ."

My words trail away, as I remember how she slipped around my questions when I was a child, how she batted away the truth to protect my father, his wounded honor. She put him before me. But I don't think she understood how important it was for me to know what my father had done in the war. I never told her what I had to put up with at school.

In the park, I measure my pace to Ernst's painful hobble, anxiously hovering at his elbow. He likes to walk with me next to his seeing eye. I dive back into the memory of his visit, long ago. I can still remember so many details. It's the one thing that links us. It's a good place to start.

"That doll you bought for me," I tell him. "I'd never had anything so exciting before."

"She was nearly as big as you." He smiles. "I was worried at the time. I didn't know anything about children. I thought you might be too old for dolls."

"Well, you got it right. I was very happy."

"It was a pleasure, buying you all gifts. I got your father a watch, and perfume for your mother."

"I'm sure they were as pleased as me. We didn't really spend much on presents. Often they were homemade."

"I admired your parents. They didn't need expensive gifts to be happy."

"No. But I'm sure Mum was secretly thrilled to have some luxury. I can only remember her smelling of talc."

"I got her a bottle of something that smelled like heaven. It was floral without being sweet. It came in a heavy glass bottle with a gold top."

The image of the empty bottle lying in Mum's drawer among her bras and girdles jumps into my head: the perfume I brought back from Paris.

"Mitsouko." I say the word without thinking.

He puts his hand to his ear. "What was that?"

I hear my father's voice. *You smell like a harlot.* Facts clash in my head; taken together they suggest an idea that makes me suddenly queasy. I want to push it away. But I can't. It's like a weed, putting down roots.

I shake my head. "Nothing."

We've come to a slight rise. Ernst is wheezing. He stops and lets me take his arm.

"Perhaps we should go back now?" He looks apologetic.

There's a sheen on his forehead. The wind pulls at his gray hair, tugging it back from his scalp; brown blotches mottle his skin. He turns to me. The half-mask of his face looms close, the distorted webbing across his cheek and the blind, pale eye blinking.

My mouth is dry. "Did you get any medals?" I work to keep my voice level. "When you were in the army?"

"I suppose I did." He curls his lips as if it's unpleasant to think of it. "Three," he admits, "if I remember correctly."

Of course they belonged to him, the brother who went into the army. And the photograph flashes up in front of my eyes. The one I can't forget: the dark girl snatching her last breath.

ERNST

IT HAD TAKEN YEARS of gentle suggestions in my annual Christmas card to prompt the invitation for my third visit. When it eventually arrived, I'd been jubilant. But as soon as I stepped into their home, I could see that Gwyn was nervous. Otto made it clear that he didn't want me there. He didn't leave me alone with Gwyn for a second. Not that I'd come with any expectations of going to bed with her. I still desired her. She was older, of course. She'd put on some weight. But the extra softness added to her lush curves, an illustration of her generous nature, her kindness. I wanted her more than ever; being near her made my throat tight, my breathing fast. But she'd made it clear that it would never happen again.

It was enough, I told myself, to love her from a distance. Loving her without touching her was a kind of punishment, and I felt I deserved that pain, because I shouldn't have loved her in the first place. But I'd been looking forward to spending time with her—going for walks in the park, helping her wash up, doing odd jobs, talking. Instead, Otto presided over every activity: a looming shadow.

Christmas Day. I stayed behind while they went to chapel. It was the first time I'd been alone in the house. I put on some Ella Fitzgerald, turned it up loud. I picked up one of Gwyn's cardigans and pressed it to my nose, inhaling the scent of her, finding the secrets of her body trapped in flecks of wool.

Their new house was a plain, mid-terraced little boxy place. I slapped my hand against woodwork, checked window-frames for gaps. It was solidly built, but there was no refinement to its design. It had pebbledash all over the front, which had become grimy with age and pollution. Inside, all was as neat and tidy as I remembered from before. Klaudia's toys were kept in boxes and put away every night. The place gave me claustrophobia. Everywhere I looked there were embroidered words from scripture or a biblical figure carved in wood staring out with a demented gaze. Otto had always needed to believe in something, to belong. It seemed ironic that he'd exchanged the Third Reich for God.

I'd been nervous about seeing Klaudia. I didn't know what to expect. I wondered if I'd know straight away if she were mine or not. But the shy girl that came into the room behind her mother's skirts, with flaxen plaits, thin limbs and clear blue eyes stirred nothing in me, except the disconcerting thought that she looked Aryan.

Anyone who didn't know me would assume she looked the spitting image of Otto. He and I were physically alike, so she looked like both of us. She was a great kid. After she got over her shyness, she followed me everywhere, asking me questions, listening intently to my answers. She was more like her mother in that respect. I'd felt a cowardly relief in deciding that she couldn't be mine. I'd convinced myself by then that Gwyn would have said something. That I would have had a feeling about it, our shared blood tugging out the truth.

After lunch there was an exchanging of presents. Gwyn opened mine with anxious fingers; she unwrapped the perfume from a nest of tissue paper and held the heavy bottle in her lap for a moment, examining the details of it, before she unscrewed the top and dipped her head to sniff. She unfolded the silk scarf and rubbed the fabric between her fingers. "It's beautiful," she said in a muted voice. "Thank you."

I felt ashamed, seeing the strain on her face. I'd been an idiot. A selfish idiot. I should have stayed away. It was me that had forced the visit. I'd encroached where I wasn't wanted, trespassed on a home and family that were not mine. I saw how difficult it was for her, and I felt like walking out, catching a taxi to a hotel or the airport. It didn't matter where. I just needed to leave them in peace. But Klaudia was already unwrapping my present; she'd ripped the Santa Claus paper apart, and she pulled out the doll with a gasp of excitement. With one bound, she flung herself into my lap, folded her arms around my neck and kissed me.

I won't forget the sweetness of that kiss, the feel of her hot arms around me. It was like a thud to the heart. A blow of love. After a second, I returned her embrace, hugging her close, breathing her in.

She wriggled away almost immediately, dropping onto the floor with the doll, tipping it to make the spiky lashes open and close, and I felt an ache inside, a yearning to have her back in my arms. I was deserted. Undone. I breathed in sharply, and at that moment caught Gwyn staring at me. Her face was blanched; her mouth trembled. And I knew.

After tea on Boxing Day, Otto went out to the shed to fetch something. Klaudia was sitting at the table in the living room with a giant puzzle of castles and knights spread out before her. I'd promised to go and help her after I'd finished drying up the dishes. Gwyn had her hands in the washing-up bowl. We'd both watched Otto disappear into the dark garden, hardly daring to believe that he'd left the house, his torch shining before him in dancing circles.

Gwyn pulled her pink washing-up gloves off, and reached for my hand. She held it tightly. "This isn't working," she whispered. "You can't come again. It's no good. I'm trying. But I have to stop myself from looking at you. I'm afraid of giving my feelings away."

I squeezed. "I know. I'm the same. I'm sorry."

"I think of you. All the time. It's not right, Ernst. I'm a married woman."

I stared down at her fingers curled in mine. They were pale and clammy from the rubber gloves. "I don't care if it's right or not. I love you," I told her, keeping my voice steady. "You could come with me. You and Klaudia. I'll take care of you. Come to New York with me."

She pulled her hand away to wipe her eyes, and gave me a trembling, frightened smile. "You know I can't do that."

"Uncle Ernst," Klaudia called from the other room. "I'm stuck! You said you'd help . . ."

Gwyn swallowed. Patted her hair. She glanced out through the blackness, through the blurred lines of our reflections. "He'll be back soon. You should go to her."

"Gwyn." I followed her stare, searching for Otto's returning shape, the tell-tale spotlight moving across the lawn. "Klaudia is mine. Isn't she?"

She gripped the side of the sink, and hung her head.

Otto would be back any moment. "Gwyn?" I couldn't control the urgency I felt. It made me sharp.

"Yes." Her voice was so low and gravelly I could hardly hear. She cleared her throat and began to empty the washing-up bowl, tipping out the dirty water. It gurgled down the plughole. "She's yours." Her words mixed with the rush of water. "Forget I told you. The only thing you can do for her— and me—is leave us alone." She turned to face me, her mouth pulling down. "Otto must never know."

Our child. A tiny flame of joy flared in my heart. I wanted to press my lips over hers, hold her in my arms. But the finality of her meaning was filtering through the pleasure.

The joy flickered out. "I'll do what you want," I whispered. "But think about what I said." I leaned as close as I dared, her hair touching my nose. "Please. My darling."

"I'll never leave him," she whispered back. She didn't yield, didn't move closer. She held herself apart. "He needs me. He needs me more than you. And I've made a promise. Before God."

By the time the kitchen door opened and slammed shut, and I heard the murmur of Gwyn's and Otto's voices, I was already sitting with Klaudia at the table in the next room, searching through cardboard shapes to find the missing piece of a turret. "Do they have castles in America?" she was asking.

I kept my eyes down, because I knew if Otto came into the room and looked at me at that moment, he would have seen through me like a glass, into the dark sediment shifting inside, bitter with envy.

Gwyn was taking Klaudia out to buy new shoes. My daughter ran up to my room to say goodbye, bursting in without knocking, and gave me a hug around my waist, clasping me in her skinny arms. I held my hands above her head, fingers flexed and hovering, wanting to touch her, to feel her hair and the curve of her skull, but resisting.

"We'll finish that puzzle when you get back." I pressed her nose as if it were a bicycle horn.

She giggled. I watched her go, following her out onto the landing and leaning against the wall at the top of the stairs: my child skipping down the steps, plaits swinging. Gwyn laughed and dropped a kiss onto her head, helped her into a coat. As I watched them from above, my heart seemed to expand until it struggled for room inside my ribcage. Klaudia held her mother's hand. The door shut behind them.

I stood at my bedroom window and watched them walking along the pavement towards the bus stop. I put my hand on the windowpane over the shape of their diminishing figures. With the brief illusion of perspective, it felt as though I could scoop them up into my palm, put them in my pocket. I let myself have the pleasure of that fantasy for a moment—taking Gwyn and Klaudia to New York with me, settling them in the apartment, showing them the sights. But I knew it was just a fantasy. Gwyn would never leave Otto, never walk away from her marriage. Even if she broke her faith, her God would come between us: his presence and his absence.

I heard the click of a handle turning behind me. Otto stood on the threshold. He closed the door. It took me a moment to see the gun in his hand. He sat on my bed, the pistol resting in his lap.

I said nothing. I watched my brother. His fingers curled around the grip as if he were holding a piece of wood, something harmless and inconsequential.

"I want you to leave," he said quietly. "You should start packing."

"I'm leaving tomorrow." I looked at the gun, his fingers. "My flight is tomorrow."

"No. Now. Before they come back."

"Without saying goodbye?"

"Exactly."

Anger flared inside. Otto the bully—blood on his cheek, smoke in his hair, glass under his feet. "What if I say no?" I fold my arms, nodding at the gun. "What are you going to do? Shoot me?"

He stood up and raised the gun, held it steady, pointing at my head. "Don't tempt me. I'm not a fool, Ernst. I know what happened in Cardiff. I don't blame Gwyn. I saw the way you looked at her."

The mouth of the gun was small and black. I waited. Otto shook his head in disgust and lowered his arm.

"I left work early, came back to say goodbye, to make sure you left." He frowned. "But I saw Gwyn at the window. She was closing the curtains in your room. I knew you were in there with her. I wanted to burst in, smash my fists into your face. Instead, I waited in the street, waited for you to go, because I couldn't trust myself not to kill you. I didn't want to frighten her, or give anyone an excuse to take her away from me. Gwyn doesn't know any of this, and it has to stay like that. For her sake." His face twisted. "This is how much I love my wife. I don't need to forgive her. She's innocent. Pure." His voice was tight; he gestured towards me with the gun. "I won't let you take her. She belongs to me. I'd kill her rather than lose her."

I felt cold. "And Klaudia?"

"Without Gwyn, nothing would matter anymore."

"Do you love Klaudia?"

He blinked. "Gwyn needed a child. In the eyes of the world, of God, Klaudia is my daughter." He licked his lips. "Gwyn and I belong together. I would do anything for her."

"Even let her go?"

He shakes his head. "Don't be a fool. She doesn't want to go anywhere. I know what's best for her. I always have." He steps closer. He has a small stain on his front tooth, like a freckle. "I saw you whispering together at the sink. I switched off the torch and stood in the garden watching. I know what you're up to. I don't want you to see either of them again. Ever. I agreed to this visit because I didn't want Gwyn to suspect that I knew. But you are not to come back. Do you understand?"

I looked at the gun. Not a rifle like the one he held in his hands all those years ago in military training, but an English pistol.

"Do you ever think of when we were boys, Otto? The farm. Hitler Youth? Everything that we did then, in the name of the Fatherland?"

Otto looked startled. He shook his head. "No. Never. I never think of it. It was another life. I did what I had to do to belong. To survive." He glared at me. "Gwyn knows about my past. I have no secrets from her. I don't expect you to understand. I helped to build a chapel in Wales. When it was finished, I sat in one of the new pews with Gwyn. She took my hand. She told me Jesus would forgive everything if I repented."

"You were always good at following orders."

He ignored the jibe. Otto took everything literally. "It was necessary to follow orders back then. You and I, we didn't have proof of our ancestry. We were in danger. You just didn't see."

He gestured towards my suitcase. "Start packing, Ernst."

I wanted to knock the gun from his hand. Rage made me shake. Adrenaline hummed through my veins. I thought of those fights we had as boys, wrestling with each other in the straw, Otto swinging a fist at my cheek. He was better at fighting than me then. But I would be the stronger one now, after my years at the Front. I'd killed men, beyond counting.

As quickly as my rage came, it went, leaving me weak, nauseous. I knew I should be ashamed of what I'd done. I was nothing but a thief. An adulterer.

I pulled my things out of the drawer Gwyn cleared for me. Shoving things into the case without bothering to fold or sort. I swept coins and passport and pens and wallet off the chest of drawers, stuffing them into my pockets.

When I was standing downstairs by the door, the case in my hand, he put the gun down on the hall table. "Go back to your rich life, your fancy apartment. I never wanted any of that. Only Gwyn. You know me too well to think I'd let you take what is mine." His expression is almost friendly, now that he has me on his threshold. "I'm sorry about the little Jew. But it wasn't my fault. You were indiscreet. You think I was the only one who knew about their cottage? You think other people didn't notice what you were up to? Stealing Gwyn wouldn't alter the past. It wouldn't change what happened to the girl."

I stared at him, unable to find words. Eventually I managed, "Sarah. Her name is Sarah."

He held the door open, gazing beyond me into the street.

I wanted him to look at me. "I don't know what's happened to her," I said. "I've tried to find her. And her brother. I haven't given up."

His face was set and hard. His eyes averted. Stubborn mouth clamped shut.

"But you're wrong if you think it wasn't your fault. It was all our faults." My voice shook. "We were all to blame."

I walked past him into the meek suburban street; and he closed the door behind me with a click.

KLAUDIA

I HEAR THE NOISE from my bedroom: the rolling fumble of something heavy falling, then a loud sharp crash. Smashing china. I rush into the kitchen, taking the stairs in jumps and slides. Ernst lies on the floor, twisted at the waist, one arm flung behind his head, his legs crumpled beneath him, surrounded by the remains of cups and plates.

My father and I half-drag, half-carry him back to bed. Draped between us, head lolling, he moans, muttering words I don't understand. He's speaking German, and I'm frightened, because he seems feverish or drugged. My father's face is closed, grim. When he dumps Ernst on the bed, he steps back and wipes his hands on his trousers as if he's afraid of catching something.

A doctor from the local surgery arrives, a short man with matronly hips, clutching his medical bag with manicured hands. I show him to Ernst's room. He shuts the door. After he's finished the consultation, he sits in the living room with my father and me, and declines a cup of tea with an impatient wave.

"Mr. Meyer has cancer, as I'm sure you're aware. Unfortunately it's no longer primary. He told me that it's spread to his bones, his liver and lungs, and that he has voluntarily ceased the medication and treatment he was receiving in New York." He makes a little cough behind his hand. "It is, I'm afraid, terminal."

I look at my father. His face is stony.

"Should he go to the hospital?" I ask.

The doctor shakes his head. "A hospice would be a more suitable option. It's about making him as comfortable as possible."

"How soon can he go home?" my father asks.

The doctor scratches his head. "If you mean New York, I'm afraid that is out of the question. I couldn't advise him to fly. Mr. Meyer has asked about employing a nurse, and I can certainly give you some contacts to help you find a private one."

"So he is to stay in my house?" My father rises to his feet.

"It is only for me to suggest options," the doctor says with a peevish twitch of his mouth. "Perhaps all this should be discussed with Mr. Meyer. Let me know if you would like me to put the paperwork in motion to find a place at a hospice, or if you would like to go ahead and hire a private nurse." He stands up, buttoning his jacket. "I'm afraid the state won't be able to provide the full-time nursing that Mr. Meyer will be requiring in the near future."

I sit on Ernst's bed. He looks sunken, his skin dull and clammy as clay.

He opens his eyes. "Sorry."

I take his hand in mine. I think about it clasped around the barrel of a gun. The frightened girl in the snow. I should feel revulsion at what he's done. But strangely the feeling won't come. Or else it's submerged under the huge weight of sadness that presses down on me. I can't connect that fuzzy, ancient photograph with this sick man in the bed before me. When I look into his face, he makes me trust him. I wish I could ask him about it. I wish he could reassure me with words, explain it away somehow.

"I thought I could manage the visit." He attempts a smile. "I didn't expect this. Otto must be . . . unhappy about it."

I move my head. "It doesn't matter. You're staying here. With us."

"Otto and I . . . we've had our difficulties. I won't impose on his hospitality longer than I have to." He plucks at the sheet with his swollen fingers. "But if I may suggest," he makes an effort to continue, "I have the resources to employ a private nurse."

I sit with his hand in mine and I want to ask him why my mother had his medals hidden in her drawer. I don't think my father knew they were there. I want to ask him what happened in Russia. What he did there.

So many questions. They clot inside my throat like frogspawn. I can't start interrogating a dying man.

Amoya arrived two days later. She breezed into the house, broad and beautiful, with her polished cheekbones and tight braids, immaculate in her white uniform. She moved gracefully, carrying her weight like precious cargo. Soon Ernst's bedroom looked like a small hospital. Amoya set up a camp bed in the corner, for those occasions when she might need to stay over, although I worried if the narrow canvas would hold her weight.

Often the two of them are shut up in there together, and I hear Amoya's laugh and feel unreasonably jealous. I linger outside the door trying to hear what they're saying. Sometimes there is nothing but silence, or just the creaking tread of her feet as she pads around the bed. When the door is open, I pop in to check on him. If he's awake I sit on the bed, and when he's up to it, we play cards, or I read to him. He welcomes me each time I come to him. I miss him when the door is closed.

Our house takes on the smell of sickness. It permeates the atmosphere. I smell it on myself, in my clothes and hair. My father shuts himself in the living room and plays loud opera, or he disappears into his shed. Weeks slip past. Having a sick person in the house has changed the way we live, draws us inwards, making us more secluded than usual. The household revolves around Ernst's needs and routine. There is a hush and an activity different from normal life. A kind of reverence has descended; time slows and the world outside retreats. Oddly, it's as I imagine it might be if there was a new baby in the house.

I don't get a job. I tell myself I can't leave Ernst, even though that's not true, not in a practical sense, because Amoya takes care of everything. The house, with a dying man at its center, exerts a hold over me, webbing me inside its slow days. We all walk with our heads bowed, as if the rooms themselves compress us.

When I'm not with Ernst, I'm managing to keep up with my dance practice, developing my two pieces of choreography for the audition. I don't like going out; I've begun to shop at the Guptas' to save having to brave the bright, busy confusion of the supermarket. Choice overwhelms me. I am unsteady amongst people. I hardly know how to negotiate crossing the road, or how to count money.

Walking home from a shopping trip, I notice pumpkin faces leering at me from behind curtains, on window ledges and tops of walls. Halloween. I'd forgotten. I stare at them: orange flesh split by roughly carved teeth, jagged eyes and holes for noses. Tonight they will flame with the light of tiny candles, lit from within as if feverish with some terrible illness.

A firework goes off with a bang in a garden nearby. I jump. I hear the rip and sizzle of falling sparks, but can't see anything against the pale sky. Ordinary life is carrying on with all its rituals and seasonal markers. I am marooned from it, as if I'm watching through glass. I allow myself to think of Cosmo. It's nearly November. Last year we were together on fireworks night. It had felt dangerous and exciting, up there on the slippery tiles with the drop below into hazy, acrid darkness. When I try and think of him in Rome, I can't imagine anything except tourist snapshots of narrow streets, ancient houses and fountains. I can't see him there. My mind offers nothing but uncharted emptiness, as if space washes against me. He's lost inside it, spinning on another planet, a different star.

I wonder what mural he's working on and I wish I could be wherever he is, standing in a dark corner, unobserved, just to see him painting. I love the focus in his body when he works: the intention of his movement, how energy flows through him and into the brush, like a dancer.

I miss Scarlett and the others too. I suppose that there'll be someone else behind the bar now, and a new burlesque dancer.

Amoya has gone home for the evening. The kitchen is full of the sweet scent of carrot soup bubbling on the stove; I have a glass of wine on the go. The nights have drawn in; darkness laps against the windows. Every now and again I hear a rocket go off. The noise takes me by surprise. Halloween isn't over yet and already people are letting off fireworks. Things slipping and sliding into each other.

I think of Ernst upstairs, the cancer eating him away. He seems to get weaker every day, and yet he holds on, almost as if he's waiting for something. I'd asked Amoya how long she thought he had, feeling oddly furtive and disloyal about it. "He's a fighter." She'd sounded protective, rolling her cushioned shoulders; and the watch pinned to her breast slipped to the side. "Could be days. Could be months. I'm afraid I can't tell you. In this job, life and death surprise me all the time." She'd softened when she'd seen my expression. "My advice to relatives is always to treat each day as if it might be the patient's last." She'd nodded. "We should do that with everyone, if only the good Lord would give us the strength."

She is right, of course. I need to be kinder to my father, try to stop being angry with him all the time. He's old. The doorbell chimes. I start, spilling a splash of wine. I push back my chair, sucking my fingers as I hurry to the door.

Two witches stand on the threshold, black cloaks hanging down, green hair sprouting under pointed hats. A sickly faced monster lurks behind, torn mouth bleeding. The witches raise sharp claws and screech, "Trick or Treat!"

I flinch, stepping away. One of the witches holds out a plastic bag and rustles it hopefully. "Any sweets, Miss?"

I smell the dank, smoke-laced air of Halloween. The night hums with excitement. I stare down the street. There are pumpkin faces flickering, small groups huddled in open doorways. Kids running down the street, cloaks flying behind them, hands clutching long plastic devil's forks.

"Wait a minute," I tell them.

A few moments later I'm dropping a couple of apples and a banana into their bag. The monster removes his mask to stare balefully at the fruit. The witches look at me as if I'm mad. "Fanks," they mumble.

I watch them wander off down the street in search of richer pickings. I sigh, guessing that I'll be answering the door a few more times before the evening is over. High over my head there's a whine, then a crackling explosion.

I go upstairs to ask Ernst if he'd like any bread with his soup. The door opens and my father comes out, grim-faced; he walks past as if he doesn't see me. They must have had an argument.

I hurry in to see if Ernst is all right. He is lying against his pillow, and his skin is nicotine gray. He doesn't look upset. His expression is still. For a horrible second, I think he is dead. I hold my breath, stepping closer. I see the rise and fall of his chest.

"Supper time. Are you ready for some soup?"

He starts and turns to me.

"It's carrot and potato. Delicious," I exclaim heartily.

I flinch. I was too loud. I keep doing that, behaving like someone jolly and brisk. He must hate it.

"Would you like bread?" I ask in a quieter voice.

"No, thank you." He smiles. "Just a little soup."

I lean over him to straighten his blanket, relieved that he's alive and accepting food. "I wish you and my father would sort out your differences," I say, thinking of Amoya's words.

He grimaces. "We've chosen to live differently. It's hard for him . . . that I'm an atheist."

"And what about my mother?"

He curls his fingers. "What about her?"

"She had your medals. They were in one of her drawers. I don't understand why she had them."

"I gave them to her, Klaudia." He sighs. "They meant nothing to me. But she said that it would be wrong to throw them away." He twists his head to one side so that he can see me properly. "She understood that your father would have found it difficult. You know of course . . . it was his ambition to fight . . . in the war."

I wonder what my father has done with them. He must have found them after she died, going through her things. I guess he's thrown them away. I don't want Ernst to know. It will be another thing to come between them.

"I'll bring your soup up," I tell him, slipping out of the door.

Going past the sitting room, I make out a slumped shape in the room beyond. My father alone in the dark. When I switch on the light, he blinks.

"It's good," I tell him, "that you're spending time with Ernst."

I perch on the sofa, thinking of how to phrase what I want to say without sounding patronizing, or making him angry. "You know, maybe you should use this time to make up with him." I open my hands. "I know you had an argument, but he's dying; shouldn't you think about forgiving each other?"

"We have talked of forgiveness," he says slowly.

I try to control the surprise in my face. "I didn't know. I'm glad."

As I stand at the stove, stirring the soup, I look out of the window. Ribbons of glitter shoot through the sky, arching over the dark contours of the shed. I turn off the heat and go out into the garden, my breath misting the air, and stand under the apple tree looking up, watching stars burn and flash between the steady arms of its branches.

Mum used to love fireworks, like a child. Thinking of her, I can almost smell lavender, hear the soft exhalation of her breath as she oohs and aahhs with each new explosion.

ERNST

PAIN SHOOTS INTO MY BONES, deep and hot and sharp as a blade. I lie still, as if by doing so I can fool the pain into leaving me alone. Like playing dead when a bear comes sniffing. I have tried curling into a ball: I have writhed and twisted, rolling and crawling from one end of the bed to the other. I wish I had one of my paintings here, something beautiful to center me. At home I would pick one and sit in silence absorbing the lines and colors, the feelings pressing in behind the image. But even that wouldn't help now. There is no escaping. Only morphine can help—blunting the edges, pulling me into muffled dreams. Amoya injects me with that sweet release. She can see when I've reached the brink of endurance. I like her firm, papery-skinned hands. I like the feel of them on my body. She knows how to handle me, the way I knew how to touch horses, how to soothe them when they startled. I long for her dark eyes holding mine as she finds the vein in my arm.

"You rest now, Mr. Meyer," she says.

I see trees picked out, dark against white, a landscape for me to fall into. I know this place. I don't want to go. I kick out under the covers, clutching the sheet, trying to struggle back to the brink, back into the spare room. Pain is safer. It's too late. The tangles of poppies have me, and I can't get free.

———

I'm here again, moving through the tall, stark forest with the others, our guns at the ready, picking our feet in and out of deep snow. Sweat prickles my back. The Russian civilian prisoner comes with us, stumbling, hands tied. His bruised and defeated face leads us on. I watch the trees on either side, alert for signs of ambush, listening to the creak of branches straining under weighty drifts, the snap of frozen wood and crunch of boots through ice.

The Russian stops and gestures with his chin. The SS *Hauptmann* leading the hunt holds up his gloved hand. His long leather coat swings at his boots.

I can make out a slight rise in the snow, and underneath a lip of darkness. We approach, and a soldier steps forward, kneeling; a grenade rolls like a nut through the slit; I hear the rattle, and then an explosion. Smoke gushes out. I sniff. Burning flesh. Scorched earth. The sound of frantic scuffling and a second concealed entrance is flung open, the stolen barn door falling back, scattering snow.

There are four of them left alive. They are bundled together, and their weapons removed. The *Hauptmann* looks pleased. "Jewish partisans. A real rat's nest."

Two others are dead inside the dugout. The ones that live are thin, dark creatures wrapped in rags, limping, wounded. The *Hauptmann* chooses his man for interrogation: the oldest, his face resigned. The remaining three he lines up, and he turns to us and clicks his fingers. "You, you and you. Get rid of them."

I don't want to look too closely. I don't want to notice that one is just a whimpering boy. There is a girl too and I pray she won't be mine. When we step forwards, rifles up, she is there in my sights.

She wears a man's jacket, done up with twine. She has no shoes. Her feet are wrapped in old bits of cloth. I think of German trains blown up. Men killed. Supplies lost. I think of friends I've known, stabbed in the back, tortured by people like these. The thoughts won't stick, won't spark into the right emotions. There is nothing for it then, but to aim straight. I brace myself, and hold the gun steady.

I see only the dwindling pupils of her eyes, the way she stares down the barrel of my gun as if she is the one with her finger on the trigger.

The butt kicks against my shoulder. The shot tears through the breast pocket of her jacket. I blink; lick salt from my lips. She is a bundle dropped in the snow.

We follow our tracks back without the Russian guide. The *Hauptmann* put a bullet through his head. Darkness webs over us, hangs between pointed branches; it is the ground that holds the light. It glows. I drag my heavy boots, head down, face stretched tight as a howl. I want to be numb, like my frozen feet.

It's evening. There are bangs and screams outside. I have never liked fireworks. I put up my hand to press the skin on my face, thin and bumpy around my eye socket. Old wounds. The morphine is receding, the world floating back with its textures and shapes: the pain duller, but nagging at me, a gnawing inside my bones.

The door opens. Otto. He rarely visits. He comes closer and stands stiffly by my bed.

"I'll be dead soon," I reassure him.

He grunts. Not even the flicker of a smile.

"I want to make sure . . . you won't tell Klaudia," he says. "You mustn't tell her."

"Not tell her that I'm her father?" I breathe carefully, skimming past the pain.

He nods tightly. "Not for me. For her. Think what it would do to the memory of her mother."

No gun this time. Just emotional blackmail. But I can see what this is costing him. The effort of it is written into his expression.

"I haven't come for that, Otto," I say gently.

The boy I used to know is somewhere there, my brother hovering below this old man's armor, anxious and ambitious, still unformed, raw with possibilities. I don't want us to be enemies. Dying erases nearly everything. It distills life. Only grit remains. A few true things.

"Then what have you come for?" He is gruff with fear.

"To say goodbye. And I wanted to tell you . . . I have news that concerns you too."

"What news?" Otto is suspicious. He's moved farther away, leaning against the closed door. I wish he wouldn't. I can't see him properly now.

"I hired a private detective to . . . help me track down what happened to the Baumanns." I cough, a rough tearing inside.

He says nothing; but I feel his tension.

"Mrs. Baumann died of typhus in the Lublin Reservation. The others were transported in spring 1942 to the Belzec extermination camp. Sarah and Daniel . . . they were murdered there. Gassed."

The words are blunt now. I've worn them away with my weeping. I remember when I first heard. Even though I'd suspected for a long time that Sarah was dead, it had been as if I was hearing unexpected news.

I catch the movement of his shrug.

"You knew them," I persist.

But he didn't really know them. And so many have died. But not him: safe on a Welsh mountain, building a chapel, falling in love. He won't understand about bearing witness. He doesn't think of the Baumanns as people. He can't let himself do that. I nod towards the glass on the side table. My tongue is dry as a piece of tinder. "Could you?"

He approaches slowly, takes the glass and holds the straw to my lips, pinching it between his fingers. Drops of moisture slide down my throat. The intimacy seems to repel him, or perhaps it's my ravaged face. He looks away.

"There's something else," I say.

He replaces the glass on the table.

"I went back to the farm. A few years ago. Meyer and his wife are both dead. Only Agnes was there. She runs it now, with her husband. They have three sons." I pause to gather strength. "After the shock, she was polite. Pleased, even. She invited me in. I shared their supper. I asked her if she had any information that might help track down our parents."

Otto breathes out, interested at last. "And?"

"She did. Her father confessed to her before he died that we weren't foundlings. Not exactly. Our father was a wealthy German. Although she didn't know his name. Meyer wouldn't tell her, and she's found no papers since his death."

I pause, sucking in oxygen; the effort has winded me. Otto hovers impatiently.

"Our mother," I continue, "apparently, she was his mistress. A household servant set up in a flat after I was born. When you were born, at his wife's insistence, our father ended his relationship with our mother. He paid Meyer to take us in and look after us . . . paid him well to conceal our identity."

"Why would he need to do that?"

"Because our mother was a Jew. Our father didn't want to be associated with his ex-mistress or us. But he did his duty, kept us alive."

"How do you know that Agnes was telling the truth?" He paces beside the bed. His face is flushed. "Or Meyer? He could have told her anything."

"What reason did either of them have to lie?"

"One of them was lying. We're not Jewish, Ernst. You forget, we passed every test . . ."

I roll my head on the pillow. "That's all nonsense. You know it is. Feeling skulls, checking eye color? There is no such thing as Aryan. The idea is ludicrous." I stare at him through the gloom. "You don't still believe in blood being pure?"

He is stiff. "But there is no proof, is there? About our parents. It's all just . . . what do they call it? Chinese whispers."

"No. There's no proof. My detective got nowhere. But I keep thinking of that woman who came to the farm. Do you remember?"

He looks irritated. "What woman?"

"We saw her standing under a tree one evening. She came to see us, I think." I swallow, rising above the pain in my ribs. "I believe she was our mother."

"Our mother?" He snorts. "We have always had different beliefs, Ernst."

I feel weary. "It's your information . . . to do with as you will." I want to sleep, to slide back into unconsciousness, but I'm curious too. "Your God, Otto. Isn't he the same one as the Jews'?"

Otto shrugs heavy shoulders.

"And will this God of yours really forgive those that repent? Will he forgive Hitler? Himmler? All those camp guards? Will he forgive the Russian soldiers, the German soldiers? The British and the Americans?" I force myself to go on. "What about the good German citizens that refused to give back the house they'd been keeping safe for their Jewish neighbor? And will he forgive the partisans that nailed German tongues to a table, the children in the Panzer division that executed prisoners old enough to be their fathers?"

I stop, panting. The list is too long. I don't have the strength.

"Only God knows what God will forgive," Otto says without expression.

He looks out of the window at the shimmering lights and explosions above the apple tree.

"People say that Hitler set himself up in God's place. They say the world was bound to fall into sin after that." He rubs his forehead, making a strange, strangled noise in his throat; I realize that it's a laugh. "You call him my God. He's not mine. He never was. He left me when Gwyn died. He only existed through her. And now my guilt sits on my back like a devil, digging its claws in."

"What are you guilty of, Otto?" I'm trying to be kind. I want to reassure him. "We were just boys. Our minds were warped. You weren't in the SS. You didn't even fight in the army. You were captured so close to the start of the war. You've lived a good and ordinary life. And you loved your wife."

"I loved her too much." He falls heavily against the bed and sinks to his knees. "I didn't tell her everything. I lied." His voice is hoarse. "Before we were sunk, we torpedoed a passenger ship bound for Canada, full of children. No survivors."

I flinch. I wish I were strong enough to sit up so that I could comfort him properly. "I'm sorry. That must be a terrible thing . . ."

He clears his throat. "They were all Jews, Ernst. Before the war I killed two more of them. On *Kristallnacht*."

I remember the blood on his head. His sleeve. *Not mine*, he said.

"A boy about my age. It felt like running a blade through butter. I hit his artery, watched him crumple . . . there was a lot of blood . . ."

Otto's hands grip my sheet. It pulls tight across me.

"And a man. The SS knew him—he'd made trouble before. They wanted to make an example of him. They rigged up a noose over a lamppost, and they said I could be the one to put the rope around his neck. Then I helped kick the chair away."

Memories flicker. Daniel is looking at me across the years behind the glitter of his glasses. I put my fingers out to touch Otto. He moves away and, with a creaking lurch, pushes against the bed to stand up.

"It was your friend's father." He rubs his face. "Baumann. He would have died anyway. Later."

"I don't . . . I don't understand," I say.

"What's so difficult, Ernst? Despite your little tryst with the girl, you know the Jews deserved to die as well as I. No. My guilt is for Gwyn. She was my wife. But her heart was too soft, like a child's. She didn't have our education. She didn't know any better." He stands over me, and the words keep falling from his mouth. "I wanted to tell her, but I had to protect her from the truth. I was afraid she might not love me if she knew. Not if she knew everything. I couldn't risk it. I couldn't lose her. And then you came into our lives, trying to pollute what was pure, forcing more lies into our marriage."

The room sways. He sways with it and I cringe against my pillow. There are so many wrongs—and no way of righting them. But he is my brother. And there are more unfinished things. I try to raise myself on my elbows. My arms are like cotton threads. "I am sorry . . . for loving your wife."

"Maybe God will forgive you," Otto says. "But I can't. I never will."

He leaves quietly. The room is thick with his words. They press against me, surrounding my bed: flapping layers of darkness, impossible to breathe through, impossible to shift.

When the door opens, my heart leaps. I think he's come back. He made a mistake. He didn't mean it. Any of it. But it is Klaudia. She creeps close, her face crumpled with anxiety. I inhale her clean scent, her youth. The room brightens. I can breathe. She plumps up my pillow and talks about soup and I nod, to please her. It isn't food I need anymore.

She asks about the medals I gave to Gwyn. She flings it out as a casual question, but I see the look on her face. She is suspicious. I want to tell her the truth. I want to tell her that I am her father. A selfish longing for it makes me tremble. But it wouldn't be fair on her. I have no rights to this beautiful creature. I've played no part in her life. I am unclean. My past is ugly. I want to keep her free of it. I'm afraid it will corrupt her.

KLAUDIA

WEEKS SLIP BY. Time has become irrelevant. I don't even read newspapers. We three exist, and Amoya comes and goes, bringing shreds of the outside with her, bits of gossip, the smell of buses and hospitals, and her good-humored common sense. Even my father is drawn to her, suddenly entering the kitchen when she's in it. She is full of life, full of ordinary human grace.

It's late. Ernst is asleep. I draw the curtains, sitting next to him on a chair because it hurts him now when the mattress tips. His face is more skull than flesh. His mouth hangs open and the thin skin of his eyelids flickers. I wonder what he's dreaming about. Was it really him in that picture? Does he ever think about the girl? Were there others? I thought I'd inherited guilt through my father. And all the time it was this man, a stranger, my uncle, that was the link. It's odd, but I feel the spooling of our blood running between us. Cosmo and I could never have stayed together—not with our two histories—not when I feel love for this sleeping man, despite what he's done. And I can't stop thinking about my mother, how she kept Ernst's medals for him, and the perfume he gave her. I'd thought she was angry when I asked where Uncle Ernst had gone; now I wonder if it had been disappointment, not disapproval, plucking at her.

He moans and opens his eyes slowly, blinking. He smiles when he sees me and moves his hand to cover mine. His touch is cold and dry.

"Beautiful Klaudia," he whispers. "I'm glad you're here. Talk to me."

"What do you want me to talk about?"

"Tell me who you love."

I'm startled. "I don't have a boyfriend," I say.

"But there's someone you think about, isn't there?" he persists. "You get a look on your face. A faraway look."

I frown. "Yes. But I made a mistake. I lied and he discovered my lie before I could tell him the truth."

"Ah." He squeezes my fingers. "Don't let him go. Love is the thing that makes us human. Don't lose it."

I shake my head. "I have lost him. It's over."

"But you must explain." His voice becomes strained. His eyes widen. "Explain your reasons. I know you would have had your reasons. If he loves you, he'll understand."

"It's too late," I tell him.

"It's never too late," he whispers.

We sit in silence, until he stirs again. "Would you do something for me, my darling?"

"Of course." I lean forward.

"I'm tired of the pain. So tired. I have nothing left to do in this life, but I seem to lack the ability to die." He gives a faint smile. "There have been so many opportunities for me to leave. But here I am. I want to die, Klaudia. Please."

I stare at him. My numb mind not understanding.

"Will you help me?"

I gasp, sitting back, pushing myself away from the bed. "I couldn't!" I can't keep the horror out of my voice.

"I know. It's too much to ask." He sighs and drifts away. "I'm sorry. Perhaps though . . . you'll think about it?"

I walk to the window and look out into the dark garden.

"You don't have to let me know right away," he says quietly.

Sometimes, in the night, I hear his low, keening wail. The morphine only takes the sharpness away. Nothing gets rid of it. I remember Amoya's shoulders shifting as she told me that he could live for months. I go back to the bed and bend to kiss his forehead. I smell the sickness, the cloying scent of death that clings to him.

Cosmo would think it was wrong. He said his family believed in saving lives, even the terminally ill. My father is adamant too: the Church teaches that we cannot make the choice to end a life. It is a sin. But I will never be free of sin. I was born into it.

I still can't give Ernst an answer. I wish more than anything that I could discuss this with someone. The only person who would listen without judging is Meg. But it's not the kind of thing you can talk about on the telephone. So I do the only thing that always helps. I pull on my running shoes.

On the pavement, the cold air hits me. I shiver, shaking my freezing hands to get some blood into them. It will be Christmas soon. Nearly a year since I came home. A plane roars low overhead, its white undercarriage a shark's belly moving through a dark sea. I begin to run in the direction of the park. My feet smack down on the pavement in long, purposeful strides. I begin to get warmer, rolling up my sleeves as I run. My back is damp. My fingers tingle. I increase my stride, arms pumping, my heart banging at my ribs. I notice the way my feet strike the ground, moving from heel to toe and pushing off. I'm aware of the sensations in my body, the healthy push and pull of muscles, the rush of blood.

Behind me, stretched out in the narrow spare bed, Ernst is waiting for my answer. He is a skeleton, too weak to even sit up. Amoya fetches and empties bedpans for him, gives him bed baths, feeds morphine into his veins. I can see the pain moving inside him: a writhing, stabbing demon. I understand now why some societies try to expel it with witchcraft. I wish I could drag it out too, chase it away with prayers or spells, sprinkling the blood of hens and hair pulled from the tail of a fox. Magic is what I need. But the only magic available is hope, and it's too late for that.

I stride out, the road passing in a blur under my feet, my focus trained on the air just before me, as if I'm racing towards a goal. It's Cosmo I want to run to. I imagine hurling myself at him, colliding with him, crashing chests, finding a way to cross borders of bone and flesh, a way to enter him. I keep running, tears and sweat stinging my cheeks.

A streetlight flickers above me. I have a stitch in my side. Trees and buildings are crow-black shapes looming over me. My legs are trembling. I drag at the air with greedy gasps. It scorches my throat. I come to a halt and bend over, hands on my knees, trying to catch my breath.

I look up into the night sky. Something comes fluttering towards me. White stars falling. A flickering cloud. Snow. I catch a flake on my tongue; it melts immediately, icy water pooling inside my mouth. I laugh aloud. Forgetting everything for a brief second. I can't remember when I last saw snow. I turn to walk home, my trainers already soggy, slipping in the fresh fall that's coating cars and bushes, sticking to trashcan lids and railings in clumps of crystals. I walk faster, breaking into a jog, suddenly anxious about Ernst, thinking of him in the darkness, the cold settling against the windows of the house like white wings, feathers folding shut.

Our house is the only one in the street without lights, dark as a rotten tooth in the row. All four windows gape black and empty. Amoya has gone for the night. I come into the hall, kicking the snow from my trainers, brushing it from my face.

He is dozing. I stand by the window and pull back the curtains to look out into the falling snow. I listen to the slow wheeze and drag of air entering and leaving his body. Somehow his heart is still beating. To stop that will be murder. But it's what I must do.

How do you kill someone? I don't know how to think about it, plan it. Then I remember the dead cat, my father's handgun in the top left-hand drawer of the portmanteau. I found the key once and opened it. Stared at the pistol, too scared to pick it up. My eyes followed the heavy lines of the barrel and worn grip. This time I'd feel the weight of it in my palm, slotting bullets into the snug nest of the cylinder. But I've seen the films; I know what happens when a bullet tears through a skull: blood, an explosion of it, and scraps of shattered bone, the gloopy insides coming out. Anyway, I've never fired a gun. I could end up maiming him instead.

I can't believe that I'm even considering this.

The garden is covered in a thick, dampening carpet of snow. Neat flowerbeds have become small white graves. The naked apple tree holds up silvery branches. The hushed world is transformed. Beyond our garden fence, streetlights gleam, catching snowflakes in illuminated fans. A car rolls past slowly, wheels crunching. The street is oddly deserted.

It has to be pills. It's the safest way, surely? I'll have to acquire them in furtive visits to different chemists. No. That won't work, because I don't have weeks, not even days. It has to be now. I need another kind of drug, something immediate and powerful enough to let his dreams drag him under, so that he drowns silently, invisibly, within his own body. I think of his lungs, his heart, his muscles, the secret core of him, unclenching, letting go at last.

I turn around and Ernst stirs, opens his eyes. He looks at me in silence. His eyes are dull and flat. But as he gazes at me, his one good eye gleams. He doesn't need to ask the question.

"I don't know how," I say quietly. "I don't know how to do it."

He indicates with his fingers for me to sit, and I lower myself carefully next to him. "Morphine." He forces the word out through his wheezing. "Amoya has it in her bag. All you have to do is take some extra vials." He stops. Spittle shines on his lips. "It should be enough. I would go to sleep . . . hopefully, not wake."

"I'd have to steal it?"

He grimaces as if a knife has sliced into his ribs. "She knows," he manages to say. "But . . . not ethical . . . I can't put her in that position. She'll never say anything. Nobody will question the . . . death of an old man riddled with cancer."

"Yes," I say.

His eye brightens. His face relaxes.

"I need to know something first." I stare into his ravaged features. "I might have got this completely wrong. But I've been thinking it for a while now."

I look at him, my heart thundering. There is no way to do this except with the plain question. "Did you and my mother . . . did you ever have a relationship?"

His eyes widen for a second, and then he nods.

It's like puncturing a balloon. All the tension leaves my body. I slump forwards, towards him.

I feel his hand on my head, stroking my hair. "My dearest," he murmurs.

Another certainty is entering me. A knowledge that is as extraordinary and familiar as my own skin seen close up.

I keep my eyes on the bed. The white fold of sheet. The woolen weave of the blanket.

"You're my father . . . aren't you?"

His hand pauses against my head. His fingers tremble.

A small noise escapes my throat. I bend over, careful not to crush him, and put my arms around him, burying my face in the thin hollow of his neck. I could lift him up. He would weigh no more than a child. I breathe quietly, smelling the sour taste of decay. I press my lips to his scratchy, sunken cheek. His arm curls around my back. We stay like that until the pain means he has to move.

I busy myself plumping the pillow behind his head. A hard lump of feeling is lodged in my throat: joy and grief.

"Your mother asked me to keep it secret . . . she thought it best . . . she didn't want Otto—"

"I know." I want him to stop talking because I can see that it hurts him. "I won't say anything."

"We didn't have an affair," he says. "I need you to know that. We slept together once. We loved each other from a distance. I loved her very much."

Enough to let her go, I think.

I used to make up daydreams when I was a child, dreams of running into my father's embrace. I imagined myself hurtling towards him: my feet swift and agile, and then the joyful leap into his open arms. He swept me up, holding me against his broad chest. And I heard the thud of his heart, felt the rasp of his chin. He wrapped himself around me, as I nuzzled into his neck, whispering against the warmth of his skin, *Daddy.*

I kept my eyes tightly closed in that moment, not wanting the dream to end, but it always faltered, because however hard I tried, I couldn't picture my father's face.

ERNST

Amoya is here; her skin gleams. I smell coconut oil, sweet. There is the pin-prick. Sharp and necessary. She finds the vein first time. She's good. She lets go of my arm. "I'll be back later, Mr. Meyer." Her voice floats away.

Cold swims through me, loosening the hooks of pain. Dark eels drift away into the murk. The liquid chill travels on; it swells into my heart, washes onwards through the narrow column of my neck, breaking behind my eyes in a wave of white. White mist. Geese moving inside a cloud, crying and complaining. Otto walks ahead. Blood trickles down his calf. My feet slip on the icy lip of a puddle. Wait for me, I call. Otto. So impatient. Striding on with bright blood running down his leg.

He was born without a sense of humor, that one, Bettina says with a wink. Bettina: impish and teasing as ever, tossing her hair out of her eyes. I look for her, wanting to return the wink, let her know we're friends. But she's moved beyond the edges of my vision.

It's strange in this borderland between living and dying. The morphine promises me more. But there is never enough. Klaudia will fetch it for me. She will take me home. My daughter. My little girl with her plaits swinging behind. Sweetheart. *Liebling. Schatz. Du machst mich so glücklich.* She holds out her hand to me. It should be me leading her to safety, not the other way around.

My bed is a raft floating across the lake. Beyond there's the forest, dark and full of wolves. But inside its thickets is the cottage. And I have to get there. I will scramble off the raft and make my way through the secret paths. Sarah and Daniel will be there, waiting for me. Sarah. The door slammed shut behind you. The train moved off. And I stood and watched. I let you go.

Gwyn moves through the trees. "Don't worry, cariad," she whispers. "It will be all right. God forgives you. Sarah is there. She's waiting for you."

She leans down and kisses my forehead. She kisses my blind eye and my scar. Her tongue is damp and warm; her breath is like honey. I wish that she would stay. I wanted to dance with her one more time. *Dancing is a joy and the heart in love laughs. Ja da pfeift der wind so kalt.* But the wind is so cold, and I'm so tired. Better that she lies down beside me and puts her arms around me. I'd like to feel the pressure of her head against my heart, the soft uncurling of her hair under my chin.

There's someone else in the room. A sturdy man moves to the other side of my bed. He's built like an ox. I smell cigarette smoke and damp earth. He puts a hand on my shoulder and squeezes. "Damaske," I manage. "There you are." His face is whole and round, ruddy-cheeked. He winks at me, moving the cigarette in his mouth.

Who is missing? There's a woman below the spreading chestnut tree at the edge of the field. But I can't get to her. The ploughed earth between us is deep and dark. It's seething with lice, rolls of wire; dead men's hands stick up out of the mire, clutching their rifles. A tank's burnt-out carcass is borne up on the swell of muck. She waves. I wave back across a drifting mist of battle smog, the stink of cordite making me cough.

And there is Otto, young and strong, running through long grass, his head tipped back. He's laughing. "Catch me if you can!" he calls out, and his voice is clear and loud inside the warm summer evening. There are woodpigeons calling, soft and throaty, and the swallows swoop and dip, blue wings flashing.

Otto looms close. He hangs over me, peering down. He's not a boy anymore. I smell smoke in his hair. The ashy stink of old fires.

"You should never have come back," he says.

KLAUDIA

THIS MORNING, WHILE AMOYA WAS out of the room, I slipped vials of morphine into my closed hands, walked into my bedroom and hid them in my sock drawer. Ernst was right. They were easy to steal. She'd left them inside an open bag, on top of other things, so that it was the work of seconds to take them. Ernst has given her the afternoon off. Amoya will return for the night. I must help him before she gets back. My job is to inject the fluid into his poor, thin arm. I've never pushed a needle into a vein before. I hope I won't hurt him.

There's nobody else in the chapel. I can sit quietly in a pew and think. I don't believe in my parents' God. But I'm not like Ernst. I do believe in something—a force for good, something higher and better in the world. Although I feel that helping Ernst to die isn't wrong, I wish there was someone else to tell me that it's right. I need reassurance. But I have to do this alone.

I've struggled all my life to make the wrong father love me. It's every child's nature to love. When it isn't returned they think it's their fault. The moment Ernst told me that he was my father, I felt that old wound heal and a new wound open: his guilt scorching me. He did something unforgivable. But it's haunted him, all this time. I know it has. What he did was evil. Yet, despite it, he's a good man. My mother said that once about Otto. This time I believe it.

It was my mother who told the biggest lie. What must it have been like to live with her lie every day? I'd thought she'd lived a dull life. I'd thought nothing had ever happened to her. Now, when I consider the choices and sacrifices she made, the agony that must have gone with each of them, I wonder how she squared it with her God. When she prayed, was she asking forgiveness? Was she asking for the strength to endure, to fulfill her duty with a man she didn't love anymore? Or did she love him? Did she love them both?

I wish I'd known Ernst when I was growing up. I wish I could spend time with him. We don't have that luxury. It's funny; he should still be a stranger to me, but there has always been a familiarity between us, a sense that I'd known him before. I'm glad that I can do this for him, that it's me who will fulfill his last request.

A shadow falls over me. There's the rustle and flicker of someone walking past and I glance up. The scent of lavender hangs in the air. I look around at the empty pews, the closed double doors into the street. I'm alone. I feel a sense of urgency, a need to get home, strong as a hand tugging at me. I struggle to my feet and walk quickly out of the chapel.

I turn and begin to run along the pavement. It's drizzling: a freezing sleety rain. I forgot to put on a coat. The chill bites at my skin, seeps inside my bones. Afternoon is drifting into evening. All the streetlights have come on. Cars pass, their headlights picking out the rain in shimmering beams. The snow has gone from the street, except the rutted, blackened remains lying in drifts at the side. Car tires leave mushy tracks through the wet.

There are no lights on. No noise or sound of voices. A deep, dense silence exists. I break it as I close the door behind me, like breaking a spell. I hear my lungs pulling air in and out, the creak of my shoes, the rustle of my clothes against my skin. I pause at the foot of the stairs, standing with my hand on the banister, afraid of what waits for me. My pulse quickens in my wrists. I drag my feet up each stair tread, my hand sliding along the polished wood.

The door to the spare room is closed.

———

There's a shape hunched by the bed. At first I think that Ernst has somehow pulled himself into a chair. Then I realize that it's my father. He's slouched low, his head hanging forward. Ernst is a motionless shape under the sheets. I stand for a moment with my hand on the door handle, hardly daring to breathe, not wanting to go in. I don't want to disturb a final reconciliation. Neither of the men moves.

I approach quietly, standing by my father's shoulder. He doesn't acknowledge me. When I glance at Ernst's face my body goes cold. I know at once that he is dead. He is vacant. Empty. His body lies on its back and his face, parched and yellowed, stares up at the ceiling with unseeing eyes. His mouth gapes. I want to close it. I want to slide his lids shut too. But I'm afraid to touch him. He looks like a creature that has been excavated from a tomb, something that is thousands of years old. His wounded hands lie over the sheet, fingers spread as if in surprise. I force myself to lean forward and touch them. There is a hint of warmth inside the skin; I feel it drawing back like a tide.

I gasp.

My father doesn't move. And I notice the pillow on his lap. He clutches it tightly, his hands curled into fists.

I shake him. His fingers curl even tighter around the fabric, and he lets out a low moan.

"What have you done?" My voice scratches the air.

A sound breaks through the gloom: the doorbell, its chimes loud and ordinary. A trilling electrical noise that echoes before it comes again. It can't be Amoya. She has a key. I stand, my heart beating. It chimes again, insistently. Someone is pressing the bell repeatedly, as if they know I'm here.

I obey its call, turning away from the bed. I walk slowly down the stairs. Through the frosted glass of the front door I make out a tall shape. The shape has its face pressed against the pane, trying to see in.

I'd expected a policeman to be on the step, rocking back and forth on the balls of his feet. I blink at the man who's there instead, a dark silhouette against the streetlight and the silver needles of drizzle.

"Eliza?"

My old name shocks me. The sound of his voice makes my mouth dry. Light catches his face, slides around his features. The face I've kept alive in my imagination for months.

"Klaudia?" he tries again in an uncertain tone.

"What are you doing here?" Longing runs through me. I want to throw myself into his arms. I want him to rescue me.

Cosmo steps closer. "Can I come in? I'm soaked."

I swallow, holding the door open. He comes into the hall, shaking drops from his hair. He looks the same. I shiver. The shiver intensifies, becoming a violent shudder that forces my shoulders to hunch and drop.

"It took me a long time to track you down—" He stops when he sees me tremble. "What's the matter?" He pushes a hand through his soaking hair. "Have I done the wrong thing by coming?"

I shake my head. "I didn't think you'd ever want to see me again."

"Not want to see you?" He stares at me. "That night. Shane turning up. He dropped a bombshell. But I didn't expect you to disappear."

"I was just about to tell you, before—" I stop. This is no time for excuses. "Shane . . . he's no friend of mine. He bullied me at school. It wasn't what you thought . . ."

"I didn't think anything. I didn't have time to. And in the end, it was Shane that gave me your address. Or I'd never have found you."

"Shane?" And then I understand what he's just said. "You've been trying to find me all this time? I thought you were in Rome."

"I didn't go. I couldn't leave you again. I got together with the others, Scarlett and Josh. We all tried to pool our resources. Put scraps of information together to help find you. But none of us had any information. Josh had paid you in cash, and the address and number you'd left for him turned out to be false." He blinks. "I went back to Leeds. But I couldn't track you down there either. Shane was my only hope. The bouncer on the door said he was from Croydon, that he had a prison record. I eventually got hold of him and he gave me your address. For a price, of course."

I press my hand over my mouth.

"Hey," he says gently. "You don't think I'd really give up the chance to hear your explanations? Miss out on you waving a magic wand, coming up with a reason for all this?"

He's trying to make a joke. He's never been good at them. But he's offering me a way back from my lies. Only he doesn't know what's upstairs. I edge away. In the spare room Otto sits with a pillow on his lap. Ernst is dead. Nausea rises and I have to breathe out sharply. I reach out and hold on to the hall table.

"I wish you hadn't disappeared." Cosmo's face crumples in concern. "None of us thought that you'd tricked us out of spite. I'd known for a while that something was wrong. Even at the beginning, the night you were drunk, you said some odd things that didn't add up with the rest of your story. You were always evasive about talking about your family, as if you were embarrassed or afraid. I began to think you must be running away from something . . ." He looks into my eyes. "Are you?"

My knees buckle and I grip the table tighter.

"What's the matter?" His voice rises. "Are you ill?"

I manage to shake my head. "My father . . . my uncle . . . he's dead. He's dead. Upstairs . . ."

Cosmo startles, his chin jerks away and he stares up the dark stairs and back at me. His dark gaze is full of pity and something else that makes my legs weak. He takes my hand, and his fingers are strong and warm.

Otto is in the chair. He hasn't moved.

Cosmo lets out a low breath. He goes to the bed and sits down carefully; he picks up Ernst's stiff hand and puts two fingers behind his wrist. Leans over and looks into his face. Places his cheek over Ernst's chest, closes his eyes to listen. He sits up and looks at me and makes a small movement with his head. "I'm sorry. We'd better call someone."

He bends to close Ernst's lids gently. "Your uncle?"

I can't explain now. I nod.

He puts his hand on my father's shoulder. "What's his name?" he asks in a quiet voice.

I moisten my lips. "Otto."

"Sir? Are you all right? Otto?" He talks clearly and loudly. Then he stops and I see him notice the pillow. He reaches down and takes it from my father's frozen fingers. Cosmo holds the soft mass for a moment, frowning, and places it on the bed.

I wait for him to make the accusation. But he stands up. "I think he's in shock. Can you get him a drink of water? I'll call for an ambulance."

I'm grateful to be told what to do. I can manage that. I walk downstairs to run the water at the sink. I fill a glass and return to the spare room with it. I bend over Otto, offering him the drink.

He ignores me. He doesn't seem to see the glass.

I glance at Ernst's body. *Why?* I bite back my question. The man I thought was my father is sitting below me, human, alive; but he's retreated. He's unreachable. I remind myself that he's in a state of shock. He looks through me, blinking.

He stumbles up out of his chair, spilling water over my hand as he pushes past me on stiff legs. At the doorway, he pauses to move one hand to his other arm, rubbing it as if he's cold. He coughs. "Must have . . . air," he says in tight gasps.

He's gone. I hear unsteady feet on the stairs.

I'm alone with Ernst. I feel his absence now, feel it as the emptying out of something irreplaceable. The loss winds me.

I slide to the floor by the bed, kneeling as if I'm praying, and take Ernst's cold hand in my own. I clutch it to me, and kiss his fingers. "I'm sorry," I tell him. "I'm sorry. I should never have left you."

But perhaps they planned it this way. Perhaps this was what came out of their reconciliation. For Otto to take a life, it went against everything he believed in. He must have loved his brother very much. I turn Ernst's hand over and bury my face in the thin, worn skin of his palm. His poor, blunt fingers fall open. His hand is wet. I'm crying.

"I love you," I murmur.

Cosmo is at my shoulder; he bends down, steadying me. "The ambulance is on its way; come on. Let's get you something warm to put on. Find a cup of hot tea. You need sugar."

I'm shivering. My teeth are rattling. I stand and lean against him and he closes his arms around me. I press my damp, crumpled face into his chest, remembering the smell of him. He holds me tightly.

I manage to stop crying and pull away, wiping at my eyes. "Amoya should be here soon." But he doesn't know what I'm talking about. "My father." I remember. "I'd better make sure he's OK. He went outside."

"Outside?" Cosmo frowns. "It's wet and cold. He shouldn't . . ."

We both go quickly down the stairs and I lead the way through the dazzling, empty kitchen out into the garden. Everything is indistinct in the dim, dying day. Shapes blur in a drizzly mist. The melting patches of snow are stained and pitted with criss-crossing tracks: footsteps and paw prints. The apple tree holds up its naked branches, and its twigs make accusing fingers that clutch at the last shreds of light.

At first I can't see him. Then I make out the crumpled shape in the slushy remains of snow at the bottom of the apple tree. I run, feet slipping on the soaking ground. He's caught in the roots, his back against the trunk. Spittle hangs from his mouth. He's wheezing, horrible, scratchy sounds rattling from his throat. I crouch by his side. He turns frightened eyes to me; he's trying to speak, slurred words. I can't understand. He's clutching his chest.

And Cosmo is there too, kneeling down beside me. "He's having a heart attack." He looks back towards the house. "Aspirin. Do you have any?"

"In the bathroom cabinet . . . upstairs."

"Right." He stands up, staring towards the house. "I'll find out where the ambulance is—tell them it's an emergency."

He's gone. I take off my jumper and wrap it around Otto's shoulders. He's been sick. It's all down his front, sticky and stinking. "It's going to be all right." I try to make my voice sound bright and hopeful. "Hold on. Help is coming."

He shakes his head. He's grimacing. He squeezes his eyes shut and moves his hand from his chest to his arm. I let out a sob. Putting my hand over my mouth. And then his eyes snap open. He focuses on me. He can see me. I know he can. His eyes drill into me. He wants to say something; I lean forwards. He can't speak. His lips move. I stare hard, trying to decipher his words.

"Ernst . . ." he struggles.

I take a deep breath. I shake my head. "It's all right," I say loudly. "He's at peace now."

He gives a tiny impatient shake of his head. His lips are moving around another word. I strain to hear. "Daughter . . ."

He reaches wavering fingers to me. I hold them, squeezing tightly, and try to smile through my tears.

"Dad," I manage to whisper. It's my last lie.

He's closed his eyes again.

There is noise and activity behind me. Two paramedics are hurrying across the garden, bright yellow jackets startling in the gloom. I step back, letting them crowd around him. There's a stretcher and the woman is talking to Otto, getting him to open his mouth, slipping a pill under his tongue.

Cosmo is there beside me. I walk next to the stretcher. Otto is ashen. His eyes sealed shut. There are neighbors peering out of windows, standing in doorways. On the pavement, they put the stretcher into the ambulance. He is being hooked up to a drip. His chest is bare and covered in wires. I glimpse his sagging flesh, a smattering of gray hair around the plastic equipment suctioned to his heart. The doors slam shut and the ambulance roars away, siren screaming.

My legs can't hold me, and I stagger. Cosmo's arms slide around my shoulders, holding me tight, bearing me up.

1997, London

January

They say grief lowers your immune system. I woke up with the flu after the funerals were over. I'm still red-nosed, with hollow, aching bones and a stubborn, ticklish cough. Huddled into my coat and scarf, I escape the bitter streets through glass doors, beginning to unbutton and unwrap as I approach the reception desk to ask the way to the auditions.

Cosmo offered to come with me. But I need to do this on my own. There's the sound of laughter and piano music in distant studios. Students hurry past, gossiping, soft-soled dance shoes whispering across the floor. I find the right room. There are three other candidates already inside, warming up in their leotards and leg warmers. Their eyes slide towards me, the newcomer, assessing my chances. I can feel their anxiety. The space is ringing with adrenaline. I put my hand over my heart. It's beating fast. But I don't feel sick or faint. My perspective has shifted. Nerves seem irrelevant in the face of life and death.

I unpeel my outer clothes, blow my nose. I go through my stretches and focus on deep, steady breathing. I'm going to do the audition in a simple black leotard and black tights; I've managed to weave my hair into a short plait with the help of hairpins. A girl with a clipboard calls me into a hall. Three people are waiting behind a desk in front of a stage: a man and two women. None of them smiles. One of the women looks over the top of her glasses and tells me that I can begin.

I have two pieces of choreography prepared. The first is for my mother. I've chosen Bach's *Goldberg Variations*. The piano notes drop into the silence, slow and gleaming. It's a piece that is dignified, delicate, but certain. I move through the music, holding positions. I create patterns, finishing every movement so that there are no untidy edges, no trailing threads. The dance has to be a shining thing. Something pristine and whole. After I finish, I look up and see the woman with glasses talking to the man next to her. She turns and gives me a nod that I should begin the second one. She's already writing notes as I look away, waiting for the music to begin.

I discover that it's easier to perform if you think of the performance as a gift. Performing is not about you; it's about what you want to give.

This is for Ernst. I've chosen "Debussy's Arabesque No. 1." The lilting, elusive music is part of me. Everything I have to say takes shape through movement. In dance there is call and response. Like prayer. The words I didn't say can be said now. The years we never had can be remembered. Past and future flow through me, and I am there as a child in the kitchen; I am Klaudia and Eliza; I am Otto, Ernst and Gwyn. They slip through the avenues of my body, meeting and mingling. I imagine that together we are dancing across a slate-colored lake, through a forest whitened with snow, over the rooftops of terraced houses. I want to make the impossible possible: to make my body sing with their stories.

1997, New York

Two months later

WE'VE BEEN HERE A WEEK and I'm still dizzy with excitement. I love the water tanks perched on top of buildings, the air-conditioning vents hanging from windows and the zig-zagging fire escapes patterning the long flanks of buildings. New York is even more densely populated and multicultural than London. The streets are seething with crowds; every road is pitted with potholes; sidewalks are dirty with rubbish; ravaged, weedy tenements exist beside vast, sweeping skyscrapers of glass and stone. We stroll past doormen in gold-trimmed uniforms, watch them tip their hats to people getting in and out of shiny limousines. Ella Fitzgerald plays in my head. I hum. *I'll take Manhattan. The Bronx and Staten Island too.* I keep putting jazz songs to this city. They just seem to fit.

We take the customary boat trip around the bay and stare up at the Statue of Liberty. I think of Ernst sailing past, an immigrant with fresh scars and empty pockets. What would he have made of her seamless, stern face and resolute arm, raised not in a salute, but in a promise? Cosmo insists on taking a photo of me against the railings as the statue slides past. The day is brilliant blue, cold and clear. I look into the blank eye of the camera, to the man standing behind.

We stop at a newsstand to buy postcards. I write one to Meg. It has a picture of the Empire State on the front, a pink sunset frothing behind the iconic building. It's an echo of the one she sent me of the Eiffel Tower. Meg kept her promise; she came to see me in Croydon before Christmas. She never got to meet my father. Otto and Ernst died on the same day. I hardly recognized her when I answered the door. She seemed incongruous against the bleak, suburban street in all her newly acquired Parisian gloss. I looked at her black pumps, the elegant coat and her sleek haircut in admiration, feeling oddly shy.

"I know," she laughed, and plucked at her coat. "Dead smart, aren't I?"

She threw her arms around me, crushing my ribs in a bear hug. "Come here, you big soft creature. We'll sort it together. Look, I've got us a bevvy." Even though it was four o'clock in the afternoon, she opened a bottle of red wine and poured us each a glass. After that she rolled up her sleeves and got on with practical jobs, helping me to contact estate agents—being Meg: flippant, sensible, big-hearted.

After landing at JFK, I went straight to a meeting with Ernst's lawyers. Sitting in a sleek, glass office on the twentieth floor, I clutched a coffee like a talisman, while a fast-talking young man told me that Ernst had named my mother in his will. In the event of her death, he said, everything went to me. I was jet-lagged and confused. The information scrabbled at my brain. My fingers squeezed the cup and before I could understand the meaning of his words, the smell of coffee imprinted the moment on my memory. Knowing that Ernst had left me his fortune tripped so many different emotions: shock and sorrow and excitement clashing together. The one that came last, the one I'll always feel, is gratitude. He'd sold his business when he became too ill to manage. His financial affairs had been neatly tied into trust funds in my name and bank accounts. He'd known he wouldn't come back.

I was given the address of his apartment and the key. He'd left instructions to his housekeeper to keep it ready. Since he'd been away, flowers had been arranged in vases, dust swept, cushions plumped, windows cleaned. Walking in through the front door, it felt welcoming and lived-in, as if he was hiding in the next room, waiting to surprise me. Paintings were crowded onto every wall. Cosmo went straight to them, opening his hands in pleasure and amazement.

"A Chagall," he breathed. "It's not a reproduction." And stepping up to a small sketch and peering through the glass, "Look at this. Picasso. From his Blue Period." He turned to me. "Your father was a collector. This is incredible."

It was too much to take in. The flat. The paintings. But I thought that when there was time, I'd choose one painting and sit in front of it, let myself get lost inside the lines and colors. I would look, knowing that Ernst had loved it, and that somewhere inside it he would be waiting.

The night that Otto was taken away in the ambulance, Cosmo came to the hospital with me. He was by my side when a doctor with a serious, tired face told me the news. At home, Cosmo held me as I cried and then he listened while I told him my story, as I explained who Ernst was, spilling all that I knew in a mixed-up gabble, stopping only to pull in air, and let out the judders and gasps of my sobbing.

It took all night. We moved through different rooms in the house while I talked, and he fed me glasses of wine, cups of tea, and sandwiches cut into tiny triangles, even though I didn't want to eat. In my bedroom, exhausted, I finally stopped and we got into my single bed. We didn't have sex. We just wrapped ourselves up in a tangle of limbs.

When I was silent, he stroked the hair from my hot forehead. "But, Klaudia, we're not stamped with the deeds of our parents, or our grandparents." He sounded puzzled. "I just don't believe that. Maybe we should learn from their mistakes, but we don't have to repeat them." He kissed my head as if I was a child, or he was administering a blessing. "And you let this come between us?"

"I made everything so complicated," I murmured.

"Life is complicated," he said. I felt his considering frown. "But it's not in the end, is it? It comes down to what you love. Who you love."

We lay face to face in the half-light of dawn, completely still, holding each other's gaze. Inside that quiet moment, between the air entering and leaving my body, I felt myself running to him. And he caught me.

There is a box filled with Christmas cards in Ernst's bedroom. Flicking them open, my heart squeezes tight as I realize that every single one is from my mother. She never wrote anything personal. Just a couple of lines with news of us: *Klaudia lost her first tooth. Otto has a new job as caretaker of a local school.* Next to his bed is a book held together with ribbon. It's badly burned, the torn pages charred at the edges. Cosmo picks it up carefully. "Einstein," he reads. "*Relativity.*" He rubs his fingers together and sniffs. "Wonder what happened. It's old, but I can still smell the ashes."

Across from the apartment, resigned horses stand in a line, harnessed into their carriages, their heads lowered, snuffling into feedbags. I'm already approaching one of them.

"You want to do this?" Cosmo gives me a sideways glance, eyebrows raised. His expression adds—the most cheesy of tourist activities? But he doesn't say it.

I shake my head. "Just want to say hello."

We've reached the first horse. Cosmo steps around the dappled gray rump cautiously. He's as ignorant about horses as me. Ernst told me he used to carry carrots in his pockets to feed these horses. He said he always patted them, keeping their smell on his fingers for the rest of the day.

I reach up tentatively to touch the horse's sleek neck, feeling the curve of muscle, the power of the animal. I feel sorry for it, standing day after day in the noise and traffic fumes. The cabbie is wearing a top hat. Sprays of plastic flowers stick up on either side of his seat. He leans forward hopefully. "Come along folks. Step up behind."

Cosmo gives an apologetic smile. "Not today."

Not tomorrow either. We're leaving for London. There are things to do at home. I'm hoping there will be a letter waiting for me from the Laban Center. The house in Croydon is on the market. I've already moved Mum's urn to the chapel. I don't want strangers stamping across the grass, ignorant of what lies beneath their feet. Otto rests beside her. *Beloved Husband.*

We stroll along sweeping tree-lined avenues, watching people going about their lives. Elderly people sit on park benches gossiping or reading papers. There are cyclists and roller-skaters. People walking their dogs. I look at them all, wondering about their stories. I can almost hear them: the clamoring of the past streaming behind us like so many ghosts.

Out of the park and back onto the busy street, buildings soar above us; traffic lights blink; the air hums with constantly sounding horns. We don't talk. I like that we can be together in comfortable silence. Both of us are too busy pulling in the sights, storing up images. I know he'll be doing it differently from me. He looks at everything as an artist does. He has a sketchpad in his pocket, and he'll nonchalantly take it out whenever he feels the desire and with a few deft marks, he'll capture an old man pushing a grocery cart laden with junk, or a swirl of pigeons around a hot dog vendor. Sometimes he sketches me. I'm not embarrassed anymore. I've come to find it comforting to sit inside the intensity of his gaze; it holds me steady. I daydream while I listen to the quick slide and brush of his pencil against paper.

We turn down another street, passing Barnes & Noble, a Jewish deli, an art gallery. Cosmo tightens his grip on my fingers. "Look," he says urgently.

I turn my head and peer at a building site on the other side of the road. Men in hard hats and fluorescent jackets cluster around a truck; a pneumatic drill screams inside a cloud of steam. A new building is going up in the middle of the city. I stand, absorbing the purposeful movements of men and machinery; they're in the process of making something solid, where now there's just a wounded space: a dank hole in the flattened ground, piles of rubble and the jagged edges of a snarling wall. Cosmo nudges me, and I see it, the logo picked out in blue and yellow: Meyer Construction. A name you can trust.

EPILOGUE

1997, London

May

THE HOUSE IS SOLD. Cosmo and I are sorting through my parents' possessions, sending bags of clothes and kitchen equipment to the Oxfam shop, offering larger pieces of furniture to friends and neighbors. I wander through the familiar rooms, trying to decide which things I want to keep. The floors are cluttered with packing cases and rolls of paper. Cosmo is clearing out the garden shed. I can see him from the window in the spare room; he's hauling out Otto's workbench, sorting through the tools, laying them neatly on the grass under swags of pale blossom. I look around me at the bare walls and dusty corners of Ernst's old room. There's not much to do in here. Amoya has already stripped his bed; she's left the sheets and blankets folded neatly on the bare mattress. I lean over to touch the pillow and my toe nudges something hard. I squat down to find Ernst's small brown leather suitcase. Amoya must have packed it after he died.

I slide it onto the mattress. My fingers move to the catch. It takes one click to open. My insides contract when I see how little it contains. There's a pile of neatly folded clothes and a small wash-bag. It's as if he'd shrugged off all his possessions when he came here: leaving behind the lofty apartment with the collection of beautiful ornaments and paintings like some ornate and palatial shell. I touch a folded shirt, and the sour scent of illness rises from the fabric. But there's something else: a narrow book slotted down the side. I lift it out and open it. When I see his handwriting, my blood begins to beat faster. I read the beginning of the first page:

1931, Germany

Beneath the cow's belly my thumb and fingers are busy squeezing and pulling. I lean against her warm flank. This is work I've done since I can remember . . .

My heart is pounding now with excitement. I can hear his voice in my head, the lilt and expression of his mixed accent. With shaky fingers, I flick back to the flyleaf:

Darling Klaudia,
    This is my story, and so it belongs to you. My daughter. The best way of explaining my life to you, the choices I made, is to write it all down. (I hope you can read my terrible handwriting.) Some things may shock you. I am sorry. Know that, despite what you read here, I always tried to do what I thought was right. The weakness of my human heart and the horror of war are not excuses for the mistakes I made. I take full responsibility for everything. Please forgive me if you can. I wish more than anything that I could have been a father to you.

I trace the swoop and line of his letters as if I could reach through the flow of ink to feel the pen, touching his battered fingers curled around it. My chest is tight. I look through pages covered in his messy scrawl. There are dates at the top of some. I calculate numbers in my head. He's written down memories stretching back to his childhood, and on through the war until he came here to London, to see Mum and me. It is all here, how his life began and how it ended. Outside I hear the muted sounds of a radio and the bangs and clinks of Cosmo sorting through the shed. Birds move among the petals of the apple tree, calling to each other. I take the book over to the window and settle in a chair. Morning light falls onto the first page.

AUTHOR'S NOTE

It wasn't until I was in my forties that I discovered who my real father was. He'd died by the time I tracked him down. But I had facts about him for the first time. He was Dutch. And he was Jewish. He'd been brought up in Friesland; then as a teenager he'd run away to Paris. He spent the rest of his life in France. His rabbi grandfather had lived in Amsterdam, where it was likely that he and other family members were killed in the Holocaust. This extraordinary and unexpected information had an immediate effect on me: not only did I wonder about the lives of all these relatives I'd never met, but the fact of them fed into my idea of myself—it changed my sense of identity. There was no obvious outer alteration. I didn't feel an urge to convert to Judaism. But the story of me had grown, had become more complicated and poignant in light of my heritage, richer for having a link with another culture. I gained a new perspective on history. My knowledge of World War Two and the Holocaust at once became more personal.

This made me think: What if I'd made a different discovery about that side of my family? What if my father had been the child of a German Nazi instead of a Dutch Jew? What if his father had been involved in atrocities? How then would my idea of myself have changed? What would I feel about my identity? Would I feel a sense of inherited guilt?

These were the questions I started with when I began to write *The Other Me*. I found the experience of writing this book a fascinating one. It was deeply personal and at times an emotional, difficult exploration of themes close to my own heart and life.

After finishing the novel, I was put in contact with someone who could help me delve further into my Jewish relatives. But immediately it became clear that the information I'd been given ten years ago was suspect, possibly even false. Suddenly, another rug was pulled from under my feet. There was no record of a rabbi going by the name I'd been given. The family name was not Jewish. It had possible German/Austrian roots. I was unable to find a trace of the Jewish connections that I'd been told about.

In trying to find out more about my new identity, I'd instead slipped further away from knowledge. I had a vivid sense of disorientation. Had someone made a mistake? Had someone lied, and if so, why?

This sudden turn of events made me understand even more clearly the need for family stories—ones handed down through generations that help to explain the story of us. When those stories are absent, or full of ambiguity, it undermines our sense of identity.

I am still searching for my ancestors, still hoping to find clarity. But whoever my father was and whatever his family were—Jews or not—I hope he would have approved of this book.

ACKNOWLEDGMENTS

A HUGE THANK-YOU to my U.S. editor, Amy Einhorn, and my U.K. editor, Emma Beswetherick. I am so grateful for their support, encouragement, and inspiration.

Also, many thanks to the talented teams at Flatiron Books and Macmillan in New York; and to Piatkus and Little, Brown, London.

I would like to thank my agent, Eve White, who is always there for me.

I'm grateful to those who took the time and care to read drafts of the manuscript: Sara Sarre, Alex Marengo, and Ana Sarginson; and my thanks to Viv Graveson, Cecilia Ekback, Laura McClelland, and Mary Chamberlain for work-shopping extracts.

Thank you to Lindel O'Neil for his knowledge of Brixton in the 1990s, and most of all for sharing his love of dance and dance philosophy with me. Scarlett's words of wisdom come from him. Thank you to Pandora Money for giving me an insight into the world of mural painting; to Dr. Andrew Low for words on music and physics; and to Peter Padfield for his guidance on useful books on the Second World War.

The following books were particularly helpful in my research:
The Forgotten Soldier by Guy Sajer (Cassell, 1999).
The Holocaust by Martin Gilbert (Fontana Press, 1987).
Soldaten by Sonke Neitzel and Harald Welzer (Simon & Schuster, 2011).

In Deadly Combat by Gottlob Herbert Bidermann (University Press of Kansas, 2000).

The Perfect Nazi by Martin Davidson (Viking, 2010).

I watched many documentaries on the subject of Hitler Youth, including the excellent *Hitler's Children* by Maya Productions Ltd.

Any mistakes are solely my own.

ML   1/2016